"POWERFUL . . . COMPELLING."
—*The Bookwatch*

"Karin McQuillan is a major new talent in the mystery world, and no reader will be able to resist the storytelling magnificence of ELEPHANTS' GRAVEYARD.... [It's] a book I couldn't put down, a story I didn't want to end, peopled with real flesh-and-blood human beings who I came to know and care about—almost as much as I did its marvelous animal inhabitants."
—*The Clarion-Ledger*

"Exciting ... The setting is beautiful and the pace never flags. Ms. McQuillan has thrown in a passionate romance to boot.... This is a deftly told story and most readers will be surprised and overwhelmed by the solution."
—*Rave Reviews*

"A perceptive, realistic, dramatic mystery set in problematic present-day Kenya, this book is an excellent selection."
—*Library Journal*

"McQuillan adds picturesque touches of Africa that stay with the reader long after the book is finished.... Like Jazz Jasper, she is a persuasive spokesperson as well as a skillful guide for our armchair safari to the ELEPHANTS' GRAVEYARD."
—*Mostly Murder*

ELEPHANTS' GRAVEYARD

Karin McQuillan

BALLANTINE BOOKS • NEW YORK

Copyright © 1993 by Karin McQuillan

All rights reserved under International and Pan-American Copyright Conventions. Published in the United States of America by Ballantine Books, a division of Random House, Inc., New York, and simultaneously in Canada by Random House of Canada Limited, Toronto.

Library of Congress Catalog Card Number: 92-54391

ISBN 0-345-38862-3

Manufactured in the United States of America

First Hardcover Edition: April 1993
First Mass Market Edition: July 1994

10 9 8 7 6 5 4 3 2

TO THE WILD ELEPHANTS OF AFRICA

The works of many conservationists, scientists, and adventurers inspired and informed *Elephants' Graveyard*. If any mistakes crept into the book, they are my own. Thanks especially to the African Wildlife Foundation; to Robert Heilbroner for his sensitive writing on African poverty; to Cynthia Moss for her wonderful books *Portraits in the Wild* and *Elephant Memories*; and to Shirley Strum for her fascinating book on baboon society, *Almost Human*.

Thanks to Claire Israel, Dominick Abel, and Joe Blades for their belief in me and their high level of professionalism in bringing this book to the public. I especially want to thank my husband John for his enthusiasm, support, and help with the manuscript.

1

DEAD BODIES DON'T last long out in the African bush. There's nowhere to hide under that big, clear sky.

A tawny eagle rose from a road kill with a raucous cry as I turned off the two-lane national highway onto the dirt track that led to Emmet Laird's camp.

"Elephants, here we come!" Inspector Omondi slapped his elegant, dark hands together. We exchanged grins.

"Watch it," I called out as the Rover lurched into a pothole and up over a series of cement-hard ruts.

Omondi braced himself against the dashboard. "A large, cold Tusker would not be amiss, either."

"All your wishes will be granted," I told him. My hair brushed the ceiling as the car bounced me up and down. "Emmet has a kerosene refrigerator, a stock of beer, and an elephant family that stays near his camp—thanks to the poachers."

Poaching had become so bad in Kenya that desperate elephants were hanging around tourist lodges and scientists' camps, where they were relatively safer.

Omondi shook his head. "Our world has gotten too small for comfort. The Soviets sell the Somalis AK47s to fight their civil war, and now when a Somali guerrilla wants money, he sneaks into Kenya and zap, zap, zap. Soon they will kill all our elephants."

"Let's not talk about it," I said vehemently. "I can't stand it."

1

"It is a great tragedy."

"It's a nightmare." I stared at the golden plains stretching before me, fighting the steering wheel as we bucked over the ruts and ridges that pass for a Kenyan road. "And they're killing the whole safari business, too. Tourists don't want to fly seven thousand miles to see more dead elephants than live ones." I'd booked several good tours lately, only to have bad publicity lead to cancellations. If my business went belly up, I wouldn't be able to stay in Africa.

"Enough of serious matters." Omondi cleared the air with a wave of his hand.

"Right. Today is for enjoying ourselves in the world's last remnant of Eden."

Fleshy baobab trees dotted the landscape like fat men waving their arms. I brushed away my gloomy thoughts. I had a tour booked for next week, which would stave off my creditors for a while. Omondi had finished a drawn-out domestic murder case and decided to give himself the day off. For both of us, driving down on a weekday gave this outing the added sweetness of stolen pleasure, and I was going to savor every drop.

We passed a giraffe nibbling the top of a struggling thorn tree, and a few tommies gazelles, but it was nearing the end of the dry season and the big herds were farther south. A long, bumpy hour later, we sighted the camp's parking area at the top of a rise. A flat-topped acacia sheltered the boxy silhouettes of two Land Rovers. I could already feel a cool beer washing the dust from my throat.

"Emmet has other visitors," Omondi said.

"It's probably Mikki Darrow. You know, my friend who studies elephants."

"Ah. A special friend of Emmet's?"

I took my eyes from the rutted tracks to shoot a glance at Omondi. "No fair! How could you guess?"

"Your voice." Omondi laughed with pleasure at his own prowess.

"It's a closely guarded secret." After a moment I added, "Mikki's been trying to decide whether to leave her husband."

"Jazz, Jazz—this is the real reason you invited me for a

drive today, is it not?" He held his hands to his chest. "You think I am a witch doctor to mend broken hearts."

I glanced over again and our eyes met with a little jolt of memory. I turned back to the road with a smile. "Well, it worked for me and Striker."

Some people think I overreacted to my divorce. Changing husbands these days is supposed to be as easy as flipping to a new TV channel. I've never cared for TV. I prefer real life, even though real wounds bleed. When my husband walked out on me, my whole life felt broken. So I bolted. I picked a fantasy out of my childhood and ran for it. No half measures: I changed continents and careers—from Dr. Jasper, art historian, to owner and tour guide of Jazz Jasper Safaris. Then I spent my first two years in Kenya circling warily around Dan Striker, calling my fear independence. It was only this past winter that Striker and I became lovers, thanks to Omondi thawing out my frozen fear of men.

"Surely you're not suggesting I use the same medicine on Mikki that I did on you?" Omondi gave a deep laugh. "I don't pass out my magic that freely. Besides, it sounds like she's doing fine on her own."

I pulled in next to the two other Rovers. One was Emmet's, with SAVE THE ELEPHANTS blazoned on the door. The other car looked almost new under its coating of red laterite dust. A gun rack held a single rifle—definitely not Mikki's car. Neither she nor Emmet carried a gun. They preferred to rely on their knowledge of animal behavior to keep out of sticky situations.

We got out of the car and found we were on the crest of the rise.

"Whooee!" Omondi flung his arms out to embrace the landscape. Emmet's hilltop held a surprise: it looked down on a permanent waterhole. There was a commotion of elephants below, rumbling and milling about on the hard-packed soil. Beyond them a group of zebras hesitated, giving the elephants plenty of room. Catching the excitement, one of the zebras kicked up its hind legs and ↑ stretched its neck forward in a toothy bray. An Egyptian goose ignored the mammals and squawked into a splash

3

landing with a flash of white and rust. A young elephant charged two jackals who were darting this way and that with the persistence of scavengers.

"Extraordinary!" Omondi flashed a delighted smile, teeth gleaming in contrast with his dark skin. "Listen to them talking!"

To our left was a picnic table Emmet Laird had set up under a feathery acacia, so that even during meal times he could watch his beloved elephants coming in to drink and bathe. A single plate sat on the table with the congealed remains of bacon and eggs. Several flies were having a feast. Next to the plate a pair of binoculars lay at hand for closer observation. I glanced toward the scattering of tents in assorted sizes for sleeping, eating, bathing, and other functions. Where was Emmet? Or his visitors? People usually don't go animal watching on foot in the African bush, especially near a water hole.

Omondi stared at the elephants below. "What's going on? Look at that big bull flapping his ears and kicking dirt up. Doesn't he look angry?"

"Animal observation is like police work," I said. "Rule Number One: don't jump to conclusions."

"But look at the way he's thrusting his tusks into the ground."

"It's not a *he*. Bulls live by themselves. The biggest elephant is the mother, and this whole herd is her family of grown daughters and grandchildren." One of the elephants waved a ripped-off acacia branch in her trunk, and was lost from view as she pushed her way into the crowd. Despite my Rule Number One, I assumed she was going to eat it, so I paid no attention.

"No grown males?"

"Exactly," I replied. "Once the males become teenagers, they're too rambunctious and aggressive and are ejected from the herd." I assumed this was Broken Tusk's family, Emmet's most loyal visitors, but I couldn't pick out individuals as they milled about, rumbling and jostling each other. "Emmet knows this whole family by name, has watched many of them grow up."

"I wonder if they have a name for him."

4

The voice spoke from behind me and I whipped round. "Alicia!"

"In the flesh." She walked to my side, eyes drawn by the spectacle at the water hole. "Those elephants are making such a racket, we didn't hear you drive up."

I tried not to look surprised. Emmet's wife, Alicia Laird, never came to camp. I knew from Mikki Darrow that Alicia and Emmet didn't spend much time together—and yet there she stood, life-size, as big as Texas, with a voice to match. She wore a sundress in an expensive fabric swirling with lions and tigers, which suited both her coloring and personality. A heavy gold chain lay against the soft skin of her cleavage, now blotchy with dust. I wondered if my friend Mikki knew Alicia was here.

"They probably call him Uncle Deep Pockets." She drew her red-painted lips into a smirk and two pretty dimples appeared. Every now and then I'd wonder how Emmet could ever have married her, especially his third time around, but those thoughts never came up in Alicia's actual presence. Alicia had the pull of a gravitational force. "I swear, he'd spend his last dime on those baggy-pants monsters." She put a hand up to her mouth like a semaphore. "Greg! Come say hello to Jazz Jasper."

Alicia's current male escort, Greg Garner, emerged from the awning of the large dining/sitting tent.

"No note," he said to Alicia. He looked at her with the doting expression of a man who's been getting great sex. Greg was barely thirty, at least five years younger than Alicia and half Emmet's age, a big burly man tall enough to tower over Alicia. His snub nose and shock of blond hair made him look even younger. If I remembered correctly, he was the chief loan officer for WorldCorp Bank. His milieu was the club golf course and bar, rather than the bush. So this was her Other Man. Why in the world would Alicia bring him here? The camp was Emmet's special place, a hideaway from Alicia and her party crowd.

"Let me introduce you to my friend," I said. "Alicia Laird—Inspector Omondi of the Nairobi police, and this is Greg Garner."

At the word *inspector* their smiles became painfully brittle. Were they afraid Omondi would whip out handcuffs and cart them off for speeding, or perhaps for adultery?

Alicia recovered herself and shook Omondi's long, elegant hand. "You're the detective who helped out with those killings on Jazz's first safari tour, aren't you?" She turned to Greg. "You know Jazz started her very own safari company, Greg. Isn't that enterprising? And on the very first tour there was this terrible—"

"I wanted to show the inspector elephants," I cut in. An old friend had been murdered on that trip. It was painful to remember, and I certainly didn't want Alicia building me up into some kind of a heroine.

Omondi shook her hand energetically. "Delighted to make your acquaintance, Mrs. Laird. I have been looking forward to this visit for a long time. Jazz tells me your husband is one of the great men of Kenya, protecting our living national treasure. Yes, these elephants are necessary for a developing country like ours to raise its biggest cash crop: tourist dollars." Omondi chuckled at his own joke.

He turned to Greg. "Mr. Garner, I hope you aren't getting too much heat today. The sun strikes." He patted his spongy hair. "You need a helmet like mine." Omondi looked toward the tents. "And where is Mr. Laird?"

"I'm not sure where Emmet is, and that's the truth." Alicia glanced toward Greg. "I haven't seen him since, oh, since Monday. I can't imagine what he's thinking of, with all the work for the party."

"Maybe he's out hunting for dinner," Greg joked.

"Don't let Emmet hear you say that. He'd have a fit." Alicia put her hand on his biceps and Greg looked pleased. "He won't even allow a gun here. That's why I never come with him." That and the fact nature bored her to death. "Imagine, all these wild animals around and poachers getting more brazen every day—and not even a pistol. I wouldn't go for a Sunday drive without my rifle."

Next she'd be telling us her daddy taught her how to shoot.

Greg rocked on his heels. "So, Inspector, you're playing tour guide to the tour guide? You from around here?"

Omondi shook his head. "No, my family comes from

north of Nairobi, tea country. The British killed off all the game there before World War Two, when I was only a wish in my mother's heart. Oooh, they loved to hunt, those white settlers. Now it is all farms, no more empty land. I myself prefer city life. It is Jazz's idea to show me the animals. She thinks it's a scandal that most Kenyans don't have a car to visit their own national parks." He showed his empty palms. "It is ironic, is it not?"

"Of all the inconsiderate things, to take off like this and leave me with a party for five hundred people Saturday night." Alicia stared at the white-gold grass shimmering in the afternoon heat, as if five hundred people might materialize on the spot. "It's the last Save the Elephants fund-raiser I'll organize for him."

I was no one to talk—I avoided doing volunteer work for Emmet myself—but I knew Mikki and Emmet had been working their tails off to make this fund-raiser a success, without any help from Alicia other than letting Emmet use their house. Today, Alicia seemed to be playing My Husband Neglects Me for all it was worth. Surely she could think of more amusing games for Greg.

Omondi returned to the crest of the hill to watch the antics at the water hole. "They're starting to quiet down a bit."

"Oh, those elephants!" Alicia said.

Several of the larger elephants fell still and the dust around them began to settle. They stood in a cluster with trunks hanging down, not moving toward the water. It was odd.

"I think I can recognize some of them." I pointed. "We call the biggest elephant Broken Tusk, for obvious reasons. She's one of the oldest surviving matriarchs in the whole country. She was shot by poachers once—you can see the scar on her shoulder—and can sometimes be cranky around people. The one next to her—see how one ear is notched at the top—that's one of the youngest daughters, Blanche. She just had her first baby." My view was blocked by a wall of wrinkled gray skin, like a tumble of granite boulders. "It may be hiding under her belly."

Omondi was studying the elephants closely. "Look on

the ground in the center of their circle. They've kicked up a big pile of dirt."

I pulled a pair of binoculars from my car and focused on the ground. My chest tightened. "They've buried a pile of branches." When an elephant dies, its family covers it and hangs around for hours, days sometimes, keeping the scavengers off. "I hope that doesn't mean Blanche lost her baby." I loved that little elephant, with its soft, floppy ears and miniature trunk that only reached to its knees.

"What kills baby elephants?" Greg asked.

"Not much." I tried to focus on the branches, but it was hard to see between the elephants' legs. "Of course, if the mother is shot and the baby gets separated from the rest of the family, it can easily be killed by lions. But Blanche is right there."

"So we are watching a funeral," Omondi said quietly.

"The closest any animal comes to it. It's obvious how much they love one another." I handed the glasses to Omondi.

"Hey, remember Tarzan and the elephants' graveyard? Is this it?" Greg took on a puppylike excitement.

"That's just an old tale, silly." Alicia slapped his arm. "Like the pot of gold at the end of the rainbow." She puckered her lips into a teasing smile. "A place where old elephants go to die and you can pick up a fortune in tusks right off the ground. Wouldn't that be nice?"

"The legend probably started because you don't see many elephant skeletons lying around," I said. "Old elephants will go to a nice, private place when they feel their death approaching—back in the days when they lived to old age."

"Nowadays, all Kenya is the elephants' graveyard," Omondi agreed sadly. He raised the binoculars, studied the dark mound on the ground, then slowly scanned the surrounding area. Suddenly his body stiffened and he spoke in an urgent voice. "There's a canvas shoe near the water's edge."

I grabbed the pair of binoculars from the picnic table. Omondi directed me where to look. There was a blue and silver running shoe lying on its side.

"People are terrible, throwing trash everywhere—" Alicia said.

"Let's get down there." I wouldn't let myself think what that shoe might mean. I ran for the car and started the engine. The others sprinted after me.

It was too dangerous to go on foot outside the safety of camp or village unless you were armed with a Maasai spear or a gun. Wherever farms abutted the wilderness people were often mauled by lions or gored by cranky Cape buffalo. A water hole—where animals congregated and lions waited in ambush—was the most dangerous place of all.

That shoe might have been thrown from a car. It might. Emmet wore blue and silver running shoes.

"Hold on a second." Alicia raced to her Rover, pulled her rifle off its rack, and fired into the air. I flinched at the sound, and the animals below stampeded. Alicia scrambled into the car, and I hurled us over the top of the rise and straight down the slope toward the center of the herd. One adolescent male took a few threatening steps in our direction, saw that all the adult females were running flat out, tails raised in alarm, and took off after them.

We approached the pile of sticks. A foot in a white crew sock poked out from below. Alicia screamed piercingly. She sounded like an animal being tortured. Greg leaped from the car and began throwing branches aside. Omondi and I joined him. The branches were heavy, some requiring two people to shift. The ends were splintered and oozing sap where they had been torn from a living tree. Thorns and branches kept catching on one another in a tangled mess. It seemed to take forever to pull them loose. There was a smear of dried blood under our feet, a boiling of flies and a putrid smell.

A moment later we looked down on Emmet Laird. His still body created a deadly silence in the middle of all the noise. His white shirt was soaked with blood. A bullet had smashed a jagged crater where his heart used to beat.

2

"**I**F EVERYONE WILL please get back in the car." Omondi crouched next to Emmet's body. I turned away, unable to watch the blanket of flies crawling over the wound, but I couldn't get away from their sound, that awful buzzing. The stench from Emmet's body mingled with the smells of elephant shit and pools of urine that dotted the hard-packed ground. I moved to the other side of the Rover, breathing shallowly, trying not to be sick, and slipped behind the wheel. Even as part of me was praying, *please, God, let this not be true,* I heard my voice, sounding dead and far away, ask Omondi if I should radio the police.

"Yes. Ask for Sergeant Kakombe. He's on duty today."

I called in and gave detailed instructions on how to find Emmet's camp. The sun came in through the open roof hatch and fell in a burning patch on my back. I could feel sweat trickling between my shoulder blades. It would be at least a few hours before the forensic specialists could get here. Alicia climbed into a backseat. A shadow passed over me, then another, bird-swift. Two vultures fell from the sky. They tipped their wings from side to side to hasten their descent, greedy to share in the possible spoils.

Greg hovered over Omondi's shoulder. Everything seemed far away, except my stomach, which was trying to crawl up my throat.

A giraffe rounded the slope with its calm, rocking gait. The pattern of its skin, rust blotches on a tan background, stood out clearly in the strong light. The giraffe stopped and stared.

"There's a tarp in the car we can use to carry him." Greg's voice brought me back.

The vultures sidled closer.

"Please, if you would get in the car. Mrs. Laird needs your help more than I do. The less we disturb the area, the better." Omondi moved along in a crouch as he studied the ground. Near the water the earth was churned into a lumpy, semiliquid, rich-smelling goo, but where we were, the dry ground had been pounded and polished by animals' feet until it was hard as stone. Omondi circled round slowly. The giraffe realized there was a man loose, grew alarmed and loped off.

"No tire tracks but ours. Mr. Laird's body was not dumped here." Omondi went back to stand over the body. "From the amount of blood on the ground, I would guess this is the very spot he was killed."

"He wouldn't have walked here," I called from the car. "Emmet was too knowledgeable to do such a dangerous thing."

No, he'd never walk here of his own free will, but he could have been forced—with a rifle focused on him from the camp above. Told to stop and turn around, and then shot through the heart. I felt a pain in my own chest. Why was it the best people, the people the world needed most, who were always killed? Who would champion the elephants now? Who would love them with Emmet's courage and energy? I didn't let myself think of Mikki, or I'd break down completely.

Did Emmet recognize his killer? I wondered. Or was it an employee, doing a day's work, hired to kill a man as a change from killing elephants? I looked at Alicia, who was leaning her head against the seat in front of her, eyes closed. The thought that it might be a domestic murder flitted through my mind, unwelcome as the buzzing of the flies. Alicia had just become the richest widow in Nairobi.

A call came in on the radio. It was Sergeant Kakombe. All the police cars were in the shop for repairs.

11

"Or being used for personal business." Omondi clicked his tongue with annoyance.

"No cars?" Greg's voice rose with disbelief.

Alicia raised her head. "Just last week some poor bastard called the police station to report that a band of thieves were smashing through his front door with machetes. You know what the police said? Come to the station and pick up some officers, we have no cars tonight." A mirthless laugh exploded from her throat like a cork under pressure. "No cars." The laugh grew, doubled her over, rose louder and shriller. Greg grabbed her to his chest and the laugh turned abruptly to sobs. "No cars," she wept.

A black shadow moved over us with a whoosh from a six-foot wing span. The marabou stork alighted on one of the branches we'd tossed aside and clacked its massive bill at Omondi, as if telling him to get a move on. The stork had the naked head of all scavengers. Its skin looked like diseased meat, ugly enough without the huge fleshy wattle that hung down from its neck, swinging and bulging as it sidled toward Emmet. When Omondi ignored it, the bird reached out and pulled at Emmet's hand.

Greg and I yelled. Alicia tried to pull away from Greg's chest and see, but he wouldn't let go of her. Omondi lunged, waving his arms, and the bird took a few hurried steps out of range.

Omondi turned to us. "I am very sorry, Mrs. Laird, that you are being subjected to this. Normally, I would leave the body untouched until the forensic team gets here, but that is clearly impossible." He paused. None of us volunteered for the job of spending the night with the body and shooing away carrion eaters. "Mr. Garner, your idea was a good one. If you would be so kind to help me with the tarp."

I helped the two men bundle Emmet into the car. Why should a dead body feel so much heavier than a live one? We brought Emmet's body back up the hill, left it in the back of the Rover, and at Omondi's suggestion, regrouped around the picnic table.

Alicia hugged herself with crossed arms. She looked almost as bloodless as Emmet. Omondi made her sit down with her head between her knees. The whole time she kept

12

saying, "I'm all right. I'm fine." When she did lift her head, she was still pale, but not that scary green color. "What possessed him to go down there?" she whispered.

"Did an animal get him?" Greg asked. "I didn't see claw marks, but I wasn't looking too closely."

I could imagine Greg in the club lounge, surrounded by other well-fed businessmen, making a long, dramatic story of it. The punch line would be how stupid Emmet was to get killed. I wanted to howl. Emmet dead? In the two years I'd known him, as Mikki's friend, Emmet had become special to me—not exactly a friend, more like a valued comrade in arms, plucky and optimistic. I could almost hear him whistling Gershwin tunes as he laid the evening campfire.

"Alicia, you're still white as a ghost. Let me pour you a whiskey," Greg said. "I'll have one, too. Anyone else? I even have ice and soda." Omondi and I opted for soda water. Greg went to his car and came back with an ice chest, a hamper of booze, and glasses.

I looked down at the water hole. A jackal was sniffing the ground where Emmet's body had rested. "If the elephants hadn't buried him," I said, "there wouldn't be a trace left by now. Emmet would have simply disappeared."

Omondi looked around the camp. "The abandoned car would have looked suspicious." His eyes rested on Greg and Alicia. "Unless the killers meant to come back and get rid of it later."

"What are you suggesting?" Greg took a step forward, as if to intimidate Omondi with his physical weight.

"Nothing." Omondi met Greg's gaze with his usual mildness. "I always raise a lot of questions. What implication did you draw, Mr. Garner?"

"You said you spoke with Striker this morning?" Alicia didn't look at me as she asked the question. "Did he tell you Emmet was upset about something he'd discovered?"

I took the cool glass of soda from Greg's large hand. "Striker didn't say anything." Much as I loved him, Dan Striker had a maddening habit of being close-lipped about his work in progress, whether it was a straightforward piece of nature writing or investigative journalism. It was one of the marks left by his many years as a loner.

13

"What's this?" Omondi's brown eyes settled on Alicia with a look I recognized, a look of professional concentration, like a basketball star measuring the distance to the net and the disposition of the opposing team. The police station might not have any cars, but I was glad Omondi was on my side. "Discovered what?" he prompted her.

Alicia frowned into her glass. "I have no idea. He and Striker were thick as thieves lately. You'll have to get ahold of him." She fished out an ice cube with her tongue and sucked on it.

"They've been investigating the ivory trade," I told Omondi. "It's probably about that, if Striker's involved. As you can understand, he doesn't advertise the fact. It was Striker who uncovered the processing plant run by those Hua brothers from Hong Kong—across the border in that so-called free enterprise zone in Somalia."

Omondi nodded. "Yes, I remember. Free enterprise— stealing Kenya's natural resources. So Striker was behind that."

I drank the rest of my soda. "He funneled the information to Emmet, who made sure it got into the papers and that the right people made a fuss about it."

"When you are as rich as Mr. Laird, you have many powerful friends," Omondi said. "And powerful enemies."

"It's an open secret that the Hua brothers moved their ivory center to the United Arab Emirates—the emirs don't give a damn about elephants, or Kenya. Striker figures there's a way station inside Kenya, linking up to a sea route along the Mombasa coast, but so far no one's been able to trace it." I poured myself more water and added a lump of ice. "If or how Emmet was helping Striker recently, I don't know." I refrained from adding it was Mikki who told me as much as I did know.

No one spoke. I heard a hunting eagle cry far overhead. It was a lonely, piercing call.

"Goddamn his stupid obsession with these goddamn elephants." Alicia swallowed her drink convulsively and slammed the glass down on the table. "You should have seen Emmet the past few weeks—an overgrown teenager playing cops and robbers. Flying here, flying there. Getting

14

himself all worked up about elephants going extinct. I kept telling him grown-ups play golf." She gave a bitter laugh. "And now some two-bit poacher found him alone out here and shot him like a dog."

"Mrs. Laird, I know you have suffered a terrible shock and loss, and you are eager to go home. I am impatient to contact my team and get on the trail of the killers. Jazz can tell you, when it comes to murder, I am a man in a hurry." Omondi put his palms together, fingertips under his chin. "I will save most of my questions for later, but for now, I must ask you to tell me exactly what transpired this afternoon: what time did you arrive, what did you see, where did you go in the camp, what did you touch?"

"I don't remember all that, I couldn't possibly tell you." Alicia held her glass out to Greg. "Be a doll and pour me another whiskey, would you?"

Omondi sat next to her. "I will help you remember, Mrs. Laird. Now, what time did you arrive in camp?"

Alicia looked at her watch. "Oh, I don't know. Just a few minutes before you did."

"That can't be right," I said. "We would have been eating your dust the whole drive up."

Alicia gave me a sharp glance. "Maybe ten, twenty minutes before, then. Not long." She took the proffered glass from Greg.

"Please bear with me. This will help us save time later." Omondi got up. "Without touching anything at all, show me what you did when you arrived at camp."

"I really don't see the point of this." Alicia's makeup was smudged by her tears, softening the emphatic eyebrows and red mouth she'd drawn on her face. "Greg, I'm ready to go home."

Omondi nodded graciously. "Yes, I understand the workings of the police can seem pointless and even brutal. We'll get this over as quickly as possible. Mr. Garner, would you like to go first?"

Greg walked toward Alicia's car. For a moment I thought he was going to defy Omondi, but he turned and headed back at a deliberate pace. "We got out. Called. I came over to the picnic table and looked down at the water hole." He

15

walked in front of the table and glanced down the hill, like everyone does when they arrive. "The elephants were milling around, making that weird rumble like the worst case of indigestion you ever heard. Alicia looked in the sleeping tent, and I walked into the big tent over there." He went over to the dining tent. "I figured there might be a note or something on the table saying where he'd taken off to."

"He was expecting you?" Omondi asked.

"No. We came down on the spur of the moment." Greg slipped his hands in his pockets. "Anyway, there was no note. There was a mess of papers on the dining table. I didn't touch a thing. When I turned around, you'd arrived."

It didn't sound like that would take ten minutes to me, but Alicia corroborated Greg's description. She added that she'd noticed a small plane flying north soon after they left the national highway.

"Did you notice what kind of plane? Anything about it?"

"Are you kidding?" Alicia raised her stenciled brows.

"No one went to the kitchen or touched anything there?" The two of them shook their heads in unison. "Thank you, very much. I won't keep you any longer. You understand, there will have to be an autopsy, but let me know your funeral arrangements and we will release the body directly to the funeral parlor." Omondi looked at the large gold watch on his thin wrist. "I am afraid I will need to disturb you again with further questions."

"I've already told you what I know, Inspector." Alicia stood up. She looked at her watch. "I'll have to get ahold of Kim—that's my stepdaughter. I hope she's at her office. Garret is undoubtedly at the club." Kim and Garret were Emmet's grown children, half sister and brother from his first two marriages. "I suppose you'll want to talk to them, too. Whatever good that will do. I don't imagine he's told them any more of what he's been up to than he told me. We're not a very close family." The brittle smile was back.

Omondi tried to get me to drive back with Alicia, while the two men drove the body back to town in my car, but I resisted his chivalry. My stomach grew queasy at the thought of the long journey, but I didn't want to be shuttled

16

away from the action, and I thought I might be useful to Omondi.

Alicia moved toward my Rover to retrieve the rifle she'd left leaning against the back seat.

"Mrs. Laird!"

"Now what?"

"If you please—leave the rifle with me. I will return it to you later."

Alicia looked at Greg. "This is outrageous. I'm not driving out of here without a gun."

Greg put the last glass back in the hamper. "Inspector, do you have the right to seize Mrs. Laird's personal possessions without a warrant?"

Omondi showed his empty palms and brought them together with a slap. "My dear sir, a man has just been shot. There is only one weapon at the scene of the crime. I would be seriously negligent if I let you drive away with it. It is in Mrs. Laird's own interest to have this rifle examined and categorically ruled out as the murder weapon." He turned to Alicia. "If you are afraid, please wait and we will drive out together in a convoy. But truly, I do not think you have anything to fear."

Alicia fingered her skirt, making the lions and tigers swing menacingly. "You saw me take that gun off the rack and fire it. The only fingerprints on it are going to be mine."

"Yes, we saw you fire one shot."

Alicia fixed him with a narrow-eyed look. "I also fired it once on the way down here. There was a hyena with cubs by the track. I just hate those slope-backed, skulking critters. I missed, in case you go back looking for a carcass." She flicked her skirt back and forth like a cat flicking its tail. "Inspector, I don't like your questions. How dumb do you think I am? I'm going to bring a witness along while I shoot my husband, and then calmly stick around waiting for you to show up?"

"I don't think you should answer any more questions without a lawyer," Greg told her.

"Damn right." Alicia turned with a swirl of skirt and marched to her Rover. Neither one looked toward Alicia's

17

rifle, still in my car. She pulled out a pocket mirror and put on fresh lipstick while Greg stowed away the booze and got the car started. They sped away without a backward glance. Their dust left a plumed track across the plain.

3

"**I**'M SURE MRS. Laird can be charming under more favorable circumstances," Omondi said. He crouched on his heels where her car had been. The dusty ground was textured with a confused overlay of tire tracks, but one thing was obvious: Alicia's car was leaking oil. A couple of feet to the right, overlapping the space Alicia had just pulled out of, was another oil stain.

"Look at those." I pointed at the two stains. "You'd almost say they came from the same car."

Omondi stood and studied them with narrowed eyes. "Most interesting. Here is a perfect opportunity for Western technology to make its contribution. We will be able to certify if they both came from Mrs. Laird's car." He continued to look at the ground. "It will take a tracker like Sergeant Kakombe to sort this out, but one thing is intriguing. To my uneducated eyes, it looks like the only tire prints are Emmet's, Mrs. Laird's, and ours."

He turned his attention back to the camp. Besides the large dining/sitting room tent, there were two smaller tents with iron cots, an open-sided cooking area under canvas, a bucket-shower stall of woven straw matting, and a similar latrine.

I followed as Omondi examined each tent, including the

18

latrine. The sleeping tent held two cots pushed together to make a double bed. Some women's clothes were hanging on hooks along one wall.

"Your friend Mikki's?" Omondi asked.

"Probably. She and Emmet spent a lot of time here."

A man's worn leather wallet was on the night table next to his bed. Omondi flipped it open with a pen. It was fat with pound notes. "It would be a strange sort of thief to leave this behind," he said. "I think it better that we take the wallet back with us."

He emptied a box of tissues lying next to it and carefully slipped the wallet into the box, trying not to smudge any possible fingerprints. He didn't need to explain that he couldn't trust his men to collect the wallet as evidence. What Emmet carried around as pocket money could support an African family in the countryside for months.

We pushed through the mosquito netting into the large dining tent. It was hot under the canvas. The table was covered with a none too clean red tablecloth covered with papers. Omondi and I bumped shoulders as we both moved to read what they were, and I pulled back hastily. Omondi didn't react the same way, for he put his hand on my shoulder as we bent over the table. It felt warm and comforting. What was I so uptight about?

There was a manuscript with red editing marks, and a red pen thrown down near it. Omondi turned to the title page. "*The Biggest Are Gone: Can Herds Survive with No Full Grown Adults?* by Mikki Darrow and Emmet Laird," he read aloud. "So they worked together, too."

"They were a great team. Emmet funds"—I hesitated —"*funded* Mikki's elephant research, produced her reports, and she donated a lot of time to Save the Elephants. They wrote an article last year for *International Wildlife* on how fifty percent of the ivory ends up in American stores. It created quite a stir."

"Passion for work leading to romance." Omondi seemed intrigued by the idea. "And the wife worked for Emmet along with his lover?"

"Not as far as I know. Alicia and Emmet didn't intersect

19

that much. I don't believe she's involved with this fund-raiser Saturday, for example."

"And yet Alicia comes all the way out here today to look for him. Why? She complains he's left her with all the work for a huge party. You are skeptical. We have not heard the true reason, I think."

He turned back to the table. There was a pile of articles on the Hong Kong and Japanese ivory business, some newspaper clippings on recent arrests of Somali poachers, and a folded *Daily Nation*.

I pointed to the date under the masthead. "If he's been here since Monday, how did Emmet get yesterday's paper?"

Omondi squeezed my shoulder. "You have sharp eyes. Either Emmet left camp yesterday or today, or someone brought him a paper."

"The killer?"

"Or a visitor." Omondi thought a moment. "Or Greg left it in here before our arrival."

Why Greg would do such a thing didn't present itself to me, but I knew Omondi's methods: examine every possibility, make no assumptions without evidence, and even then, keep your mind alert to alternate explanations.

The ground between the tents was polished by wear into a hard, smooth, almost lacquered appearance that left no visible tracks. But just outside the dining tent Omondi noticed a tiny half-moon pockmark.

"That could only be from Alicia's heels," I said. "I'm sure Mikki doesn't even own a pair of shoes that make a mark like this."

"Except for one thing. Mrs. Laird's shoes this morning had wider heels that wouldn't puncture the ground in this way."

I pictured Alicia's feet: cute, chubby toes nestled in gold sandals that matched her dress. Omondi was right. The sandals were low-heeled. "If you find she has a pair of shoes that match these marks, along with the two oil stains from her car . . ." A creepy feeling came over my skin. If we hadn't arrived when we did, would Alicia and Greg have noticed and removed these signs of an earlier visit? Could it really be this easy? I thought of Mikki. Would losing Emmet be even worse for her if Alicia was the killer?

At the same time, half of me felt guilty relief. The country couldn't afford any more awful publicity about poaching murders. A white man killed mysteriously in the bush would stop tourism dead. Jazz Jasper Safaris would go belly up—but if the murder was personal and solved quickly, the damage could be contained.

Omondi's voice brought me back to the present. "You have the makings of a fine detective," Omondi teased. "Have you considered changing professions?"

"Don't joke. I might have to, if my tour company doesn't get some more customers."

Leading the way to the kitchen lean-to, Omondi said, "Ah-ha. Look at this."

The fry pan, holding two half-cooked eggs, sunny side up, sat on the gas canister camping stove.

"Emmet was cooking another round of eggs."

"Yes." Omondi nodded. "You noticed the used plate out on the picnic table. One set of eggs half eaten, another in the pan half cooked." Omondi tapped his teeth with a fingernail as he thought. "I doubt the killer was cooking himself some eggs and broke off to shoot Emmet. It's more likely he pulled out a gun while Emmet was facing the stove."

"Emmet must have been halfway through breakfast when a stranger arrived, and I imagine he offered to cook some more eggs."

"So we think it was an unexpected arrival by a person or persons Mr. Laird did not perceive as a danger."

The half cooked egg yolks stared at me like accusing eyes.

"He turned off the flame." I tried to picture the sudden threat, a rifle focused on his chest, Emmet calmly turning off the fire under the eggs. Something was wrong.

"He might have hurled the pan at his assailant. Instead, he saved the eggs from burning." Omondi shook his head. "There is such a thing as being overly civilized."

"Emmet wasn't like that. Bandits tried to ambush him

once on his way to camp. Instead of halting, he accelerated, ran right through them. He was an aggressive man."

"Yes, he'd have to be, to try and fight the world ivory trade." Omondi frowned. "And yet he let himself be trapped here and shot, without signs of a struggle."

My eyes ached with unshed tears. I rubbed them, trying to pierce the grief fogging my brain. "Maybe he knew the person so well he wasn't scared, wouldn't dream of throwing a burning skillet at them."

"You are thinking of Mrs. Laird."

"It fits, but I don't know. It seems so incredible—she was so cool when we arrived."

"Nothing here speaks to me of a bandit or a poacher. Would Emmet offer a thief breakfast? Would a bandit leave that wallet behind, in plain view, easy to find? Would a poacher, killing in revenge or warning, try and make the body disappear away from camp by forcing Emmet down to the water hole?"

"Why would Alicia kill her husband? Unless Mikki and Emmet had finally decided to divorce their spouses and get married." Mikki had been talking about that last week, but I'd let her tell Omondi herself. "What a disaster."

Omondi interlaced his fingers and shook his joined hands. "Murder is an act between two people, and to find the truth, you must recognize their relationship and their context. This is the African way—we uncover who they are, who their families are, what rip in the social fabric has given a doorway to evil. It is not enough to find a killer in traditional society. It is more important to mend the tear, to restore society to wholeness, and to do this, one must understand all the forces at work."

He turned his back on the kitchen lean-to and extended his arms to the enormous landscape that surrounded us. "Like the diviner with his magic, the police must use imagination, psychology, yes! But we are also modern professionals. We benefit from Western science and logic. Every fact must be examined and acknowledged, whether or not it seems at first to fit in with our theories. At the end, facts and theories will come together to show the truth." He brought his open palms together as if gathering in a sphere.

22

"So, we shall test Alicia's rifle because it was here, and because she is his wife. I found Alicia's reaction rather interesting."

"She's always a prima donna."

"Yes, but she talks too much when she is angry. It is useful to know that." Omondi studied the camp. "I think we have seen all that we can see, for now. This is a beautiful setting, but rather spartan for a permanent camp, wouldn't you say?"

"Emmet said simplicity was the one luxury few rich people could achieve. He used to compare this hilltop to living on a boat." I looked out at the sere hillside vibrating in the heat. A giraffe was slowly walking to the water hole, perhaps the same animal we'd scared earlier. "When the grass gets tall after the rains, and the wind blows, it looks like waves."

It was strange to think I'd be leaving town Monday with a load of carefree tourists who knew nothing about this, who just wanted to enjoy the wildlife and go home with beautiful memories. Maybe by the time I got back, the investigation would be over. There was one part of this job, though, that I couldn't leave to Omondi. I was Mikki Darrow's friend. I had to tell her myself that Emmet was murdered and that all signs pointed to his wife.

4

WE DROVE BACK to Nairobi in the glaring afternoon light. First I kept my window wide open, but the wind felt like a hair dryer blowing in my face, so I closed

23

it; but that was worse. It was impossible to get rid of the flies, and in the closed car their insistent buzzing around Emmet's body was louder. I opened my window again and concentrated on the road. After a while my hands stopped trembling on the steering wheel, and I realized I'd been clenching them so hard they hurt.

We passed a boy with a herd of black and white sheep, and later a peasant woman with a basin of potatoes balanced on her head, walking down a dirt track to nowhere. From the national highway Kenya looks empty, although it has the world's fastest growing population, exerting intense pressure on the land. Even a few years ago this area was richer in game, but we didn't see any animals except for a few tommies, a goat-sized, honey-colored gazelle with two stripes down its ass and a cute habit of looking at you over its shoulder.

Omondi wanted to know everything I ever knew, said, thought, or did with Emmet and the people surrounding him. Considering that I'd worked closely with Emmet as a volunteer on several occasions, and that he was Mikki's lover, I was surprised at how little I actually knew him. Emmet was one of those well-bred old Connecticut money types who gave the impression of being friendly but who actually considered intimacy impolite.

Our relationship was like the hamlets the road swept through now and then. There'd be a one-block stretch of turquoise, yellow, and red-painted shops with murals to entice the passing motorist: frothing beer steins, soft beds to sleep in, or steaming dishes of stew painted in bright colors. Behind the main street, shabby mud-brick houses surrounded by straw fences straggled a ways and then petered out into empty scrub land. What did I know of Emmet's reality behind his pleasing front? It was an odd feeling because I genuinely liked and admired him.

I was able to give Omondi the outline of Emmet's life, but none of the insides. I knew that his family sent him on a hunting safari to Kenya as a present after World War II, before going on to Yale; that he fell in love with the country and returned as soon as he got his inheritance, in the late Forties or early Fifties. He married some rich settler's daughter, had his son Garret, and was a rancher for a while before he moved to Nairobi and founded Kenya Trading Corp.

He hadn't become involved in animal conservation until he retired in the 1980s, when it suddenly became obvious that elephants would be extinct in another decade unless people did something about it. It was almost like a religious awakening for Emmet, though of course he never put it that way. He made a total commitment to halt the extinction juggernaut. He poured his fortune into Save the Elephants, funded research, funded educational campaigns, funded political campaigns. And it worked: Americans, who'd been fifty percent of the market, stopped buying ivory almost overnight; conservationists won a temporary proclamation that elephants were endangered; there was a two-year worldwide moratorium on the wholesale ivory trade; and for the first time, poaching was going down. That's why I was hopeful that if only I could keep Jazz Jasper Safaris afloat a little longer, the tourist trade would pick up again.

My throat was sore from the dust and so much talking, but at least it kept my mind off Emmet's body in the tarp behind us. Omondi kept throwing me one question after another.

When it came to Emmet's personal life, I had much less to tell. For example, I knew he had a daughter named Kim, from his second marriage, who was black and who wasn't on speaking terms with her father. But something about Emmet's manner had always made it impossible for me to ask about Kim, and Mikki said she had no idea what father and daughter had quarreled about, that Emmet didn't like to discuss family problems even with her.

"The daughter is black? African?"

"Her mother was an American black. Kim grew up mainly in the States, but after her law degree, she came back here to work with poor people. That's all I know about her. And that she has a temper. That's it."

Omondi made a thoughtful clicking sound. "Okay, tell me about something you do know—tell me the story of Mikki and Emmet."

"Mikki and Emmet." A wave of pity swept over me. "I

25

don't want to talk about Mikki, if you don't mind. With her it's the opposite—I know too much personal stuff."

Omondi answered sharply. "Nothing is private when murder knocks."

"You can ask her yourself."

"I intend to, but it is best if I have some background first. How did she and Emmet meet?"

"No, really, I don't want to talk about her."

Meeting Mikki—was it over two years ago?—had been a stroke of luck for me. When I first came out to Kenya, half crazy after the breakup of my marriage, she'd been a stable and sympathetic presence despite her own problems. Her situation, torn between a husband and lover, made divorce and celibacy look good. That was before Dan Striker and I became lovers, when I was in my super-independent period. Mikki encouraged me when I started my own safari tour company. She helped me get through the tough period earlier this year, when two of the people on my first tour were murdered. She was as passionate as I was about saving Africa's wildlife. In short, Mikki was a good and loyal friend, and a staunch ally in our common cause. Telling her Emmet was dead would be like plunging a knife into her.

Omondi's voice cut into my thoughts. "This is a murder investigation, not some gossip session. You think Mikki is off limits?"

I'd rarely heard Omondi voice annoyance so directly. I glanced over and was met with a steady unsmiling look. I turned my eyes back to the road. "I'm not saying she's off limits, but I'm the wrong person to ask, especially right now. I'm feeling really bad for her. I'm going to visit her after I drop you off, to tell her about Emmet, and I'm dreading it."

"Excellent. If you'll be so kind as to wait while I arrange for the body, I will go with you. I, too, want to tell Mikki about Emmet's death in person."

"Come on, Omondi. Don't be an asshole." I glanced over again and instantly saw I'd overstepped some cultural boundary. It struck me, too late, that Omondi was much more formal than I am, that politeness and respect were synonymous to him. I apologized and tried to explain, but

26

it did no good. We covered the rest of the trip in an uncomfortable silence.

When we got to the police station and Emmet's body was removed, Omondi stuck his head back in the car and told me to wait, that he'd be driving to Mikki's with me. What could I do? I waited.

While he was inside, I found a public phone and put in a quick call to Striker to tell him about Emmet. There was total silence.

"Striker?"

"I heard you." More silence. "Emmet. Goddamn it." I could hear a sound like a chair being kicked over. "I'm real sorry that you had to find him. We can talk more when you get here."

"I'm going over to Mikki's first, to tell her." For some reason, I didn't mention that Omondi was going with me. "I'll be too bushed to drive up after. How about you coming down to Nairobi for a change?"

Striker lived a few hours north of the city, in a cabin on the slopes of Mount Kenya.

"I have a better suggestion. I'll fly down to Nairobi, pick you up, and fly you over to the Darrows'. Then you can come home with me afterward."

"Striker, I'm just asking you for once to come to my place."

"You know your bed is too short for me."

I'd just found a friend murdered, and my bed was too short for Striker to come over? I knew he hated the city, but this was unbelievable. "Okay. Forget it. I'll talk to you later."

"Honey, don't be like that. You know I love you. I want to see you tonight. Don't be unreasonable."

We hung up without making peace. Great, here I was fighting with two men at once, when all I wanted was to be folded in warm, loving arms. I walked back to the car. Was this the old familiar me, pulling on my armor and retreating to the castle alone? Shit. But it was Striker's fault, too. *Honey, don't be like that* had become a refrain lately, but I was always the one who was supposed to change, to give way to his needs and his inner logic. If you love me, do it

27

my way. Shit. I didn't know who I was angrier at, him or me. And now I was going to have to sleep alone tonight. After facing Mikki with the horrible news.

By the time Omondi got back to the car, he found me weeping over the steering wheel. I felt like everything was going down the tubes: Emmet dead, my relationship with Striker full of problems, my business so bad I didn't know how long I could stay in Africa. Omondi didn't say anything, just put a warm hand on my back and let me cry till I was finished, then quietly handed over a large, white handkerchief. It broke the spell of coldness between us, and the ride up to the Darrows' was warm and companionable.

Residential streets whirred by in a blur of stucco verandas and untidy tropical gardens, punctuated by rows of single-story public housing along alleys of beaten earth. Children ran back and forth, babies strapped to the older girls' backs, while their mothers waited to fill basins and pails at public faucets. The city ended abruptly and we were in the open grasslands. Omondi, who was a widower, entertained me with stories about his twenty grandchildren, and I told tales about my tourists.

It was nearing sunset as we rumbled down the dirt track leading to the Darrows' house. Their property was surrounded by an immense cattle ranch whose owner believed cattle and wildlife could coexist. A big male baboon sat on a fence post, his little eyes bright with aggressive intelligence. In the gold of late afternoon light his fur looked wonderfully deep and lustrous. I thought I recognized him as one of the alpha males in the troop Mikki had studied before switching to elephants.

I pulled into the parking circle and paused a moment to gather my courage. A grove of gum trees, now giants, had been planted around the house long ago. It was dim green among the trees, and the spicy smell of eucalyptus engulfed us as we climbed the porch steps. As soon as we entered the house, I knew something was wrong, and it wasn't just the smell of burnt food. Mikki's husband Henry descended on me with an outstretched hand and hearty bellow of welcome, but he seemed to have shrunk. The last time I'd seen him had been last Christmas, at the Darrows' annual party.

He'd looked fine then, although he'd been unusually quiet. Was he ill? He'd lost a brother to cancer the year before; I hoped there was nothing wrong. He hadn't lost weight. It was more as if he'd contracted into himself.

Henry's handshake was as strong as ever. As he grabbed me and administered a sloppy kiss, I saw he'd hung an ivory gewgaw around his neck, a crudely carved elephant hanging from a string of ebony beads. I pulled back as if I'd been slapped.

Henry laughed and patted his beads. "I see you noticed my necklace. Nothing wrong with a man wearing jewelry, is there?"

This was why I didn't like visiting Mikki at home. I usually saw her the days she came into Nairobi to teach at the university. Henry was a contrarian, to put it kindly. He was a seventy-five-year-old naughty boy, putting a frog down your dress and laughing as you squirmed. For the thousandth time I wondered how Mikki could stand him. Presumably he hadn't always been this bad. People said that Mikki had married him to get ahead in her career, back when he was the Grand Old Man of primate studies and she was a struggling grad student, but I knew there was a lot more to it.

I gave him a crooked smile and asked, "What kind of game is this, Henry? Next you're going to tell me you've insisted on elephant steak for dinner."

"I bought Mikki an even longer string, but she wouldn't wear it."

"Did you buy that ivory recently?" I asked him, tired of the pretense that this was amusing.

Henry's eyes glittered with malice. "Ah yes, you're one of Mikki's lost causers, aren't you? When are you going to stop fooling yourselves?" He squeezed the ivory elephant around his neck and one of its legs broke off with a snap. He laughed. "Cheap little things. No matter. There's plenty more where this came from."

I looked at his yellowed teeth and wondered if killing his wife's lover would be Henry's idea of gallows humor. Time to change the subject before I murdered him. I introduced

29

Omondi as a friend. Henry bellowed a welcome at him, too, but without the kiss.

"Of course you'll stay for supper, though don't ask me how we're going to feed you." He gave an exaggerated sniff and waved a hand in front of his nose. "Mikki has been in a complete muddle lately. Last night she mislaid her field notes. You can imagine the hysteria. Turned out they were sitting right on her desk the whole time. This morning she disappeared for hours without telling me where she was going. She came back and burned dinner to a crisp, didn't even notice the house had filled with smoke. You picked a bad night to take pot luck, Mr. Omondi." Mikki, he added, had gone out for a sunset ride.

5

WE FOLLOWED HENRY's directions, drove down a track that started behind the stables, due west through a stand of gum trees, and there was Mikki, on a large bay horse, gazing into the western sky. This was going to be awful. At the sound of the Rover, she trotted down to meet us, her long auburn hair gleaming like bronze.

"Jazz, you must have been reading my mind! I was just wishing I could talk to you!" She swung off the horse and extended a muscled arm through the window to shake Omondi's hand. Her nails were bitten to the quick. "Come back up the hill and catch the view," she suggested, "before the light goes."

The three of us stood side by side and looked down into

the Great Rift Valley. On the hill below us a mixed herd of zebra and tommies grazed quietly, motionless except for the flicking of tails.

Mikki's horse inhaled with a snort to test the air. She patted him absent-mindedly on the neck, pulled the reins over his head, wound them loosely around her hand. He took a step or two away and began to graze. A moment later I realized there was a big troop of baboons picking among the grasses, probably searching for favorite herbs before climbing a tree for the night. I wondered if they and Mikki met on this hillside each evening to watch the sun go down.

I tried to find the words to start. This was a good place to tell Mikki, if any place is good to break someone's heart. At least she'd have time to react without Henry gloating in the background.

"That's the baboon troop I studied for about a decade," Mikki explained to Omondi. "I used to know every single baboon by sight. Now there are new youngsters and young males who have joined from other troops that I barely recognize."

A large baboon walked over to where a female with a tiny baby on her chest was feeding and made a sudden grab for the infant. "The bigger one is a higher ranking female," Mikki explained, "who lost her baby a few weeks ago. She's been hounding Sally, trying to hold her baby all the time." The mother screamed and held on. A large juvenile ran up screeching and darted at the interloper, but she ignored him and managed to wrest the baby from her mother's arms.

"Will she adopt the weaker one's baby?" Omondi asked.

"Probably not, although of course they're always surprising you, doing something you've never seen before."

The decibel level rose as more baboons rushed in to take sides. Then a large male, his mouth stretched wide to show chisel-sharp teeth, and his hair standing on end in an angry ruff, waded into the center, and everyone else scattered. He grabbed the infant and bit the would-be kidnapper on the thigh before she had time to get out of his range. He then calmly cradled the tiny baby in his lap while the mother inspected his hair for lice.

31

"The chief restores order among his wives," Omondi said.

Mikki's horse moved up behind her, rested his nose on her shoulder and breathed in noisily. Mikki gave him a light kiss on the side of the nose and shoved him away. "Actually, that big male isn't the dominant male in the troop, he's just one of Sally's two boyfriends."

"You mean they have reverse polygamy? The wife has two husbands?"

Why was Omondi encouraging this digression? He was making me very nervous. The longer we talked about baboons, the more the awful words stuck in my throat.

"My husband Henry was among the first to study wildlife in the field," Mikki said. Despite all that had happened since then, I could still hear the pride in her voice. "The first model they developed was sort of a harem, the strongest male mating with all the females, but what I learned with this troop is that male strength effects access to food but it's unrelated to reproductive access."

"Not a harem at all." Omondi shielded his eyes from the glare of the sun, which, as it neared the western horizon, seemed to take on speed as if eager to be gone.

"Do you want to hear more?" Mikki asked.

"Well, actually—" I began.

"Please, this is most fascinating," Omondi cut me off. Why was he doing this?

Mikki tossed back a windblown lock of her bronze-gold hair, a Botticelli in jeans and khaki shirt. Only her strong jaw and a certain unbending, clear-eyed look in her eye hinted that this was a hardworking, accomplished scientist. "A young male has to leave his family troop to join a strange troop where he can mate. His first problem is how to be accepted as a new member of the troop. How does he do it? If he's very aggressive and spends all his time fighting the other males for position, he scares off the females. It's a challenge for an adolescent male to calm down. He has to slowly win a female's friendship by hanging around her family, being nice to her children, taking her side in fights—like we just saw. Once she accepts him, the whole

32

troop will, plus she'll sneak off and mate with him when she's in estrous."

Omondi slapped his palms in appreciation. Mikki's horse shook his head, rattling his bit noisily. The closest zebra raised its head, studied us closely, then slowly walked farther off. Omondi kept exclaiming and asking more questions, noticing something new about the troop and asking Mikki to explain it, until she cried for release and I was ready to explode.

I finally caught Omondi's eyes and he nodded. I gave Mikki a little hug around the shoulders, gathering my courage.

Before I could talk, Mikki burst out, "I'm so glad you're here. I don't know what to do. Things have reached a crisis point. Could I talk to you for a few minutes alone, Jazz?"

"Sure."

Now it was Omondi's turn to frown, but he volunteered to wait by the car.

I only got out two words when Mikki cut me off again. "Emmet's suddenly decided we should marry, after all this time." My heart sank. "He's already told Alicia and he's moved out of the house. He's been after me to say yes and leave Henry. I agreed, but then I changed my mind. When it came down to it, I just couldn't tell Henry." She made a small fist and pounded her other palm. "God, am I a coward. I hate the thought of hurting anybody. And I love both of them, in different ways."

"Mikki—" I had to tell her.

She talked right over me, her words rushing out, hungry for a sympathetic ear. "Emmet says we can't keep leading double lives, and I know that's right. But I'm afraid Henry would never recover. He's so dependent on me."

"I don't know how—"

She hunched miserably. "Right and wrong seem all tangled together."

"Mikki." I pulled her around awkwardly to face me. "I don't know how to tell you this. We've come with very bad news. About Emmet."

Her eyes went round with fear. She swiveled to look at Omondi, who was a few paces away, leaning against the

33

Rover, then looked back at me. "What is it? Is he all right?"

"I'm sorry," I said. "Someone shot him. At his camp."

"Shot him? My God. Is he badly hurt?" Her eyes were pleading with me to say no.

"Oh, Mikki, he's dead."

She started shaking her head back and forth, no, no, no, face hidden by her long hair. All the life seemed to drain out of her body and she sagged heavily. "I knew she'd never let go of him."

"You mean Alicia?" Omondi asked softly. He'd instantly rejoined us. He must have been listening to the whole conversation.

Mikki said dully, "Emmet said she didn't care, as long as he paid her off."

She didn't say anything more. The robin's-egg blue of the sky deepened to cobalt, the lowering sun grew into a huge, wobbly pumpkin balanced on the far side of the rift. Mikki's bronze hair took on a molten glow.

Omondi prompted her gently. "I know this is a terrible moment. I would not intrude on your grief, except that time is a crucial element in finding the killer. Please, Mrs. Darrow, was there a particular reason you expected trouble from Mrs. Laird?"

Mikki pulled herself up, arms hugging her waist. "I didn't expect her to shoot him, if that's what you mean." As the daylight waned, her eyes looked dark and hollow.

"But you thought she would never let go of him?"

"Did I say that?" Her horse moved uneasily, rattling his harness. "I can't even think right now." The horse butted her with his long nose. She ran her fingers through his dark mane, but in such a frantic way, it made the horse more agitated.

Omondi asked what she knew of Emmet's recent whereabouts and actions. She told us in a slow, sad voice that she hadn't seen as much of Emmet as usual the last week. At the beginning of the week he'd been incredibly preoccupied with some new project that involved the ivory business—Mikki hadn't heard any of the details yet. Mostly they'd talked about getting married or not.

34

"Was it unusual for him to embark on a project and not tell you about it?"

"Yes, but given the circumstances—it's not every day you end a marriage. Emmet didn't show his feelings that much, but I could tell he was feeling tremendous strain. It was his third marriage, you know."

"It seems strange he asked Alicia for a divorce just before an enormous party at their house," I commented.

"I know. I told Emmet the same thing, but once he decides"—her voice faltered—"*decided* on something, he couldn't bear to wait. He only knew how to do things full speed ahead."

Omondi asked her some more questions. Mikki tried to be cooperative, but her voice kept fading away, she'd get distracted by the horse and lose track of what she was saying. Finally she asked, "Have you told Henry?"

"No. We wanted to tell you first."

"Would you mind terribly going ahead of me and telling him? I'd like a little time alone."

The thought of Mikki out here in the dark by herself didn't seem that great to me, but she swung up on her horse and reassured us he could find his way home blindfolded. It wasn't the horse I was worried about, but there was no point insisting. I wished I hadn't told Omondi I was coming here. I felt a complete failure. I hadn't been any comfort at all.

By the time we neared the house, the piercing voices of the peepers were in full chorus. Light spilled from the windows onto the sere front lawn. The house was an ample square with a wraparound veranda under the broad overhang of a corrugated metal roof. A row of battered wicker rockers were lined up to face the view of rolling grass and distant volcanic hills, but no one sat there.

"An impressive woman, your friend Mikki," Omondi said.

"It would have been better if she'd screamed or cried," I said. "Holding everything in like that worries me."

"She's in shock. The tears come later."

"I couldn't believe you kept asking about the baboons."

Omondi took my elbow and guided me toward the porch

35

steps. "I wanted to lead up to the bad news gently, not knock her over with it before she'd even met me."

I pulled my arm out of Omondi's grasp—I hate being gripped above the elbow—and slipped my arm through his. Our footsteps matched. We were almost the identical height. "You wanted to size her up."

Omondi ignored my remark. "Also, the fables people tell about animals reveal most about their own human nature. I did not know about these changing scientific theories. Most fascinating cultural keyholes."

"So what did you see through the keyhole?" I waved Omondi ahead of me through the screen door.

"Mikki told us a sweet story of the female choosing her own mate, who is also her best friend. She wants to see a world of love, not power or violence. But what we saw among the baboons with our own eyes was a violent fight."

6

HENRY WAS SITTING on one of the shabby couches in front of the fireplace, cradling a glass of whiskey and soda. He got up as we entered. "Sounds like Mikki's been expounding her theories to you. I couldn't agree more with your comment, old man. You can't understand animal or human nature without explaining aggression."

"And cooperation. Both exist." I sank down onto the other couch and let my head fall back, feeling utterly weary. Sammy, the Darrows' pet mongoose, jumped up on my lap and nosed at my pocket, skittering out of reach when I tried to pet her. She fixed me for a moment with her shiny round eyes, then disappeared under the couch.

The room was a curious mixture of African artifacts and European antiques, dominated by two Maasai spears crossed above the fireplace. To their right were faded photographs of Henry's early days of Kenya. My favorite was a group portrait of the first baboons studied in the wild. Against the far wall was a dark oak sideboard displaying a Georgian silver tea set flanked by life-size silver pheasants. Above the sideboard hung a row of oil paintings in gilt frames.

Omondi went over to look at them. "Your ancestors? Imagine these paintings being crated up for the long voyage from Europe to Africa, down the English Channel, through the Straits of Gibraltar, the Suez Canal, down to Mombasa and then overland to their place on this wall. They must feel quite displaced."

"Not at all, my dear man. My family has had a long history in Africa, you know, going right back to the seventeenth century. The family fortune was founded on the slave trade." He smiled, ready to enjoy Omondi's discomfort.

Omondi returned to the oldest portrait. "Truly, the face of evil is so often banal." He turned. "There is no sign of your wife in the room. Most unusual."

I'd noticed that, too, and puzzled over the reason. Henry dominated here, as if he'd never made room for another personality in his home. Maybe at first Mikki was overawed, and later she didn't care. Emmet's house was the opposite, or rather, the same: it was completely Alicia's creation. This room was full of beauty, and yet it made me uneasy.

Henry, for once, was at a loss for words, and hid it by bustling about bringing whiskey and sodas.

I took my drink over to study Henry's grandfather, the Victorian paterfamilias, with his corseted wife and six cherubic children in velveteen suits and crinoline dresses posed under a tree. He was tall and broad-shouldered, like Henry, with the same bushy brows and a pudgy air of prosperity.

37

The family mansion stood on a knoll in the distance, complete with tiny sheep clipping the greensward.

Omondi came next to me. "Ah, the Victorians! With their simple and self-serving view of the universe."

"Yes, doesn't he look virtuous and pleased with himself?" In a way, I envied the Victorians. They saw nature as a bountiful mother whose limitless treasure was theirs to grasp and consume like a greedy baby. They worked to control and possess nature, to domesticate her as they domesticated their women. Lucky for them, nature was big, far bigger than man in those days, and they were safe from realizing their goals. Our generation was left to reap the marvels of such science and industry—an overpopulated and poisoned planet, heading toward mass extinction.

And now there was one less person to hold back the tides of death.

Henry looked at the door. "What's taking Mikki so long?"

Omondi returned to the couch and I followed. "I told Mikki some bad news. She wanted to be alone for a bit." I took a deep breath. "It's about Emmet Laird."

Henry eyed me brightly. "Well? Go on." He took a sip of whiskey and sat opposite us. "I wondered if there was a reason for your dropping in on us tonight. Don't be so mysterious."

"Emmet has been murdered."

"Murdered! You don't say!" Henry got up and fidgeted with some carved wooden animals lined up on the mantelpiece. "Murdered? How did you hear of it? How did it happen?"

Sammy slipped from behind our ankles and started inspecting the room, running rapidly under the couches, under the chairs, poking her nose in every dark space and hole, all the while talking to herself in a flow of squeaks, grunts, and chatter.

"He was shot through the chest. I was there with Omondi when we found him."

"Where?"

"At his camp," Omondi said.

"You don't say." Henry tossed a wooden hippo in his

38

hand. "Bad business. Bad business all around. Any more of these murders and we can kiss our whole tourist industry goodbye. They keep blaming it on Somali guerrillas, but I say: who's being paid off?"

"It's not the usual story," I insisted.

"Why do you say that?" Henry put the hippo back on the mantel.

"They didn't go after the elephants, just Emmet, and they dumped his body next to the water hole."

"The water hole? Heavens, why?"

"Probably to make sure the body disappeared fast, but it backfired. Broken Tusk's family group was milling around when we arrived, creating an enormous rumpus. They'd buried Emmet as if he were a family member."

"But that is extraordinary! Nothing like that has ever been reported in the literature. Burying a human being?" He gave a nasty laugh. "Not that I imagine Mikki will be writing it up for her favorite quarterly journal."

It was just the sort of tasteless reaction I'd expected from Henry. I hoped he wouldn't keep it up once Mikki returned, but I wouldn't put it past him. Sammy provided a timely diversion. She began to stalk the silver pheasants and was on top of the oak sideboard in a fluid leap. Omondi crossed the room with his quick stride, scooped her up and deposited her in my lap, a small, furry gift of comfort. Her coat was a coarse gray-brown, marked with the dark stripes that give the banded mongoose its name. She struggled for a moment and then gave in to my petting, even deigning to let me scratch her under the chin.

"Truly extraordinary," said Henry. "Still, it might be poachers. Who else would shoot Emmet?"

Neither Omondi nor I said anything. I wasn't about to share the evidence against Alicia with anybody, let alone Henry.

He looked at us and gave a long wicked-sounding laugh. "You don't suspect me, do you?"

"C'mon, Henry. Why would we suspect you?" I asked.

"Manly honor may not be what it used to," said Henry "but still, Emmet Laird has been diddling my wife all these years." He walked stiffly to the bar and spoke over his

39

shoulder as he poured himself another drink. "Maybe I finally got fed up and decided to put an end to it. Ha, ha. That is rich."

"Mikki thinks you don't know," I told him.

"Oh, that's a good one." He sat down opposite us with his free hand making a fist on his knee. "What does she think I am—deaf, dumb, and blind? I might be old, but I'm not that old. She comes back from those Save the Elephant meetings with this certain unmistakable glow that I haven't seen in years, and all the time thinking she's pulling one over on me. That's rich!" He gave another cackle and took a big slug of whiskey. "Emmet's death is bad news. I'm in big trouble now."

"In trouble?" Omondi asked.

"That affair was the only thing keeping this marriage alive. With Emmet gone, Mikki will walk out on me. You see what it's like here. This place is a time capsule. History has passed me by. I have even less future than the elephants." Henry returned to his spot by the mantelpiece and gave the hippo a poke. "Damn!"

He moved to sit down, then suddenly swiveled and hurled his half-full glass into the fireplace. The glass shattered against the stone, splattering shards around our feet. Sammy scrambled over my shoulder, digging in with her sharp claws. Henry flung open the screen door, muttering something about finding Mikki. His steps thudded on the porch. He was gone.

Mikki and Henry returned together, she stiff and hollow-eyed with grief, he hovering and solicitous. I made an omelette and salad for supper, and somehow the four of us managed to get through it. Over coffee Mikki announced she'd like to go to Nairobi with Omondi and me and sleep over at my place. At least she offered Henry some face-saving excuses: it was her official responsibility to see what had to be done at Save the Elephants, since she was now the top officer and there was the year's big fund-raising party only three nights away. Henry tried to persuade her to cancel, but Mikki insisted that if Alicia would still let them use the house, the event should go on, dedicated to Emmet.

Mikki set her jaw and kept repeating it was her responsibility.

Finally Henry got her to agree to sleep in her own bed with the offer that he'd fly her into Nairobi the next morning. I was to pick her up at the airport and we'd go together to the Laird mansion, ostensibly to pay a condolence call and talk to Alicia about the fund-raiser. Going to the Laird's was the last thing I wanted to do, especially since I had a full day planned to get ready for Monday's safari, but what did that matter next to giving Mikki all the support I could? We agreed to meet at eleven.

She bent into the car to give me a goodbye kiss. Her cheek felt cold. "Thanks, Jazz," she whispered. "I hope you understand. I have to see Alicia's face for myself. Once I see her, I'll know. I'm sure I'll be able to tell."

7

IN DAYLIGHT THE drive home from the Darrows' is one of the most beautiful on earth. My favorite view is halfway along the A104, where the road runs along the edge of the Kikuyu Escarpment and the earth plunges two thousand feet straight down to the floor of the Great Rift Valley.

I'd come this way many times with Striker, to go bird watching at Naivasha, to take the turnoff for the B3 and the long, hot drive across the Rift valley to the Maasai Mara plains, or just as often, heading for Lake Nakuru, with its flamingo-bright beauty. Tonight all Omondi or I could see was the unrolling black stillness of the road. It matched my thoughts.

The car pounded on, mile after mile through the dark, sleeping countryside. The way events were shaping up, I wouldn't have time to go to Striker's place this weekend. Unless he deigned to come down to the city, we wouldn't see each other before I left. Accepting each other's independence was great, but sometimes . . . I'd been over it so many times in my mind, the thought followed a well-worn groove without requiring any response from the rest of my brain. I concluded, as usual, the problem was that Striker and I were too alike.

Omondi exclaimed and threw up a hand to block the glare of oncoming headlights dead center in the narrow road. The worst risk at the moment was not moving smartly enough when one of the hard driving truckers decided to avoid a pothole by borrowing my lane. The concept of defensive driving had never caught on here. Truckers especially seemed to rely on their magic charms to an alarming degree. Luckily there was little traffic at night. I squeezed right, hoping not to hit the road's scalloped soft shoulder. The truck roared by with a whoosh.

"Are you worried about your friend?" Omondi raised his voice above the roar.

"My mind had drifted." I felt embarrassed. "But I am worried about Mikki. I wish, for her sake, that Alicia wasn't the prime suspect. It makes the horror of losing Emmet more personal and bitter. It's as if Alicia finally won."

Omondi shifted to face me. "I hope you're not going to tell Mikki what we saw at Emmet's camp and our preliminary conjectures." He emphasized the last two words. "Remember what I told you last time. Examine everyone, suspect no one, until the final evidence is in. There is no chief suspect yet, as far as I am concerned."

"Of course I won't tell her. That's police business." I don't like keeping secrets from a friend, but I can do it.

"We will know a lot more in the next day or so. Sergeant Kakombe should have arrived at Mr. Laird's camp with the forensic team while there was still light. And the pathologist promised to do the autopsy tomorrow." He looked at his watch. "I mean today."

"I thought there were no cars for Kakombe to use."

"Oh, I located a car for him." Omondi sounded grim. "The fellow in charge of records is a cousin of a cabinet minister. He thinks he can reserve a police car and driver for his own personal use."

"Will you get in trouble for taking it?"

"No. The mechanic is a friend. The would-be Wabenzi thinks the car is being fixed." Wabenzi was the nickname for the new African elite, made up of government officials whose symbol of social arrival was a Mercedes-Benz.

We were still in the vicinity of Nakuru when I had to slow down to a crawl. The road was all torn up for repairs, or maybe a bomb had hit it. The truck that appeared behind me from out of nowhere didn't feel slowing down was necessary. His headlights flooded the Rover, catching Omondi's alarmed turn as if in a spotlight. It sounded as if there was a diesel locomotive in my backseat, and coming closer.

On pure reflex I threw the wheel over to the right, crashed through a yellow sawhorse, bounced over the torn-up pavement and careened onward, tires half on, half off the road. I watched with slow motion horror as the car hurtled toward a mountain of gravel. I pumped on the brakes and fought for control. Inches—well, a few feet— from the pile of stone, the Rover came to an abrupt halt at a forty-five-degree angle, the near tires in the air, the far tires sunk to the axle in a sand shoulder. I guess that's what the gravel was there to fix. The trucker didn't stop. His rear lights gleamed like angry red eyes and then blinked out as he rounded a bend.

Wanting to howl with frustration, I got out to assess the damage. Omondi stumbled over something in the dark and cursed.

"On the bright side, at least the engine's still running," I said. Both upper tires were flat, but, prepared for safari out in the far bush, I always carried two spares.

We set to work and changed the tires by the hissing white light of a portable gas lamp. But then even with four-

43

wheel drive, the car was at such an awkward angle, I couldn't get enough traction to pull out of the soft shoulder.

It was forever until another car came by, and it was a pip-squeak Morris Minor. We didn't even bother to flag it down. By the time a passing truck stopped and pulled us out, it was past two in the morning. I drove a bit farther, but I couldn't keep my eyes open, no matter how hard I tried. It had been an exhausting day, and even at the best of times I'm no good at staying awake once my body has decided it's time to be asleep. It's as if I have an automatic turnoff switch in my brain. It used to drive my ex-husband crazy, but I don't mind, except for the odd time like this, when falling asleep could be downright dangerous.

The second time I startled awake at the wheel, I told Omondi there was no way we could make it back to Nairobi that night. He was ready to head for a Nakuru hotel, but agreed with my suggestion we camp by the lake instead. We could drive into Nakuru in the morning to fix the tires before heading home, and I'd still have plenty of time to meet Mikki by eleven. I found the campsite, an old favorite, and pitched a small two-man tent. I'd never been there without Striker.

"Where do you want me to sleep?" Omondi asked.

Where, indeed? I was acutely aware of our privacy. A lion grunted in basso profundo, maybe a quarter mile away. Closer at hand, a tree hyrax shrieked like the damned. It's a tame little creature that looks like an oversized guinea pig, but it sounds scarier than the lion. I remembered the smooth warmth of Omondi's chest and thighs, the way we'd laughed together.

"Your choice: the car or the tent," I told him. "I'll sleep in whichever you don't."

"You're sure?" Omondi stepped toward me. I could have moved away, but I didn't. He encircled me in his arms and kissed me tenderly, then harder. He started a row of little kisses along my throat, and as I flung my head back, the stars filled the sky above us. Decision time. I could conjure up the memory of Striker and say no, or I could remind myself I was a free woman and say yes. Omondi kissed the pulse at the base of my throat and I could feel my heart beating under the soft pressure of his lips.

I pulled back and rested my forehead against his cheek. "No. Not now, not here. It's too confusing."

"Do you want a declaration of my intentions?" Omondi smiled. "I intend to make love to you." He moved my hand to his lips and kissed the palm.

"Yeah, I got that part." I dropped my hands.

He encircled them in his and kissed them again. "And then—is it all right if we don't know? We feel something special for each other in our hearts. Who can tell the future?"

"Omondi, I can't. I feel the special link between us, too, but as long as I'm involved with Striker ... I just can't make love to two men. It's not fair to anybody. It makes a mess and hurts people too much. I don't want someone to do that to me—and I won't do it to Striker. Or anyone."

"You can't make life act so neat and tidy ..."

I started to protest, and he put a finger softly on my lips.

". . . but we do not have to be the same. This is how you are. It is understood."

Omondi gave me a small, good-night sort of kiss. I was both disappointed and relieved. Luckily, I was too tired to spend time feeling virtuously frustrated. Omondi generously opted for the car, and I crawled into the tent. Seconds later it was morning.

I awoke before Omondi and started coffee going on my gas canister stove. Near the water's edge the silver branches of a dead tree carried dozens of pinkish-white baby pelicans, looking comical with their Jimmy Durante bills. I filled my lungs with the cool morning air, pungent with green and rotting scents from the acacia woods behind us. It was the first time since Emmet's death that I'd been able to really breathe comfortably. I felt a rush of confidence and strength. Omondi woke up and reached out with both his arms to embrace the lake.

"Look at this!" he exclaimed. "We are in paradise."

The lake was shrouded with sweeping tendrils of mist. As we watched, a long line of lesser flamingos floated into view, heads held in a graceful curve reflected in the perfect stillness of the water. The sky was crisscrossed with wavy lines of greater and lesser flamingos, looking like shadowy wraiths in the distance where the mist robbed them of color, turning a clear pink as they drew closer. A deep murmur, accented with gooselike honks, rose all about us. Omondi pointed as thirty greater flamingos flew over us with a slow flapping of their scarlet-lined wings.

When they passed, he turned to me with a beatific smile. "The mattress was a bit hard, but no hotel could compete with this. Shall I get us some water?" He gestured toward the flat shore.

"Not from there. Nakura is a soda lake. It's worse than sea water." How could he not know that? How could I have a relationship with him? We had nothing in common, knew none of the same things. I showed him where the water barrel was stowed.

Omondi filled his palms with water and splashed it on his face. "Ah, that feels good."

I leaned against the Rover. "Flamingos are very ancient and unique. They live on a microscopic shrimp that can only survive in this special environment. There are three other soda lakes in Kenya's Rift valley, and that's it. That's their whole world."

Omondi must have read something on my face. "You are thinking I'm an ignoramus." I handed him a towel and he dried his face. I braced myself, fearing I'd insulted him again, but all he said was, "I am such a city person. To me, this is like a foreign country."

The coffee smelled ready. I poured out two mugs. Omondi added three teaspoons of sugar and stirred vigorously. "I was in school before independence. We learned all about Europe, nothing about Africa. On my time off I visit my family, in tea country. All the animals there were exterminated back in the Twenties and Thirties by the British. No one minded then. We just minded them taking our land."

Omondi didn't spell it out, but I knew that it was mostly white tourists and the occasional Indian family who had a car, as well as the time and money, to enjoy Kenya's wild

46

places. No wonder it was mostly Americans and Europeans who cared about conservation.

A black and white fish eagle took off from a drowned snag, plunged headfirst toward the water, pulled up at the last moment as it grasped a fish in its sharp talons. It gave a cry of triumph as it bore off its heavy catch with powerful wing beats.

I sipped my black coffee. "I'm going to be back here the second week of my next safari. If the investigation is finished by then, maybe you could take the time off and come with me. We're going to do a figure eight, visit mountains, plains, lakes, and forest."

Omondi laughed and shook his head. "You are overly optimistic about my talents as a detective. But I will remember your offer."

And I said I didn't want to complicate my love life? What in the world was I doing, inviting Omondi to spend a week camping with me? I couldn't pretend to be just pals with him, not after last night. Was I inviting Omondi along because I was mad at Striker? Or was Striker's refusal to come through for me this weekend the death knell of our relationship? The thought of giving up on Striker made me sad. He was such a special person. I thought of Mikki losing Emmet. I thought about making hard choices—and missed opportunities.

We drank our coffee and watched the mist burn off the lake. A pale blue mountain rose on the far shore, with what looked like a pink sand beach at its foot. It was a million flamingos gathered in the shallows. Closer at hand a flock of roseate spoonbills bathed and preened their feathers, and a circle of pelicans fished in unison.

Nakuru was once a pleasant country town, I hear, before Kenya's population bomb exploded. Now it wasn't so much a city as a way station for lost humanity, a jostling mass of desperately poor people, most of them children and teenagers with no past, no present, and no future.

Even before we reached the edges of the national park, my eyes started to water from the newly built sewer system, an open canal leading away from the city right up to the park boundary. It threatened to replace the Eden we'd

47

seen that morning with a lot of dead animals and an open sewer of human shit. There was no money to do any better. Emmet had been trying to find a sister city in America that might help, but these days Americans were too tight-fisted even to build their own sewer systems.

I gripped the steering wheel and controlled my urge to run people over. This is what Nakuru always does to me. I'd be a raving lunatic in a week if I had to remain here. I needed to find a garage, get those tires patched, and get out.

The mechanic was a jovial fellow with a missing front tooth and oil-stained hands, full of smiles and jokes. He tried to sell me two spares so bald they were as thin as playing cards, but it was just for the fun of it. Then he tested my Swahili by asking if I knew the words for cock and cunt, with an open good humor that had me laughing as hard as everyone else. He carried off my two dead tires for patching, while Omondi and I waited at a little table set up near the gas pumps. We talked with a few youths who were hanging around, bored and sociable. One sweet-faced man in his mid-twenties confided he had an uncle in Nairobi who had good connections and was working on a government sinecure for him. He used the word *job*, but since neither qualifications nor work came into the concept, it seemed a misuse of the term.

Finally the tires were done, and Nakuru city grew small in my rearview mirror. I dropped Omondi off at his place, with just enough time to go home and shower. When I got out of the shower, the red message light on my answering machine was blinking. I had the horrible thought it was the tour group canceling. Or maybe my landlord threatening to cut off my electricity again. Lately the messages seemed to be mostly bad news.

I pressed the rewind button with trepidation. It was Ibrahima, my safari manager and cook, calling to tell me the driver we'd lined up for Monday had taken another job, but he thought my old driver, Chris Mbare might be available. I groaned. It would be great if we could get Chris, but otherwise—I hated the thought of setting off with a driver I didn't know. It could ruin the whole trip if he wasn't good

48

in cross-country game drives, or, even worse if he wasn't safe. If worse came to worst, I could do both the driving and the game spotting myself. It wasn't ideal, but maybe it wasn't such a bad idea. It would be one less salary to pay. I looked at my watch. I had no time to deal with this crisis. I barely had time to get to the airport by eleven.

8

MIKKI WAS PACING up and down the sidewalk in front of the terminal. She got into the car and gave me a quick kiss. She looked exhausted and miserable, but what did I expect? She was in a somber brown dress which set off her bronze hair as if burnished, but she'd tied it severely at the nape of her neck. The pulled-back hair made her face seem exposed and vulnerable.

"You still want to go through with this visit to the Lairds?" I asked. "If you like, I'll coordinate with Alicia about the fund-raiser."

"Don't worry about me. I can handle seeing her." Her voice lowered and grew intense. "I told you, I want to look her in the eye."

I edged into the traffic on Langata Road. I thought Mikki was being irrational, but she had a right to act weird. Death affects the survivors in funny ways. As her friend, it was my job to be sympathetic and make sure she didn't get into too much trouble.

The Laird mansion was only a few miles out of town, smack against the southern border of Nairobi National Park. As we approached the park gates, Mikki asked me to pull into the park for a moment. I showed my season pass at the ticket booth. A hammerkop—whose large head does bear an uncanny resemblance to a mallet—flew past with a stick in its beak, heading for an enormous, messy nest it had built right next to the parking lot.

"Any particular spot you want to go?" I asked Mikki.

"I don't care. I need to talk to you about something important before we see Alicia. It won't take long."

The park's main road led through a stretch of woods and then to an open plain, where a mixed flock of zebra, wildebeest, and Thomson's and Grant's gazelles grazed with seeming concentration, ever alert for predators. The details of the animals' coats stood out in the clean air with the luminous colors of a Van Eyck's newly invented oil paint. I pulled over to the side and cut the engine.

"Jazz?" Mikki looked out her side window, so all I saw was her bronze hair and a bit of her elegant profile. "I have something rather unusual to ask you. Please consider it before saying yes or no."

Nairobi's skyscrapers formed a jagged silhouette across the horizon like a mouthful of broken teeth. I agreed uneasily, wishing she would face me.

"Emmet's murder could be a complicated business—maybe involving his family." Her fingers plucked at her skirt. All her nails were bitten to the quick, like a child's.

"I know what you mean, but really, it's too soon to say."

"It was you, not Omondi, who cracked that murder case on your first safari."

A jackal trotted across the road, nose up, tracking a scent.

"Only if you consider getting shot as cracking a case. What are you getting at, Mikki?"

She stopped fiddling with her skirt and looked straight at me. "I want to hire you. To catch Emmet's killer."

"What?" A gazelle that had drifted next to the car was startled by my exclamation and trotted off rapidly, tail flicking across its neatly striped rear end.

She cut me off. "Hold on. I've been thinking about this since last night. I *need* to do something. You understand."

That wasn't a question. We were the same in this regard,

50

and I did understand. Sitting around and waiting for other people to solve a lover's murder would drive me crazy, too.

"I'm a suspect, of course," Mikki continued. "I can't investigate without looking even more suspicious."

"You, a suspect?" But even as I questioned it, I knew she was right. That was why Omondi insisted on coming along with me last night, and why he let her talk on and on before telling her about Emmet. "Okay, you're right. You probably are a suspect at the moment, along with dozens of other people who were close to Emmet. It doesn't mean anything at this stage. Please leave it to Omondi. If he gets stuck, then hire a professional investigator. It's not that I don't want to help you, but—I mean, I'm not the right person."

Mikki set her jaw. "You are. You're the best person. I told you, I've thought this all through." She shifted in the bucket seat to face me more directly. "You've solved two murders, the one here and that one in Sicily. You're as experienced as anyone I could find in Nairobi, and twice as capable." She looked into my eyes, measuring my reaction, willing me to agree with her. "You have an entrée into the family—they know you, you've worked with Emmet, you found the body. You can get information informally in a way no one else could." She broke her gaze and looked down. "You can probably get information from Omondi, too. He was very willing to include you last time."

"It's a crazy idea. I'm not a professional investigator. I have my own business to run—"

"I'd pay you, of course—generously. You could use the money. You were just telling me last week that you don't have enough work to keep Jazz Jasper Safaris afloat much longer."

I laughed. "So what else is new?" Mikki knew the hole I was in. Still, I loved running my own business, worries and all. I like being my own boss. Working for a close friend, and on what seemed like a personal vendetta against a rival, was a recipe for disaster.

"And besides, I trust you. You're the only person I can turn to. Please, Jazz, don't say no to me." Mikki covered my hand with hers. "It will help us both out. I want to find

Emmet's killer—whether it's Alicia or someone else. If we wait for the police to mess up before even trying—the trail will be stone cold by then."

I'm a sucker for being needed. Maybe one reason I like Striker is that he's so independent he never exploits my rescuing impulse. With women, I have a harder time saying no. This time I was saved by my schedule. "Mikki, I'm leaving Monday on safari for two weeks."

Her face fell with disappointment. "Shit, I forgot all about that. It slipped my mind completely. But when you get back—"

"Let's discuss it then," I said like a coward. Mikki would probably feel calmer in two weeks. "Who knows? The police may have it pretty much sewed up by the time I get back."

"And if they don't? Tell me you'd at least consider it."

Mikki looked so hurt, my heart went out to her. I couldn't bear to turn her down flat. "I'll consider it."

I started to turn the car around to head back the way we came. Mikki stopped me. "Go straight, then take the next right. I'll show you a secret route to Emmet's through the southern boundary. Very few people know about it. You'll see why."

A flock of helmeted guinea fowl scuttled into the tall grass, checkered in black and white like op art chickens. We left the plains and entered a heavily forested area. The road climbed and twisted. Then just past an old Cape chestnut tree, Mikki directed me to take a sharp right. Faint ruts along an overgrown track showed that an occasional car had passed this way before.

I glanced up at the chestnut as we passed, and there was a spotted leopard lying along a branch in the dappled shadows. The carcass of a Thomson's gazelle dangled under its front paws. I was so close, I could clearly see the leopard's chin matted with fresh blood.

The track plunged down the far side of the ridge, requiring all my attention, through a rocky gorge, and then climbed steeply up the far side. We were surrounded by dense undergrowth that cut off vision on all sides, when I saw a green archway of foliage framing blue sky. I headed for the opening and we popped out of the forest onto the Lairds' rough-cut lower lawn. Mikki jumped out to swing a gate shut behind us, annoyed that someone had left it open.

"I can see why Emmet didn't advertise the existence of this route to his back door."

"He liked to be able to visit the park without having to go all the way around, deal with traffic and visitors."

Faint tire marks led past the pool pavilion, where we picked up a graveled drive, passed through an allee of jac-aranda trees, a shrubbery—and there was the front of the mansion ahead of us. As far as I could tell, no one had seen us.

"The guards at the gate will be awfully surprised to see us leaving when we never arrived," I said.

Mikki gave a tense smile. "Oh, they're used to my com-ings and goings. They'll just assume we drove in during an earlier shift."

My feeling of dread grew stronger as I parked in the semicircle in front of the Laird mansion. A crested crane rose with a cry from a grove of flame trees that flanked the house. Beyond it a series of garden terraces flowed down to a sweeping lawn, cut off by the wild trees of the National Park. The pool wasn't visible from the house. Above the treetops I could see the open grasslands we'd come from, dotted with miniature wildebeest, zebra, and gazelle. A breeze brought the smell of jasmine from the garden and the sound of zebras neighing from below.

"I would kill to keep this property, wouldn't you?" said Mikki.

I gave her a sharp look. She smiled tightly.

"Not Alicia." The gravel crunched under our feet as we walked under a portico of white pillars to the front door. "Bet you anything she sells this place and buys a big house on Embassy Row."

"You're assuming she stays in Kenya."

I shrugged. "Who knows?"

Before we could ring, the door was opened by a short, fat, dark-skinned man all in white.

"Hi, Joseph. We've come to pay our respects to the fam-

53

ily." I stepped cautiously onto the marble floor, polished highly enough to reflect the crystal chandelier hanging twenty feet above our heads. Did Emmet go through culture shock each time he returned from his camp to this house? *Alicia's Palace* he used to call it, but that was long after he'd fallen out of love with her. I thought it unfair to pin all this on Alicia. It was his house and his ego, too. Africans give cows as a bride price; we give houses.

Joseph greeted us quietly, saying how sorry he was about Emmet.

Mikki gave him a quick hug. "You've known Emmet longer than anyone, haven't you?" she asked.

"That's right, miss. He hired me the day he arrived in Kenya. For many, many years I was his personal driver. Did you know that? Then one day he took pity on all my gray hairs and said, 'Driving is too much hard work. From now on, you will be my personal man.' You see? He was a good man," Joseph added sadly. "I never thought I would bury him first."

"It feels strange to be here without him," I sympathized.

"Makes me feel very bad." Joseph walked heavily across the foyer and opened the sitting room door. "Me and the elephants, we're going to miss him the most of all."

Not as much as Mikki, I thought, as we followed his ample back. It sounded as if Joseph didn't know about Emmet's hopes to marry Mikki, or maybe he was being diplomatic. Although it wasn't too diplomatic to say he'd miss Emmet more than Alicia, was it? He must have known most of what went on in this family, might even have been in Emmet's confidence about the breakup of his latest marriage. I imagined that in their long time together, through Emmet's three wives, Joseph had protected many secrets. He'd have a lot to tell the police, if they could get him to open up.

The sitting room was at the back of the house, commanding the view. I had to admit it was a beautiful room, although far too formal and ornate for my taste. There were two smaller crystal chandeliers. The walls were painted a soft green, with garlands of fruit and antelope heads in stucco around the top. There were several seating areas with matching couches; pale pink and green Chinese rugs, the requisite coffee and end tables, each with their collection of silver-framed photos; carefully arranged silver boxes and candle snuffers or whatever it was that you were supposed to scatter around to show that you were wealthy, of old family, and had good taste. I didn't think that was Alicia's background and wondered if she had copied it all out of a magazine. It had that too-perfect look about it.

When we first entered the room, it appeared empty, until I noticed a tendril of cigarette smoke rising above a tall-backed armchair at the end of the room. Joseph announced us, and Garret Laird popped up from the chair like a startled hare. His large white hand hung flaccid and damp in my own as I shook it and offered condolences. He mumbled something I couldn't catch and then flopped back in his chair.

A second servant appeared. "You rang for refreshments, sir?"

"Oh yes, good idea. Just the thing. I would like a lager, Nelson." Then remembering his manners: "What can I offer you? The lager is very good. I special order it from a small family brewery in Kent. I daresay this is the only place in Africa where you can get the stuff. First rate."

I asked for a club soda with lime instead, but Mikki took up the offer of lager. That settled, Garret sank back in his chair, looking exhausted.

Mikki and I offered our condolences.

"Shakes you up, doesn't it?" Garret put a hand to his midriff. "I feel like I've been kicked by a horse."

"How's Alicia bearing up?" I asked.

"Just as you'd expect," Garret drawled sarcastically. "I'm jolly sorry for you, Mikki."

"Thank you." Mikki looked around the room. "Is Alicia home? I was hoping to talk to her about the fund-raiser."

Garret mashed his cigarette into a pink and green china ashtray and immediately pulled another out of the pack with his thick white fingers. "Alicia made an appointment to see the lawyer this morning. Greg took her. Losing not a minute." His fingers trembled as he put the cigarette to his lips. "I overslept. Took some sleeping pills I found in

Father's dresser. Terrible stuff. Look how shaky it's made me. Old boy was hooked on them. With his manic personality, it was hard for him to turn off and go to sleep."

"I'd say energetic rather than manic," I said, wondering if Garret routinely poked around in Emmet's dresser.

Mikki got up and began to stride about the room, picking up and putting down small silver objects. I'd noticed Garret have a similar effect on Emmet, the few times I saw them together in the same room.

Garret looked at his watch. "Wonder what's keeping them?"

Our drinks arrived. Mikki took hers and went to stand at the long row of French doors that gave onto a balustraded terrace. Garret slurped down a third of his glass and wiped the foam off his long upper lip with the back of his hand.

A silence fell. It was never easy to find a topic of conversation with Garret, even at the best of times. I searched around for something to say. "I hear you've launched a new enterprise?"

"You mean Father complained to you about my latest crazy scheme." Garret's lips twisted in a self-mocking smile.

Garret knew Emmet's attitude toward himself all too well. It was not that Garret's ideas were stupid. The trouble was that he saw his role as lord of the manor, counting the profits without doing any actual work. Emmet had stopped giving him loans long ago. Poor Garret was reduced to surviving on the interest from his mother's trust fund, which he stretched out by living with Emmet and Alicia. With free room and board, he could save his own income for essentials, like lager from Kent and club dues.

"No, Emmet didn't tell me. What is it?" Mikki was stalking the room again. She walked through a shaft of sunlight from the French windows and her hair briefly flamed red.

"I'm building a luxury resort on Umar Island, just up the coast from Lamu. It's going to be the ultimate tropical paradise getaway. We've dredged a nice little harbor. The dock is finished—big enough to handle the construction equipment."

56

"You're doing this on your own?"

"It's my brainchild, although, of course, I don't have the capital for a scheme of this size." Garret waved a hand. The lit cigarette slipped through his fingers onto the Chinese rug. He groped for it ineffectually. There was the sharp smell of burning wool. By the time he picked up the butt, it had left an ash-sized black scar on the pink and green carpet. "Alicia is going to have a fit when she sees this." He tried to scuff away the mark with his foot. "Oh, my." He gave up on it. "Where was I?"

"Umar Island."

"That's right. One of my backers pulled out, and for a while the whole project looked rather dicey. Father was rather annoyed with me at the time. I thought he might have said something."

"No, Emmet never mentioned it to me," Mikki said. "Look at this, Jazz. They're feeding the kites." Mikki made room for me at the window.

Below us, a servant was out on the lawn with a great bowl of red meat cut into chunks. Above his head there was a swirl of kites. The hawklike birds were as common as pigeons in Nairobi. He flung the morsels high into the air and the birds swooped to catch them in mid-flight. The air was filled with piercing cries, acrobatic twists, dives, and ascents as each one tried to grab the meat and then keep it from being stolen.

The sound of a woman's heels rang out on the marble floor and Alicia strode into the room. No bright colors, no swirling skirts, no jewelry, no cleavage. She wore a collarless gray suit with a straight skirt, and high-heeled shoes that I imagined would pierce tiny half-moons even into beaten earth. Instead of her usual knock-'em-down smile, her jaw was clenched so hard that the muscles bunched and quivered.

Alicia stripped off her gloves and threw them with her pocketbook on a chair. She hardly gave Mikki or me a glance. "Garret, you will never believe what Emmett has done to us. I am contesting the will, that's all. I am contesting the will."

57

"Alicia, don't. You're scaring me." He reached for a cigarette. "How bad is it?"

"As bad as it could be."

Garret groaned. He was older than his stepmother, but the only clue was his thinning hair. If anything, in her presence he grew more babyish than ever.

Joseph came in with fresh drinks on a tray. Alicia practically grabbed the whiskey glass from him.

Garret reached for a lager. "Joseph, quick, give the condemned man his last drink."

A look of contempt crossed Alicia's face. "Oh, stop whining before you even know what's happened."

"Tell me, for God's sake."

Greg spoke from the doorway. He looked more like a banker than a jock today, dressed in a well-fitting black suit. "He hasn't disinherited you . . . completely."

"Greg, come get a drink." Alicia strode back and forth angrily. "That bastard and his goddamn elephants . . ."

At the word *disinherited*, Garret looked as if he'd been slapped. "Don't joke like that. Emmet told Kim he'd taken handsome care of all of us."

"You mean before they stopped talking," Alicia said.

"He changed his will?"

"No, this bill—this will, I mean—was written years ago. Handsome! Handsome!" Alicia sloshed her drink as she turned on Garret. "I don't know what Emmet told Kim, or why you believe that crazy sister of yours."

"Will you two tell me what he did?" Garret broke in.

"Greg, you tell him. I'm so mad I can't talk straight."

Greg obligingly sat down in the wing chair facing Garret. In a matter-of-fact voice he said, "He left half his money outright to Save the Elephants."

"And the other half?" Garret rose partway out of the chair. "What about the rest of the money? What about the house?"

"The house and the rest of his investments are in trust." Greg seemed to be playing out Garret's rising hysteria like a fish on a line, while flaunting his own complete self-control.

58

Garret sank into the chair and held his head with both hands. "Damn, damn, damn."

Greg went on in his calm banker's voice, "The house is for all or any of you, including Kim, to use for as long as you live. After your collective demise, or if no one chooses to live in it permanently, it, too, goes to Save the Elephants."

"And the money?" The words rose without hope from Garret's hidden face.

"We each get a stipend from the interest," Alicia said. She mouthed the word *stipend* as if it were a bug. "The capital is being saved for guess who. God, I could kill every elephant I see." She threw back her head and emptied her glass with an abrupt motion and then turned for the first time to Mikki. "I bet you know, don't you?"

Mikki stood tall. "No. I can't say I do."

"Funny. I thought Emmet told you everything." She let the silence dangle. "The elephants, obviously, can't spend the *endowment* themselves." Her mouth curled over the word. "You have sole discretion, little Miss Scientist. Sole discretion over a goddamned fortune!"

9

I CONVINCED MIKKI she needed to eat, even if she wasn't hungry, and we headed over to Shabaan's Bar and Grill, hidden in the warren of streets behind the old market. A short flight of steps led down to a sort of ante-room presided over by Shabaan himself, splendid in an embroidered grand boubou and Muslim cap. He had pockmarked skin, dark as espresso, that caught gleams of light from the street door. Shabaan was from Mombasa, on the Indian Ocean, once home to the Arab slave traders who dominated the coast and left behind a heritage of Islam and Swahili, a part-Arabic trading dialect. His kitchen was famous for fresh fish brought in daily and grilled over a bed of hot coals.

Shabaan's warm greeting turned solemn as Mikki murmured to him that we needed a very private table and there was something she wanted to tell him. Shabaan didn't say another word, but led us past the long mahogany bar. The bartender, a broad, slow-moving Indian called Raj, nodded in greeting, his right hand never stopping in its rocking motion, slicing orange after orange with a sharp knife as he prepared the famous Shabaan screwdrivers.

It was early for lunch, and we passed only one or two tables of people we knew, and greeted them without stopping. It was dim and cool inside. We walked under a broad arch into a back room. Shabaan led us to a small alcove that held only two tables, and the three of us sat down.

The waiter glided up moments later with our freshly squeezed screwdrivers. A busboy appeared to fill our water glasses and serve rolls, and at a sign from Shabaan, he scooped the place settings off the nearby table to ensure our complete privacy. A red-coated waiter with grizzled hair announced the catch of the day, rock cod or parrot fish, and went off to place our order.

Shabaan folded his hands and quietly waited for Mikki to begin.

Mikki took a breath and said all in one go, "Emmet was shot to death yesterday at his camp. Jazz can tell you more."

"Yes, I have heard this sad news. It is in the paper." Shabaan's face betrayed no sign of emotion, but his big soft shoulders drooped. "It is sad news, indeed. Mr. Laird was a fine man, a friend of Kenya."

I told him in a few words about driving down to Emmet's camp the day before and finding the body.

Shabaan blinked his eyes knowingly. Giving information to Shabaan was a form of currency that he could be trusted to spend wisely and repay in dividends many times over. This time, the payback was immediate. "And to think just last week here he was, at that very table," he pointed his chin at the table next to us, "having lunch with his beautiful daughter, for the first time in a long time."

Mikki leaned forward. "With Kim?"

"Yes. They sat right there." We all looked at the stripped and empty table next to us. Mikki and I exchanged a curious glance.

"Do you think they made peace with each other?" Mikki asked.

Shabaan looked doubtful. "A fine thought—Allah be praised," he intoned. He got up heavily and took his leave.

Mikki. and I lifted our glasses. "To Emmet."

The drink was cool and redolent of oranges. I looked at my watch. Service at Shabaan's was never rushed, and I'd have plenty of time to call into my answering machine before the food arrived. There was a post office a few doors down that had public phones. I wanted to see if Ibrahima had left any more news about finding a replacement driver. This afternoon was going to be incredibly hectic as it was, with all the necessary reconfirmations and rechecking of supplies to be absolutely ready for the tour group's arrival Sunday night. As always in Africa, there were sure to be both major and minor disasters requiring last minute attention.

I excused myself and trotted over to the post office, heading straight for the newspaper kiosk. I had a morbid curiosity to see if Emmet's death had made the front page of the *Daily Nation*. It had, with a grainy photo of Emmet and a banner headline: ELEPHANTS BURY BENEFACTORS BODY. They played up the animal angle, but they also rehashed the spate of poachers' attacks on tourists in revenge for the ban on the ivory. This was going to be terrible for business.

I called in for messages. One from Striker, to say hello. One from Omondi, saying I should come in to headquarters to give a formal affidavit at my earliest convenience.

The last one was from the U.S. Adventure Travel Agency, whose group was arriving Sunday night. Betty Ann's voice, usually bubbly, sounded businesslike and terse. "Call me as soon as possible."

Kenya is eight time zones later than New York, minus an 1our for daylight savings, so if Emmet's obituary was on the news wires yesterday evening our time, it would have hit their afternoon papers, a day ahead of breaking here. It also meant Betty Ann must have set her alarm for two A.M. to try and reach me first thing this morning. It was not going to be good news.

I called the operator and she got me a long distance line in only five minutes. Five minutes of purgatory. I stared at the scruffy wall opposite the phone booth, trying not to think of the repercussions if I lost this job. I couldn't borrow any more money. I could sell the Rover to pay the rent, but then what happened to my business? Striker and I wouldn't last a week if I moved in with him. This was the end of the line. Goodbye, Jazz Jasper Safaris. I supposed I could try to get a job working for another safari company, but everyone's business was suffering. Did this mean goodbye Kenya? I wouldn't accept that. The phone rang and I picked it up. The operator told me the call was going through.

Betty Ann didn't waste any time. "Bad news, I'm afraid. You probably know what it is."

"You're canceling the tour."

"There's no way to pull it off. We've lost half the people, and there's no time to make up the number, even if the waiting list folks were willing to go on safari with a killer on the loose. There are more murders in New York City in a week, in a day probably, than Kenya has in a year, but try telling them that. Why waste your breath?"

"Half the people canceled after one news report?"

"Considering your name was in the paper—after that, forget it. You discovered the body? Was there a tour with you?"

"No. The man who was killed was a friend."

"I'm sorry. Dreadful thing. And they think it was poachers again?"

"No, actually they don't. They think there might be a personal motive."

"Well, that does us no good, I'm afraid. With the elephants burying this poor guy, it makes it into a big story. The afternoon papers gave it a lot of play, and it even got onto the eleven o'clock news. Like I said, after that, forget it. I had the first cancellation before the station break."

We exchanged pleasantries about working together, and Betty Ann said she'd wire me my half of the late cancellation penalty fees. That wouldn't even pay for a ticket home.

As soon as Mikki saw me, she asked, "What is it, Jazz? What's wrong?"

I picked up my crumpled napkin and slipped into the chair. "My tour is canceled."

"Oh, no!" Mikki was a good enough friend to think of me first. "What will you do now?"

I shrugged and smoothed the napkin over my thighs. "I really don't know, Mikki. I needed the work."

"Jazz?" Mikki studied her knife, tilting it back and forth, as if watching her reflection appear and disappear in the narrow silver blade. "My offer to hire you to investigate Emmet's murder still stands."

"To tell you the truth, I don't think it's a good idea. You're all upset right now, and you want to do something, but . . ." I shook my head.

"But what?"

"I'm not qualified. I'm too involved myself to be objective."

"You're selling yourself short. I have confidence in you. I know you can do this job if you're willing to take it on."

"And I think you're gunning for Alicia."

She stared into the knife's bright surface. Tilt, tilt. A band of light bounced off the silver knife and moved across her face. "So what, as long as you have free rein to examine all possibilities? I'm not asking you to frame her, for God's sake. You know I'm not."

"That didn't even cross my mind."

She put down the knife. "Well, then?"

She'd out-argued me, and she could tell. "Just think about it for a minute. Honestly, Jazz, wouldn't you like this job? Not just for me, but for yourself. You know you're good at this stuff. And I'm sure you want Emmet's killer

63

found almost as much as I do." Emmet and the elephants seemed to be staring beseechingly through Mikki's eyes. "I mean, otherwise, you're just going to be hanging around, going crazy."

I was wavering.

"If it comes out soon that Alicia did it—and I'm just saying *if*—tourism would pick right up. People are afraid of being killed by poachers in the bush, and who blames them? It's not just you whose business is affected. Think of the whole tourist trade, all the people who work for you."

Pretty soon she'd be telling me all of Kenya depended on me.

The waiter pushed through the beaded curtain into our alcove carrying a whole parrot fish on a platter. He deftly skinned and boned it, and slipped the filets onto our plates.

Mikki bent toward me. "Are you afraid? If it's that, just tell me, and I'll drop it."

"No, I'm not afraid. It's just . . ." Just what? Mikki's arguments made sense. Corny as it sounds, I did want to bring Emmet's killer to justice. Still, part of me didn't want to get involved. I'd come to Kenya to catch hold of the last remaining bit of Eden in the world, to get away from heartache and human betrayal after my divorce. I knew all too well the murderous feelings divorce could bring up, no matter how civilized you thought you were. I admired Emmet, but I had the impression he had hurt a lot of people, his children as well as his wife. Did I want to uncover the underside of his life? Would Mikki thank me if I did? On the other hand, looking for the killer was more constructive than sitting around in mourning for Emmet, for elephants, or for Kenya's future. You can only run from problems so far—at what point do you turn and fight to protect what you love?

I picked up the lemon half and squeezed it all over the fish. I had thought I wouldn't be able to eat, but I was suddenly ravenous. "Let me think about it. You'll be at your office this afternoon?"

Mikki jumped up and wrapped her arms around me. "You're a wonderful friend."

"Whoa! I haven't said yes."

"Yet." She went back to her seat looking as if a great load had been taken off her mind.

"You know the adage: never mix business and friendship," I said as I dug into my fish. "I don't want to do something we'll both regret."

"I'm sure we can handle it. I won't tell you how to do the job. I'd like to be kept informed, but that's up to you."

"Seriously, you should think this over, too. Do you want to feel responsible for finding the killer if it turns out not to be Alicia? Garret and Kim, for starters, also expected to inherit a fortune."

"I think Kim wrote Emmet off long ago as a neocolonial elitist, or whatever her jargon is."

"That doesn't mean she'd written off his money."

We tossed that one around for a while. The waiter appeared to whisk away our plates and pour us small cups of strong Turkish coffee from a long-handled brass pot. I took a tentative sip and almost scalded my lip. "Or what if Henry found out that Emmet asked you to marry him?"

Mikki gave a crooked smile. "Henry? He talks mean, but he's so transparent, he's like a big baby, really. Besides, I didn't tell Emmet yes." Mikki started fiddling with her silverware again. "But listen, Jazz, I'm not hiring you to pin this on Alicia. I want to see justice done, whoever the killer is. I mean it."

Mikki insisted on paying the bill and took off. I sat staring at the white stucco wall, letting the full disaster of the canceled tour sink in. Then I started to mull over what I knew about the murder and Emmet's situation. I felt the stirring of excitement at a challenge, and yet also a sense of foreboding, warning: keep out. Like the sign near the witch's castle in *The Wizard of Oz*. "I'd turn back if I were you," I muttered out loud.

"Pardon?" The waiter stopped at the arched entrance, smiling at having caught me unawares. He was a man in his fifties, with a dignified manner. Heavy black-framed eyeglasses perched incongruously on a neat, round nose.

"I was just talking to myself." I smiled back. "You served me last time I was here with my friend, Mikki, didn't you?"

He came up to the table, pleased to be recognized. "That's right. You two usually order pudding, but not today." He cleared away Mikki's empty cup and whisked off some invisible crumbs.

I wondered if he'd also served Emmet and Kim. "May I ask you something?"

"Of course." Not a moment's hesitation or qualification. If I asked for a loan or a place to sleep that night, he'd probably agree, like most Africans, without a second thought.

"Do you know Emmet Laird?"

"That's an easy one," he said in his soft African-British accent. "Everybody here knows Mr. Laird. I am terribly sorry to hear he's passed beyond. May the Lord bless him."

"I feel very sad, too. Shabaan told me Mr. Laird had lunch last week with his daughter, Kim." I nodded at the table next to me. "I heard that in the past they didn't get along too well."

The waiter shook his head as he picked up my Turkish coffee cup and balanced it on his wrist next to Mikki's empty one. "Oh, there are always mischief makers ready to talk about everybody's business. Myself, I am not the gossipful type."

Shit! It would be my luck to find a waiter who disapproved of gossip. I slipped a couple of hundred bob notes under the salt shaker. The waiter shifted his weight from one leg to the other and made no move to leave. "Do you think it was a lunch of reconciliation between them?"

The waiter put the two hundred shillings in his pocket. "Thank you, memsahib. To tell you the sad truth, I felt very bad for Mr. Laird. The younger generation doesn't show the respect they owe to their elders. With my own son, it is the same way. Always answering back. In my day, if you dared speak to your father like that, the strap would teach you a different way, that I can assure you, and if there was no strap handy, a fist would do. The young women are even more shameless—their husbands beat them and they are back in their mother's hut the next morning complaining and saying they won't go home again, that the bride price

66

must be returned. How is harmony to be preserved in the family if the man is not respected?"

"Kim was not respectful? What did she say?"

"Oh, I wouldn't like to repeat her language. Where there is no shame, there is no honor. That daughter, she is a girl who leaves home without bringing her father cattle." He thrust out his lower lip. "A girl her age should have many children by now. It is not as it should be."

"So they were arguing about marriage?"

The waiter looked puzzled. "Marriage? Perhaps. Of course, I was back and forth, serving many tables." He thought for a moment. "No, I can't say they mentioned marriage."

I wondered if I'd misunderstood, or if two hundred bob wasn't enough money, or if he was just taking his time getting around to the actual lunch between Kim and her father. I'd never quite gotten the etiquette of giving bribes. I always feel awkward, even when I know it's expected. Or maybe there was no etiquette—just the more the better. I pulled out another hundred shilling note and slipped it under the salt shaker. "What did they talk about?"

The waiter shifted his weight, still balancing the coffee cup on his wrist as easily as if it were attached there. "They discussed Mr. Laird's oldest son. Now, there is the same problem. He is living in his father's compound, like a good son, but where is his wife? I have a son the same age, and with only one wife, yet they have produced eleven sons and also many daughters, and he is paying the school fees for his younger brothers. What good is money if you have no wives and no children?"

The more he told me, the less I knew. I was beginning to wonder if the waiter overheard anything at all. One more try and I'd give up. "With your wonderful memory, I bet you could tell me Kim's exact words to her father."

"I heard her words, but this I cannot repeat." The waiter pursed his lips.

I shifted the note that I'd put under the salt shaker. He slipped it in his pocket. I waited expectantly.

"Mr. Laird wanted his daughter to do something to help her brother, as is natural. That brother, it is well known, he is foolish with money. One cannot both feast and become rich. The daughter, she is a hard worker."

I nodded. "A hard worker, but not respectful."

"No respect. I was bringing coffee and pudding when Miss Laird jumps up like she had cockroaches in her pants—and that big girl, she shouts right in her father's face. I tell you, a demented person would behave better. We have a saying: if your mouth turns into a knife, it will cut off your lips."

"Umm," I agreed. Inside I was screaming, What did she say?

"Can you imagine, to say such a thing to her father?" He faltered.

"Yes?"

Visibly reaching for his courage, he whispered, "I don't care what you found. Take the goddamn tusks and shove them up your ass."

I went back to the post office and left a message for Mikki at her office: I would take the job.

10

THE NAME FLOATED by itself in the middle of a smoky glass window in the oak door: KAMARIA LAIRD, ATTORNEY-AT-LAW. I could hear the sound of an old-fashioned typewriter clacking away.

Four Maasai filled the small waiting room. There was a young man in an ill-fitting Western suit, nervously tapping one foot. The others were old men, draped in red or red-checked blankets knotted over one shoulder. One of them carried a knobby club. He hawked loudly and spat on the floor. The old men's earlobes had been stretched into open hoops, decorated with loops of silver. One of them, his face as wrinkled as a fallen leaf, also had a wire triangle dangling from the top of his ear. The young man had the same stretched-out earlobes, but he'd taken out the jewelry.

I gave my name to the secretary, who nodded and kept on typing. Her beaded braids rattled each time she moved her head.

It looked like I was going to be here for a while, so I sat next to the young Maasai and said hello. He spoke English. The oldest man was his father, he explained.

"He's very old to be your father," I said.

"Yes, the oldest of my father's twelve brothers."

"Ah." And I'd thought father only meant one thing.

They'd come to Kim for help in a land dispute with a brother-in-law, who claimed the old man had sold him a piece of land and had a deed with the old guy's thumbprint to prove it. The old man was illiterate, but he could tell a swindle when he saw it. He claimed he'd signed a deed for another, smaller, parcel. Now it was a question for the Kikuyu-dominated courts. Chances for justice were slim, but at least the nephew could speak English and help with the lawyer.

"I think you have come to the right place," I reassured him. "This lawyer is very powerful, on the side of the people."

The young man relaxed a notch at my words, and translated them into Maasai. The old man gave me a snaggle-toothed smile and said something.

"What did he say?" I asked the young man.

"He says, you are not a young girl and yet your breasts are still standing up."

"It's because I have no children."

They discussed this new fact. The young man turned to me. "He is very sorry. There is a woman with strong magic who lives not far from Narok. Maybe she can help you."

A plump woman in none-too-clean clothes came weeping out of Kim's office, cutting short the medical referral and the Maasai filed in. A copy of the *Daily Nation*, with its

69

grainy photo of Emmet, lay on a scuffed table next to me; I turned it over.

A woman with a big-eyed baby on her back came in, unslung the baby and started nursing. A while later a woman in a tight purple dress and a pungent cloud of cheap perfume joined us.

Kim certainly had an unusual clientele for a graduate of Harvard Law. I admired her for her values and her guts, and imagined Emmet would have, also. Yet something had gone terribly wrong between them. How had Kim become a sore subject he never mentioned?

At last the Maasai left and it was my turn to go through the inner door. I must admit I was a bit nervous.

The sight of her stunned me into silence. Mikki hadn't told me she was such a beauty. Of course, Kim had grown up in the States, only returned to Kenya a few years ago. Had she and her father quarreled almost immediately? Maybe Mikki had never met Kim. I'd have to find out. Emmet was too much the gentleman to tell Mikki his second wife was gorgeous, and so was their daughter.

Kim was around thirty, a woman in the full force of her physical prime. She had a high brow, elegant cheekbones, and wide, shapely lips. Her features were perfect to the point of coldness, but her warm brown skin had a lustrous shine, and her body was full of life, rich, curving, with an athlete's sense of latent power and confidence.

She came around the desk, gave me a firm, businesslike handshake, and signaled me to take a seat. "How can I be of service?"

I gathered my wits. "I'm a friend of your father's. Let me tell you how very sorry I am about your loss. He was a wonderful man."

"Is that what brought you here?" The voice turned a shade colder, and her clear, intelligent eyes narrowed.

"Not just to offer condolences, no. I went to visit Emmet at his camp, and was there when his body was discovered." I figured she'd ask me some questions, but she didn't. I plunged on, feeling my palms begin to sweat. "There are indications he was killed because of an investigation he'd recently undertaken." Still no reaction. "Into the ivory trade."

Kim didn't so much as blink. "Were you working with him on it?"

"I've been working with Emmet for the past few months." And did I just set myself up as the next victim? a small voice inside me asked. "I'd heard he'd contacted you recently about the subject."

"You know I have no sympathy for your pro-elephant movement?" Her voice had turned to icy cymbals.

Trying to keep cool, I said rather stiffly, "That's not why I'm here. I'm trying to find out who he talked to, what he found out, so we can find his killer."

"Who's *we*?"

"We? I hope it includes you. Everyone who'd like Emmet's murderer caught."

"I don't think your *we* includes me. A white man gets killed and everyone's in an uproar. Two black men were shot on sight yesterday as poachers, but that's considered good news." She didn't raise her voice, yet each word was like a fist. "So don't come crying to me about how noble my father was, and what a big loss to Kenya. I don't think Kenya needs people like him."

"People like him!" I jumped to my feet. "Your own father?" My hands were shaking. "And you preach about respecting people's lives?"

Her eyes glinted with tears, but her mouth tightened. "Get out of here."

"Wait." I sat down and tried to still my trembling hands. "Kim, I saw your clients out there in the waiting room. I don't believe you really feel this cold-blooded about Emmet, about any human being."

"Spare me the soap opera."

At least she wasn't throwing me out. "As a lawyer, surely you don't condone premeditated murder? Besides, your father wasn't killed for politics; he was killed for money."

Kim thought about this for a moment.

"If it was because of poaching, we want to find the

71

higher up, the guy who ordered the killing, so it won't be pinned on some poor, defenseless person."

She nodded grudgingly. "What do you want? I have five minutes."

"Why did Emmet contact you about the ivory trade?"

"He didn't. There's no reason that he would. I know nothing about ivory."

All I had to go on was the waiter's report of one overheard sentence, but I was going to use it for all it was worth. "Emmet thought you knew something about the tusks he found."

"If so, he was mistaken."

Aha, so Emmet had found tusks. "What did he tell you about them?"

"I'm not about to repeat libelous hearsay."

The second tiny piece of information. Emmet had accused someone, someone Kim knew, or why go to her? I racked my brains for a clever follow-up question and came up blank. "He accused you?"

"I've said all I'm prepared to on that subject." She started playing with a stray paper clip on her desk.

"What else did Emmet want to talk to you about?"

"I wouldn't know. He's the only one who could tell you what was on his mind."

"What made me think I could worm information out of a Harvard lawyer?"

We both smiled.

"All right." Kim threw down the paper clip she'd uncurled into a wiggly line. "Emmet and Alicia were splitting up, and he needed advice about a prenuptial agreement they'd signed before getting married."

Thrown off by this complete change of topic—as she undoubtedly intended—I blurted out, "Why would he consult you on his divorce plans when you two weren't even talking? That makes no sense."

Kim raised a softly arched brow. "If I don't want to tell you something, I'll say so. You can take everything I've said as the truth."

"You're playing word games with me."

"Look, do you want me to tell you about this or not?"

"Please ..." I gestured for her to continue.

"He and Alicia were married when I was in law school. Prenuptial agreements were a new phenomenon. I sent his lawyer some information on them. I don't know what final form they came up with. And you're quite right, Emmet was not consulting me as his lawyer."

There were whole chapters missing in Kim's story. The prenuptial agreement probably existed, since she knew I or the police could check it out, but that wouldn't prove Emmet had gone to talk to her about it.

Kim looked at her watch. "I've given you all the free time I can afford. I have important clients waiting." She stood up.

"May I make an appointment to continue our discussion?"

"I see no point in that."

If she'd decided to talk to me only to find out how much I knew, it was pretty obvious to both of us that I knew little or nothing. But I did know a hair more than when I'd started. Emmet had talked to her about tusks, and her evasiveness, even her volunteering information pointing to Alicia and away from ivory, told me she was hiding something. But what? I wasn't going to get the answer here. I needed to start at the other end and discover, from friendlier sources, what Emmet knew, what led him to Kim. I had a few ideas.

"Your five minutes are up." She opened the door, said "Next" to her secretary, and stood aside to let me pass. "Goodbye, Miss Jasper."

She didn't add, "Good luck."

11

WHETHER I FELT like seeing Striker or not, it was time to talk to him. If Emmet had told anyone what he'd discovered recently about the ivory trade, it would be Striker. I headed north on Murango Road to the A2 and the familiar route through Thika and Kiganjo to Mount Kenya.

Winding up the red dirt flanks of Mount Kenya, I passed an elephant family browsing among the trees. They'd knocked one medium-size acacia completely over. Two other trees had been stripped and would soon die. Bark hung from their oozing trunks in long tatters. The elephants were slowly and methodically tearing off branches with their clever trunks and stuffing them into their mouths.

I was almost there. Striker had built his cabin on an ancient migration route. For millenia, every dry season the elephants moved onto the mountain, then returned to the plains with the coming of the rain. Now that most of the plain was taken over by people, the elephants were stuck here year-round, not giving the forest time to recover.

I pulled up next to Striker's Land Cruiser, composing arguments in my head to convince him he had to break his rule and tell me about his current investigations. It's not safe for you to know this until it's public knowledge, he'd say. And I'd say . . .

A crown-of-thorns bush resplendent with hundreds of small scarlet flowers bulged into the parking area and gave my arm a sharp poke as I squeezed out of my car. All was quiet, except for the ever-present whine of insects and a distant birdcall off in the jungle. A flock of superb starlings crowded a feeding pan set on a stump by the kitchen window. Their sapphire feathers threw off sparks of light as they fluttered and darted for the last remaining crumbs. A black and white hornbill many times their size landed in the center of the pan with a squawk and set the starlings flying.

I was smiling about the birds as I pushed open the door, anticipating Striker's welcoming hug. There was no welcome. It was quieter in the house than outside.

"Striker?" No answer.

The little cabin fit Striker like an old glove, its every surface contoured to his personality. The living room was comfortably cluttered with magazines and newspapers, abandoned coffee cups, and well-used furniture. Odd rocks, seashells that had caught his fancy on long-ago vacations, and twists of sun-bleached wood jostled for space on the bookshelves that covered two walls. The place reeked of coffee, but then Striker was known to concentrate so hard on what he was doing that he let his coffee boil down to sludge.

"Striker?" I glanced into the bedroom. It was empty. The mattress was half off the bed. Odd. He obviously wasn't home. But his car was here. I pushed against the study door. It didn't open. I pushed harder and heard the slither of paper across the floor. The racket in my brain saying something was wrong rose to a shout. I shoved my shoulder into the door and got it wide enough to wiggle through. An avalanche of books had come off his shelf and jammed against the door. I took a step forward, unbelieving, not wanting to believe. The innards of his computer crunched under my feet. The fireplace poker lay across what remained of the computer monitor. Books lay open and mashed into the floor. Papers were strewn everywhere. His radio had been ripped from its cabinet and stomped on.

I went to the kitchen, almost running. A pot of coffee had been knocked over and spilled across the stove and floor. A chair lay on its side with one leg snapped off amidst a litter of broken dishes.

I turned and ran for the radio in my car to get the police. All I could think was: he may still be alive, he may still be alive. But if his Land Cruiser is here . . . Before I could get the car door open, I heard something moving in the brush next to the driveway and dropped to a crouch, my heart pounding. The sounds were coming slowly closer. A man walking cautiously? Or a foraging animal? It sounded big, and I didn't want to come nose to nose with a wild boar any more than with whoever had trashed Striker's house. As silently as possible I snuck around to put my car between me and whoever or whatever was approaching. I peered under the car. The rustling got louder.

I heard a familiar voice yell "Damn," and out stepped Striker's black high-top sneakers.

I jumped up. He was giving the crown of thorns a dirty look and sucking the side of his thumb.

I rushed to him, threw my arms around his chest and pulled him close, breathing in his spicy masculine smell. His chest felt hard and solid as a rock. I never wanted to let go.

He nuzzled my hair. I turned my face up to his and we kissed long and fervently. Striker's green-brown eyes reflected the forest around us. "I don't need to ask," he said. "You've been inside."

"Where were you?"

"Checking to see if the bastards who did this came through the woods." He took off his wide-brimmed safari hat and slapped it against his thigh. "Goddamn bastards."

"Who was it?"

"Shit, I don't know. I didn't find anything. It looks like someone waltzed up the road, found the place open, and—goddamn." He yanked open the door, and as we went in, the smell of spilled coffee assailed us.

I went to the office door and looked in at the mess. "I guess we should leave it untouched for the police."

"No, I'm cleaning it up. I don't want the police."

"But Striker, this must be connected to Emmet's murder. It's too big a coincidence that one day he's killed and the next your place is searched and smashed. Weren't you two working together on some new ivory trade investigation?"

"Nope. Nothing recently." He headed for the kitchen. "Coincidences happen more than people realize. It's called the laws of chance."

76

"What if you'd been here? They may have been looking for you!"

"Don't let your imagination get carried away," he called from the kitchen over sounds of rummaging. "There's been a lot of problems with Somali bandits around here." He re-emerged with a broom and large trash can. "Ever since we've squeezed their poaching revenue. You should see what they did to the Stedmans' place."

"A thief would have taken your computer and radio, not smashed them. Whoever did this wanted to destroy information, or else send you a warning."

"Or they were pissed off there was nothing much to steal. These guys want money, a TV, something they can sell—not a computer." He pushed past me into the office.

I couldn't believe he was ignoring my opinion so totally, especially since I knew I was right. He picked up the remains of his computer and dumped it with a loud noise into the trash. "C'mon, Striker. Stop that, and stop this bullshit about thieves. It's just too big a coincidence." He ignored me, started gathering papers and piling them in neat stacks. "Listen, I know Emmet was working with you on the ivory trade."

Striker looked up for a second. "Who told you that?"

"Alicia." I didn't tell him it was more of a guess on her part. But she did say Emmet was upset about something he'd discovered, and asked if he'd called Striker. She must have gotten the idea from somewhere. "Plus, he contacted his daughter Kim and they exchanged words about tusks he'd discovered. This presents a whole different angle on why he might have been murdered. I came up to see what you knew about it." I looked around me. "This looks like the murder has an ivory connection to me."

Striker started putting books back on his shelves. "Different angle from what?"

"There could be personal reasons, too," I said reluctantly. "He decided to ask Alicia for a divorce and marry Mikki, although she hadn't told him yes. Who knows, maybe Alicia or one of his kids decided to stop it."

"Wait a second." Striker turned with three books in his

hands. "Why are you so up on all this? How did you find out about his conversation with Kim?"

"I went to see her at her law office and I asked her."

"Oh, no. No, no, *no*." He put the books on the shelf and came over to face me. "Jazz, you are not going to get into investigating this murder. Once was enough—you almost got killed last time."

"Almost doesn't count." I smiled, but he wouldn't smile back.

"If it's a family feud, you don't want to get in the middle—and if it's about ivory, you are dealing with very serious, very deadly criminals."

"Like whoever destroyed your computer," I retorted. "They might have left fingerprints or hair or something. We've got to call the police."

"Listen, I'm going to take care of myself. I suggest you take care of yourself. And leave the police to take care of themselves."

"And what about Emmet? Don't you care that he's dead?" I could feel my face getting hot.

"Whoa, Jazz." Striker put his hand on my shoulder and I shrugged it off. "Hey, let's not fight about this. That's not fair. You know I care about Emmet."

I fought the impulse to apologize. I could guess what his next words were going to be.

He said, "I don't tell you what to do, and you don't tell me what to do."

I knew it. "It seems to me you are telling me what to do."

"Okay, fine. I'll stop. You're right. What you do is your business." He gave me a special look. "I love you, baby." He tried to hug me again, but I flung his arm off. "Let's not be mad. Won't you help me clean up?"

"Destroy the evidence, you mean." It was just as well I was in the doorway with nothing handy to throw. "I can't stop you, but I'm not going to help you." I took a deep breath and tried to speak in a normal tone. "Did Emmet talk to you about anything he discovered recently? Do you know what he was looking into?"

Striker looked at me as if I was testing his patience. Finally he said, "Yeah, Emmet called me earlier in the week to say he might have located the coastal way station we've been after, and that he'd know for sure after he checked up on a few things." He turned his back to me and picked up another load of books.

"That's it?" Striker would never lie about anything important, but he was not above leaving things out.

"You mean did I throw a fit like you're doing now and try to force him to tell me everything he had before he was ready? No, I didn't. I don't operate like that."

"What else did he say?"

"That was about it."

"Do you know why he might have contacted Kim about tusks?"

"About tusks? That's the word he used?"

"It was implied by what she said."

"That sounds pretty flimsy. You better get some corroboration before taking her word for anything, since you seem to think she's also a suspect."

"Striker, do me a favor and stop being so condescending, okay? That's exactly what I'm in the process of doing." Suddenly my self-control slipped and a magma of hot anger rose from my chest and exploded. "Goddamn it, you make me furious sometimes. You talk equality, but that's not how you act. You act like a complete asshole." I turned to stomp out. "And I'm telling Omondi about your cabin. He should know."

Striker followed me to the driveway. "You tell Omondi, and that's it, Jazz." He raised his voice as I turned on the engage. "You hear me? Finito."

I leaned out the window. "I've got news for you, honey. It's finito right now." I put my car into reverse and roared out of there.

I got halfway down the mountain in a blur of anger, fuming goodbye and good riddance like an eight-year-old. A string of black and white guinea fowl skittered across the road, and in my distracted state I hit the brakes a little late and a little hard. The car fishtailed on a patch of loose soil. I decided to pull over to the side until I regained my composure. I couldn't believe that Striker and I had just called

79

off our relationship. I was still too enraged to feel loss, but I knew it would hit me soon and would not feel good. And what a lousy, stupid way to end. Why did we seem to bring out the worst in each other? Well, maybe it was just as well, but even as I had that thought, I recalled our kiss when Striker came out of the woods just now, and I knew I was lying to myself. For all his faults, I thought he was a special, wonderful man. It was a goddamn shame he was so pigheaded. My being pigheaded was, of course, different. Maybe we just wanted two different kinds of relationship, and that was that.

I sighed, put the Rover back into gear, and checked the rearview mirror. I could tell from a plume of dust that another car was coming down the mountain, probably the van from the tourist lodge farther up the slopes. The car came around the bend. It was Striker's beat-up old Land Cruiser. He pulled up alongside of me.

"I'm sorry, honey. Come back up to the house and we'll start again."

The mattress was still halfway off the bed, but one big heave and it was back in place.

I pulled off my sneakers without untying them, threw my jeans over the back of a chair, and pulled up my T-shirt. "Why can't we get along better?"

"It's a sign of life. At least we're not bored."

"Isn't fighting half the time boring?" I threw the T-shirt on the floor. "We have the same old fight over and over."

"Yeah, but what about the other half?" Striker was stretched out naked on the sheets, hands behind his head on a nest of pillows. "You look great."

"So do you." I perched on the edge of the bed and put a hand on his chest.

"Mmm, baby. Come here." Striker's chest vibrated under my hand like a jungle drum.

I leaned over to kiss him. He grabbed me and pulled me on top of him so that my breasts pressed against the hard smoothness of his chest. He kneaded the tense muscles along the length of my spine. Slowly my body began to relax, then to respond. Our anger flowed into longing, flowed into passion, and we twined around each other like great cats, fierce and supple and free.

12

THE RINGING PHONE pulled me out of sleep. For a second I didn't know where I was and felt gripped by fear. Moonlight came in through a window on the wrong side of the room and fell on unfamiliar furniture. Then it clicked: a hotel room. Despite his pretense yesterday that mere thieves had broken into his cabin, when I'd said I'd feel much safer booking a room up the road at Mt. Kenya Lodge, Striker had agreed without a fuss. That told me more than any words how seriously he took the break-in.

Mikki was the only person who knew where we were. I'd called her to see how she was doing, which was lousy, as could be expected. The phone rang again. Why would she be calling me back now? I fumbled for the receiver.

"Jazz! Thank God you're there." It wasn't Mikki's voice.

Striker stirred and murmured, "Who?"

"Shhh, go back to sleep. It's for me."

He put the pillow over his head.

The illuminated dial on the bedside clock read one A.M. "Who is this?" My tongue felt too thick and slow to form the words clearly, but even as I asked, I recognized the voice. "Garret?" I searched for Striker with my foot and felt his calf, hairy and muscular.

"Oh, did I wake you? Terribly sorry. I didn't know who else to call and I couldn't find you at home. Mikki told me

81

where you were. You must help, or I'm afraid there'll be another murder."

I sat up. "What are you talking about?"

Garret giggled. "The police have released the body. The funeral is tomorrow. Alicia is screaming bloody murder because she expects a huge crowd at the house afterward."

"Why—"

"It's a disaster: Joseph has quit."

It sounded like Garret had been drinking steadily since I'd seen him that afternoon. "Joseph has quit," I echoed, for want of a better response.

"Yes, you know, Joseph, our butler and staff manager. He spilled some hot water on his foot or some such nonsense, and anyway, he's decided some jealous rival has used bad medicine against him, and that's that. He didn't even give notice. He just disappeared. Alicia is absolutely frantic. Then I thought of you and your marvelous safari staff, all sitting around costing you money, waiting for your next trip."

"Aha." Suddenly the phone call made sense. "Yes, my staff is free right now." And for the foreseeable future. I pulled my thoughts together. "I could ask Ibrahima. He's actually the cook, but he's a very mature, responsible person. His English is good, and I'm sure he could handle the job with very little guidance." And be my eyes and ears in the Laird house.

This was a lucky break. Yesterday I'd had to tell Ibrahima I couldn't pay his salary anymore. It had been a bitter moment for both of us. I hated firing him with the whole tourist industry in such a slump. The thought crossed my mind that he could end up working for Alicia or Garret permanently, but I pushed it hurriedly away.

". . . are a darling," Garret was saying. "If he could be here by eight, it would be a tremendous help. See you and Striker at the chapel at eleven."

"Garret? I wonder if you could tell me something?"

"If it is within my means."

"Kim will be there?"

"What's gotten you interested in my tiger of a baby sister?"

"I was just wondering why she and Emmet weren't on speaking terms."

"You've come to one of the few people who actually knows," said Garret, with the puffed-up pride of the drunk.

"And?"

"After she moved back to Nairobi and opened her law practice here, she really tried to start a relationship with Father. She really did."

"I believe you."

"Really." Garret was starting to sound teary.

"And what happened?"

A snort. "Father made it impossible. I mean, here she is, working with these displaced village girls who have turned to prostitution to feed themselves and their children to survive, and now they've all got AIDS, and there's no one to take care of all these orphans."

"It's a terrible situation." Garret, I recalled, had lost his own mother as a child.

"And Father's sitting there at the table stuffing his mouth with food, and he says AIDS is a blessing in disguise if it starts people using birth control. Can you imagine? She lost herself completely. She slapped him, but I mean, can you blame her? That's the last time she's been in the house."

"So that's why he never mentioned her."

"Father never liked to deal with problems in the family. If he wasn't getting along with someone, he bought a later model. If he couldn't replace you, he pretended you didn't exist." He gave an unconvincing laugh.

"I'm sorry." And I was, too. Garret's mercenary facade had cracked for a moment and shown me scars of pain and bitterness that could never be healed. It was confusing to admit that Emmet, a man I'd respected so much, had been such a shit as a father. Of course, Emmet was right. Africa desperately needs birth control, whether to conquer poverty or to save the environment, but why use that to undercut his daughter's compassion? Thinking long-term is no excuse for callous disregard for the living. Or the dying. To be so insensitive to your own daughter, and then so unforgiving—that was hard to understand. "I'll find someone to replace Joseph. Don't worry," I said gently. "See you

83

at the chapel tomorrow." I put the phone back in its cradle and padded into the bathroom to get some water.

It was only when I got back into bed that the implications of Joseph's sudden flight sank in. He'd been one of the people I needed to interview about Emmet. Now I moved him to the top of the list. There had to be a persuasive reason to make him leave such a cushy job. Did he quit because he was scared, because he knew too much? It wouldn't be too hard to find out where he lived.

When I awoke at dawn, Striker's long legs were taking up most of the mattress. We made love in the sunshine spilling over the sheets, making a long, leisurely time of it, playing with rhythms of hard and soft, fast and slow, inventing little riffs of pleasure we'd never done exactly that way before. Then we joined in one rhythm and stuck to it, built together to a roaring waterfall of a climax that spilled over and dropped me into a calm, clear pool—a warm, happy feeling to carry through the day.

I sang in the shower, forgetting the past and the future, and emerged to find Striker at the breakfast table on our balcony, a gleaming ripe papaya with fresh lime at my place. Below the hotel a delicately spotted bush buck was nibbling salts next to the water hole, while several Cape buffalo wallowed luxuriously in the mud.

"I figured if we're here, we might as well order room service." Striker looked at me appreciatively. "Love that robe. Love them legs." He hooked out a long arm, pulled me next to his chair, and pushing aside the heavy silk of the short kimono I kept at his place, kissed my belly just below the navel.

I kissed him on my favorite part of his neck, the back where the hairs are soft and prickly against my lips. He protested happily that I was tickling him.

I sat down and squeezed lime juice over my papaya. "I've got to get going. I don't want Mikki to have to wait for me."

When I'd spoken with Mikki yesterday evening, she'd told me she had to go to police headquarters to give her statement. She asked if I'd go with her for moral support, and of course I said yes. I liked the way Mikki could ask simply and directly for help. I'd never gotten the knack of letting other people take care of me.

Striker poured us each a fragrant cup of Kenya AA coffee from a white china carafe. "So you're going to go ahead with this loony scheme of working as Mikki's private eye, even after I've asked you not to?"

"I can't believe you said that!" I grinned broadly with amused disbelief. "Striker! What about personal freedom, what about we're each responsible for ourselves, what about—"

He smiled back. "Okay, you've made your point. I don't know what came over me."

I scooped out the last remaining shreds of papaya from the smooth skin and told him the gist of Garret's call, ending pointedly, "The funeral is at eleven."

"So that was the cause of the Great Rift between Kim and Emmet. Jesus, she'd be the last person in Nairobi he'd ask out to lunch to discuss his divorce."

"He must have uncovered something that involves her personally."

A half-tame vervet monkey climbed onto our balcony, looking for handouts. Striker shooed it away and leaned against the railing. "Jazz, are you going to tell Omondi about my place being trashed?"

Was that a look of worry in Striker's green-brown eyes, worry that I was about to trash our reconciliation? With the light behind him, it was hard to see. I answered slowly, "No. I guess it's your story to tell or not tell. I won't lie for you, but I won't bring it up."

"Thanks—and I really mean it." He leaned over the railing. "There's a beautiful Sykes monkey down there with someone's papaya."

Maybe we would learn how to remain independent but together. Maybe all this fighting was just growing pains.

"The funeral's at eleven. Will you come?" I asked.

Striker didn't look up from watching the monkey. "You know I can't stand Nairobi anymore. I'm allergic to the place."

I stared at his broad back, wondering if it was worth a

fight. Independent but together would only work if the together part was two-sided, also. Striker wouldn't be much support anyway, I told myself. I'd be focused on Mikki and picking up what information I could. Striker would just get in my way, and afterward I'd have to hear about his hating crowds. Who needed the aggravation? I'd be better off on my own.

"That's fine," I said, feeling a bit depressed. I wondered if Omondi would be there.

13

ONCE I SET off, my spirits rose. I love driving by myself. We were nearing the end of the dry season, and the grass was sere, straw white and pale gold. A yellow-billed stork stood stiff and unmoving inches from the car as I whisked by. His gaudy yellow bill was topped with a band of bright red across his face, and I couldn't help but smile at such a cheerful sight.

I caught a glimpse of a village with a mix of tin and thatched roofs that reflected the morning light. Wisps of smoke arose from the cooking fires. A patchwork of fields had been hacked out of the woods, and the bare soil expectantly awaited the first rains. Farther along, I passed a peasant woman carrying firewood on her head. The long, thick branches almost touched the ground before and behind her.

Around the next bend, a baboon troop had spread across the road and were going about their business: family members and special friends groomed one another, youngsters played jungle-gym on the patient back of a big male, an adolescent female presented her rear end to a male. He examined the pink sexual swelling with interest, saw she was too young, and turned his head. She moved off in disappointment. Adolescent females are sexually receptive, but the males won't have anything to do with them until they're more mature. I honked the horn, but it made no impression, so I inched forward until the baboons reluctantly moved and let me pass.

By the time I reached Nairobi, the world was long awake and the road bustled with sagging trucks, overcrowded buses, cars belching oily smoke, and the unpredictable matutu—taxi vans with handpainted names across their rear—that darted in and out of traffic, picking up and discharging passengers. I threaded my way to police headquarters behind a matutu named Hatari Safari. *Dangerous Journey.*

The desk sergeant told me with a gold-toothed smile that Mikki hadn't arrived yet, so I spent some time getting a sore butt on their hard wooden bench. A middle-aged Kenyan in shabby clothes, a wool ski cap, and one shoe, lay motionless on the floor in front of the duty sergeant's desk. At first I thought he was drunk, and didn't look too closely until he moaned in pain. There were some nasty gashes on his face.

"Sergeant, this man is bleeding."

"He is a purse snatcher," the sergeant said. He didn't need to explain further: the previous week, nine street thieves had been punched and kicked to death by an angry crowd in the market. The sergeant, preoccupied with finding the right forms to fill out, was cursing the ambulance for being so slow. "If he was dead, I wouldn't have to do this paperwork," he complained to his subordinate.

At last Mikki arrived, looking tense and miserable. She wore her dark brown dress, which set off her lustrous bronze hair and reminded me I had to change before going to the funeral. To my surprise, Henry was with her, looking less shrunken than yesterday.

"The old girl needs some bucking up," he told me. "Saw she was in no condition to come in by herself."

Having a chance to take care of her seemed to be doing Henry a world of good.

Mikki gave me a quick hug. "Thanks for coming, Jazz. I'm afraid I sort of wasted your time asking you to meet me. We realized Omondi would probably want to talk to Henry eventually, so we decided to come in together and get it over with."

"That's okay. I want to talk to Omondi anyway, after you're done. Henry, would you excuse us for just a moment?" I turned to Mikki. "Let's go outside for a second."

We stood against the chipped stucco wall near the front steps. "No new developments, just some ideas from yesterday."

Mikki nodded, but she seemed distracted. She didn't look at me, but at the crowd pressing by, blandly dressed in pastel prints for the women, black pants and white shirts for the men. A legless man wheeled himself over on a homemade wooden pallet, ankle high. I gave him some coins and he pushed away through the crowd.

"I can tell you some other time, if you want." I said.

"No, not at all." Mikki gave my arm a little squeeze. "I'm sorry, I'm just having trouble concentrating on anything. Go ahead."

"You remember Emmet told you he was busy with a new ivory project?"

"You want to hear something weird?" Mikki cut in. "I was going to move the location of the fund-raiser from the Lairds' to Louise Carruthers's house after Alicia's fit about Save the Elephants yesterday, but Alicia insisted it go ahead tonight at her place, as planned." Mikki brushed a lock of auburn hair back from her cheek. "Why would she want it at her house? Is she trying to get control over Save the Elephants?"

So much for discussing the ivory angle. "That doesn't strike me as so strange. Maybe Alicia wants to show she's honoring Emmet's memory to avoid gossip." I wanted to squelch Mikki's assumption that everything Alicia did was a sign of guilt. "So did you agree?"

Mikki shrugged. "Sure. It saves us a tremendous amount

88

of work and confusion. Seeing Alicia has never bothered me, and I don't see why I should start now."

Yeah, sure, I thought to myself. "We better get back inside."

As soon as we walked through the doors, the desk sergeant told us that Omondi wanted to see all three of us. Together.

"Hello, hello, hello." Omondi jumped up from behind his desk and came forward with an outstretched hand. As he held my hand in both of his, his eyes peered into mine with equal parts sympathy and pleasure. "How are you bearing up, my dear girl? Yesterday was not pretty."

Omondi was neither tall nor broad, and yet his presence filled the room, brightening and pushing back the drab green walls. "I have just now been talking to your friend, Striker." He gestured at the old-fashioned black desk phone. "He says some of his papers were disturbed, as if someone searched his house."

So Striker listened to me after all, at least partially. "Yes, I was there. Do you think it might be connected to Emmet's murder?"

"Maybe, maybe. There are many pieces to this puzzle that we must collect before we get a coherent picture."

"We're all eager to give you what help we can," Henry said pompously.

"I thank you in advance. Rather than conduct a formal interview, since all three of you are here at once, I thought we could hold an African style palaver to look into Emmet's murder."

"Don't we need a witch doctor to do that properly?" Henry asked.

"A diviner would come in most usefully, yes." Omondi laughed. "And we should also have the whole family, all the neighbors, distant relatives from near and far." He gestured us into stiff wooden chairs arrayed before his desk, and circled around to his place behind it. "And not to forget the spirits of the ancestors. But we shall do the best that we can." He gestured broadly. "Everyone comes together, everyone gets a chance to talk, to say what they know and

89

what they think. Big fact, small fact, recent, or the distant past—anything that comes to your mind. I am not taking signed statements." He crossed out the very thought with his hands. "No, this is three people talking who knew Emmet, who saw him recently, perhaps."

I'd seen Omondi do this before. It could be quite an effective way to get people to say more than they planned to, but in this case I thought he was making a big mistake. How could Mikki and Henry talk freely in front of one another, let alone in front of me and Omondi? We didn't live in a thin-walled, crowded African village where a secret was something everybody knew but nobody talked about—although, now that I thought about it, Mikki's affair with Emmet actually was like that.

Mikki began in a low voice. She described Emmet as a dedicated, hard-driving businessman who'd devoted the last decade of his life to halting the rapid extinction of elephants, winning love and admiration from like-minded people and the enmity of others, especially his own family.

"Was he ever threatened?" Omondi asked.

"He got a few anonymous calls last year, but nothing we took seriously," Mikki said. "Elephants have a lot of enemies, but Emmet personally? Not really. Killing him at this point won't stop the momentum for a permanent ban on ivory."

In response to Omondi's questions, she reluctantly sketched in the main players in the ivory trade. In the first years of Kenya's independence, the president's own daughter ran an ivory poaching business from a downtown office. Those days were over, and the new president had appointed a trustworthy conservationist—Leakey, the unbribable son of the famous archaeologist—to head the wildlife service. Presumably, many government workers, high and low, who used to live off poaching bribes weren't too happy with the new order. Nor were the Somali poaching squads, the Hong Kong ivory traders who acted as middlemen, the Arab emirs who gave cover to the laundering centers, or the Chinese and Japanese ivory merchants who fed a huge Asian market and exported jewelry and trinkets to Europe and America.

Omondi listened with a finger pressed against his lips and chin, lifting it every now and then to press for more details. When Mikki ran dry, he turned to me. "Do you want to add anything, Jazz?"

Palaver or no, I wasn't about to tell all I knew to Omondi without getting information in return. "Alicia said that Emmet was upset over something he uncovered recently. I think that's our best lead. Did Emmet discover something that threatened a particular individual or organization with ruin?"

Mikki fidgeted in her chair. "What I wanted to bring out is that Alicia and both his kids saw Emmet as a crackpot. Far from respecting him, they resented every penny he put into Save the Elephants. It created tremendous ill will in the family." In a faltering voice Mikki described the last time she'd seen Emmet. "He told me he was divorcing Alicia, that their marriage had self-destructed. I asked what he meant, but he wouldn't tell me."

"Is that when he asked you to marry him?" Omondi asked.

Henry sat with his head held high, eyes focused on a spot above Omondi's head.

Mikki nodded assent. "I was very confused." She bowed her head, hiding behind the cascade of her hair. "I asked for a few days to think about it, and Emmet was supposed to call later in the week. I'd decided to tell him no."

"And when did he call?"

Mikki shook her head. When she spoke, it sounded like she was choking back tears. "He never did."

Omondi swiveled his chair to face Henry. "Mr. Darrow, what did you know of all this?"

Henry cleared his throat with a harumph. "Inspector Omondi, these questions are very hard on my wife."

"Yes. Murder is a brutal experience for all the survivors." Omondi waited with an expectant look on his face.

Henry asked Mikki if she'd like a glass of water. She got a tissue out of her bag and said she was fine, to ignore her and go ahead.

"As I told you at our house, I guessed long ago that my wife was having an affair with Emmet."

"You didn't mind?" asked Omondi.

"Naturally I resented it. The man was taking advantage of Mikki's vulnerable state. Given the circumstances, I felt the best course was to ignore it with a gentlemanly silence."

"The circumstances?" Omondi prompted.

"Well"—he darted a look at Mikki—"my wife had suffered a serious setback to her career and needed to find a new research animal. Emmet stepped in with an offer of money if she'd switch to elephants."

"Explain this to me."

"My wife unfortunately studied an anomalous baboon troop and came up with a bunch of strange data about friendship and pseudomarriage among the baboons. Needless to say, this didn't go over well with the grant committee."

"It wasn't pseudomarriage," Mikki said.

"I told her she'd wreck her career if she published that twaddle." It seemed Henry had momentarily forgotten his role as Mikki's protector. "She marginalized herself by letting her politics contaminate her research results, and"—he snapped his fingers—"there went her chances for funding."

Mikki set her jaw. "I charted every troop member's behavior in a random five-minute sequence. It was the most rigorous, most scientific method ever used with baboons. The academic establishment didn't want to let go of their self-affirming notions of males ruling primate society as the natural order."

"Cooperation is simply the latest fad," Henry said. "These feminists even want to emasculate the baboons."

"That's ridiculous."

"I grant you, in my first generation of ethologists—the pioneers, if you will—we didn't yet have the most objective observation tools, but we managed to come up with data that has stood the test of time."

"No one belittles your achievements, Henry."

Was that wifely pride mixed with irritation that I heard in Mikki's voice?

She continued, "I simply showed that the dominance hierarchy you found among males didn't lead to reproductive

92

success. That doesn't mean there's no competition. The best way to compete for females is to have good social skills and cooperative bonding."

Henry's mouth tightened. "You can't base science on one single troop." He appealed to Omondi. "I told Mikki that. I warned her it would damage her career, but she wouldn't listen to me. And then she was heartbroken when no one would renew her grant." His voice grew acid. "Emmet Laird started throwing research money at her, pulled her away from primates into elephants, and the next thing I know . . . well, it's pretty low to take advantage of a woman's hurt vanity."

Henry was right in a way—if he had given Mikki the support and affirmation she deserved, she probably wouldn't have switched study animals, or fallen in love with Emmet—but he didn't get it. Yesterday, Henry declared to us that Mikki's affair was the safety valve that kept her in the marriage. Now he was blaming Emmet for seducing her in a vulnerable moment. In neither case did Henry see Mikki as an active player in her own life, or take responsibility for driving her into Emmet's arms.

I tried to picture this muddle of feelings leading to murder. Would you call it a crime of passion if Henry knew about the affair for years? Can't feelings fester underground and suddenly explode? But what would have set Henry off? It's not as if Mikki had decided to leave him. Henry was obnoxious, but he seemed more pathetic than dangerous.

"It sounds like you had much cause to hate Mr. Laird," Omondi said.

"Yes, but I figured out a way to get my revenge." Henry laughed self-consciously, showing large yellowed teeth. "I'm also going to start research on elephants. The role of aggression among male elephants, like what we did for baboons. I want to explode the myth of the gentle, matriarchal elephant clan that all these lady scientists have been perpetuating."

Lady scientists? Was Henry trying to win Mikki back, or drive her even further away? He seemed even more confused than Mikki.

Henry misinterpreted the silence that followed his boast.

93

"Don't relegate me to the dust bin yet. Just wait till I get my new research team in place." He pointed at me. "You better get ready because I'm taking you on, all you elephant lovers. The gentle elephant, hah! An elephant is not some plushy children's toy."

Omondi pointed his finger at Henry. "Watch out. I think elephants are hard to resist. You'll find yourself falling in love with them, too."

"And getting pretty upset when your study animals are picked off one by one," I added.

Henry gave a bark of a laugh. "I'm a realist, old girl. There's no room for all those elephants, anyway. Save the Elephants, my arse. Save them for what? To knock down every tree in the Maasai Mara and then starve to death? We must cull the herds; why not make money while doing so? The poachers are simply pragmatists." He smiled smugly.

"Oh, Henry. Stop being the enfant terrible," Mikki said. "I'm afraid we've gotten way off the track here."

Omondi dug for any bits of gossip about the Lairds. Henry, of course, knew Emmet from the time he'd arrived in Kenya, and seemed to take a certain relish in describing Emmet's first two wives and his messy divorces with each of them. Throughout the recital he snuck little glances at Mikki, who sat there lost in her own thoughts. He then went on to paint unflattering portraits of both Garret and Kim, and how they both hated their father.

"Mr. Laird sounds like a man successful in his public life, but a failure in his personal relations," Omondi commented. "Would you agree, Mrs. Darrow?"

Mikki turned limpid blue eyes on Omondi. "Emmet was the sort of man who was willing to appear in the wrong, rather than stoop to complaints about his wife or children. He was a wealthy man who didn't worship money himself. He was also rather stupid about the pull money has over other people. I don't think he ever realized that Alicia had married him for his money, or that Garret was basically hanging around waiting for Emmet to die and leave him a fortune. Anyway, it seemed to me Emmet was naive about how easy it would be to divorce Alicia. He was blind, blind, blind."

94

"Was it so foolish to expect an amicable divorce?" asked Omondi. "After all, the marriage was what you call one of convenience. Mrs. Laird had another man in her life."

"Yes, a young man with expensive tastes and only a bank salary," Mikki said. "Alicia probably spends more than that on parties and clothes every year. And how long do you think she would keep Greg's interest if Emmet divorced her without a penny?"

"But you are exaggerating, Mrs. Darrow. Without a penny?"

Mikki sat back in her chair. "Not in Alicia's eyes. Without children, he had no obligation to give her any alimony at all. And he wanted to turn the house into a study center."

"That shows you what sort of fellow he was," Henry said. "Turning his own wife out of her house. Heartless."

Mikki ignored him. "You've met Alicia, Inspector. Tell me your impressions. Do you think she'd let one small bullet stand between herself and a fortune?"

Omondi tilted his chair back and addressed the ceiling. "Aren't you forgetting one person, Mrs. Darrow? Some people would say that if anyone has benefited materially from Mr. Laird's death, it is not his son, not his daughter, not his wife"—he let his chair crash forward and leaned across the desk—"but *you.*"

I expected Henry to leap to Mikki's defense, but he sat there seemingly dumbfounded.

Mikki gave Omondi a hard look and said, "The theatrics are uncalled for, Inspector. I'm the last person in the world who would want Emmet dead." Her voice got a little wobbly on the last two words, but she held her stare and didn't break down. "I want to do all I can to find out who did."

Omondi picked up a pen and tapped it lightly against his fingers. "A fine sentiment, Mrs. Darrow, but then why are you hiding evidence from me?"

"What do you mean?"

"I mean"—Omondi tapped the desk in rhythm with each word—"that you were at the camp."

Mikki didn't say anything.

"Why didn't you tell us you were there, Mrs. Darrow?"

"I didn't think it mattered. I dropped by briefly Tuesday

morning." She blushed pink to the roots of her hair. "I—" She pressed her lips together to keep them from trembling. Her breathing became ragged, and I thought for a second she was going to cry, but she managed to reassert self-control. I'm sure it was obvious to all of us that they'd made love. My heart went out to Mikki.

"Look here. I won't have this." Henry raised his voice, which was rather booming at the best of times. The clipped words bounced off the walls of the small office, and must have been audible halfway down the hall. "We understand you have a job to do and so we have been very forthcoming with you, but a woman is entitled to a bit of privacy. You are distressing my wife needlessly and cruelly. It is utterly ridiculous to think that she's the killer. Utterly ridiculous."

"It is natural that you should defend your wife . . ." Omondi said calmly.

"Utterly ridiculous." I could see bits of saliva propelled from Henry's mouth.

". . . but we know she was at the camp, perhaps the last person to see him alive . . ."

Mikki pressed her lips tighter.

"Other than the killer!" Henry retorted.

". . . and that she didn't tell us of her presence."

"I will not have you humiliating her! I will not have it!"

Mikki nibbled on her pinky fingernail. "I'm all right, Henry, I'm all right. I don't mind discussing it. I dropped by for a short visit and to pick up an article we were writing together about orphan herds that I wanted to finish up this week. I didn't think it was important or I certainly would have mentioned it."

"I believe we saw that article among Emmet's papers at the camp," Omondi said.

Mikki blushed again. "I know—I forgot to take it back with me, after going all that way."

I didn't believe her. Mikki was too bright to claim she thought her visit to the camp unimportant. She'd been like a zombie ever since I told her of Emmet's death, but still . . . Maybe it was too painful for her to even think of the last time they were together. It must have been very

96

emotional—trying to decide whether to say yes to his marriage proposal, and now, looking back, knowing it was the last time they would ever make love. No wonder she hadn't talked about it.

I wondered what else Mikki hadn't told me.

14

"**D**O YOU HAVE a few minutes?" I asked Omondi, as the Darrows filed out of his office.

"Of course." He came around to perch on the front edge of his desk, close enough for me to notice how smooth his skin looked and the elegant structure of his hands. "That was a most fruitful interview, don't you think?"

"You don't really suspect Mikki, do you? You were pretty hard on her."

"You know my method. I ask every question that occurs to me. I don't worry is this a good question or a bad question. Sometimes you are surprised and get an answer. Keep asking and eventually the truth will come out. Besides, one must not ignore the old wisdom: *cherchez la femme*. In this case we have two *femmes*, Alicia and Mikki."

Old wisdom? I caught myself in time. I was not here to argue about sexist proverbs. "Mikki has no motive. What's the big deal about being made the trustee for Save the Elephants? It's not the same as inheriting money."

"She has research money on tap now. She need depend on no one."

"But she didn't know she would be put in charge."

"You have only her word for that. Not good enough."

97

"It's ridiculous to think Mikki would murder Emmet—a man she loved passionately—to get control over research funds." I didn't like the defensive tone in my voice or the way this conversation was going. It was getting more and more awkward to tell Omondi that I was working for Mikki.

"She looks like a romantic young girl, that one, but underneath she is not only unbreakable, but I suspect unbendable. I am not surprised she would not leave her husband for Mr. Laird. That marriage is a complex one. He loves her, but is angry and bitter. Still, he wants to win her back, that is clear. As for her, a strong lover is fine, but for a husband, a weak one like Henry is easier to manage. And it seemed to me that Mrs. Laird still has a genuine soft spot for her husband."

"Yeah, in her head. I don't think you're right about Mikki wanting to dominate Henry. It's more a protective, maternal thing she has toward him, now that he's old. But it wasn't always like this. She once told me it was her life's dream to work under the famous Henry Darrow. When he accepted her as his research assistant, and then started courting her, she thought she'd been admitted to the halls of Olympus and miraculously attracted the attention of Zeus. He thought he'd found an acolyte. He dominated everything then, and they were very happy together for a long time." I made a face. This wasn't a part of Mikki I liked to admit. "But it all fell apart on them. The acolyte overthrows the master's work, becomes a cause célèbre, at least among women scientists. Then she drops baboons for a more macho animal, and starts cheating on him. I wonder if Henry could have killed Emmet, out of pure spite."

Omondi listened attentively. "This plan of Henry's to start studying elephants himself is most curious. Is it to court his wife or compete with her?"

"Both, although he probably told himself it's to compete with Emmet. He's never respected Mikki enough to admit she's competition."

"Yes, perhaps he was trying to recapture the past." Omondi held his hands out, one high, one low, and then reversed them like a seesaw, in illustration of the Darrows' relationship. "But it won't work now. It's much harder to compete with a ghost than a living man."

"Speaking of which, what did the autopsy show? Did the bullet match Alicia's rifle?"

Omondi crossed his arms. "My dear Jazz, your question is highly irregular. I can't tell you police business."

"But last time—"

"Last time was different. This is not the bush, you know. You are in police headquarters." He counted off on his fingers: "Last time the murders took place in your safari, you knew all the suspects, I was working under a severe time pressure, I had only Sergeant Kakombe to help me, we were far from the rules and regulations of the capital." He held up his outstretched palm, a five-fingered stop sign. "It was a unique situation."

I listened impatiently. "If I hadn't gotten involved, the murderer would never have been caught."

"Nor would you have been shot. No, Jazz, I will not let you be my junior assistant this time."

"I'm a grown woman. I'm not interested in any junior positions, thank you." I could feel my face flush hot with anger. I thought of telling him Mikki had hired me, but I was afraid he would laugh in my face. "If he was killed because of ivory—and I think that's the likeliest possibility—I have valuable contacts." Meaning Striker, and Omondi probably knew it, too. "I'm sure I have a lot to contribute." God, why did I sound so defensive? I had the right to take on this job if I wanted to. At least Mikki had confidence in me, and she was no idiot.

"Jazz, calm yourself. I did not mean to be condescending. I respect your abilities, but let me be perfectly clear: I will not involve you in this investigation."

"I won't stay out of it. If you don't fill me in, I'll work blind."

Omondi got to his feet. "Now it is my turn to be offended. That sounds like a threat."

I ran a hand through my hair. This meeting was not going the way I'd imagined. "I'm sorry. It's not a threat." I didn't sound very apologetic. I took a breath and tried a more conciliatory tone. "I can do things, go places, talk

99

with people informally. Don't you see? I know I can do a lot to help. Of course, I understand that you have to follow your personal discretion in what you tell me—"

"That is just the point, my dear Jazz," Omondi interrupted. "It is not my personal discretion." The old-fashioned black phone on the desk gave a tinny clang. Omondi picked it up. "Inspector Omondi speaking. Yes, sir, it is being typed right now. I will bring it to you personally as soon as it is ready. Thank you, sir." He turned to me. "You see, the chief inspector is following this case very carefully." He got up. "Jazz, be reasonable. If it was a domestic murder, you don't want to get in the middle. If it was a professional killing, the danger is very grave."

"I don't scare easily."

Omondi looked at me sorrowfully. "No, you are not as reasonable as you might be. Stubbornness is not often associated with wisdom."

"I prefer to think of it as commitment." I looked at my watch. If only I could talk to Omondi away from the police station, maybe he'd open up. "Are you coming to the funeral reception?"

"I'm afraid I don't have time."

"How about getting together for a coffee break later on?"

Omondi thrust out his lower lip and shook his head. "No. No breaks for me today. Not until we have made some headway."

"Drinks after work, then?"

He shook his head, smiling this time. "I wish you were asking me out for another reason, but you are too transparent. You think if you can get me alone and practice your wiles on me, I will tell all. It is no use." He took my elbow and hurried me toward the door. "Now, you mustn't be angry with me. This is a very serious business indeed, and I want to keep you out of it."

He walked me through the empty outer office to the top of the staircase. I started down and waved goodbye. When he was out of sight, I paused and listened for the click of his office door as it shut behind him.

Heart pounding, I climbed back up the stairs, stopping myself from looking left and right like a criminal, and walked into the secretary's vestibule. Sure enough, there was a pile of typed sheets on the desk, one page still in the scroll of the typewriter. I picked it up, one ear alert for footsteps. It was the scene-of-the-crime report. I scanned it as quickly as I could, struggling with the technical jargon.

There were two sets of tire tracks, not to mention the oil leaks, from Alicia's new Rover, and the heel marks around camp came from two sets of her shoes, one high-heeled and one low-heeled, as Omondi and I had guessed. When we found Alicia and Greg there, it was her second visit to the camp. Of course, that didn't prove she killed him. For what it was worth, the bullet that killed Emmet didn't come from her rifle.

There were marks on the flat strip of road approaching the camp that Emmet used as a landing strip. A small bush plane had used it recently. That was probably Mikki's Tuesday morning visit. They'd found her fingerprints all over the *Daily Nation*.

The phone on the desk gave its hollow clang and I jumped, scattering some pages on the floor. As I stooped to gather them up, I heard the secretary greet someone in the hall outside.

I scuffled the disordered pages into a neat pile, put it on the desk, and was almost at the door when Omondi's secretary entered. He was a keg of a man, and I banged smack into his solid belly. My shoulder bag fell to the floor. We had a flurry of retrieving my bag and apologies, making enough noise for Omondi to open his door. He gave me a sharp look and his eyes immediately went to the secretary's desk.

"What were you doing here?"

"I came back to invite you to lunch. Won't you reconsider?"

Omondi's dark look reminded me I'm a lousy liar. His secretary started to edge around me to get behind his desk. I was certain that he'd immediately notice the pages were out of order. I'd never seen Omondi openly angry and I didn't look forward to the experience. I leaned awkwardly against the desk, as if to give the secretary more room, and managed to scatter the report to the floor a second time. Apologizing profusely, I edged out the door.

15

STRIKER DIDN'T SHOW up at the chapel for services, not that I really expected him to surprise me. I was so used to going everywhere without him, that I only noticed it for a moment. After that, I was too busy shoring up Mikki to think about myself. Just as the minister finished the first prayer, Kim walked swiftly down the aisle and slipped in next to Garret in the family pew. She sat stiff and frozen through the eulogy, which praised Emmet's contributions to his adopted land and to the entire world in his fight to save the elephant. Mikki gripped my hand all through the service.

There was no burial since Emmet wished to be cremated and have his ashes scattered in his beloved elephant country. Alicia had the grace not to fake intense grief, but her face was strained and pale as she accepted condolences. She made a point of approaching the Darrows and inviting them to the house to join a small circle of family and friends. Mikki declined, claiming publicity work for tonight's fund-raiser. I'd signed on to supervise the setup of a tent and dance floor in the garden in the afternoon, so I had to be there.

I pulled up behind a Jaguar XKE and followed the cortege filing through the Lairds' gates. Ibrahima, my cook from Jazz Jasper Safaris, was at the door playing butler with panache as he directed the stampede for the drinks table. A long frock coat bulged over his stomach, instead of his usual uniform—a T-shirt cadged off the back of a tour client. I hovered near the door, greeting people with half my attention, hoping for a private word with him.

There was a pause in the arrivals, and Ibrahima turned to me. "I have already learned something." Another carload of people arrived, and Ibrahima was busy for a moment greeting people and announcing their names. "Will you be home later?"

"If it's important, I don't want to wait that long."

"Okay, you will come back when I am not so busy and we will talk."

Still I didn't move.

"Go and get something to eat and drink, my child. When Striker arrives I will tell him to look for you."

"Striker's not coming," I said, and got out of there before Ibrahima could say anything. The green-walled salon with the antelope frieze was abuzz with conversation and the somewhat frenetic laughter of funeral receptions. I circulated for a while to see if I could pick up any useful information, but I felt ridiculous, and after a while I gave up and carried my drink out to the terrace. The wash of conversation poured through the open windows and drove me down the steps into the garden.

An English-style flower border billowed in equatorial colors that dazzled the eyes. Kniphofia, the red-hot poker, thrust flower spikes six feet into the air. A rapid, jingling warble drew my eye to a malachite sunbird, nine inches of emerald feathers sipping nectar with a needle bill. Above the flowers, red-rumped swallows swooped in long arcs, hunting for insects on the wing.

Despite the tropical blaze of life, Nairobi's high altitude kept the climate temperate. There was a delightful breeze, and I closed my eyes for a moment and held my face up to the sun.

"Yoo-hoo." Garret waved and trotted down the stairs from the balustraded terrace, whiskey and soda in hand. "I've been looking all over for you. I want to thank you for Ibrahima. He's been a perfect gem."

"I thought he would be. I'll say hello to him later, when

103

he's not so busy." We walked along the flower bed as we talked. "He's happy to get the work. I'm surprised that Joseph would quit such a great job."

"Oh, he's been saving up his money to go into business with some relative, I think. Emmet left him enough money to do it right away."

"I thought he'd burnt his foot and got scared."

"Oh, really? Who told you that?" Garret emptied his whiskey in one go.

"You did, Garret. Last night on the phone."

Holding his glass awkwardly, he snapped off a daisy and started shredding the petals. "God, I must have been drunker than I realized. I don't remember saying that at all. I must have made it up." He giggled. "How funny."

Today's version sounded more plausible—except that I knew inheritances take months to get through the legal formalities. There was no way Joseph would have the money this quickly, unless somebody—Garret?—had paid him off. Garret was working mighty hard to explain Joseph's leaving, and I wondered why.

Garret threw away the denuded yellow center of the daisy. "Tonight will be an absolute zoo. Mikki is hoping for twice as many people to show up than usual. Alicia was mad to agree."

"Why did she? I imagine she'd like nothing better than to see the whole organization collapse."

"Oh, I think she asked for some sort of financial compensation for use of the house."

Why hadn't Mikki told me that? I was going to have to talk to her about being more honest with me. She had been rather distracted, I remembered, but she had brought up how weird it was for Alicia to go ahead with the party. Was Mikki so certain of Alicia's guilt that contradictory facts didn't make any impression on her mind? I hated to think she was doing it on purpose. It wasn't making my job any easier.

Garret giggled. "Poor Alicia is going to find it very hard to live on her stipend. She's used to bathing in money, not counting it. I doubt she remembers how to subtract."

104

"I'm glad to see you laughing about it. You seemed pretty shaken by the will yourself."

Garret flapped a pale white hand. "It was a disappointment, of course. Now that I've got over the rough spot I told you about—thanks to a rescuing angel who appeared in the nick—soon I won't have money worries ever again." He sighed. "Won't that be lovely." He looked back at the house. "I'd better go in and check up on my baby sister, make sure she isn't clawing anyone." He started walking back, and I had no choice but to follow. "I hear you two met yesterday," he said over his shoulder.

"She told you about that?"

Instead of answering my question, Garret exchanged a few words with a group that had spilled onto the terrace, then paused a moment at the French doors. "Perhaps you know her boyfriend, too? Robert Thiaka."

"No, I don't think I've met him."

"He's only interested in animals people can eat, so perhaps you don't move in the same circles."

"And I prefer animals that eat people? What does he do?"

"He's in the zoology department, with Mikki, but he only teaches every other semester. His big thing these days is developing a model ranch. Before that he was some high muckety-muck in the government, until the bureaucracy and corruption got to him."

I grabbed Garret's arm and pulled him to one side before he could plunge into the room. "Wait a second. I'm not sure Kim wants to meet me again. Did she tell you she threw me out of the office?"

Garret snickered. "It's happened to me, too, dear. Don't worry about it."

"What's your relationship like with her?" It was hard to imagine a conversation between them.

"Kim likes to give me good advice: move out of here, break my chains, grow up." Garret abandoned his empty whiskey glass on a handy table, pulled out a cigarette and stuck it into the corner of his mouth. "You know how popular good advice is. Plus, the advice giver always gets mad when you don't rush out and immediately do what she says." He lit the cigarette and inhaled deeply. "I love Kim dearly, but she is so terribly earnest."

"Do you know why Emmet went to see her?"

"I hadn't even known they'd talked until Kim told me about your visit." Garret's eyes shifted around, studying the crowd beyond my shoulder.

"You must have asked her what she and Emmet discussed."

"No. Truthfully, I assumed it was some confidential lawyer's business."

"C'mon, Garret. Your father wasn't consulting her as a lawyer!"

Garret fixed a tight smile on his face. "That's the impression I got."

"I hear he found out something he wanted to talk to her about, something connected to the ivory trade, something about tusks."

Garret's eyes widened and his smile became more fixed.

"What are you hiding?"

"Why are you bugging me about this? Aren't you being a bit nosy?"

"I don't know," I said, trying to think of a plausible excuse and failing. "I told the police about Emmet seeing Kim, and they wanted to know why. Listen, I'll just tell Omondi to contact you to find out more about it."

"Please don't bother. He called me in for questioning yesterday. That man is like a smiling pit bull. And of course I have no alibi for the time of the murder." His lips narrowed into a tense smile. "But then neither does Alicia." He flipped his ashes nervously onto his pants legs, the pavement, and my shoes. "I'll tell you what Emmet and Kim talked about if you promise you won't tell where you heard it."

"Promise."

"Father wanted to tell Kim in person he was getting divorced." He blinked rapidly. "It was about a prenuptial agreement Kim helped Father draft when he and Alicia got married."

I still couldn't believe Emmet would call up his totally estranged daughter to confide in her about his personal

106

problems, and certainly not to get her legal advice. If he wanted to discuss his prenuptial agreement, he'd do it with his own lawyer. Far from corroborating Kim's version of the lunch, it sounded like Kim had prepped Garret. The prenuptial agreement was a useful lie, because it deflected attention back to Alicia's possible motives.

"That's bullshit, Garret. Emmet was on to something connected to Kim or a client of hers, something about ivory—it could be the key to his murder."

"I tell you it had nothing to do with Kim!" Garret talked faster. "It was about the divorce."

"Do you know what this prenuptial agreement said?"

"You've twisted my arm enough. You're not getting any more out of me." He threw his cigarette on the ground, stomped it, and marched into the house.

A waiter told me the caterers had driven up with a large truck. I was busy for a while helping them set up the wooden dance floor and refreshment tent. They were a good crew. At last the red-and-white-striped tent popped up on the lawn like an elegant mushroom.

I left them to the banging of hammers on the dance floor and went to find Ibrahima. In order to avoid the few remaining guests, I crossed to the far end of the terrace and entered the house through the library. Despite its tall windows, the room seemed dim after the brightness of the sun, and I was inside before I noticed it was occupied.

Garret, Kim, and a tall man were talking intently in the far corner. They shut up at the sight of me.

Again I was stunned into shyness by Kim's beauty. The balanced planes and lines of her face were still, almost impassive, but her clear, dark eyes flashed with energy. Towering next to her, a very black man with powerful shoulders rocked on the balls of his feet.

Garret was repeating our names. The other man was Robert Thiaka, Kim's boyfriend. He wore heavy black-framed eyeglasses and had a receding hairline that gave his forehead imposing dimensions. "Would you care to join our discussion?" he invited me. "We are plotting how to—"

"Shhh—" Garret flapped his hands at Robert. "Don't give away my business secrets."

Robert Thiaka continued with a broad, teasing smile. ". . . increase foreign investments in Kenya. Are you in business, also?"

"I'm starting to wonder. I started a small safari tour company this year. So far I've managed to exhaust my own savings and a loan I took out."

"Capital is a great problem. I myself am trying to introduce the Maasai to commercial ranching. The problem is water. If we expand the herds and keep them year-round, we need more water, and the damned national parks won't let us have access to their land. Building reservoirs or wells costs money we don't have, money that should be going to the people."

"Can the land really support large scale ranching? I thought it was badly overgrazed already." Until modern pesticides, the tsetse fly had stopped cattle from taking over all the prime grazing territory. The wild animals were immune to sleeping sickness and not as destructive as cattle. Since we'd removed the natural checks and balances, and hadn't put anything in their place, unlimited human expansion led swiftly and directly to famine.

Kim's face tightened like a clenched fist. "You think all the land should be for wild animals, don't you? What should the local people do? All move into Nairobi slums?"

"Let's not fight," I said. "I think we all want a good future for the people of Kenya. Perhaps we disagree on the approach, but that doesn't make us enemies."

Kim smiled tightly.

Garret looked right into my eyes as if to impress me with his sincerity. "You're not our enemy, darling." Somehow his reassurance was the more disturbing of the two.

Robert Thiaka seemed unaware of their hostility. "Of course we do not want everyone moving into the cities. Nor do we want the cattle bringing the Sahara south. Exactly. You have put your finger exactly on the problem." He rocked on his heels. "You have more cattle, and instead of having more food, you get starvation. And it's no use telling people to keep smaller herds, because for us the cattle

108

is an icon, like money to Westerners. The more you have, the more you are respected. You use cattle as a bride price to get a rich man's daughter for your wife, for your son's wives. Can you imagine telling an American that if he had less money and was less of a consumer, it would be better for the environment? They won't even waste breath to say you are crazy, they will simply ignore you. The Maasai are the same with cattle. Am I right?"

I nodded. "Absolutely." Robert must be a wonderful teacher.

"So what is the solution? For there must be a solution if only we can look at it creatively. We want to provide food, avoid desertification—let the Sahara stay up north, we don't want it coming south to Kenya, and that is exactly what is happening now—and give the people some income to replace the use of cattle as money. Can you guess what we have come up with?"

"You're ranching gazelle."

"Excellent! You are very, very close." Robert Thiaka smiled delightedly. "Impala. They can live on almost no water, they step lightly on the earth, and their flesh is delicious."

"I've had it at the Carnivore," Garret said. "A light gamy taste, but not too tough."

"You go to the Carnivore?" Kim asked.

"I know it's a tourist trap, but I think the meat there is really rather good, as long as you avoid hippo."

"No, you must not discourage him," Robert told Kim. "We want everyone to discover how good impala meat is. It is going to replace beef as standard fare. Cattle do not belong in Kenya. The nomad life is finished; we are too many people." He turned to me. "By next year, if I get the funds, we'll turn the old ranch house into a beautiful guest lodge. You must come visit us with your tourists. They will be very interested in the ranch, I think, and also, there is much wildlife to be seen—lion, leopard, buffalo, elephant, everything, except rhino, of course." There were so few rhino left, they'd all been moved to the best-secured parks with individual guards. "You see? We have an integrated scheme: food, commercial herds, and tourism, all from the same piece of land. It will provide an income for many more families. So you will come?"

"If I'm still in business by then," I joked.

"You must visit sooner. You will come with Kim." He put his arm around Kim's waist. "She works too hard and doesn't take enough time off to see me."

Kim didn't seem to think much of Thiaka's idea that we visit together. She looked at me with the flat, bright eyes of a cobra measuring the striking distance to a mouse. I decided it was time to go find Ibrahima and find out if he'd learned anything useful.

Ibrahima pulled me toward the back of the entrance foyer, in the shadow of the curving stairs, where we could see anyone who entered before they noticed us.

"You've already found out something?" I asked him.

"Everyone who works here has their idea of why Joseph ran away."

"Do they know anything?"

"There is a mystery about Joseph's departure." Ibrahima's big fleshy face took on the seriousness proper to talk of black magic. "Some say a rival put magic on him, but no one knows exactly how. He was not sick. There was no hot water on his foot, as Garret said to you."

So Garret had made up that first story out of thin air. "Garret also told me that Joseph got a lot of money from Emmet and left to start a business with some relative."

"I don't know." Ibrahima looked dubious. "From what I am hearing, Joseph didn't have the face of a man who has been given money. Yesterday, after Garret came back from the police, he calls Joseph into his study. With the door shut. When the door opens, Joseph walks out with a face like a stone. The housemaid said he walked past her with no greeting. He changes clothes, leaves the house, says no goodbyes, and this morning, I show up. Is that the way a man acts who has received good news? I think Garret warned him of danger."

Or threatened him. "The best way is to talk to Joseph himself."

"I will find out where his family lives."

"Excellent." When we saw him yesterday, Joseph hadn't seemed nervous, just sad. Why was Garret so eager to get him out of the house? Did he think the police were so stupid they wouldn't trace him? I hoped Joseph hadn't disappeared entirely. "Yes, I'd very much like to talk to him."

"We can go together."

I squeezed Ibrahima's arm. "You are a good ally."

Ibrahima put two fingers together. "We are a team."

"Okay, team, what else did you find out?"

"It is a feeling. The son, Garret, is a soft one, and his sister, Kim, she is a strong one. They have lost a father; it is natural they would cleave together. But I see them talking, talking, many phone calls. When I come in the room, they fall silent. Are they helping the wife to arrange for their father? No, she complains loudly she has had to do all the work herself. Are they grieving? No, they are worried and excited, like children with a naughty secret."

"I know exactly what you mean. See if you can overhear anything, but don't take any chances. Promise?" Ibrahima nodded. "Now, what about Emmet and Alicia? Did you hear about his asking for a divorce?"

"I have saved the biggest for last." Ibrahima patted his belly with satisfaction. "The evening that he left, there was much shouting between him and his wife. He told her she must go back to her father's house, and she was not at all agreeable, not at all. That same evening, he went to his camp. Next day, she was like a thundercloud rumbling around the house all morning, but when she came home at the end of the day, the black cloud was gone. The next day you found him dead." Ibrahima said in a loud voice, "All is going very well. Do not worry about me. You should go home now and rest."

"I'd better check on the dance floor before I go." Following Ibrahima's eyes, I glanced up at the staircase.

Kim stepped onto the landing and rested her hand on the curved banister. A silver African bracelet encircled her wrist like a crescent moon glinting in the light of the chandelier. She looked down at us impassively. "What are you two whispering about?"

"Hi, Kim. Have you seen Alicia? I want to say goodbye

111

to her." It was only a half-lie. Seeing Kim on the stairs gave me an idea, and I needed to ask Alicia's permission to do one thing before I left.

"She was on the terrace a minute ago." Kim stalked down the stairs with feline sureness. I expected her to brush past me, but instead she held out her hand. "Goodbye. We probably won't be meeting again. Robert told me I was coming down too strong on you. I'm very frank, and sometimes it comes across wrong." She gave an embarrassed smile. "Maybe I was dumping some of my anger at Emmet onto you. So I just wanted to tell you that."

I thanked her and said something about anger being part of grieving, yet I couldn't help wondering if this olive branch was sincere. I wondered if Garret and Thiaka had told her to stop being so openly hostile toward Emmet and all conservationists because it would arouse suspicion.

I had more questions. I wondered how Kim got there from the library without crossing the hall. In a house that size, they must have a back staircase, but why would she go up one set of stairs and down another? How long had she been watching us?

16

"**H**ONEY, YOU CAN take his papers and burn them, for all I care." Alicia leaned back in the terrace chair and waved a beautifully manicured hand toward the first floor and Emmet's study. Although Save the Elephants had an office downtown, Emmet preferred to do most of his writing at home. "In fact, you can tell Mikki I want all the Elephant stuff out of here, pronto."

"Thanks. There are just a few key things I need now." Seeing Kim on the stairs had reminded me of his study, crammed full of Emmet's meticulous records. The answer to what tusks he'd discovered might lie right above me.

I went back inside and hurried along the upstairs hallway, my footfall cushioned by a thick Oriental runner, past a man-size Chinese vase and an ancient chest holding a bowl of cut flowers from the garden. Africa seemed strangely distant.

Entering Emmet's office was to enter yet another world. A flat oblong of sunlight illuminated the grain of a mahogany desk, or at least the bits that showed. Most of the desk was covered by stacks of papers that overflowed plastic in-boxes in red, blue, yellow, and green. Two easy chairs faced an old couch under the window. I looked out onto the terrace below. Alicia was alone. She had let her head fall back against the flowered cushions, face angled up to the sun. It was the first time I'd ever seen her in repose and I immediately pulled back, feeling that I'd intruded on her privacy.

Despite the daunting clutter, Emmet's study felt warm and homey. I'd spent many an hour in this room working with Mikki and Emmet on Save the Elephants, although less often since I started Jazz Jasper Safaris. Afterward, we'd sit in those chairs as the sun went down, tossing out ideas, making plans for future projects, talking strategy. I pushed aside my sadness that those times, that Emmet, would never return. I was here on business. I wanted to collect what I'd come for and get out before Garret or someone else came by and asked me what I thought I was doing.

I sat at the desk, pulled the in-boxes closer and began to flip through the contents. Checks, bills, circulars, magazine articles, newsletters, drafts of the article Emmet was writing with Mikki. Nothing on a recent ivory investigation. The drawers yielded pens, paper clips, and blank stationery.

I turned to the row of filing cabinets beneath a spotlighted mask from Zaire, a face with slitted eyes and a great square mouth with iron nails as teeth. I usually spent some time admiring the piece, but today it seemed all too real. I bent to read the labels on the file drawers.

One whole cabinet was for Save the Elephants. The next one held research papers on various African animals and news clippings documenting the population explosion, the AIDS epidemic, conservation, and antipoaching measures. There was a drawer of financial papers where I found the checkbook, bills, and a folder neatly marked FUND-RAISER EXPENSES, which I placed on the desk. There were drawers on varied projects he'd funded, and another on all the trips he'd ever taken, stuffed with stained coasters from forgotten restaurants and old road maps.

It looked like Emmet saved every piece of paper he touched, all alphabetized and color coded. I returned to the cabinet devoted to Save the Elephants, looked under *I* for Ivory, and there was a nice tidy manila folder with a blue-rimmed label announcing IVORY—ILLEGAL TRADE. Congratulating myself for finally thinking of the obvious, I pulled it out and went over to one of the easy chairs.

The folder was filled with newspaper clippings, some yellowed with age, some as recent as last week. There was nothing on Emmet's own work.

I went back to the cabinets and looked again under Save the Elephants. Nothing else under Ivory or Investigation or Poaching or Trade. I was running out of subject headings. I knew Emmet had a file on the poaching ring he and Striker broke up last year. I'd added notes to it myself. Shit. It must have been misfiled, and finding it was going to take ages.

I'd resigned myself to reading through all the file headings when I noticed all these files were red-labeled; the one I'd pulled out with the poaching clippings was blue. I turned to the other drawers. Green, yellow, blue. Blue was for the news clippings on assorted topics.

Emmet wouldn't have put his blue news file in the red Save the Elephants drawer. And even if he had made such a mistake, where were the files on antipoaching projects that ought to be there? Omondi and I hadn't found them in the camp. It looked as if someone removed all the files on ivory and tried to hide it by sticking the folder of news clippings in there.

The implications started to hit me. It had to be someone who knew Emmet's habit of squirreling away records on everything. Someone who was familiar with this office. Someone with access. Someone with a secret about ivory tusks. Someone who knew Emmet wouldn't be coming back.

The two tracks I'd been following—the family motives and the tusks Emmet had found—were starting to intersect. The mask above the filing cabinets grinned down at me with its mouthful of iron teeth.

"Knock, knock," Alicia said from the doorway. "My, it's taken you a long time. Everyone else has gone home." She'd changed out of black into a jumpsuit with a halter neckline and a heavy gold slave collar. Instead of lions and tigers, today's silky fabric draped her voluptuous figure in red and yellow hibiscus.

I froze for a moment, as startled as if a flashbulb went off to capture my snooping on film, but if Alicia noticed I was standing there with the red-labeled file in my hand next to an open filing drawer, with my mouth hanging open, she wasn't letting on.

She plopped down in one of the easy chairs. "Whew, I'm plumb tuckered out. I think I'll go down to the pool for the rest of the afternoon and worship the sun." She examined a tanned arm.

I decided to push her a bit, to see if she was as unaware of the missing files as she seemed. "Alicia, I've found something funny."

"Good. I could use a laugh. Funerals." She made a face. "It all seems unreal, doesn't it?"

I waved the ivory trade file at her. "I found this under Save the Elephants. It's the only file in there on the whole huge topic of poaching, which is odd in itself. And see." I pointed to the contrasting colors. "It doesn't even belong here. It was moved from this other cabinet."

Alicia focused on me for the first time. "I thought you were picking up some papers for the fund-raiser tomorrow night."

"I got those out." I nodded toward the desk. "Then I remembered what you said about Emmet being upset about something he'd discovered last week. I thought I'd look under Ivory and see if he'd made notes."

"Why? Are you going to carry on where he left off?"

I shrugged. "Curiosity."

"Curiosity killed the cat, you know." Alicia got up to look over my shoulder.

I gave her a sharp glance, wondering if that was a threat, but her demeanor seemed neither threatening nor defensive.

"Couldn't Emmet have done that himself?"

"But then where are the missing files? Mikki doesn't know anything about it, and there weren't any papers on this at the camp."

"Are you saying that Emmet was murdered to get these files?"

Alicia was sharp. "That's a big jump. Let's just say that someone with access to this office removed the ivory files and stuck this other one in there."

"It wouldn't have fooled Emmet for a second."

"Exactly. So it must have been done after the murder was discovered, or after Emmet left for camp—"

"By the killer." Alicia looked sobered and a little scared.

"Did you see anyone come in here the last few days?" I asked.

"You've got to be kidding. Do you know how many doors this house has that are always left open?" Alicia waved toward the window and the terrace below. "Ask Joseph. He's the most likely one to know who's been coming and going. Hmm. I don't rightly know when he'll be back. His mother is sick and he had to go visit her, way out in the boonies. You can try asking one of the maids, but they don't spend a lot of time lurking around this hallway."

"Joseph told you his mother was sick?" This was version three of the butler's disappearance. I hoped this version was as false as Joseph's burned foot, or it would be very hard to find him.

"Garret. Joseph left in a darned hurry."

"Garret told me Joseph quit to start his own business."

"He did? Now isn't that funny. So is Joseph coming

back to work or not?" Alicia looked annoyed. "This is one more headache I don't need. If Garret chased him off and is lying about it, I'm going to be one very angry lady."

"Maybe I misunderstood." I wasn't a practiced liar myself, but at least I knew the basic rule was to be consistent. It seemed like Garret said the first thing that came to him each time: for me, Joseph had merely to leave the house, while for Alicia, he had to be out of Nairobi entirely. I should have kept my mouth shut. I didn't really want Alicia using my name to confront Garret, but I'd already said too much.

"Back to these missing files." I tapped the file I was holding. "Either Emmet was murdered for personal reasons"—Alicia's expression didn't change—"in which case it has nothing to do with these poaching files, or it could have been connected to this discovery you said had him all upset. Did he say anything about it at all?"

Alicia bit her lip. "Not to me, but he was in the worst mood I've ever seen him in last week. He and I had a big fight over a personal matter, which was very unusual for us, but he was in a piss-poor mood even before that." She looked at me as if to gauge my reaction. "Emmet and I always got along smooth as a baby's ass, you know. Too well, maybe. I think if we'd fought more we might have gotten on better, but that's water under the bridge. He was always a gentleman—very fair, very civilized—that's why this sorry excuse for a will . . ." Tears welled up in her eyes. She gave an embarrassed laugh. "I'm not just crying for all the millions I thought were coming to me. I never thought Emmet would be so mean." She fished a tissue out of her pocket and dabbed her eyes, carefully so as not to smudge her mascara. "Mikki must have really sunk her claws into him."

That was not a line I wanted to pursue. "Would Garret know what pushed Emmet into such a bad mood?"

"Do you think Emmet would tell his firstborn anything important? He was on Garret's case, too, last week, chewing him out about some fool thing he'd gotten into with that Treasure Island deal of his."

"Do you know what it was?"

Alicia thought for a moment. "I overheard Garret whining that Emmet shouldn't have gone into his things. I got the impression he was bribing government officials with expensive gifts or something like that; maybe it was some gifts he'd received, as thank-you for a hefty bribe? Emmet wouldn't stand for that. He thought government by corruption was killing Africa's future, sure as a bullet. Westerners doing it really drove him mad."

"Pardon me for surprising you, Mrs. Laird. Ibrahima told me you were up here." The unexpected sound of Omondi's voice went through me with a flash of memory. He was dressed in a short-sleeved gray tropical suit that showed off his finely muscled arms and smooth skin. I hoped he couldn't tell what I was thinking.

"Inspector." Alicia shook his hand.

I shook hands without saying anything, and Omondi's eyes flicked quickly past my face. "A pleasure to see you, Jazz, and to meet you once again, Mrs. Laird. I wanted to let you know we'll be questioning all your servants this afternoon, and must ask you to come into headquarters for a formal interview, as well." He looked at the big gold watch on his wrist. "Perhaps when I finish here?"

Alicia hesitated. Her hand fluttered up to lightly touch the heavy gold necklace she wore. "Would tomorrow morning be acceptable, Inspector? I'm very tired after the funeral."

"That is fine." He gave a slight bow with his head. "Shall we say, ten o'clock?" He looked at the files scattered over the desk. "May I ask what you were doing here?"

"Oh, Inspector, you're not going to believe what Jazz found—someone's been messing with Emmet's papers."

"Oh, really?" Omondi walked over to the desk.

"I came up to collect the receipts and bills and things we need for the fund-raiser, and seeing all the filing cabinets—Emmet keeps notes on everything." I heard myself stammer defensively.

Omondi looked me in the face for the first time. "Jazz, I hope you're not trying to get involved in this investigation. We don't know yet who we're dealing with, but they could be very nasty people."

118

"Looking through Emmet's file cabinet hardly seems dangerous."

"Anything connected to a murder investigation can be dangerous. You should know better than to come in here without checking with me first. Show me what you've found."

Being bossed around doesn't sit well with me, but I swallowed a retort. I showed Omondi the color-coded file drawers and the misplaced file of news clippings. "See? Someone removed all the files relating to ivory, and tried to hide it with these news clips."

"You want me to be impressed by how clever you are. To thank you," he said. "What I see is that you've touched everything, destroyed any chance we had of picking up fingerprints, and contaminated the evidence. How will the court be certain you and Alicia didn't find the relevant files and destroy them?"

"Why would I do that?"

"To protect your friend Mikki."

"Is Mikki a suspect?" Alicia asked.

"Everyone is a suspect at this stage," Omondi told her. "That's why we collect all the evidence systematically. Like testing the filing drawers for fingerprints."

"Don't tell me you would have tested these drawers before opening them! Some dutiful sergeant would have brought you that file full of old news clippings and you'd have concluded there was nothing suspicious."

Omondi tightened his lips. "We would have followed correct procedure, procedure you obviously know nothing about. Luckily I arrived before either of you had left, and I can testify you removed nothing from the room."

"Really, Inspector, I'm feeling downright alarmed about this, and all you're doing is picking on two defenseless women." Alicia sat down and crossed her legs; the silky fabric of her jumpsuit draped in new patterns over her shapely thigh and showed a bit more cleavage. She gestured at the four walls. "Emmet's killer was in this very room!"

"Unless your husband removed the files himself."

"We already thought of that," I said. "Why would he

119

bother to stick the news clippings in their place? If so, it means he didn't trust someone in the household."

"Ooh, I hate to think that," Alicia said. "I would trust everyone on the staff with my life. I mean it. I don't want you scaring them with accusations, Inspector." I'd been thinking of family, not staff, but there was no point antagonizing Alicia, since Omondi surely knew what I meant.

Omondi reassured her he would question the staff without accusations or alarms. "It is good you've noticed this," he admitted grudgingly. "Now we will also ask everyone who they saw coming down this hallway or into this room."

"I saw someone unexpected coming downstairs during the reception," I said. "Kim."

"What was she doing upstairs?" Alicia asked. "Of course, it's her father's house—she can go wherever she wants," she quickly amended. "But what would bring her up here?"

Omondi nodded. "We will ask her."

And she'll come up with some convincing excuse, I thought, remembering how adept Kim was at evading questions. If she came up here to get rid of Emmet's notes, she must have hidden them somewhere in the house. She wouldn't have wanted to be caught with an armful of files, so the quicker she was able to dump them, the better. I looked around the office. Hiding them among his other papers seemed too risky to me. I pictured what lay between here and the stairs.

"This is a crazy idea," I said, "but come with me for a second." I led Omondi and Alicia into the hall and pointed to the man-size Chinese vase swirling with blue-painted tendrils and blossoms. "Wouldn't that be the place to hide something you didn't want found for a long time?"

Omondi pulled out a big white handkerchief and, holding the vase by the far side of the rim, gingerly tipped it over so we could see inside.

Nothing.

Alicia let out a breath. "I feel like I'm with Sherlock himself."

"Except his ideas worked," I said. Omondi kindly re-

mained silent. I looked down the hall. The only other furniture was the heavy old chest with its bowl of bright flowers. "We might as well try that, too."

The chest's dark varnish was thick and crackled with
age. It was also spotted with drops of water. My chest tightened. A careless servant might have spilled the water when
placing the flower bowl there. Or the water might have
been spilled by someone hurriedly moving the flowers in
order to open the chest. Omondi reached for the flower
bowl.

"Notice there's water on the chest already," I said.

As he moved the bouquet, we could see the bowl had
been filled too close to the brim, and a bit of water sloshed
over the side. Omondi knelt and carefully, slowly, with the
help of his handkerchief so no fingerprints would be lost,
opened the iron clasp and raised the lid.

At the bottom of the chest lay several thick manila files
with blue labels reading: IVORY—TRADE ROUTES, IVORY—
MARKETS, IVORY—INVESTIGATION.

17

FINDING THE MISSING files with Omondi
there turned out to be a stupid move. He wasn't angry at
me anymore—big deal. All I got out of it was to watch his
back as he walked away with the files under his arms.

The rest of my afternoon was equally frustrating. I spent
it running all over Nairobi before everything shut for the
weekend, looking for evidence that linked Kim, Thiaka, and
Garret to an ivory trade scheme. I visited the Tax Assess-

or's office, the Registry of Deeds, the university, even Garret's club. I needed to find out more about Thiaka's commercial ranch and about Garret's Umar Island development plans. More? I needed to find out anything, starting with where they were located, let alone their financial status and possible illicit backers.

I kept hitting dead ends. I should have known better than to try a government office after noon on Friday. Most African bureaucrats consider their job an outward show, a symbol of the patronage they'd received, involving little work and less personal responsibility. Many government services, even health clinics, are closed for much of the day so as not to tire their staff with the annoyance of citizens' needs. The Registry was especially maddening because I could see the staff chatting, cracking jokes, even snoozing at their desks, while the desk clerk fended me off by repeating, "We are closed for cleaning." Finally I gave up and left. The university offices were empty as a ghost town.

Trying to tap the gossip circuit was more useful. I couldn't get my nose through the front door at The Grosvenor, Garret's club, so I went around to the delivery entrance, talked my way into the kitchen, and struck up an instant friendship with the head waiter. He gave me the names of several high government officials that Garret had been wining and dining frequently over the past few months. Garret had also played host to a Japanese businessman several times recently. I slipped the waiter some money, and he agreed to sneak a look at the guest log and leave the businessman's name on my answering machine.

Three days had passed since we discovered Emmet's body. Although I'd found out many things, they were a teasing jumble of facts and suspicions that pointed in all directions. Which were the false trails, which the true one? I slept fitfully, and dreamt I chased Emmet through a strange city, chased in turn by an undefined menace, then the buildings turned into a forest and Emmet was a wounded elephant. The bad guys were about to catch me when I woke up, with the sun pouring through my window and the usual dawn sounds of a donkey braying and children's voices floating up from the shacks and cottages behind my apartment building.

It did feel as if I was chasing Emmet in nightmarish slow motion, trying to retrace his last steps without ending up where they had led him. I tried to think of a way to get a look at Emmet's files, now safely locked away in Omondi's office, and failed. The next best alternative was to talk to Joseph, the Lairds' butler, the only person likely to know what shenanigans Garret was up to and what Emmet had found. As soon as I'd showered and ate, I went directly to Ibrahima's to pick him up and head over to Joseph's. Ibrahima was an early riser also, and if we found Joseph in bed, that would be better than not finding him home. But here again I was stymied. Ibrahima had already checked out Joseph's address and had some bad news for me: Joseph had packed his family and left for parts unknown.

Striker would be up, too, of course, and I gave him a quick call. He'd slept in his cabin last night, and there had been no unexpected visitors. To my relief, he was scheduled Monday—the day I should have been setting off with my tour group—to do a story on the nesting colony of Goliath herons at Lake Baringo. It was a top-dollar assignment for *International Wildlife*, which meant a photographer was going along, too. Even better, they'd be staying with some old friends who ran a luxury safari camp on an island in the lake. Striker was nice enough to ask if I'd prefer he cancel the trip and stay closer to home, but that struck me as ridiculous. This was my job, not his. Besides, what was the point of Striker's staying if he wouldn't come to Nairobi? At least this way I wouldn't be worrying about whoever trashed his cabin coming back for him. It was only when I hung up the phone and my apartment seemed emptier than usual that I realized his absence would matter to me.

The only other person I needed to talk to who'd be up at this hour was Mikki, and I headed for her place without bothering to call. It was shortly before nine when I arrived, and Henry bullied me into having another cup of coffee with him on the veranda before going off to talk to Mikki, who was already out with the elephants.

Henry's coffee wasn't bad. I leaned back in the wicker

123

rocker and watched him toss bits of breakfast roll to a troop of long-limbed vervet monkeys. The gum trees rustled in a pleasant way, adding their eucalyptus fragrance to the morning breeze. If he wanted to talk to me, let him begin. A monkey with a tiny black-haired baby hanging on to her stomach got the biggest piece of bread and ran in triumph up the tree before one of the males could grab it from her. A male sat on his haunches and sucked a stalk of grass like a country hick. The soft-looking white fur of his belly didn't extend over his testicles, which were a bright robin's-egg blue.

"Look at that fella. I know how he feels." Henry cackled, showing his big yellow teeth and watching me to see my reaction.

"Then count yourself lucky, Henry. Most men your age would be glad to have that problem."

"You're as young as you feel, I always say, young as you feel."

"That must put you around twelve years old."

Henry threw back his head and laughed a great braying, "Ha, ha, ha." The monkeys scattered. "Please, fourteen at least. You can't deny I've hit puberty."

He patted my knee with a wrinkled hand, leathery and spotted with age. How could Mikki stand him? I wondered for the thousandth time. I gulped down the rest of my coffee.

Before I could move to go, Henry said, "Mikki told me she hired you to look into the killing. I won't ask if you've found anything yet . . ."

Because you know you'll do better getting it out of Mikki than out of me, I thought.

". . . but I did want to tell you that I don't approve of Mikki trying to pin this on Alicia. It's natural that she feel upset, and all that, but this giving way to emotion just won't do. It's not healthy. Cooperating with the police and all that is fine, but not going off half-cocked like this. I know I can count on you not to encourage her. 'Nough said."

I had been all ready to rankle, but the trouble was, I agreed with him. Not the half-cocked part, but about Mikki

124

gunning for Alicia. I patted his knee. "Don't look so worried, Henry. We'll try not to be too overemotional. And I'm not planning to pin this murder on anybody—except the killer."

I drove through a belt of scrubby acacias, their seed pods rattling dryly in the wind, and spotted her Land Rover parked near a circular area of smooth-beaten bare soil where a large elephant family was busily digging mineral salts.

I could make out the back of Mikki's head, a flash of auburn as she flicked her long hair away from her face, then her fine profile, then the back of her head again. It looked like she was marking down timed observations, a method she used to protect against observer bias. I hated to interrupt her at work, especially if she'd managed to lose herself in the world of elephants for a while.

The elephants, too, seemed completely engrossed in their work, except for one. When I pulled up next to Mikki's car, a large adult stopped gouging the earth with her curved ivory tusks and headed toward me. She rumbled, shook her head so that her crepe-thin ears flapped emphatically, and lifted her trunk. I looked over to Mikki for a sign of whether I should worry.

"Hi, Jazz. Three minutes," she called, holding up three slender fingers with their childlike bitten nails, and checked off something on her chart, perhaps: *9:22, Snaggletooth lifts trunk, 9:23 overturns unfamiliar car and tramples driver.*

The elephant was now so close I could see the wiry lashes over her eyes. She trumpeted at me, a short derisive hoot, and came to a halt. The other adult elephants ignored her, but some of the youngsters caught her excitement and began sparring. Snaggletooth found a small branch amidst the dry grass and began whipping it about. I put my car into reverse, just in case I had to leave in a hurry. She flung the branch up and down, over her head, onto her back, in between her legs, and into the air. Then she dropped it, snorted loudly through her trunk, lost interest in threatening me and went back to tusking the ground.

Mikki slipped her pen into the wire spiral binding of the

notebook and called to me with a welcoming smile. "Juno seems to be feeling jolly today. Earlier she mock-charged some tourists who didn't take it as calmly as you did." Her blue eyes were clear and direct, but the skin around them looked bruised with strain. "Come in here where it's easier to talk."

I transferred from my car to hers. "How are you, sweetie?"

She flicked back a strand of hair that fell across her cheek. "As long as I'm working, I'm okay." She gave an uncomfortable, almost embarrassed, smile. "Evenings are the worst. It helps to know you're doing something about finding who did it." Her delicate brows rose in a question mark. "Have you come up with anything?"

"Lots of information," I told her, relieved to see her more able to focus than yesterday. "I'll tell you what I've got so far." I'd jotted down notes on a small pad, which I pulled out more as a prop than a memory aid. I flipped through the pad, stalling for a moment. There were two separate lines of inquiry that kept cropping up: Alicia and the divorce, on one hand; Emmet's interest in ivory smuggling, on the other. I tried to pick out the bits that didn't include Alicia to go over first.

By now the elephants were on their knees, reaching into a hole deep enough to hide their trunks. The tip of the matriarch's trunk came up curled like a fist with a gob of rich gooey mud, which she popped into her mouth with obvious relish.

I started with the ivory track, reporting verbatim on what the waiter at Shabaan's had said about Kim's lunch with Emmet, my meeting with Kim at her office, finding Striker's place trashed, my conversation with Garret, Kim, and her boyfriend, Robert Thiaka, after the funeral, then seeing Kim come downstairs and finding Emmet's ivory files taken out of his study and hidden in the hall chest, and now locked away at police headquarters. I also mentioned Joseph's disappearance and the chance he was scared off, although it wasn't clear yet if he knew about ivory, or anything else for that matter. There had to be a reason, though, for Garret to tell so many lies about Joseph quitting his job.

I could see that getting back to work had been good for Mikki. Yesterday she'd been unable to concentrate on anything I said. Today she listened carefully, nodding and asking questions if she needed to clarify anything.

When I finished, Mikki's shapely mouth turned down in a bitter smile. "I can see Garret getting involved in the ivory business to raise some quick money—and take a sneaky sort of revenge on Emmet at the same time. Then, if he were discovered, pulling a gun on Emmet in a panic—yes, I could imagine that."

"But Emmet made his discovery and had a confrontation with Garret days earlier, when they were both in Nairobi, according to Alicia. If Garret went with a gun to surprise Emmet at his camp, he planned to use it with malice aforethought."

She fell silent. At the salt lick a chubby young elephant was trying to dig its own hole with ineffectual jabs of its small tusks, then gave up and wedged its way in among the adults for a taste of the yummy mineral-rich mud.

Mikki came out of her thoughts and asked, "How does Alicia figure in?"

I took a breath. "I got a look at the police report. They have indications that Alicia was in the camp earlier. She wore different shoes, and her car was there twice."

Mikki's eyes got hard and she set her jaw. "So they've caught her."

"Wait a second. Her first visit could have been the same day you visited, the day before Emmet was killed. The ballistics test showed it wasn't her rifle that was used to shoot Emmet."

Mikki flicked off this objection. "She'd hardly bring the murder weapon back to the camp, would she? It's easy enough to get rid of a gun in the bush."

"Now just listen calmly. Kim and Garret both told me that Alicia and Emmet had a prenuptial agreement."

Mikki nodded. A lock of auburn hair fell over her ear. "I knew that."

"Mikki, you've got to tell me what you know! Don't you

127

see? This really gives Alicia a motive, once Emmet asked her for a divorce. She'd expect a lot more money as a widow than as a divorcée."

"That nails the motive down." Mikki gripped the steering wheel with both hands until the knuckles whitened. "Too bad they couldn't find the gun." She turned back to me. "Have they dredged the water hole, do you know? Maybe I could offer to pay for it myself."

"Or, there's a nice set of circumstances for a frame-up."

"You're not talking about me, are you?" Mikki looked shocked.

"No, of course not. Why would you even think that? I'm talking about Garret. He probably knew Alicia went to see Emmet at the camp, making her a prime suspect. Or maybe she was never there: for all we know, he could have borrowed Alicia's car. His little MG would hardly make it to camp. He could have borrowed her shoes, too, if the murder was premeditated. He and Kim are uncooperative in every way, yet both of them made a point of telling me about the prenuptial agreement, which deflects attention from them to Alicia. And then there's the whole ivory angle. We can't ignore that. It seems much more likely that Garret and Kim are involved in tusk-running than Alicia."

Mikki thrust her chin forward. "As long as we're spinning hypotheticals, Alicia could be involved in the ivory trade, too. Her friend Greg Garner used to be a loan officer for WorldCorp in Hong Kong, and he's always going over there."

"And? Is that it?"

"You know Hong Kong is a center of both money laundering and the ivory trade." Her jaw muscle bunched and quivered. "You're looking at me like I'm raving. Why are you so set against investigating Alicia?"

"Hey, wait a second. That's unfair. I'm giving you as complete a report as I can, with the evidence that points toward and away from each person. I told you that she was in the camp before and didn't tell us—but so were you. In itself, it doesn't prove anything. I also told you the prenuptial contract gives Alicia an even stronger reason to kill him, but that simply doesn't clinch the whole thing, Mikki.

I have to trust my own senses: I'm sure she didn't know about the hidden ivory files. And Garret has a strong financial motive, too. That Umar Island development scheme could have ruined him. He says the money he needed came through recently. From where? Could it be from some ivory sales? I'm not ruling anyone in or anyone out at this point, that's all I'm implying."

An elephant scuffed up some dry earth with its big saucer-shaped foot, sucked the dust into her trunk and then sprayed it over her back. Her gray skin took on a pale ocher cast.

Mikki bit the skin on the side of her thumbnail. "Maybe you should go down to Lamu and look this Umar Island over."

"That's just what I was thinking. I wanted to check in with you before spending the money to go down there."

"If you wanted, Henry and I could fly you right now."

"You want to get Henry involved in this?" I could hear the incredulity in my own voice—not too diplomatic, but asking a husband to help investigate your lover's death seemed a bit much.

"I told him I hired you. He's been very understanding." Mikki avoided my eyes. "He offered to help in any way he can."

I never could understand why a powerhouse like Mikki played the little girl and enjoyed being taken care of so much, but she probably didn't understand my phobia about dependency, either. One of the challenges of friendship is to accept differences, I thought, and my mind flashed briefly on Omondi's face.

"Look, Mikki, please don't take this the wrong way, but I think it's better if you don't tell Henry all the stuff I've just told you. If it seems important to visit Umar Island, I'll take the overnight train down, or go on a commercial flight."

"But why? You don't have to go around with him once you reach the coast," she added. "It'll save a lot of time and money. He'll be glad to do it."

"Mikki. He's a suspect. I don't want him to know what I'm doing."

Mikki bit the already red skin at the side of her thumb nail. "I know you've never liked Henry."

"Don't make this personal. You hired me as a private detective. I'm trying to do a job here, and my reports have to be strictly confidential. It's all right for you to be sure Alicia did it, but I have to keep an open mind. That means Henry's still a suspect—and so are you."

As soon as I said the words, I wished I could grab them back. Mikki looked as if I'd slapped her. She stared straight ahead through the windscreen, but I doubted if she noticed that the elephants were filing out of the area, matriarch in the lead.

"I keep thinking, if only I'd joined him at his camp. If only I'd been there, too. Maybe whoever did it would have shot me also." She began to cry. "At least we could have been together."

18

A TREMENDOUS CROWD showed up that evening for the fund-raiser, as Mikki had predicted. She stayed only long enough to greet people, and then Henry took her home. Even I had to admit he'd been very sweet and solicitous.

The caterers had done a marvelous job, and Louise Carruthers, one of Save the Elephant's stalwarts, had taken on the job of supervising. I'd spent a frustrating day. In the morning I failed to find Garret's Japanese businessman, and in the afternoon I failed to get any more leads on Emmet's discovery. I was primed for a big party.

By midnight I had danced with a lot of different partners, finding again how much fun it is to flirt. Above the dance floor a jungle cactus climbed a palm tree and flung erotic scarlet blooms into the night air. Champagne, moonlight, and the insistent rhythms of the African dance band made an intoxicating mix. I swung my bare shoulders to the beat, reveling in the music. From the wildness of the party, it seemed a lot of other people were having the same reaction to Emmet's absence.

Omondi appeared from out of the night, his slight frame elegantly clad in a formal suit. I could see a glint of amusement, and something more, way back in his eyes. "You look shockingly stylish, Jazz. This is the first time I've seen you out of bush clothes."

"All for a good cause." I used steely determination not to check the nonexistent neckline of my strapless gown. "You look quite smashing yourself. I'd wondered if you'd be here."

The band began a Latino-inspired number, Omondi put out his hands, and suddenly we were on the dance floor, moving in a syncopated rhythm. Omondi slowed down a notch so I could keep up with him, and skillfully clued me in with his hands and hips. We danced belly to belly, then he'd swing me out, behind him, around, side by side, never losing the beat. I didn't know I could dance that well.

There was another fast number, then another, until I was flushed and panting. Just as I suggested we retire in victory, the band switched to a lower gear, and Omondi moved closer and enfolded me in his arms. We glided, seemingly inches off the floor; his ear brushed my cheek, soft and intimate.

The dance ended and we moved apart. I charged off the dance floor toward the drinks tent, with Omondi behind me, feeling false to both him and Striker. Flirting was fine, but having Omondi's arms around me again was a whole different category. Safely surveying a tray of barbecued shrimp on toothpick skewers, I apologized for pressuring him to tell me about the case, that I did understand he had to follow police rules.

"There is no need to mention it." Omondi took a skewer

and pulled a shrimp off with his teeth. "All is forgotten. It is over and done with."

"Well, not quite," I said.

"What do you mean?"

"Mikki has hired me to look into Emmet's murder for her." I wandered down the buffet table, unwilling to face Omondi. "I seem to be pretty good at this detecting stuff, and I need the money, and I'm helping her out at the same time, so I figured, what the hell? I just wanted to let you know. Of course, if you decide to share Emmet's files with me, I wouldn't argue. Maybe we could trade information."

"Aha, so now you are being a Mata Hari, dancing with me so that I go crazy over you and tell you whatever you ask."

Our eyes met.

"If I thought it would work, I might give it a try," I joked feebly.

"Give it a try anyway."

"I'm glad you're not angry with me."

"Why be angry? You are not trying to hurt me, but to help your friend. I admire your courage and loyalty. I have seen this side of you before. Besides, you're also a most stubborn woman. Why should I hit my head against yours?" He took my hand. "Come, let us find somewhere quiet where we can talk."

We took a mossy brick path that wound along a hedge of jasmine, its sweet scent heavy in the soft night air, and led to a hidden garden. It was a garden of all white flowers that I remembered as somewhat affected and bland. Under the moonlight it was a magical, luminous place.

Omondi bent his face to mine and kissed me. His lips felt soft and wide, so different from Striker's. Even as I joined in the kiss, I panicked inside. I hate emotional messes that end up hurting everyone. Not that Omondi meant anything serious. My lips parted, and Omondi began to kiss me more deeply.

Against the dark of my closed eyelids I saw my ex-husband kissing his grad student. The image, for the first time ever, made me want to laugh. It had lost its power to hurt me. I was free. Even more, it didn't fit me. I wasn't

132

married to Striker. We weren't getting along, except in bed. Any fool could see that Striker wasn't going to be in my life forever. I was allowed to kiss a man at a party without getting uptight. That's all this was, a delightful kiss.

The champagne fizzed in my brain, mixing with the moonlight and the distant music of the band. I slipped my arms around Omondi's back, ran my fingers over the soft skin on his neck and the beginning of his cushiony hair, and melted against him.

The band finished their number. In the moment of silence that surged around us, I heard a nightjar calling, a rustling of fabric, and a woman's voice from one of the shadowy recesses beyond the flower beds. This was the second time today Alicia had interrupted me at an interesting moment.

"Buckaroo, you know I never would dream about asking for a favor from the bank, but he is pressuring me something fierce. I can't even enjoy the party in peace, without him threatening to make trouble for me. Normally I'd handle that little two-bit pip-squeak without breaking a sweat, but with that devil sister of his getting into the act, he's—"

The lower rumble of Greg's voice was less distinct.

"You're so sweet." A brief rustling pause. "I do hate to ask you for help, but I don't know who to turn to."

"Perhaps I could help." Omondi walked toward the voices.

Greg and Alicia were sitting on a low bench framed by tall white delphiniums. Greg wore a white suit, and with his shock of blond hair, he stood out clearly in the moonlight. Alicia was more shadowy in black velvet.

"Oh, Inspector! Jazz! You've found my favorite place in the whole garden. Isn't it lovely here? There's no scent like jasmine, is there? Did you hear me complaining about Garret? That boy—I say boy, he'll never see forty again, but I swear, he's more like a teenager than a man, with all his dream schemes, one loonier than the next. I wish you could throw him in jail for me and get him out of my house and out of my hair. My husband not cold in the ground and he's asking me for money—which I don't have. Now do you think that's right?"

I looked at Alicia with awe: the woman could talk faster

133

than I could think. Things looked bad for Alicia, and maybe she killed her husband, but I couldn't help liking her verve and brains.

Omondi commiserated with her and asked what sorts of threats Garret had made.

Alicia put a hand on Greg's arm. "Really, Inspector, jokes aside now, this has nothing to do with police matters. Garret asks for money easier than breathing."

"You say he's threatened to make trouble for you. Do you know what he means?"

The unspoken thought of blackmail hung over the moonlit flowers.

Alicia hesitated for just a second, and I could almost sense her switching gears. "I haven't the foggiest, Inspector. He's touched me for a loan once or twice before, but this time is different. . . ." She paused dramatically. "He wants a lot of money, and he seems desperate. That's why I was asking Greg if he could help. I'm worried Garret might have gotten himself into serious trouble. He almost scared me, he really did, like he was ready to go out and do some plumb crazy thing."

Greg hugged Alicia around the shoulders. "Now, bunny, don't start letting your imagination run wild. Garret's always desperate for money, you told me that yourself." Alicia pushed him away. Greg quickly tried another tack: "But if you're scared about having him in the house, you just tell me. He can sleep in the club, if that makes you feel safer. You tell me, and I'll take care of it."

Alicia slipped her arm around Greg's waist. "Isn't he sweet?" she asked me. "I just love it when a man says he's going to take care of me. It makes me feel like a little girl."

I remembered what Omondi said about Alicia talking too much when she's angry. It might be useful to shake up her control—if I could. Yes, and let Omondi know that I had useful information, too. "Alicia, there's a nasty rumor going around that Emmet made you sign a prenuptial agreement. I thought you might want to squelch it before it spreads any further."

"Who told you that?" Alicia let go of Greg and straightened so that her bosom pointed aggressively toward me.

134

"Some brunette in a black dress was telling some other people. I think she's one of the stringers for *The Nation.* That's why I thought I should mention it." Lying makes me feel like a five-year-old, certain everyone can tell. But this one went over well. "Are they allowed to print a rumor like that without checking with you?"

Alicia pulled out a cigarette and a gold lighter, which she clicked several times without producing a flame. "What's wrong with this darned thing?"

Greg took it from her and lit her cigarette.

"Explain this prenuptial agreement to me," Omondi asked. "I have not heard of it before."

"I think it was started in California," I said, "by movie stars who don't want to hand over their fortune to some passing spouse. The couple agrees in a legal document that in case of divorce, the poorer spouse has no rights to the fortune the rich spouse amassed before the marriage."

"But this is a dangerous thing to do!" exclaimed Omondi.

"Oh, come now, Inspector," Greg said. "It's a common practice among the very wealthy."

"It provides a motive to murder: who would not rather become a rich widow than a poor divorcée?"

"But from a rich wife, I have descended to being a poor widow."

"According to our information, Mr. Laird asked you for a divorce shortly before he was murdered."

"That's a vicious lie!" Alicia snapped. "Or else servants' gossip." She shook the glowing end of her cigarette at Omondi. "You know how they love to embroider a whole cloth from one overheard thread of conversation." She inhaled a sharp drag from her cigarette and exhaled through her nose. The smoke looked like night mist curling about her head in the still air.

"You don't deny you had one of these prenuptial agreements?"

"I'm not trying to deny it. But Emmet wouldn't have asked me for a divorce right now." She put a hand to her stomach. "Not when I'm expecting his baby."

19

GREG GOT UP abruptly. "I think you should tell the truth, Alicia." He sounded pained and young. "You're making things look worse for yourself."

So the big hunk could have an opinion of his own. I agreed with him: Alicia's pregnancy sounded to me like a great reason for Emmet to ask for a divorce, if he suspected—as we all did—that she was carrying not his, but Greg's child.

"Greg, come sit back down, right here next to me," Alicia cajoled.

Greg sat down, put his elbows on his knees and his head in his hands. Alicia tugged at his biceps, but he wouldn't look up.

"Mrs. Laird, you have been given excellent advice," Omondi said softly. "It is time to tell the truth. I am still waiting for your explanation of what happened during your first visit to Emmet at his camp."

Interesting. When Alicia went to headquarters this afternoon, Omondi obviously hadn't gotten any answers from her. Goose pimples rose on my arms.

Alicia tugged on Greg's wrist, but he wouldn't move. "Buckaroo, how can you say that? You know I'm telling the truth."

Greg turned his head sideways to address Alicia as if in a private conversation. "The whole truth, Alicia. I can't take this anymore. I'm proud it's my baby. I don't mind telling the inspector we planned to get married."

Not one to cry over spilt milk, Alicia patted Greg's broad back. "Okay, buckaroo, you want me to, I'll lay all my cards out." In the moonlight her face was a pale heart shape with a dark slash for her lipsticked mouth. "Like I said, I went down to discuss some personal matters with Emmet. You see, I'd asked him for a divorce."

"You asked Emmet for a divorce!" The words flew out of my mouth.

"Yes. The servants must have overheard the word divorce and assumed I was being kicked out, instead of walking out on my own two feet."

"How did that effect the prenuptial agreement?" I asked.

"It didn't apply if I was pregnant." Alicia's hand strayed to her belly and rested there. "Emmet and I were working out what kind of settlement I'd get." Her other hand circled protectively on Greg's back. "The baby is Greg's, but I didn't tell Emmet that, I said it was probably his."

"He believed you?"

"Emmet was too much the gentleman to start a paternity suit, but I can tell you, he was horrified at the idea of raising another child." She tugged at Greg's arm, and this time he let her take his hand. "He was only too happy to learn Greg wanted to marry me. I went down to the camp to hammer out the details."

"What was your agreement?" Omondi asked.

"I'd give up the house, which he wanted as a nature center, and he'd give me a two million dollar settlement and a trust fund for the baby."

"Do you have any proof to back up these statements, Mrs. Laird?"

Alicia spoke confidently. "Proof? I have a letter of understanding in Emmet's handwriting that we both signed—it was the day before he was killed. I went back with Greg, when we met you, to iron out some details about the furniture and so forth and to discuss the timing of our divorce. Instead, I found a dead man."

"You were foolish to remain silent about this, Mrs. Laird. You have drawn needless suspicion against yourself."

"Surely you can understand, Inspector. Once Emmet was dead, I needed to find out from the lawyers what took precedence, this letter of understanding or my role as the widow. Since there was no legal separation, I was legally a widow. Why bring out our plans for divorce and provide a lot of busybodies with a gossip fest?"

"They're sharks. You've just got to ignore what people say," Greg told her.

"So that's the whole story, Inspector. I didn't hate Emmet; he was a decent man. Why would I risk murder if I was getting such a sweet deal anyway? And would I ask for a divorce if I planned to murder my husband?"

My first thought when I woke up Monday morning was of the Lairds' butler. With Alicia now above suspicion, I was more interested than ever in talking to Joseph. I wanted to ask about Garret's fight with Emmet, what he knew about Emmet's ivory discovery, and why he'd quit his job so suddenly—or had Garret fired him? I wanted some solid information to report to Mikki when I called up to tell her Alicia was off the hook.

I controlled my curiosity, though, and decided to first revisit the government offices that had been closed Friday, distasteful as the thought was of hassling with the bureaucracy again. If I had to go find Joseph while he was visiting his mother in the bush, I was willing to do it, but depending where she lived, I might be able to combine it with a visit to either Garret's or Robert Thiaka's land, or both. So first I needed to do all my homework.

It took the whole morning, but I did find the records on Umar Island. Garret had paid top dollar for his undeveloped dot of an island. He'd bought just at the peak of a speculative real estate boom, and prices had come down since then. I had less luck with Robert Thiaka. His department secretary was out for a long lunch. I waited, and surprise! She didn't bother to come back to work at all. No one else there seemed to have ever heard of Professor Thiaka's commercial ranch. I banged my head against the wall of their indifference for a while, and finally gave up in disgust.

It was mid-afternoon by the time I picked up Ibrahima. We headed over to Joseph's apartment house: a four-story stucco building dwarfed by a hundred-foot euphorbia tree that grew out of a dusty scrap of front yard.

Ibrahima got out of the Rover, repeating once again that we wouldn't find him there. I hadn't told him yet of my plans to follow Joseph to his mother's. "I am telling you, when I got the address yesterday, I came by to make sure. His whole family is gone. Joseph came home, made his wife pack everything, and they left in a big taxi that his wife's uncle owns."

I headed for the front door. "Who told you that?"

"His sister's son also lives there, but he knows nothing, or pretends to know nothing. He was afraid. It is on the fourth floor."

We headed up the dark staircase, blinded after the bright mid-afternoon sunlight outside. "We have to track down this uncle with the taxi and find out where he took them." Something small skittered away down a dim hall; I banged my feet on each stair to announce our presence to other life forms that might be using it.

"Joseph has another wife in Ngong. Perhaps they went there." He flicked his hand, as if dismissing a long story. "But the two wives do not get along. That's why he keeps them in separate cities. He probably went to his first wife's village." He started to pant. "One more flight."

By now my eyes were adjusted, and I almost wished they weren't. This part of Nairobi wasn't that old. How could the building have gotten this crumbling and grimy in only a few years? "I hope the cousin or uncle will be willing to tell us."

Ibrahima pointed to the left and we walked down the hall. "If we find out where Joseph went, we will go there together."

I paused in front of the door. "No, Ibrahima, that's too much to ask of you. I might be gone a couple of days, or more. If others are searching for Joseph, it might be dangerous. I'd rather go alone."

Ibrahima looked at me mournfully. "What silly things you say." He gave the flimsy wood door a loud rap.

The cousin, a small man with an enormous triangular nose, invited us in and replied to our questions with a barrage of words. Ah, Joseph. A fine man, a generous man, a good man. A hardworking man. He had worked many years for Emmet Laird, also a fine, good, and generous man. And he could tell by looking at Ibrahima that he, too, was a good sort. How many children? Joseph would be so sorry he had missed us. In twenty minutes all we learned was that Joseph's wife was named Margaret. He pretended not to know the name of her village, an unabashed lie from which he would not budge. He shook his head regretfully over the name of her uncle with the taxi, but unfortunately he had been away at the time; he didn't know of this uncle, had never met the man, and, in fact, didn't believe it was a real uncle, but rather an honorific uncle, no relative at all.

I tried outwitting him. I tried bribing him. At last I burst out that Joseph might be the only one who knew the identity of a killer, and that we had to find him. After that he kept cracking his knuckles with a horrible pop and repeating what a pity he could not help us, until we gave up and left.

"Don't worry." Ibrahima put a warm hand on my shoulder. "The neighbors will tell us. We should not have bothered with this foolish coward."

So we knocked on the neighbor's door, but when she opened, the cousin quickly came into the hallway and said in a loud voice that once a certain person got rid of the witchcraft on him, it would be safe for us to mention his name. The door slammed in our face, and no one else on the floor would answer.

We picked our way down the stairs, which smelled of piss and damp. A three-inch cockroach scuttled down the wall, and I thought I could see other shapes moving in the corners. I took the steps as fast as I could in the dim light.

An extremely large woman in a baby-blue blouse and white pleated skirt, looking as fresh as a detergent commercial, waited near the bottom step. She told me to take my time, that she was in no hurry for the climb to the fourth floor. Ibrahima made a bawdy joke about her mounting the stairs while it was filled with his own ample body. In five minutes we learned that she had lived two doors down from Joseph's family since independence; that Margaret had

140

taken the children home to her mother, who lived near Nyahururu, while Joseph moved in with an uncle of Margaret's for a while; that the uncle, Martin Chege, indeed owned a few taxis, and that Joseph planned to work for him. The uncle usually worked out of a taxi stand near the Kilimanjaro Palace. I probably could have learned how many times a week Joseph and Margaret had sex, but we were in a hurry.

"There is no Chege here. Get in, get in. I will take you anywhere!" The cabbie jumped out and pulled open the back door. For a moment I thought he was going to grab me and throw me into the backseat.

Ibrahima said, "My brother, we are not looking for a ride, but for Martin Chege, or his nephew, Joseph Muranga."

"You must take the first cab in line. That is the rule."

A knobby-jointed driver got out of the second cab. "You come with me. That man, his taxi will not make it as far as the garage. And he must go there tonight before it falls apart completely!"

"You liar! At least I have enough gas to reach where I am going," the first driver yelled into his colleague's face.

Within moments we were surrounded by cab drivers taking sides or playing peacemaker between the two men.

So much for keeping a low profile. I signaled to Ibrahima and we wormed our way to the periphery, where we asked a bright-eyed old man if he knew Joseph or his uncle. We were in luck. He told us Chege had just left with a fare, and he offered to let us sit in his cab while we waited, at no charge.

I sweated on the torn plastic seat of the old man's cab, starting up and sinking back in disappointment as cab after cab arrived and departed. I forced myself not to worry about the time, just to focus on the task at hand. We would soon find Joseph, and then we'd find out if and why Garret fired him, and why he'd moved out of his apartment. He must know something important. Was it something he'd found in the house? Something Emmet told him, or he'd overheard? Would he talk openly to me, or would he be too scared?

Three or four times the old fellow started up his engine and we moved up in line, but business was slow at the tail end of the afternoon. Surely Joseph's uncle should have returned from his fare by now, even if it had been to the airport.

When I asked the old cabbie why Chege wasn't returning, he shrugged and said he'd be back, if not now, later; if not later, then tomorrow; not to worry, we were welcome to stay in his cab. He hawked and spat out the window, and returned to dissecting the latest soccer match with Ibrahima. They were both Leopards fans and equally unhappy with the new goalkeeper.

Was the old fellow keeping us blinded while someone else tipped the uncle off? I shook off my paranoia. His relaxed attitude toward time was nothing unusual, nor was his kindness in giving us shelter in his cab.

Though I'd learned to cultivate patience since moving to Kenya, this didn't seem like the time to practice it. I joined a few of the drivers who'd gotten out of their cabs at the end of the line to smoke and chat. A long-jawed fellow with a droopy eye said he knew Joseph's uncle well, and that Joseph had started working for him that morning.

"Joseph Muranga? Out of this cab stand?"

"Why are you looking for him? He is old and also fat. Perhaps I can help you." He hitched up his pants with a bawdy smile that set the men to laughing.

Pretending not to notice, I took him to one side and pressed a hundred-shilling note into his hand. "I must find Joseph Muranga right away. If you can take me to him, I will double this, and the same for him. He will thank you."

Minutes later Ibrahima and I were bouncing around on the sprung backseat of Droopy Eye's cab, heading for the long-distance bus and taxi station.

"Why did the old man tell us to wait in his cab? Did he even know who we were looking for?" I shouted to Ibrahima above the complex drumming and hot electric guitars of the juju music blaring from the car radio.

"He was trying to be nice. He could tell you wanted to find Joseph very badly, and he didn't want you to be disappointed that no one knew him." Ibrahima held on to the

142

frayed strap above the window and swayed toward me and away as the taxi bucketed along. "But you see, if he had not made us wait, this other driver would not have come. We would never have found out where Joseph is driving a cab."

We drove into a chaotic plaza, filled with buses, matutus, taxis, travelers, beggars, and hawkers. Our driver sped up, cut across a lane of moving traffic and two lanes of parked Peugeot station wagons, the bush taxis waiting for passengers to trickle in heading for the same destination, or at least the same direction. He slowed down enough to stick his head out the window and yell a question to a fat woman selling cooked maize cobs, then sped on. We came to a section of taxis discharging and loading customers with mounds of cheap luggage, crates, chickens tied by the ankle, and even a dismayed goat.

"Wait here," the driver directed and hopped out. I watched him move down the line talking to the drivers until my view was cut off, first by a madwoman in a ragged shawl, her hair a filthy mat of ringlets, then by a roving peddler who came up to the window to offer single cigarettes from an open pack, followed by a boy selling peanuts in a twist of newspaper, and a woman thrusting a few silver bracelets and wooden beads temptingly in front of my face.

Ibrahima reached across and closed my window to within an inch of the top, and told me to sit back and stop making myself hot. Droopy Eye returned grinning, started up the engine without a word and began to reverse at high speed, almost running over a row of women selling used clothes arranged on the ground.

"What did you find out?" I asked him.

"Joseph was here, but he got hungry. Luckily, you have asked the right man to help you. I know his favorite restaurant."

The taxi station was amply endowed with kiosks selling food, beer, and soft drinks, and I wondered if Joseph really bothered to go any farther to eat, or if Droopy Eye was being kind like the old man, or worse, leading us on a long, fruitless search in order to hold me up for more money. I

143

wished Ibrahima or I had gone along with him in questioning people, but it was too late now.

"Where is it?" I asked the driver sharply, but he was already pulling to a stop in front of a block of one-story shops and restaurants. This time I jumped out right after him, and we entered the tiniest cubbyhole of them all, called Mama Magdelena Adoyos. There were six plastic-covered tables, each with a single man silently and solemnly eating a generous portion of *githeri*, a porridge of beans and maize. They were all medium-age, nondescript working men in cotton shirts and dark pants. The place was rigorously clean and well-lit with a blinding, naked light bulb.

The cabbie evidently knew two of the men, who welcomed him loudly. We all shook hands, and Droopy Eye rattled off the back and forth greeting ritual, asking after health and family, and calling down peace and blessings. He fended off their efforts to have us sit down and join them.

"Joseph isn't here?" he asked, looking around the four walls as if Joseph might spring out from the homemade mural of steaming stew bowls and loaves of bread.

"He ate and left." The man made an obscene gesture and guffawed. "He has gone for dessert."

"Where does he go?" I asked. "Does he have a special friend? Is he a regular customer anywhere?"

The two men looked at each other reluctantly. "He is too cheap to have a special girlfriend," one told me. "He goes to Majengo."

I cursed inwardly. Majengo is Nairobi's oldest and most notorious slum. A quarter of a million people are jammed into a maze of tin-roofed shacks and dark alleys, equally famous for the number of thugs and the aggressiveness of its whores. It was the last place I would expect the dignified Joseph to go for recreation, but obviously, up till now I had only seen one side of him.

We would never find Joseph in Majengo. We would be lucky to come out alive.

I turned to Droopy Eye, "I guess that's that. Let's go."

"Back to the taxi station? Or to Kilimanjaro Palace?"

"We go to Majengo."

20

TAKE YOUR AVERAGE American family and their suburban home. Now throw away the house and move everyone into the garage. Throw away the car, the bikes, the lawn mower—indeed everything. Put up a few thin walls, move in several beds and cooking pots. Keep the hibachi: you'll be doing your cooking with wood, charcoal, or dung from now on. Throw away the family pets. Add dozens of cockroaches long as a man's finger. Throw away everyone's clothes, except for two pairs of pants and two dresses for the grown-ups, one ragged outfit for each kid. Quadruple the number of kids. If Mom is between menarche and menopause, she's either pregnant or nursing. Now throw away the roof. Replace it with rusty tin that turns the house into an inferno when the weather is hot. Throw away the garage walls. Replace them with flattened oil cans, some odd bits of used lumber, and a few scavenged cinder blocks. Throw away the floor—and don't replace it with anything. Add a bundle of twigs with which to sweep the packed earth. Throw away the electricity and plumbing. The sink is a public spigot shared with hundreds of other people. The toilet is the dirt alley outside the bedroom wall. Add the stench. Now throw away everyone's job.

Welcome to Majengo.

No major road runs to Majengo. No tourist sees it. I'd lived in Nairobi over two years, and although I'd heard of it, I couldn't have found it on my own. Droopy Eye thought taking me there was the week's best joke. He kept turning around to ask, "Where do you want to go?" and guffawing each time he made me repeat the name. I didn't care, as long as he got us there.

We followed the street until it became too narrow for cars, and there was our first hopeful sign, a taxi parked in front of a neighborhood store. It was actually a closet-sized shack crowded with gritty merchandise, the type of store that sold tomato paste by the spoonful from an open can. Several men with nothing better to do sat on the dirt sidewalk outside.

I leaned over Droopy Eye's shoulder. "Could that be Joseph's cab?"

He swerved, more abruptly than necessary, I thought, and pulled up behind it. "The very same. It is Joseph's. I am sure of it."

"How can you tell?" I asked, not wanting any more kind-hearted lies, or self-serving ones, either.

"One car is not like another," he said. He sounded affronted, as if I'd asked how he could recognize Joseph himself.

Indeed, on closer look the beat-up old Peugeot in front of us couldn't easily be mistaken for another. It had been made homey by the addition of gauzy curtains with pink pompoms around the back windows, a yellow fake-fur dashboard cover, and two oversize dice hanging from a stump where the rearview mirror should have been. Somehow it didn't look like Joseph. Had Garret fired him without references? Or had he chosen to work for his wife's uncle because no white would find him in this world? My pulse quickened. Joseph must know something.

A skinny boy in a ragged T-shirt rushed to my window with a happy grin. "Watch your car?" Three other boys appeared by his side, to stare and jostle one another. Their seniors stopped talking and watched from their post by the store.

We got out and Ibrahima gave him a coin. "Are you watching that car, too?" He indicated Joseph's taxi with his chin.

The boy tied the coin into a corner of his stretched-out

146

T-shirt. "Aboge is watching that one." He pulled at the shoulder of one of his companions, a slim boy with the elegant profile of Nefertiti.

"We want to know where that man, that taxi man, went," I told them. "Can you lead us there?"

Screams of assent and offers to take us arose from the crowd of pushing and staring children that had now grown to over a dozen. I could see still more youngsters running in our direction. This was taking on the dimensions of a friendly riot.

A teenager in a polyester shirt disengaged himself from the group of adult street gawkers and offered to lead us to Joseph. The children knew they couldn't compete, so they subsided into a lower volume of excitement.

We all shook hands and introduced ourselves. "What does he look like?" I asked, just to be sure.

"Fat, with gray hair, and this tall," said the teenager, whose name was Nelson. He raised his hand to measure off five-foot-six.

It sounded like Joseph. We were closing in!

"I know that man, too well," continued Nelson. "He comes often. He walks every time the same way." He pointed to an alley opposite the little store.

The crowd of children snickered. Several gyrated their hips and yelled: "Come with me!" "See you at casino!" Two of them pretended to copulate. It was clear everyone knew exactly what brought Joseph to Majengo.

Our cab driver, forgetting neither his promise nor his tip, was not about to abandon us to these local guides. Ignoring the first boy we'd spoken to, he picked out a pleasant-looking old fellow with a club tied to his wrist by a thong, hired him to guard his taxi, then hurried to get in front of our crowd.

We made a nice little parade: Nelson, the teenage guide, Droopy Eye, Ibrahima and I, and about twenty giggling, screaming children.

"What's this they keep yelling?" I asked Ibrahima. "There's no casino here, is there?"

"That's what they call the VD clinic." He was huffing to keep up the enthusiastic pace set by our leader. "These

147

Majengo whores are too dirty. Joseph is a stingy fool. For fifty cents he is buying himself a dose of Slim's." Slim's was the local name for AIDS. "Ah-ee. When a man's cock calls, his brains fly out the window."

We went straight for a hundred feet before the alley was blocked off by a tin wall. Through a gap, I could see a woman washing a toddler in a basin, while several young men sat on a straw mat on the ground playing cards. We turned right and went into a yet narrower lane. At the first doorway a woman in a ripped nylon blouse lifted her breasts and said something invitingly to Ibrahima. When he ignored her, she pulled at his arm so forcefully that he took a step into her house before he dug in his heels and freed himself. This whipped the children into a frenzy of giggles, lewd invitations, and pantomimes of the portly Ibrahima in the sexual act.

Nelson, our teenage guide, told the kids to scram. They fell back all of three feet. He then scooped up a handful of pebbles and hurled them with great force into the dirt at the children's feet, aiming to demonstrate his seriousness, not to hurt them. To my surprise, it worked. The entire crowd of little ones turned and ran down side alleys, to regroup and follow us almost quietly a good fifty feet back. Meanwhile, Nelson asked another whore, a plump woman with a five-year-old playing at her feet, if she'd seen Joseph, and she directed him farther down the alley.

A burly fellow with a mashed nose and the eyes of a drinker came out of a dark space between two of the houses and purposely bumped into me. He smelled like dead fish overlaid with cheap wine. Ibrahima yanked me to his other side and told the fellow to watch where he walked. The drunk muttered something, a threat or a curse, but let us pass on.

We took another turn. I was trying to keep track of how we'd come, in case Nelson evaporated for some reason, but I wasn't sure I'd gotten all the zigzags. A radio blasted Zairian music up ahead, where a group of young roughs watched us approach. One of them had a machete with a broken handle and a gleaming blade tucked into his belt. I didn't think he'd just returned from hacking brush. There

148

wasn't a twig of living green in miles. Near them was a pit of open sewage, but they must have been inured to the stomach-churning foulness. I struggled not to gag or grimace, for fear they might take it personally.

We passed on. The afternoon began to wane, and in these narrow alleys it was growing dim. I linked my arm through Ibrahima's. I wanted to talk and joke as usual, but no normal conversation would form in my mind. I was hyperalert, watching equally for Joseph and for trouble. Was I leading Ibrahima into an ambush, where we'd be mugged and left for dead? I'd never known Ibrahima to be so quiet. I wished the children were back around our ankles, as if they afforded us protection. How far would we have to penetrate into this dark, crowded sea of misery?

"I hope we get out of here before it is night," Ibrahima said. "The whores do only a daylight business in Majengo. After dark, the customers are afraid to come."

The smell of cooking fires overlaid the fetid odors of garbage and human filth. I asked Nelson if it was much farther. Only a short ways, he assured me. Two more turnings. I was completely lost by now, and the light was perceptibly waning. I hoped we hadn't missed Joseph already—*if* our guide really was leading us to him.

Nelson questioned a group of children playing in the dirt. They pointed to the mud-walled shack next door. He poked his head into the open doorway and was greeted with yells of abuse. He turned to us with a grin of triumph. "It is the man you want. He will be finished in a minute."

It was then that the young toughs who'd been listening to the radio appeared on both sides of us. Several more of them now had machetes, which they gripped upright in meaty fists.

Nelson put up his hands in a placating gesture. "Now, brothers. No trouble. These people are here on some private business."

A taut member of the gang waved his machete and told us to empty out our pockets. I hoped they hadn't been drinking. Someone lit a kerosene lamp nearby, and the soft light caught the gleams of the sharpened machetes. Heart pounding, I pulled a wad of cash out of my jeans. Let them

149

take the money and run, I prayed, before Joseph is finished. I can't afford to lose him now.

A weasly-faced fellow planted himself in front of me. I handed him all my cash, and he stuffed it in his pocket. "Your watch, too."

Someone else was shaking Ibrahima down, and he began to argue about giving up his watch.

"Give it to him," I said.

I happened to know that Ibrahima wore a charm against thieves, and wondered how he was going to rationalize this away. He fumbled reluctantly with his watchband, and the young tough hit him along side the head with the handle of the machete. Ibrahima reeled and clapped a hand to his temple. The young fellow raised his machete as if to strike. I swiftly scooped up a handful of dirt and flung it into his eyes.

He cursed and staggered backward. I lunged for his arm, with some crazy idea of getting the machete away, or at least immobilizing him. I hit what felt like a wall but was only the chest of a massive man. He crushed me up against him and laughed. I tensed, imagining a machete blow against my back, but it didn't come.

"You fools to kill a European," yelled Droopy Eye.

"No killing," the giant holding me shouted. "Get the money and watches." I could feel an enormous erection through his pants. He rubbed it against me and laughed again. "You come here looking for a good time?"

"You bother me and the police will eat you alive," I told him. "Your pecker will fall off in jail and your girlfriend will cry."

Droopy Eye, bless him, ran up and pulled at my shoulders, as if to peel me off the giant's chest. "Don't mess with her, brother. She has big connections among the Wabenzi. We don't want no trouble. We have paid you all we have. Show yourself to be a true friend and take us out of here, as our guards. See, we have hired you to help us."

The giant let Droopy Eye pull me away. Ibrahima was bleeding, but not too badly. Everyone loved the cabbie's suggestion.

Except me. "We can't go without Joseph Muranga."

"Who is this man?" the giant asked.

I looked around, but Nelson, our guide, had disappeared. "He is in there." I pointed to the mud shack.

The giant pointed to one of his men. "Get him."

The man plunged into the dark interior and returned immediately. "He went out the back."

I cursed at the top of my lungs. We had to get to his taxi before Joseph did. I turned to the giant. "You must get us to his taxi, fast, before he gets there. Don't forget, we have paid you to help us."

The giant grinned. He was enjoying himself. He turned to his companions. "I will take them back. You head that way"—he pointed left and right—"and try to catch this Joseph."

"Fat, gray-haired, this tall." I marked his height in the air.

The giant whooped and raised his machete. We began to run.

21

THE TAXI WAS pulling away when the band of robbers burst onto Majengo's one street. Several jumped unhesitatingly onto the moving car. Despite the blockade of human bodies covering the windshield, Joseph kept driving. Then the giant jumped onto the trunk and shattered the back window with one blow from his machete. The taxi stopped with a squeal of brakes.

I ran up as the giant opened the car door and yanked Joseph to his feet. *"Asante,"* I panted. "Thank you for getting me this cab. You may leave the driver."

The giant laughed and let go of Joseph, who slipped behind the wheel and gripped it with trembling hands. I got into the front seat and called for Ibrahima to get in next to me. There was a nasty scrape along his temple where the thief had hit him.

The giant closed Joseph's door and wished us a good ride. Droopy Eye came around and clung to the window on the other side. "What about my reward?"

"Follow us. I will pay you, don't worry. You have been a hero today." He let go and sprinted for his cab.

"Thank the Lord, what are you doing here?" Joseph pressed his foot on the accelerator.

"What are you doing driving a cab?" It seemed wisest to pass over in silence my role in setting the robbers on him. Droopy Eye did a three-point turn and pulled in behind us.

"You showed up just in time." Joseph ignored my question in turn. "Those villains were about to rob me. Look how they have broken my window."

"Are you okay?" I whispered to Ibrahima. "Do you need to see a doctor?"

He touched his wound gently. "This? It has already stopped bleeding. I will wash it later."

I turned to Joseph. "Can you take me to my apartment?" I gave him the address. "I need to get some money, and then I'll continue with you to drop off Ibrahima."

I ran upstairs and got money to pay Droopy Eye, while Ibrahima quickly washed his wound in the bathroom. His bloody shirt looked worse than his head. Ibrahima agreed to invite Joseph in for a restorative cup of tea at his place, which would give us a comfortable setting in which to pump Joseph for what he knew.

Joseph blithely cut off a dilapidated delivery van to make the turn into Ibrahima's street. "Luckily I am still a good driver, and my uncle has long wished I would drive for his fleet."

He accepted Ibrahima's invitation to park the taxi and come in. Ibrahima led us into the courtyard of a sprawling blue stucco house, through a low wall that created a sort of porch in front of the apartment of his first wife, and gestured toward a mismatched collection of wobbly wooden chairs, stools, and rattan furniture. There was barely room to sit. Ibrahima lit an unshaded hanging light bulb that filled the porch with crazy shadows. He disappeared inside for a moment. Joseph and I settled ourselves among the clutter of pots and pans near a dripping outside faucet, a charcoal brazier still hot from the midday meal, and mounds of assorted household items that had landed here long ago and remained.

Ibrahima shared this house with his two wives and eleven children, several brothers and their families, his widowed mother, and a changing collection of distant relatives come to Nairobi for a visit that could range from several days to several decades. No exaggeration. What with friends and neighbors also constantly passing in and out, despite the many meals I had eaten in this house I still did not know exactly who lived here and who didn't. Perhaps at any given time Ibrahima himself didn't know.

Joseph and I related our adventures in Majengo that day. I edited my version, but then, so did he. He pretended he'd gone there to pay off a gambling debt.

"Are you a missionary?" Joseph asked.

"You are wondering what I was doing there. I came searching for you."

"For me?" Joseph looked flabbergasted.

"I felt so bad when I heard you'd been fired. I was worried you might be in trouble. How could Garret do such a thing?"

A shutter came down over Joseph's round, open face. "Ah, miss," he sighed, shaking his head. "The young are ungrateful."

"Did he give you a reason?" I asked, hiding the triumph I felt inside.

My tactic of assuming he'd been fired had worked, but as soon as the next words were out of my mouth, I realized I'd made an elementary and deadly mistake. I'd asked a question that invited *no* for an answer, something any experienced interviewer knew to avoid, and even worse, I'd given him a perfect excuse to stonewall me completely.

And stonewall he did. He had no idea why Garret had fired him, none at all. As to why he'd moved his family out of his apartment without leaving word where he'd be: his wife had decided to visit relatives in the country, and his kind uncle had invited him to stay at his place rather than face a week of restaurant meals. All neat and tidy, all reasonable. He seemed so sincere that for a moment I wondered if I'd let my imagination get the best of me. Then I remembered the knuckle-popping cousin in his apartment pretending not to know anything. Joseph was hiding all right, but how to make him trust me?

Ibrahima returned, carrying the fixings for tea. He'd changed into a clean T-shirt with the legend CHEFS ARE SAUCIER in a banner across his potbelly. He added some more charcoal to the brazier, blew the coals into flame, and filled a beat-up tin kettle from the dripping faucet. A toddler—a child? a grandchild?—shyly peeped from the doorway and came to lean against Ibrahima's thigh. Finished with his work, Ibrahima capped the little girl's head with his big palm and she stared up at us past his fingers.

"Joseph doesn't know why Garret fired him," I told Ibrahima. I turned back to Joseph. "You see, I'm sure it has something to do with Emmet's murder, which might mean you are in danger."

Joseph put a hand up to his chest, and I could make out the outlines of a good luck charm hanging on a leather thong under his shirt. He gave an unconvincing laugh.

Ibrahima picked up the toddler and sat her on his lap, clapping her feet together till she giggled. "My brother, you are safe with us. Did you not see how Jazz was able to get rid of that villain who broke your window and would have robbed you of every penny? She has strong magic that makes strangers treat her like family. You can confide in her as you would in your mother."

Voices laughing, arguing, talking, lapped into the courtyard and mingled with the shadows. I pitched my voice low. "You saw how we were able to find you? It is not so easy to hide."

Joseph didn't say anything. Ibrahima's hands went still and the little girl's legs fell straight. She clapped her own feet together, trying to tempt Ibrahima back into the game, but he put her off his lap, and she wandered back inside. He said to Joseph, "You will always be looking over your shoulder. It is better to have a white person on your side. Help Jazz hunt down the danger and she will destroy it."

Joseph looked at his hands for a long time. Seconds stretched to a minute, two minutes. He wasn't going to talk. Ibrahima and I exchanged frustrated looks. The water started to boil. Ibrahima threw some tea leaves in the pot, along with many lumps of sugar.

I leaned toward Joseph. "They killed Mr. Laird. Why would they let you live?"

Another long moment of silence. "What I tell you must not be repeated." He gave a pointed look at the nearby doorway into the house.

Ibrahima called out a staccato phrase, and Mary, his first wife, came to the opening. I didn't know her very well, since she had never gone to school and her English was as limited as my Kikuyu. He went to whisper in his wife's ear. She fetched one of the old women—her mother? her mother-in-law?—and the three of them held a whispered conference.

He returned to his chair. "I told them that a killing ghost had chased Joseph from his job and would turn on anyone who spoke of it, or mentioned his visit to us. They understand very well."

Joseph's voice came out hoarse and whispery, but with the cadence of one prepared to tell a long story. He'd made his decision. "When I began to drive for Mr. Laird, he was the best bachelor in Nairobi. Every night was a dinner party, and I drove him to them all." Ibrahima poured and handed around the sweet, dark tea. Joseph took a sip and his voice grew stronger. "Then Mr. Laird married. His wife's father gave a whole ranch as a bride price, a big piece of land good for cattle, not far from Maasai Mara."

A group of five long-legged teenage girls sedately dressed in school uniforms burst giggling into the courtyard. They caught sight of us, came over to shake our hands, then disappeared into several of the doorways. A radio clicked on and Michael Jackson's girlish voice reminded us to watch it.

But once started, Joseph couldn't be deflected. He looked into the dark courtyard as if seeing a far distance. "There I drove a big truck. Garret was born the first year, and everyone was happy. But there were no more children. The marriage died. Mr. Laird left and never went back. He never went back even once." His voice grew hoarser and faded into silence.

"And Garret?" I asked.

"Garret stayed on the ranch with his mother. One day when she was riding, she got off her horse to tend to a sick cow, and a snake bit her. Garret was twelve. It took his mother a whole day to die."

He took a small, careful sip from his teacup and placed it on the ground next to his chair. "He was twelve then, when he came to live with us in Nairobi. Mr. Laird had his new family, his new business. He was happy, and Garret was like a darkness to be avoided. Kim was the only one to welcome her big brother. Ooh, how she ran after him on her wobbly baby legs."

"And what happened to his mother's ranch?"

"The manager stayed on until Garret came of age to run it for himself, but he never did."

So the bad blood between Garret and Emmet went way back, into a bitter history. It was much uglier than the surface appearance of a successful father disappointed in a lazy son. I focused on the facts embedded in Joseph's story. "You're saying that Garret now owns the ranch?"

Joseph nodded. "Yes. When Mr. Laird divorced her, he had to return the bride price, of course, and when Garret's mother died, it passed to her son, but she made it so it could not be sold. This ranch is now giving Garret money for his pocket, for his airplane and club fees, and all the other things he likes, you see. Oh, yes, she was clever, that mother. If he had sold that ranch, all the money would be gone long ago."

So Garret owned a ranch. Funny he was so quiet about it. "Does he go out there, supervise things?"

"Maybe once a month. It used to be less, recently, more. He goes in his little plane, sometimes for overnight."

I was glad Joseph was talking, but what did all this have to do with Garret firing him? "Was this ranch of Garret's a problem with his father?"

"No, because Mr. Laird trusted the manager, you see. He knew him well from the days when he was first married. That is why he went to his funeral."

"Emmet went to the manager's funeral? Recently?"

"Yes, this same month, maybe two weeks ago."

"At the ranch?"

"Emmet flew out there, his first visit in thirty years. He saw many old faces. Perhaps it was his wife's spirit that had kept him away, I don't know, but it was bad luck to go back. After that visit, Mr. Laird was not at peace." Joseph tapped his chest. "In here, there was something wrong."

A reaction to memories of his first marriage? Or something current, something deadly? "Something wrong," I echoed.

"On the surface, all is normal, but underneath, Mr. Laird is like a stew pot that has been forgotten on the fire. One day, he invites Garret out for a drive, and when they return, they are both stiff, with staring eyes." Joseph shuddered. "One would say, dead men. The next week, Emmet tells his wife she must move out. And a few days after that, he is dead." He rubbed the back of his neck.

"And a few days after that, Garret fires you. Why, Joseph?"

"He said it was for my own safety, that it is best if I disappear for a while. He said I could have my job back after everything is settled."

"After what is settled?"

He didn't answer.

"The murder investigation?"

"I don't know, but I could smell his fear. I have known Garret his whole life, and he would never wish me any harm."

"But why you, Joseph? What put you in danger? Do you know what Emmet and Garret discussed on their drive?"

"No." His voice bounced around the shadowy courtyard.

157

It was too loud, too emphatic. He did know more. Ibrahima and I both worked on him, but he wouldn't say. He kept shrugging his big, sloping shoulders and saying how could he know?

"Joseph, you've told us this much. Why not tell the rest?"

"I have said everything I know." He made an abrupt move, knocking over his teacup with a clatter. "If you want to find out more, you must also go to Phantom Ranch."

22

GARRET'S RANCH APPEARED below us as a neat Monopoly board of fences, barns, staff quarters, a main house, signs of new construction, and the endless plains extending in all directions. A gust of wind buffeted the plane as Henry Darrow banked and turned to begin landing. I stared at the back of Mikki's head and counted the different shades of bronze and red in her hair, praying we'd land before my stomach decided to take a flying leap of its own. Mikki twisted around and gave me a sympathetic look. She knows I hate bush planes.

"Why did I let you talk me out of my plan to drive here?" Alone, I added silently.

"Because my idea for a cover story was better than yours," she reminded me. "Also, this is much quicker. Also, if Garret is doing something fishy here, it's safer with three of us."

This is why people tell you never to do business with friends. It was too late for regrets now. The ground rushed at us in a blur of roaring speed, breaking off our conversation and focusing my misgivings on the miracle of flight. Given that the landing strip was simply a mowed piece of field marked off with white-painted steel drums, Henry's landing was probably as soft as they come, but I was glad to step onto solid ground.

There were some thorn branches piled nearby that we packed around the wheels to keep them from being gnawed by hyenas. By the time we'd finished, a car had driven up and a sweating round-faced fellow ferried us the short way to the main house. Mikki trotted out her story about looking for a private ranch that coexisted with wildlife, where she and Henry could do a short study on elephant migration patterns at the end of the dry season. It seemed to go over well with the driver, who said that many elephants congregated at the north end of the ranch this time of year, because they could dig water holes in a dry riverbed there.

Another man ushered us through a pleasant living room with faded chintz sofas and the usual clutter of a working farm, and onto a shady back veranda. He said word had been sent to the bwana that guests had arrived, and offered us a cool drink while we waited.

Footsteps sounded in the room behind us only moments later, too soon to be the returning servant. The screen door was pushed open, and a tall man with massive shoulders, receding hairline, and heavy black glasses stepped onto the veranda. We all rose to greet our host. It was Kim's boyfriend, Robert Thiaka.

"Jazz, how wonderful! You took me up on my invitation! And you have brought old friends." He turned to the Darrows. "You have come to see my impala ranching?"

I stared. Robert Thiaka's impala ranch and Garret's Phantom Ranch were one and the same! It was disorienting, like two superimposed photos creating a third, unexpected image. Of course there was nothing illegal, immoral, or incriminating about a leasing arrangement between Garret and Thiaka. Kim undoubtedly served as a link between her brother and her lover. Nevertheless, I felt a prickling along the back of my neck.

Thiaka didn't seem to notice my shocked silence. "How

159

lucky that you found me here! Tomorrow I must go to my natal village to attend the boys' circumcision. One day more and you would have missed me."

Meanwhile, Mikki and Thiaka exchanged some small talk about Nairobi University and exclaimed over how long it was since they'd crossed paths there, given that they were in the same department.

Henry gave Thiaka one of his overhearty handshakes. "Yes, Jazz told us about your marvelous efforts out here in ranching with wildlife. Sounded positively fascinating— way of the future and all that." He smiled, showing his big yellowed teeth. "Love to see your setup, if it's not interfering, of course. But we also have a proposal to make to you."

To my surprise, Henry actually nodded to Mikki, giving her the cue to take over. Was this a new, reformed Henry, ready to work with Mikki as a coequal? Mikki trotted out the story about studying elephants' dry season migration. Thiaka thought it might work out, although he warned us that poaching had been severe recently.

He offered to show us around the ranch buildings himself, and then, if we wished, he could lend us a car to check out the north end of the ranch, where an ancient elephant migration route crossed the property.

"Emmet Laird would have loved to see it," I said. "One of his projects was to map the ancient seasonal migration routes before they're all blocked by human settlement."

"You know he was out here at the beginning of the month, to attend the old manager's funeral?" Thiaka asked. "I did tell him about this one spot where the elephants dig for water—where I am sending you—and he was most interested. He planned to come back and visit it one day, but"—Thiaka shook his head sadly—"who dreamed he had such few days left?"

We were given a most thorough, and increasingly hot, tour of the premises, from the facilities for controlled breeding to the fleet of trucks for transporting the impala to market. Nothing struck me as suspect, although I suppose the trucks could be used for transporting ivory. Without the liberty to examine each truck closely, or question the driv-

160

ers, there was no way to tell. Had Emmet been free to wander around on his own the day of the funeral?

The corrals of impala made me both happy and sad. The gazelles were a burnished bronze, almost the color of Mikki's hair, with delicate black horns—entrancing creatures. It was painful to see them half domesticated, but surely better than seeing them wiped out and replaced by cattle. At least the impala belonged here and wouldn't destroy the grasslands.

Despite Robert's constant moaning about needing more money to carry out all his ideas—including turning the main farmhouse into a tourist guest lodge, complete with horse stables and an internship program for farmer's sons—the place was already amazing. I wondered how Kim reacted to all this capitalist zeal. Robert Thiaka had grown up in a tiny village himself, near Lake Nakuru, and was quite proud of all the jobs he was creating for country people, as well as developing impala into a new food source. They had a model vegetable farm and fish ponds that fed the staff, and they produced a surplus sold in the local market.

It was damn impressive. I couldn't imagine that any of what we had seen sent Emmet Laird home heartsick. On the contrary, Robert Thiaka said he and Emmet had talked at some length about the viability of the farm, his financial resources and so forth, and the whole issue of saving wildlife by making it commercial. He'd gotten the distinct impression that Emmet was intrigued enough to consider a major contribution to the project.

"Was that the first time you'd met?" I asked as we walked back to the main house.

"The only time," Robert said sadly. "You know that Kim and her father were not talking. Such a pity. And now it is too late for them to make peace."

"Did Emmet know who you are—I mean, your relationship with Kim?"

Robert pushed his glasses up on his nose. "No. I wanted to tell him, but I could not find the right moment. So I let him go away without knowing." He had an engaging smile. "I was a coward."

161

Henry grunted. "Emmet's loss, cutting off his daughter like that. Hard-hearted fellow."

Robert was intrigued by Henry's comment. "It is not up to the father to apologize to a daughter who strikes him. I told Kim she was wrong, but of course she is too modern to listen to me. In my mind, they were not hard-hearted, those two, but hardheaded." He tapped his broad temple.

Thiaka insisted we join him for lunch, and then we borrowed a car and headed north to find the elephants. I wondered if we'd find whatever it was that had affected Emmet so deeply. Something here had led to a big fight with Garret? The day grew hotter and our conversation shorter. Heat waves raced over the ground before a driving wind, and watery mirages shimmered where the road met the sky. I balanced a canteen between my thighs and I sipped the tepid water in a fruitless effort to clear the dust out of my throat.

The track led on and on across the rolling plains, detouring now and then around a rocky spine or to avoid a ravine. The river was a dark line of trees, now near, now far. We rattled over tributary streambeds, dry at this season, but still a challenge to cross with their loose, round boulders which rocked the car and threatened to smash our crankcase or an axle.

We saw very few animals. Except for impala, most other grass eaters had migrated south, and wouldn't be back till the first rains. We glimpsed a pride of lions asleep in a patch of shade under an acacia, as if prostrated by the heat. They appeared grumpy to me, but it was probably projection. Still, they did look skinny. Lions stay behind to guard their hard-won hunting territory, even though the great herds leave; the dry season is hunger season for lions.

In the early afternoon an enormous cloud came over the distant hills, flat-bottomed and billowing into the stratosphere. It was brimming with light, so brilliant it hurt the eyes, a harbinger of heat, not water. Still, it was the first cloud any of us had seen in months.

Like a shadow from hell, we passed for miles across a blackened expanse of earth. Wind whipped dust and ashes against the windshield with a stinging sound. Dry season was the time of fire. With good grazing for their cattle getting scarce, local people set bush fires to force the grass to send up green shoots in advance of the rain. The fires rage for days, blown by the wind until they ravage hundreds of miles of the plains. The delicate balance between elephants, trees, and grass is swung off the scale to erosion as baby trees are burnt to a crisp.

The road swung in toward the river, passed a crude airstrip hacked out of the brush and marked by barrels, which I was very grateful we hadn't attempted, and then there was the sound of human activity, a sprawl of trucks and sheds and earth-moving equipment. We were at a dam-building site that Robert Thiaka had insisted we stop to admire, close to the elephants' watering place.

I pulled up next to a cement mixing trough, got out of the car and stretched. A black and yellow weaver flew past my face with a bit of straw in its beak. It joined a colony of its fellows busily constructing their gourd-shaped nests, suspended like Christmas ornaments from the branches of a small acacia. The river had carved itself a deep trough, dry now, but a rampaging flood in the rainy season. There was a wooden form built from bank to bank. The air was noisy with the sounds of workmen and the high thrumming of insects.

The foreman stood with his back to us, hands on hips, shouting instructions to bare-chested workmen as they poured a slurry of wet cement. "Slow, slow, slow. Allah be praised. Keep steady, you sons of whores." He turned and saw us, looked startled, and came right over, rubbing his big hands against his shorts before shaking hands with us.

"Rashid Husseini." He was a handsome man, but there was something unpleasantly self-aware in his manner, as if he used his good looks to assert his power over women, even to take revenge on them. I didn't like the way his eyes slowly gravitated to my breasts, and then Mikki's, as if by right.

Mikki launched into her explanation about a study of elephants in the dry season.

Rashid Husseini glanced back at the workers, turned back to us. "I will ask one of the men to make tea for you,

163

but I am very sorry—this isn't a good time for me to talk. I must apologize for being a bad host. We are at a delicate point."

"Tea would be lovely, but we don't wish to disturb you. If you'd be so good as to point us on our way . . ." Henry said, with an ostentatious look at his watch.

"No, you must have tea. You are my guests. I am honored by your presence. As for elephants, I am afraid you will be disappointed. If you want to see where they dig"—he gestured with the edge of his hand—"you follow the riverbed, about three miles upstream. There is no road and the going is very rough. You won't see much. Poachers were active here a month ago, and all the elephants left."

"Mr. Husseini, one question," I said. "You know Emmet Laird, the ranch owner's father?"

"I never met him, miss," he said, looking coldly at me with his almond-shaped eyes. "He was at the main house for a funeral a couple of weeks ago, I heard, and then we heard he'd died himself, Allah be praised."

"Did he come up to see the dam or the elephants when he was here?"

"No, as I said, I never saw Mr. Laird." He fixed his eyes on mine. "Be careful about running into poachers. If you surprise them in the act, they'll shoot on sight."

We turned down his repeated offer of tea and returned to the car. Henry started to grumble that this last three miles could take us hours. He was right, of course. But as Mikki pointed out, we had to be scrupulous about our alibi for coming—and besides, this late in the dry season, elephants were probably back digging for water, poachers or no.

I turned the car around and was about to head out when a workman with dark, almost black, skin stepped from behind a parked truck and signaled to me surreptitiously. I pulled into the shadow next to him and he leaned toward my ear. "Memsahib. Mr. Laird did come. The day of the funeral." He whispered so softly I could barely hear, though his warm breath brushed my face. "He was here. That Somali is a liar." He looked at me with sad, expectant eyes. I thanked him and handed over a tip. He ducked and ran.

"What'd that fellow want?" asked Henry.

"He offered to be our guide," I said.

"What'd you tip him for?"

"Why not? He looked like nothing good had come his way in a while."

As it turned out, the first part of the drive wasn't too bad, since there were some car tracks to follow through the grass. It was when we headed into the trees along the *donga*, the dry river course, that the going became slow.

As we passed into the shade of the trees along the *donga*, the temperature immediately dropped. There was the heavy, sweet smell of ripe figs. A vulture landed in a spindle-shaped palm and the fronds clattered under its weight. Both palm and vulture were survivors of an age before mammals ruled the earth. We passed deeper into the shadows.

We heard elephants grumbling ahead, but the undergrowth was too dense to push through, so we left the car and proceeded along an animal trail on foot. The imprint of the round pads of a big cat were pressed deep into the dry clay from the last time it rained, many months back. We passed on in silence. A knee-high dik-dik antelope stared at me from under a bush, its long nose twitching uncertainly, then burst out of cover and zigzagged down the trail.

There was a big crashing sound and we dropped to our haunches. It grew closer and I caught a glimpse among the tangled brush of a rough gray surface. More crashing came from behind and to the side. It was an elephant family. They passed on ahead of us and a moment later I heard a loud, throaty rumble.

"The water must be just ahead," Mikki whispered.

"This is damn-all dangerous and stupid," said Henry.

We broke through the last foliage and found ourselves at the edge of a high, sandy bank above the riverbed. It was dry and boulder-strewn directly below us, but a little way ahead was a sandy area pockmarked with holes. A small group of elephants were congregated around the holes, dipping their trunks in to reach water. Scattered around them were elephant skeletons in various stages of decay, partly or mostly covered with sand. Poachers had obviously been at work here. We dropped to our bellies.

Three elephants clambered down the bank and broke into

165

a lumbering trot toward the other group, which started toward them. They writhed their trunks, flapped their ears, screamed and trumpeted. The two biggest elephants, rather small to be matriarchs, pushed through their enthusiastic offspring and rubbed their heads together, clicking their tusks, rumbling deep in their throats and entwining their trunks. One baby elephant whirled round and round in excitement.

"This looks like the reunion of a family that's lost its matriarch, and even the next generation," Mikki whispered. The extended family splits up in the dry season to forage for scarce food and water in smaller groups, but you'd expect each group to be led by a more mature elephant than any we were seeing. She studied the group through her field glasses. "I doubt if the oldest are even in their twenties. Goddamn it."

I knew why Mikki was swearing. Poachers have wiped out all the larger, hence older, elephants over wide areas. A family group without an experienced matriarch is vulnerable. When the going gets tough—especially in an extended drought like the one we'd been having for the past few years—the herd's survival depends on the lifelong experience and wisdom of the oldest elephants.

Before starting to drink, the newcomers cautiously approached the largest pile of bones. They grew quiet. First one, and then all of them, reached out with their trunks to smell the skeleton, especially the skull with its hacked-off tusks. They delicately felt along the jaw and into the hollows.

"I wonder if that's their mother?" Mikki whispered.

"They're remembering the shape of her face." I clamped my lips shut so I wouldn't start bawling.

The elephants kicked some more dirt onto the bones, and then finally went to drink from the shallow wells already dug, sucking water up in their trunks and squirting it into their mouths. A young calf, not yet skilled enough to use its trunk, climbed into a hole, curled its trunk back and drank with its mouth.

"Let's see if there's any place nearby suitable for a

camp," I whispered. "We can report back to Thiaka and it will make our interest more believable."

"Let's hope we don't succeed *too* well and find the local poachers," Henry said, with his usual pessimism.

We threaded our way back along the bank. Ahead of us the crown of an enormous fever tree pierced the underbrush, its airy canopy spread like a circus tent fifty feet off the ground. I signaled with my hands to indicate tent shapes under the sheltering tree. Mikki nodded in agreement. It was a beautiful spot to place a camp. We approached carefully, just in case Henry was right.

Even at a superficial glance the clearing showed signs of heavy use.

"Hey, look here." Henry kicked a bit of wood that was charred at one end. "There's a deep pile of ashes here. More than one campfire, I'd say."

Mikki walked around the perimeter of the clearing. "And more than one meal. Look at all these impala bones."

"I think we better get out of here," Henry said. "Damn foolishness, coming into poaching territory without a gun."

We picked our way back to the Rover, ever mindful of animal noises. The elephants had begun to feed. We could hear the ripping sound of branches as we detoured around the water hole. It almost masked the fainter sound of a slithering rustle through the grass, but Mikki's experience in spending hours on foot with the baboons had made her ears more sensitive than mine. Her hand shot out and grabbed me, halting me in my tracks. A long green snake slithered across the game trail in graceful curves, beautiful and deadly.

The drive back to the ranch was hot and we were all quiet. I thought over all that Joseph had told me last night: after his visit to the ranch, Emmet had a confrontation with Garret. If Emmet had seen what we'd seen today, would he have returned home morose and quarreled with his son? I doubted it. He must have stumbled across more than a poaching camp—those were easy to find wherever there were elephants. If that's all he saw, he'd have told Thiaka he should guard his north corner, or even that his dam foreman was acting suspicious. Nothing we'd seen implicated either Thiaka or Garret.

I still had to find out what roused Emmet's suspicions and what pointed them at his son. I didn't even know if those were two separate things, or one and the same. There was only a short time gap between Emmet's visit here and his drive with Garret, when Joseph saw them return home looking like dead men. My best guess was that Emmet found something here, went home and investigated further, and discovered that Garret was involved. I needed to work from both ends, but how? The fire-scarred plains gave me no answer.

As we took leave from Thiaka, I asked him if he'd given Emmet the tour of the ranch while he was here for the funeral. Thiaka said regretfully that it hadn't been possible, given the circumstances, but that he'd noticed Emmet poking around a bit on his own.

As the plane reached altitude, I looked down at the sprawl of buildings. I'd be back. Next time I'd drive in myself, avoid Thiaka, and poke around on my own, as Emmet had done. And afterward I'd tell Mikki what I'd found.

23

I WAS IN the bathroom splashing cold water on my face when the phone rang. It was Ibrahima. I told him we'd found Thiaka running Garret's ranch. I described the signs of the poacher's camp we'd found. "The foreman at the closest worksite, where they're building a dam, said he'd never seen Emmet—but one of the workmen told me the foreman was lying. Emmet explored the area around there the same day as the funeral."

"You have found where Emmet uncovered the poaching headquarters!"

"Maybe. The timing fits what we know of Emmet's last two weeks alive, but Emmet must have seen more than elephant skeletons and a deserted poacher's camp. Most of Thiaka's trucks are for transporting live impala to market, but at that dam worksite, they have closed vehicles that could carry a lot of ivory. I'm going to go back and stake it out, see if that foreman provides a lead."

"I also have interesting things to tell. I have been serving cocktails at Elephant House. Garret has a Japanese guest, a business associate. They have been talking about Garret's island and his ranch, and also about ivory."

"About ivory?"

"Yes. That Japanese man likes ivory very much. They are on their way to Shabaan's. Let us, too, meet there."

I looked at my watch. "Thanks for the offer. And the information. It's better if I go to Shabaan's on my own. It's safer for you if Garret doesn't see us together."

The first person I glimpsed as I walked through Shabaan's arched doorway was Garret. He weaved his way unsteadily through the tables, apparently on a trip back from the men's room. I couldn't see who he joined, because Shabaan came up and blocked my view with his ample back.

"Good evening and welcome." Shabaan bowed. "May I show you to a table?"

I returned his greetings as I perched on a bar stool. "I'm fine here; I'm not eating. Tell me"—I lowered my voice so Shabaan had to lean over to catch my words—"do you know anything about Robert Thiaka's ranch?"

"A little." Shabaan signaled to Raj to serve me. I didn't need to give an order; I always get one of Raj's fresh-squeezed screwdrivers.

"I have heard he has a large and magnificent farm, way out, near Maasai Mara," Shabaan said, "where he is raising impala for market. I occasionally buy some of his meat.

Many customers like game here in Nairobi, and they don't mind paying for it, but he is a dreamer if he thinks that herders will give up their cattle. How will they purchase brides with no cows?"

"Do you know who funded him?"

"He is very secretive about this. The university didn't give him much money."

"Do you have any ideas where he got all that dough? He's spent a fortune on new buildings, fencing, all sorts of equipment."

"Some people think he got the money from Kim and is sensitive about sponging off a woman." He glanced into the restaurant. Tables had been pushed together to accommodate a few big parties, which filled the place with raucous laughter and raised voices. "I think, maybe Kim helped him start out, but as you say, he has expanded, built many buildings, is making a dam—I am thinking these things require very large sums."

"Those are my thoughts, also."

He gave one of his magisterial nods. The outer door opened and a party of late-night revelers came down the steps. Shabaan rose to his feet. "I must greet my guests. If you wish, we will talk more later."

"Thanks, Shabaan." I took a gulp of my screwdriver, which was sitting untouched in front of me. I looked around.

I felt mildly self-conscious. The other women I could see were dressed in flashy, tight-fitting evening dresses, as if come from dancing or a party. I'd considered throwing on a dress, but that meant ladylike shoes, and I wasn't in the mood to have my toes pinched. At least I'd exchanged my jeans for a stylish jumpsuit and a heavy Navajo necklace, my one good piece of jewelry.

I strained my neck around to glimpse Garret. He and a gray-haired, gray-suited Oriental man were toasting each other with sloppy, drunken movements. I wondered what the two men were celebrating.

A small hush fell on the buzz of conversation and heads turned toward the door. Kim Laird stood framed by the entrance. She was wearing a raw silk tunic that caressed her figure. If she noticed the stir, she made no sign.

Kim joined her brother's table amidst a flurry of handshakes and bows. Time to make my move. I skirted the raucous center table and went over to Garret's, bringing my drink as a signal that I expected to be invited to join them. It worked.

Kim looked frosty, but Garret gave me a warm welcome. Mr. Hanyo insisted I sit next to him on the bench. He pushed aside my screwdriver and poured me a glass of champagne.

I raised my glass. "What are we drinking to?"

"To Umar Island," Garret said.

"Paradise Island," Mr. Hanyo corrected him.

"To Paradise Island and all the pale German tourists who will come to bake themselves silly on her sands." Garret clinked glasses loudly with each of us. The bubbles trembled and sped upward like tiny beads of gold.

"Turning empty land into jobs," Kim added before taking a sip.

"To the Ranch of Ghosts," toasted Mr. Hanyo. We all raised our glasses again. Was it only my imagination that Kim signaled caution to Garret with her eyes? Garret called the waiter for another bottle.

"That doesn't sound like a tourist attraction," I said.

Mr. Hanyo patted my knee. "You never hear of Ranch of Ghosts, but when we change the name to Elephant Paradise, you will. You will bring all your tour groups there. It will be luxury hotel, five-star, deluxe, plus all the wildlife. Like Mount Kenya Safari Club started by Hollywood star, but even better. We will have armed patrols, keep out all poachers."

"That sounds wonderful."

"We will have biggest elephant herd in Africa. Two businesses in one. Best way to grow ivory is from live herd, not dead herd." Mr. Hanyo laughed. "Let elephant grow big, elephant dies natural death, collect tusk, big tusk. That way, much ivory."

The second bottle of champagne arrived and conversation stopped as we watched the waiter ceremonially rip away the foil, untwist the wire cage, and wiggle the cork out slowly. It gave a satisfying pop and emitted a plume of misty champagne.

Kim turned the discussion to their plans for Umar Island. The dock was finished, the machines and matériel were in a warehouse in Lamu, all set to be ferried across, and they'd be able to start digging foundations as soon as the final building permits were issued. Until the work started, it sounded like an ideal staging point for smugglers.

The conversation flowed on to less interesting matters. I turned to Mr. Hanyo. "I'm intrigued by your plan for raising elephants as a sustainable resource. This idea is very much the rage among some conservationists—"

"Wildlife will have to pay its way to survive," Garret intoned pompously.

"Kim's friend Professor Thiaka," I went on, "is experimenting with ranching impala; they can subsist on dry rangeland that would starve cattle to death. But elephants . . ." I shook my head. "They're different from gazelles. If ivory is allowed to be legally gathered anywhere, it will be impossible to stop illegal killings, and all you'll be left with are tiny remnants in well-guarded safari parks."

"Exactly." Mr. Hanyo held his champagne up to the candle so that the swirling bubbles gleamed and flashed. "They will kill every elephant, ten more years, no ivory anywhere. Everybody will have to come to us for ivory. We will be very very rich."

"How will you keep out the poachers from your ranch?"

"That is not so difficult. I will pay. The game parks have no cars, no staff, no guns, no salaries. How can they keep their animals safe? One million dollars a year would save all the elephants in Kenya." He nodded his head for emphasis. "Yes, this is true. One million dollars, and there would be no problem. Also, most important, you must smooth the way with the government officials." He rubbed his fingertips together in the universal sign language for money.

Was Garret leasing Phantom Ranch long-term to Mr. Hanyo as part of a package with Umar—soon to be Paradise—Island? What about Thiaka? Was he part of this deal, too? Was Kim here as Thiaka's proxy? More questions pressed in on me. Was Mr. Hanyo the ivory mogul orchestrating the death of Kenya's elephants? Could Hanyo be the person who surprised Emmet at his camp? I hated to think of the alternative: that it was Garret and Kim who murdered their father.

The waiter arrived to take supper orders. Fending off Mr. Hanyo's friendly entreaties to be his guest, I took my leave. I had a lot of questions. It was time to find some answers.

24

IT WASN'T HARD to convince Ibrahima to help me carry out my plan. I figured with Garret and company just ordering supper, we'd have plenty of time for what I wanted.

Ibrahima stopped the car before we reached the Lairds' gate house. I took my flashlight, climbed into the back and scrunched up on the floor, getting my jumpsuit covered with dust. Ibrahima called hello to the gatekeeper and exchanged jokes about working for Alicia. The gate clanged shut behind us. We drove up the graveled drive to the side road that led to the servants' quarters. The car stopped and Ibrahima greeted the roving guard, who climbed in next to him. The back door was kept locked at this time of night and the staff were let in by a guard, armed with billy club and pistol.

"I can guess where you have been, you old dog," the guard said with a rowdy laugh. "Your girlfriend uses a sweet scent."

I promised myself to go easier on coconut hair conditioner in the future. Don't look on the floor behind you, I prayed. I tried to breathe silently. As long as I didn't make a sound, I was safe. Unless his nose led him to turn around.

"Why do you think I took this job?" Ibrahima joked back. "You think it was for the pleasure of sleeping at the Elephant House? My second wife is a jealous woman. Oo-ee, that one! She gives me a hard time."

"I have one wife, two girlfriends, and they are all jealous," the guard boasted. "Do you have a cigarette?"

"Here, take as many as you want." Ibrahima handed over his pack. The two of them climbed out. We'd arrived at the servants' entrance. The guard unlocked the door, declined an offer to come in for coffee, saying he'd lose his job if they found him indoors, and set off on his rounds. Ibrahima clicked off the entrance light, waited several minutes, then stole out and wordlessly opened the car door. I unwound from the pretzel shape I'd crammed myself into and followed him into the house.

The easy part was over.

I'd never been in Garret's rooms, although I knew he occupied the second floor of the west wing. As the stand-in butler, Ibrahima had made himself familiar with the whole house. He made a quick pass through the downstairs to make sure no one was up and about, while I waited in the butler's pantry.

"All clear?"

"I went up to Alicia's corridor to check, and there was no light under her door. She usually goes to bed by eleven, so she should be long asleep by now."

And according to Ibrahim, Garret rarely came home before one, which gave us a little less than an hour to snoop around and get out of here. Long enough, I hoped.

Ibrahima led me through the narrow servants' corridor to an equally narrow staircase. The stairs climbed into a pillar of darkness and I paused, illuminating it briefly with the flashlight.

"Step softly. The stairs creak."

I gripped the banister's smooth surface, feeling with my toes for each step before I trusted it with my weight. We

174

passed through a silent swinging door. Now there was a thick carpet underfoot.

Ibrahima stopped and I took an awkward half step and trod on his heel. He breathed into my ear, "Flash your light for a moment."

I clicked the button on and off. My retinas flashed orange in protest against the burst of light. The moment of illumination showed a spacious corridor that ended in a curtained window. It was empty except for the giant roses gamboling over the carpet, a man-sized Chinese vase in blue and white that matched the one near Emmet's study, and an antique table with cut flowers that filled the air with a heavy sweetness. At least no one would sniff out my presence here.

Ibrahima's warm hand pressed over mine. "The door on the left," he breathed.

We passed the looming vase safely, and turned into the room on the left. Ibrahima swung the door shut behind us. I put on the flashlight again, muffling it against my belly. Heavy curtains obscured the windows.

We were in Garret's study. Nothing could have provided a greater contrast with Emmet's home office, with its shabby, comfortable couches and no-nonsense filing cabinets. I was expecting a men's club look: tufted-leather couch and high-back chairs, leather-bound volumes that you knew no one had ever read. Garret had done something much more charming. We were in the 1920s, with the spare geometries and naked ladies kicking up their heels of art deco. Seventy years ago one of the rich white settlers must have shipped all the latest furniture straight from London and Paris. Garret's grandparents perhaps? I didn't think Garret had the money to buy art deco at today's prices.

I put the flashlight on a chair, where its beam spotlighted a chrome and ebony desk, casting an elongated shadow against the wall. Ibrahima pulled out a pencil flashlight. He took one side of the room, I took the other, and we methodically opened every cabinet and drawer. One glass-topped display table held a collection of Japanese netsuke in cinnabar, ivory, jade, and quartz, cunningly carved into fantastical figures.

175

"Look at this," Ibrahima whispered. I joined him in front of a black lacquer credenza. On top of it sat a long wooden box with Oriental carving, big enough to hold a saxophone. Its ornate surface was completely out of place in this room of sleek, pared-down lines. He raised the lid. The box was lined in blue velvet. Inside nestled a pair of small elephant tusks.

The polished ivory gleamed in my flashlight's beams. Hardly a centimeter remained intact. Each tusk was carved into the shape of a Chinese pleasure garden with paths, stairs, pavilions, wisteria—covered arches, and tiny human figures. I'm certainly not an expert on Oriental antiques, but to my eye the ivory looked as pale as if they had been carved yesterday.

The hairs on my arms stood up with a prickle of fear. "If his father ever saw this . . ." I ran my finger over the ivory. There was no denying its beauty. Was it beautiful enough to kill for?

I wiped my fingers on my pants, feeling angry and sick at the thought of losing elephants forever so collectors could have their carved tusks on display. Alicia said Garret was whining last week that Emmet shouldn't have gone into his belongings. After his visit to Phantom Ranch, Emmet must have become suspicious and looked in here. He took Garret for a drive afterward, from which Joseph said they returned like dead men. Was that when Emmet confronted Garret? And was it over these tusks, or also for slaughtering elephants out at Phantom Ranch? Did Emmet say he'd disinherit Garret? Did Garret decide to kill his father? The tusks lay silently in their wooden case, disclosing nothing.

I shut the lid. We could leave now, but we still had a safety margin before Garret returned. It would be nice to find some of his business records on the ranch. I returned to the desk at the far end of the room. I opened drawer after drawer, only to find stacks of creamy stationery, thin blue airmail paper, letters bound in fat stacks by fraying rubber bands. Garret seemed to be quite the correspondent. I quickly glanced at the stamps and addresses. Most were from England, a few from America. None from Hong

Kong, China, or Japan—world centers of ivory carving. None from Somalia or the United Arab Emirates, havens for laundering the ivory en route to the Far East. Surely Garret must keep the records of his business ventures somewhere, but not here. I closed the last drawer and turned to Ibrahima.

The door to the room swung open and the lights blazed.

Garret was framed in the opening. I hit the floor almost before seeing the stubby gun in his right fist. He fired without a moment's pause. It sounded as loud as an explosion, enough to blast the room apart.

At almost the same instant there was the sound of breaking glass, a thud and a shout of pain. Ibrahima and Garret were tussling on the floor, the shards of a broken lamp all around them. I scrambled to my feet. Garret still gripped the gun.

Ibrahima was older, but he fought all out. He wrestled his way on top of Garret, pinned him down with his greater weight, and grabbed his right wrist. I yanked the gun from Garret's grip. Garret used his free hand to go for Ibrahima's eyes.

I held the gun in two hands and pointed it at his head. "Stop or I'll blow your head off, goddamn you!"

He glanced away from Ibrahima for a second and took in my face. I could see the change from murderous rage to recognition. He dropped his arms and went limp. "What the hell are you doing here?" He sat up and rubbed his wrist. It was bleeding from a gash on the forearm. "You almost broke my arm with that goddamn lamp."

Ibrahima went into the hallway and picked up the gun. "Shall I call a doctor?"

"No! I don't need a doctor!" Garret levered himself to his feet. He reached for the gun. "I'll take that back."

Ibrahima removed the bullets and handed it over.

"And the bullets!"

Ibrahima ignored him and slipped the bullets into his pocket. "May I bring you a brandy, sir?"

Garret was momentarily nonplussed by this sudden change in identity. I smiled from behind Garret's back, but Ibrahima met me with this newfound air of impassive dignity. Where had he learned to imitate an English butler? Had Alicia given him lessons?

"A brandy for you, too, miss?"

"Perhaps it's best if I just leave. Garret, I'm awfully sorry I startled you. I hope your arm is all right." I started down the hall. "Ibrahima, thank you for protecting me—and saving Mr. Laird from an unintended homicide. You were wonderful."

I liked that *unintended homicide.* I hoped it would shut Garret up long enough for me to get out of here without awkward questions. Questions like: what were you doing in my room at midnight?

I got as far as the man-sized Chinese vase when a uniformed guard ran into view, dropped to one knee and aimed his gun at me. "Drop your weapon," he commanded.

I showed my empty hands. "Garret!"

Garret marched down the hall. "That's all right. The gunshot was me. I thought we had an intruder." He cast a sidelong glance at me to make sure I got the sarcasm.

Alicia's voice came up the stairwell. "Is everything safe?"

So much for slipping out of here. The guard got to his feet and put away his gun. "Yes, Mrs. Laird. Mr. Laird is up here, and all is under control." He turned to Garret. "Would you like me to check through the house, sir?"

"Come on up, Alicia!" Garret went to the head of the stairs to meet her. He talked over his shoulder to the guard. "No, thank you. That's all for now."

"Thank you, sir." The guard looked at us curiously and left.

Alicia paused with her hand on the newel post. "Your arm is bleeding. What the hell is going on here?"

Garret massaged his wrist. He thrust his chin at me. "I didn't recognize Jazz in the dim light and took a shot at her."

"What?" Alicia looked toward his rooms. She was trying to make sense of my presence here. She wasn't succeeding.

I had two choices: lie or tell the truth. I tried to think of a good lie, but nothing occurred to me, so I settled for the truth.

"I was doing some snooping while Garret was out."

Alicia gave me a cold look. "Maybe we should go into Garret's study and hear what this is all about while we wait for the police."

"Good idea. But you may not want to call the police before you've heard me out. Do you have a license for carrying that handgun, Garret?"

"The gun belongs to me." Alicia tightened the belt of her silk robe. Her breasts bobbled under the thin fabric. "I lent it to him."

"Were you expecting trouble tonight?"

"No, just being cautious." She tapped the pockets of her robe as if looking for cigarettes, but didn't find any. Garret offered her his pack. "The police haven't come up with a single suspect." She accepted a light from Garret and took a long drag on the cigarette. "One of us could be next."

"Especially with a gun in the house. It's usually a family member who's shot."

"You're in no position to be sarcastic, Jazz," Garret said. "I would say you owe us an explanation. I for one am absolutely riveted." He pulled the desk chair closer and sat on it sideways. "Pray, do begin."

"I think the police would be equally interested in your explanation. Why would you fire a gun with no warning at a woman in your room?"

"I found the back door unlocked, which it shouldn't be, and lights on in the kitchen. I figured I better check and see if an intruder was in the house." Garret started to gesture, found he was waving a gun, and dropped his hand. "What do I see in my study? It looked suspicious." He was starting to whine. "The lights are out, drawers pulled out all over the place, and someone's down at the far end of the room riffling through my desk. I ask you . . ."

Alicia and I waited politely, but there was no finish to that sentence. Finally I asked, "How did you come to shoot?"

Garret blustered, "I just explained—"

"You saw a dim figure, you didn't recognize who it was, and you fired a shot?"

"Yes, but . . ." He started to wave the gun again.

179

"Would you please put that gun down before it goes off again?" Alicia said. Then she turned to me. Alicia pulled herself to her full height, her breasts thrusting forward aggressively. "Garret did not seek you out and attack you. He'd surprised an intruder. I want to know what you were doing sneaking around my house in the middle of the night."

"I apologize for sneaking into your house, Alicia. I was looking for information connected with Emmet's murder. But Garret, it wasn't pitch-black in here, especially after you turned on the lights. You fired right at me. I find that rather disturbing. You can't call it self-defense: I had no weapon, I wasn't attacking you."

"I think I'll consult with my lawyer before answering those accusations," Garret said.

"Look, I'm not planning on pressing charges, unless you bring the police into this; then it'll be up to the police, I guess."

"Look, no one is pressing charges here, either," Alicia said. "You know Garret didn't mean to hurt you. Nothing happened, right? Except we've all lost some sleep."

"And that I found some elephant tusks among Garret's things," I said.

Garret looked defiant. "That was a gift. It doesn't prove anything."

"You have what!" Alicia stamped out her cigarette. "Let me see."

"You have no right to look through my things!"

"You sound like a thirteen-year-old, Garret. I seem to remember you shrieking the same thing at Emmet last week."

"Oh, forget it." Garret flapped his large pale hand. "You might as well look at the blasted tusks. I wish I'd never set eyes on them." Alicia walked over to the credenza. "Watch out for the glass all over the floor," he said, shooting me an acid look.

Alicia raised the lid on the case and looked silently at the velvet-swathed carving. She turned to Garret. "You are an idiot, Garret. Emmet would have killed you if he ever saw this."

180

"I didn't buy it. It was a gift. From my new business partner. Ask Jazz. She met him tonight."

"Mr. Hanyo." I nodded. "When did he give it to you?"

"A week ago Thursday. The same day that my father visited my ranch and came back with his nose out of joint. Next thing I know, he snooped among my things and"— Garret gestured roughly at the tusk—"and had a bloody fit."

He pulled open the door of the credenza, which revealed a well-stocked liquor supply, pulled out a bottle of Courvoisier and a brandy snifter, and poured himself a double. He didn't offer a drink to me or Alicia. "He even went out to look over Umar Island and decided it was a smuggling base."

Garret swished the brandy round in his glass. "I told him about Hanyo. I showed him the enclosed card from Hanyo, but that wasn't enough for him." Garret's mouth twisted bitterly. "From the way he carried on, you would have thought I'd killed all the elephants in Africa single-handed."

"Because he'd also found evidence of poaching at your ranch," I prompted.

"So what? That had nothing to do with me." Garret stuck out his jaw. "Thiaka runs the place, not me. I'm hardly ever out there."

"I heard you've been there often lately."

"You really have been busy snooping, haven't you?" Alicia said.

I didn't answer.

"I've been out there showing the place to Hanyo. We didn't go around checking the place with white cotton gloves like Emmet did. How the bloody hell was I supposed to know the closed lorries were being used to transport tusks?"

"What did Emmet find?" I asked quietly.

"He found scratches on the bottom of one bloody lorry at a building site way up in the northeastern corner of the property, one tiny shriveled-up piece of elephant hide and a few bloodstains, and he was ready to close down Thiaka's whole operation as a poaching headquarters. Never mind about all the work Thiaka put into that place. Never mind that I'm about to close the biggest deal of my life! No, Emmet found one pinky nail of elephant skin in a lorry, and that's it! Flush all our hard work, all our dreams, down the drain." Garret emptied what was left in his brandy glass in one chug. "My new partner gives me a beautiful gift, made in his own country, that I didn't even take out of its box, and my dear father decides I'm a monster. Is that right? Is that fair?"

"What about all the money that's been poured into the ranch? Where did that come from?"

"Emmet asked me the same thing. Thiaka didn't get it from me, I can tell you that. I showed Emmet my bank accounts. I don't have two bloody dimes of my own to rub together! Why would I be selling the majority share in Umar Island to Hanyo, if I'm making millions out of poaching? Why would I be living in this bloody house?" Garret gave a hollow laugh.

"Did he confront Thiaka, too?" I asked.

"No. He told me not to tell Thiaka until he'd collected more evidence."

"You told him anyway, didn't you?" Alicia asked.

"No." Garret draped himself against the black lacquer credenza and folded his arms with a thin smile. "I promised I wouldn't tell Thiaka, and I didn't. I told Kim."

25

I'D BEEN DRIVING into the high, forested hills for hours, and just when I expected Thiaka's village to appear around the next bend, the dirt track petered out half-way up a rough ravine. A thrashing sound told me I'd startled an animal, and I caught sight of a giant forest hog, four feet at the shoulder, disappearing into the dense vegetation. I checked my map. Had I missed a turning? Damn. Backing down this road wasn't a joke.

I saw an animal in my rearview mirror that promised help. It was a scrawny sheep. If there was a sheep, there must be more, and where there was a herd, there would be a small boy. I wasn't disappointed. A dusty child wearing torn shorts and nothing else slapped at the wandering sheep with a peeled stick, and ran up to stare at me with open curiosity.

"Enderit?"

He nodded and pointed straight ahead, the way the Rover faced, then raised a leg to show me his callused foot. I got the message. If I wanted to reach Enderit, I'd have to walk.

I put on hiking boots and a wide-brimmed hat, plus a full canteen of water which I hooked to my belt. There was no telling how long a hike lay ahead of me. I found the footpath, dotted with sheep turds, leaned into the steep hillside and started to climb. Just then I heard the sound of a car. I waited to see who else had decided to drop in on Thiaka. I had some guesses.

A rented Suzuki Sierra with black and white zebra stripes painted on it pulled up behind my car. Sure enough, Kim cut the engine and got out.

She was wearing tight jeans with a boldly colored African print blouse, and big copper earrings that set off the elegant planes of her face. She radiated that same sense of latent power and confidence that had struck me before.

I felt scared for a moment, then talked myself out of it. Whoever killed Emmet had gone to great length to hide the very fact of murder; no one was going to kill me in cold blood and think they'd be able to cover it up.

"I've been eating your dust for hours. Peeuw." She wiped off her face with a tissue and swatted at her clothes, setting off a cloud of red laterite dust.

"I figured Garret would call you about last night. You've come to warn Robert that Garret spilled the beans?"

Kim started up the path. "So you decided to get here first, and see what you could trap Robert into saying?"

"Are you here as his friend? His lawyer? Or his co-conspirator?"

"Robert Thiaka had nothing to do with my father's murder, and I'm not going to let you drag him into it."

Kim passed me and kept on walking. I followed, deep in thought. All during the drive up I'd been trying to figure out the best way to approach Thiaka. I could either confront him or try to win his confidence. With Kim here, either approach seemed doomed. How would I find the key to get him to open up?

Kim disappeared around a bend in the trail. The sun beat down, and the acrid smell of dust mixed with the rich green and rotting smells of the woods. Aside from the liquid warbling of sunbirds, the landscape seemed empty of life, until I came to a treeless, rocky area, rounded a large boulder and heard the unmistakable sounds of baboons screaming and gecking in fear. Kim stood stock-still in the middle of the path and looked glad to see me for the first time.

I grabbed her arm, signaling silence, and looked around for a place to hide. The sounds grew louder. I pointed upward, and we scrambled onto the top of the boulder and fell flat. If it was a lion after them, I didn't want to give it any ideas about a more substantial mouthful of primate.

From our vantage point we looked down on a confusing scene that centered not on a lion, but on a female baboon with a swollen red behind, a public announcement that she was fertile. Her readiness to mate seemed to be more physiological than a personal inclination. She was screaming in protest as she ran among the bushes with the largest male close behind her. He, in turn, was harassed by a mob of competing males. He looked like a battle-trained gladiator with a shield of thick hair and sword-sharp canines. I was glad they were too busy to notice us up on our perch.

The big male turned with grunts of rage to face his attackers. His ruff stood on end and he opened his mouth wide in a flash of enormous teeth that sent the other males running and screeching, but as soon as he turned back to the female, they were after him again. Family groups looked on from the sidelines, ready to escape if the roiling group headed their way.

I looked for the female in estrous, but all I could see in the center of the mob were two males, pounding the ground and threatening each other. I heard a panting noise close at hand. Kim signaled for me to look over the edge of the rock. There was the female, mating calmly and cooperatively with a medium-sized male. They finished and snuck off together.

It was time for us to be going, too. Boiling male aggression still blocked the footpath. I picked up a few small rocks, whispered to Kim, and at my signal we both leapt to our feet with a yell and a fusillade of stones. Our threat display worked instantly. Startled faces looked up in fear, and with cries of alarm the troop melted away.

"That was amazing!" I exclaimed happily as we began to climb again.

Kim fell into step next to me. "You know that's the first time I've seen wild animals actually behaving, you know what I mean, leading their lives in front of you. It is interesting," she added grudgingly. "I loved the way the female picked a small, quiet Mr. Nice over Mr. Bully."

"I'll have to tell Mikki. This is what she discovered, you know, that ended her career in baboon studies and led her to work with your father."

At the mention of Emmet, Kim's face shut down again. "No, I don't know."

"As you said, that Mr. Nice wins over Mr. Bully. Mikki learned baboons have permanent boyfriends—a male hangs out with a particular female all year-round, acts gentle with her, exchanges grooming, protects her family in troop squabbles. And when it's time to mate, the big males fight each other while the female sneaks off and mates with her friend."

"So much for the bullshit that male dominance is natural in primates."

"Yeah, except in academia—Mikki's work was ignored and she lost her grant money. That's when Emmet started funding her research into elephants."

Kim fell silent again. The only sound was our labored breathing as we climbed up the steep path.

"What about Robert? Did he have trouble getting funding from the orthodox sources?"

Kim darted a glance at me and laughed. "He didn't get it from poaching ivory, and the rest is none of your business."

"Since it's all aboveboard, why so secretive?"

"Because we don't owe you any damned explanations."

"Kim, if Robert Thiaka isn't involved in poaching on his ranch, then somebody else is. That somebody murdered Emmet. Robert could be in danger himself."

Kim didn't answer, but at least she didn't flatly contradict me. I tried to tell myself it was a sign I'd gotten through to her, but since she pulled ahead again, I couldn't even gauge by her face.

Another two miles of hard climbing and we came to an open patch of bare earth in neat furrows, waiting for the next rains. Beyond the field, I spotted a thatched roof. We'd arrived in Enderit.

We immediately attracted a wide-eyed band of children, too shy to yell, a welcome change from Majengo. We made our way through a dirt lane between family compounds until we came to an open plaza graced by the high canopy of a stately fever tree. Its mustard-yellow branches spread out like the spokes of an umbrella, providing shelter from the midday heat. Two men lay on their backs under the tree, dead asleep.

One of the children must have alerted the headman, for he appeared, shuffling along in plastic sandals and hitching up a pair of baggy pants with a rope for a belt. He greeted us politely, and invited us to share some home-brewed fermented maize beer. When Kim involuntarily made a face at the thin, sour taste, the headman slapped his sides and rolled around laughing. He proceeded into a round of friendly inquiry about our journey, our health, and our family's health, before a small boy was assigned to lead us to the Thiaka compound.

A sagging straw mat fence surrounded several thatched mud huts and a large tin-roofed house with a row of kitchen huts behind it. We were introduced to a confusing welter of smiling people, from the wizened grandmother, her eldest son—who was a soothsayer and respected elder—to paunch-bellied, middle-aged sons and their overworked skinny wives. All the while big-eyed children looked on. They greeted us as warmly as if we were longlost relatives.

Robert Thiaka was in seclusion with the boys at the secret circumcision retreat, but we were invited to remain the several days until his return. Kim and I looked at each other with dismay. Would Robert be told we were here? Yes, someone would be dispatched to tell him. We decided to be patient and wait, since we had little other recourse.

They led us into a mud hut and sat us on low wooden stools. Every woman and child in the village crowded into the hut, sat on the floor facing us and stared with great energy and concentration, as if watching a good movie. Every now and then someone would nudge their neighbor, whisper something, and giggle.

"Do you feel self-conscious?" I whispered to Kim.

"I've been through this before," she whispered back. "It's even worse when the food comes."

A small girl sidled up to me, waited for me to look away, pressed her forefinger into my arm, then studied her finger with interest.

It was an hour before lunch arrived: a large enamel basin filled with *ugali*—a heavy mass of boiled maize mush, left to harden and covered with cooked greens. I suggested we put it on the floor, where everyone could gather around and eat it, but the robust woman who brought it said in a nononsense voice that she'd made it especially for us, their honored guests, whereupon she sat down in the front row. It was the only moment I doubted the wisdom of embarking on this search for Thiaka.

A mental fog overcame me as my stomach grew more and more distended with ugali. At last the meal was over, and a satisfied audience dispersed. The boy who'd been sent to tell Thiaka we were here had not yet returned.

Released from the hut, we joined a group of men lounging under a tree. There was a lively conversation that ranged from village gossip to world affairs. As the afternoon wore on, they began to ask us questions. Can you see the ground from an airplane? Are there blacks in America? Are they rich, too? Are Russians black or white? Did men really walk on the moon? Kim and I took turns answering. America seemed like a distant planet.

One of Robert's aunts approached with a sweet smile to tell us that the girls, too, were having their coming-of-age ceremony this afternoon. Would we like to go? Kim immediately said yes, and we were led through the village paths that snaked around each family's compound and into a small clearing in the woods.

A small crowd of women and girls formed a disorderly circle. They swayed to the rhythm of their clapping and sang a melody of complex harmonics. Two pretty ten-year-old girls knelt naked next to one another on the fallen leaves. One smiled, showing dimples. I moved closer, and saw a third little girl flat on her back, surrounded by kneeling women. She was a skinny kid, with ribs showing, and just the beginning of breasts. The little girl's head was cradled on the thighs of an old woman, with a kola nut stuffed in her mouth and a cloth over her face. A feeling of dread knotted my stomach.

The girl lay stiff as the women around her reached out, pinned her legs to the ground and pulled them apart. My heart started to pound, but I couldn't look away. Kim made a smothered sound of protest. A second old woman straddled the little girl, her back to the child's head, one foot on each side of her waist, and bent over her with a knife. My pulse was beating loud in my ears.

The old woman at the girl's head let out a shout and beat on her stomach. At this, all the women made noise and the one with the knife sawed away at the child's sex. She straightened with a grunt of satisfaction, and I caught a glimpse of something small and pink on the edge of the knife: a detached clitoris.

The girl was helped to her feet, blood running down her thigh. She had wide-apart eyes, trying hard not to cry. She was too wobbly to stand on her own, but the women supported and encouraged her as she pretended to dance a few steps to shouts of approval. They brought her over to the other two girls kneeling on the leaves and signaled for the next girl. She tried to smile, too, but it was a lopsided effort.

Kim staggered, then caught herself. All the blood had run out of her face. Her skin looked a ghastly pale tan.

"Put your head down," I commanded her, "or you're going to faint."

"Let's get out of here. I've got to get out of here."

Feeling sick myself, I took her arm and half supported her out of the clearing. When we were out of sight, she grabbed a tree trunk and heaved her half-digested lunch onto the ground. The sound of her retching set me off, and I starting puking right next to her.

I handed her my canteen and she washed out her mouth, spitting over and over as if unable to escape the taste of bile. "That was . . . that was the most . . . awful thing I've ever seen."

"Me, too." I felt like someone had kicked me in the belly. "To think that old woman was doing what was done to her."

"It's horrible. Generation after generation."

"Why? What starts a tradition like that? Why make life crueler than it already is?"

"They think a clitoris is masculine." Kim bit off each word as if it hurt. "Or maybe they figured out women are more docile this way. Just because something is traditional doesn't make it right."

"Yeah, but it sure makes it hard to change." Especially if it involves sex, women's roles . . . or magic.

I thought of Thiaka returning to Enderit for the boy's circumcision and wondered how strongly he was tied into his community's traditions and beliefs. At Ibrahima's I'd once met a brilliant African student in Nairobi on semester break from Oxford. He blew his return fare carousing with friends, then went to see Ibrahima's uncle, the famous witch doctor, to buy a charm that would make him invisible. He figured that way he could slip past the stewardesses onto the airplane. I never heard how it worked out for him, but I would bet anything that, for all his education, Robert Thiaka also believed in charms and spells.

A germ of an idea was beginning to form in my head. At the moment I had absolutely no leverage to make Robert tell me anything. I couldn't very well march up to him and ask if he was running a poaching operation out of Phantom Ranch, or if he'd accepted bribes to allow someone else to do so, or even to account for all the money he'd lavished on his impala operation. He and Kim would just tell me to go to hell.

But what if I approached Robert from his non-Western side? Magic—especially from the hands of a village elder —exerts unimaginable power over those who believe in it. I needed magic, and Enderit was just the place to find it.

26

As I ENTERED the soothsayer's mud hut I could hear the women singing off in the woods, and tried not to picture what they were doing. I took off my boots and walked through a bare anteroom into a small, dark space lit only by the indirect sunlight from the outer door. The air smelled of dust, dried herbs, and time.

Old Thiaka, the soothsayer, sat pasha style on a moth-eaten rug, half-lidded eyes lowered as he murmured a prayer or perhaps an incantation below his breath. The room brimmed with an aura of power, visceral even to a confirmed rationalist like myself. Maybe what I felt was merely the mysterious atmosphere—the shadowy room, a couple of wooden chests against one wall, faded sheaves of paper in piles on the floor, dusty bottles of magic potions. Or maybe it was the way he murmured under his breath even as he spoke to me, ceaselessly caressing a handful of cowrie shells and small stones from his diving gourd.

After greetings, I complimented him on the feats of magic we'd heard about after lunch. According to the villagers, Old Thiaka could make a charm to find a lost cow, vanquish a rival in love, return a straying husband, cure the sick, win the national lottery, gain admittance to the university, become impervious to knives or bullets, or even become invisible to tax collectors and bus conductors. You would think with all this magic power, Enderit would be the richest, healthiest town on earth, but strong magic was very expensive, and the charms so complicated that something often went awry.

Old Thiaka knew his craft well. He didn't ask me what I wanted the charm for. He smoothed the rug in front of him and cast the smooth stones and shells upon it. They looked secretive and female, tiny humpbacked domes with a smooth slit on one side. "You have come to Enderit to seek help," he pronounced.

"I need help in finding the truth," I specified. Now came the tricky part. Should I mention Emmet's murder, or would that scare the old man off? If he already knew about it, I had better mention it, or I'd seem dishonest. Should I try to maneuver him into helping me, or try to engage him openly as an ally? Would he have any motive for helping me get his nephew to talk? Would he care about finding Emmet's killer?

Old Thiaka looked me straight in the eye. His glance was strong as a young man's, sharp with intelligence but softened with compassion. I made my decision: I would try openly to win his power to my side. That was the only possible way to succeed.

So I began a long, roundabout story, African style. After all, time was not in short supply. I don't know why, but I began way back. I told him about coming of age in the Sixties, our rejection of convention and search for better values, serving with the Peace Corps in West Africa, about growing older, becoming an art historian, happily married,

191

a lover of old paintings and bustling cities. I told him that my husband left me to marry a pregnant student of his, how that betrayal almost killed me. I told him how I decided to start a new identity and ran off to Kenya to realize a childhood dream of living among the animals. I told him about the wonders of Kenya's wilderness parks, their uniqueness in all the world, their healing power for modern life.

I told him about starting my own safari company, about the double murders in the first tour group, meeting Omondi, and how I caught the killer. I told him about the ivory business, that eighty percent of the elephants were already gone and the rest weren't expected to last out the decade unless the poaching was stopped. I told him about Leakey, the new head of the wildlife department, how there was a glimmer of hope after years of despair about the elephants' fate. I told him about Striker and me—and how things weren't going too well. I told him about Emmet and his work and his death. And at the end, I told him how Emmet's murder was connected to the secret poaching operation at Phantom Ranch—the place where Old Thiaka's nephew, Robert, the distinguished animal scientist, was developing his wonderful ideas of how to ranch impala, serving both wilderness and people.

The rush of words stopped, and I realized with embarrassment that I'd been staring into Old Thiaka's eyes the whole time. My face was wet with tears, although I hadn't known I was crying. The shadows in the room had shifted. How long had I been talking? Why had I told him so much?

"Do not be shamed, my daughter. Sorrow is like a precious treasure, shown only to friends." His voice rose into a falsetto song: "Enjoy the world gently, enjoy the world gently,/If the world is spoilt,/No one can repair it,/Enjoy the world gently."

We nodded in unison, then both smiled.

"So you'll help me?" I asked.

"You need a lot of help," he teased, "but I'll see what I can do. Before shooting, one must aim." He bent over the diving stones, picked up a few more piled at his side and cast those over the existing pattern. "You have chosen well by coming to Enderit. Here you will find the answers that you seek."

"Do you have any magic to make people answer my questions with the truth?" I asked. We stared into each other's eyes. I was asking his help in getting Robert to talk.

"The right question will find the truth you seek, if you have eyes to see it."

"What is the right question?" I tried to read his face. Did the old man know whether or not Robert was involved in poaching? Would he help me if he thought his nephew might be guilty?

He picked up one of the little white shells from the center of the pattern and held it up between thumb and forefinger. "The stone in the water does not know how hot the hill is, parched by the sun."

I stared at the black slit in the tiny shell and willed myself to concentrate. I wasn't used to thinking in aphorisms. Did he mean he could no longer understand his nephew, whose world was so far from the village? That Kenyans didn't value their wildlife because it was so abundant here? No, he was telling me how to find the right question. "You mean I must understand the killer's world in order to ask the right question?"

"You must understand the killer's hunger." He threw the shell down and exclaimed with satisfaction as it came to a rest nestled against another shell. "This is very good. You see?" He pointed to the two shells. "When spiderwebs unite, they can tie up a lion."

That sounded good, but was Robert a web or was he the lion?

Old Thiaka turned his back to me and fumbled among his dusty bottles on the floor, some stoppered with twists of raffia, others made of tiny gourds stopped with black goat's horn. He murmured under his breath as he selected two small vials. "These are special herbs that I learned from my father." He unstoppered one of the vials and measured out a few seeds onto his palm. "Take seven of these and a pinch of the other I shall give you, just before you speak with my nephew. Then you can be sure that he is telling you the truth."

193

He poured the magic into a tiny leather pouch and hung it around my neck with a throng, so that the pouch was hidden under my clothes.

"That will be ten pounds."

I paid up, wondering if I was a spider or a fly. When he'd sung that little song, I felt we were united, but I knew very well that his allegiance to his nephew was far stronger. If Old Thiaka was confident his nephew was innocent, he'd give me strong magic and act as my ally. But what if he thought—or knew—Robert was guilty? Was the magic designed to make his nephew tell me the truth? Or to fool me into accepting whatever lies Robert Thiaka decided to feed me? Or worse, was it bad magic, designed to silence me forever?

27

SUNSET ARRIVES THE same time each day on the equator. One minute it was light enough to see every detail of the forest foliage pressing in around the village. The next minute the sun turned into a blood-red disk, touched the horizon, and bloated into a monstrous shape. Hundreds of bats awoke at the edge of the village clearing and took off from their roosting tree, filling the sky with their high-pitched twittering. Then the sun sliced through the horizon and plunged the world abruptly into darkness.

Whether Robert showed up soon or not, there was no way we could negotiate the path down to our cars in the dark. We were stuck in Enderit for the night. I watched with a certain amount of dread as Robert's mother put a heavy black caldron of ugali to boil on her cooking fire. Kim's face looked beautiful but severe across from me in the flickering light; she'd deflected all my attempts to start a conversation. I tried to contain my sense of urgency and frustration.

Both fear and relief shot through me when a small boy ran out of the gloom, excitedly shouting that Robert was here. Kim leapt to her feet and suddenly there was Robert Thiaka, even taller and more massive than I'd remembered, hugging Kim and greeting us with cries of surprise and pleasure. He was dressed in a long traditional robe tied over one shoulder. With his stature, he could carry it off in style.

He certainly didn't act like a man with a guilty conscience, but then Robert was a confident man on his home turf; even if he was guilty as hell, the mere sight of me was probably not enough to inspire terror. I fingered the bag of magic around my neck as Kim pulled Robert aside and talked to him in a low, urgent voice. I would need magic to get any useful information out of these two.

Robert came back into the firelight. The flames reflected in his heavy black eyeglasses, so I couldn't see his eyes. "Kim tells me you've come with many questions for me. Perhaps it is best if we go to my hut to talk these things over before we eat. Otherwise, your worries will sit heavily on your stomach."

He led the way to one of the mud huts at the side of the compound. He lit a kerosene lamp, revealing a single, almost bare, circular room. Geckos scurried up the walls, hunting for insects. There was a bed large enough for several adults, made of tree branches lashed to poles that were stuck in the dirt floor, and a couple of low wooden stools, hand-carved from a chunk of tree trunk and decorated with an incised pattern. A half-dozen children had followed us and now gawked through the door; there were no windows. I sat on the edge of the bed, leaving Kim to sit on the low stool, while Robert squatted on his haunches, peasant style. It looked incongruous with his professorial black glasses and Beethoven forehead.

How was I going to slip the magic into Robert's food or drink when there was none? Magic was supposed to be administered secretly, and gossip spreads the news to the intended victim; I had neither secrecy nor gossip to make sure Robert took the magic and afterward to let him know he'd swallowed it. I'd have to convince him somehow to take it voluntarily.

I began by thanking Robert for his family's hospitality, complimenting the beauty and peacefulness of the village, and remarking especially on the kindness of his uncle, Old Thiaka, who I'd had the chance to visit for a couple of hours.

"My uncle is a very respected man."

"A very impressive man," I answered. "I could feel his power." I stopped talking and let the silence lap around us, copying Omondi's style: let their anxiety build.

Kim shifted on her stool. "Cut the bullshit and play your hand," she said. In the dim light of the kerosene lamp, her face was all planes and shadows. Her big copper earrings stood out like the big round eyes of a night creature.

"My throat is sort of dry. Would it be possible to have some tea?" I asked.

Robert pointed to one of the kids poking their heads through the doorway and ordered her to go and bring us some tea. "And make sure the water is boiling before you pour it!" he commanded. "Otherwise you will get very sick," he said to us.

"Thanks." I leaned forward. "The reason I came to see you is that I've reached a crucial point in figuring out the sequence of events that led to Emmet's murder, and I think you may have some vital information to fill in the gaps."

"I do not know what this information might be, but I would be happy to help." Robert's deep voice sounded completely relaxed and sincere.

"First of all, the police have determined by the evidence at the campsite that this was a premeditated murder." It occurred to me that Robert was a cool-headed person who planned ahead, witness his long-range plans for Phantom Ranch. "The killer knew about animals"— again, like Robert—"since he or she tried to use scavengers by the water hole to dispose quickly of the body. The killer knew about Emmet's camp, knew he was

196

down there last Thursday, and was on friendly enough terms to drop in and have breakfast with him."

"That leaves me out," Kim said with a harsh laugh.

"You had lunch with your father his last day in Nairobi. And you argued with him about poaching."

"You've just made my point. A human being could drop dead from starvation at his feet—"

Robert interrupted her. "No one in Kenya is starving; you are making false analogies and showing disrespect for your father, who gave you life." He turned to me. "We have no fear in knowing what you have learned. Please go on."

"Okay. For various reasons, the police have ruled out Alicia as a suspect."

"I don't accept that at face value"—Kim glanced at Robert—"but for the purposes of tonight's discussion, go on."

"We know that the week prior to his death, Emmet visited Phantom Ranch and discovered evidence of a major poaching operation."

Robert said, "Yes, I told you there were signs of extensive poaching where the elephants congregate for water."

"This was more than elephant skeletons. Emmet believed he'd found a poaching network. He was actively pursuing an investigation to try and identify the kingpin. There is good reason to believe that whoever is masterminding the poaching ring is the person who killed Emmet."

"And he thought this operation was run from my ranch? This, I cannot believe."

"Emmet found a semipermanent poaching camp, signs that your trucks were being used to transport tusks, and perhaps more. I don't know all the details because Emmet's notes were removed from his study and hidden elsewhere in the house; they are now in the police's hands."

I looked at Kim to see how she was taking this. Her chin was a notch higher than usual and she scarcely seemed to be breathing.

"Kim was seen leaving the area of the house from which the files were taken and hidden," I added.

"Seen by whom?" Robert demanded.

"By me—and also the new butler."

Kim leaned forward. The light from the kerosene lamp threw spooky shadows over her face. "Isn't it odd, then, that the police haven't arrested me, or even called me in for questioning about these files you say I hid. I should think they'd be coated with my fingerprints."

"All I said was—"

Kim didn't let me finish my sentence. "That house is open as a sieve, and everyone who knows Emmet has been in and out of there recently. And then, for anyone who wanted to enter secretly, there's always that back road through the national park."

"So you know about that road. I doubt many people outside the family know it exists."

Kim's earrings seemed to stare at me like angry eyes. "Go ahead. Make a case about my visiting the upstairs bathroom. Let's hear all the shreds of so-called evidence you're trying to weave into something."

I could hear rats rustling in the palm fronds of the thatched roof above our heads. "My point is that Emmet stumbled on some criminal activity at Phantom Ranch—and that both of you knew of his suspicions."

Robert cut in again. "You said that Emmet believed my trucks were being used to transport tusks. This is very disturbing. How did he get such an idea? Why didn't he come to me?"

"You know nothing about it?"

Robert held his face very still and said, "No, nothing." I didn't need magic to guess he was lying.

In the silence that followed, three small girls arrived, each bearing a steaming, enameled tin mug of tea. Robert supervised their handing out the mugs, then shooed them back to join the audience of children staring from the doorway. While Robert was distracted, I put my mug down, pulled out the leather bag Old Thiaka had given me, and poured the magic herbs into my palm.

He returned to his place and saw what I was doing. I held back the pinch of herbs meant for me, then extended my hand with the seven seeds toward Robert. "Old Thiaka gave me these seven seeds for you to take."

Robert automatically put out his palm and I spilled the seeds from my hand to his. "What is this?" he asked.

"They're from your uncle. He gave me something for both of us to take before we talk." Robert stared at the seeds in his palm. "What are you worried about?" I asked him. "It's not love medicine."

"What are you up to?" Kim asked.

"I'm just trying to be polite and do what Robert's uncle told me to do." So saying, I showed the pinch of dried herb meant for me. "I really liked Old Thiaka. I don't want to have to tell him we threw his medicine away. Do you know what mine is?"

"No." Robert said. "Old Thiaka knows many herbs, many not yet known to science. He has quite a reputation as a healer."

"Well, here goes." I put the herbs onto my tongue and swallowed them with a gulp of hot tea.

"Don't take it," Kim told Robert.

Being bossed by Kim was the extra push he needed. He tipped the seeds into his mouth and swallowed.

"Do you want to know what you've just taken?" I asked.

"I thought you didn't know," Kim said with a dirty look.

"I don't know what they are, but I know what they do. It's . . . well, not exactly a truth serum; let's call it a sort of lie detector."

"Seven small seeds instead of all those wires and gauges!" Robert chuckled and shook his head. "You are trying to trap me in my traditions! You have set village elder against Westernized nephew. If I lie and it doesn't work, you will have proved that I've lost my roots. But what if I don't lie? Then you will never know whether or not the magic works."

"Shall we continue?" I asked.

"I'd say this has gone on long enough." Kim got to her feet. "You're insulting local beliefs."

Robert waved her back, saying he wanted to hear what I had to say, and she subsided gracefully onto the low stool.

"I don't have much more." I counted off the points on my fingers. "So: we know—leaving aside for the moment whether it's true or not—that Emmet believed there's

199

poaching going on at Phantom Ranch, that he was conducting a personal investigation, that he found a carved tusk belonging to Garret and threatened to close down Phantom Ranch."

Robert nodded judiciously. "Yes, I follow you."

"As you can readily see, you and Garret have prime motives to get rid of Emmet. He was threatening to shut down the culmination of your life's work, to ruin Garret's dream deal—involving Umar Island and Phantom Ranch—in short, to destroy the two of you."

"Your picture fits with what I know," Kim said, "except for one thing. Emmet suspected Garret of dealing in finished ivory, not misusing Phantom Ranch; it had nothing to do with Robert." She turned to Robert. "Emmet never confronted you, did he?"

"No, never." Robert's voice seemed to catch on the last syllable, and it came out as a burr.

"You see?" Kim gave me a tight smile. "And I never told Robert, either. You've mistaken a family quarrel for a poaching investigation. Emmet was just being an asshole toward Garret, as usual."

"Good try, Kim, but that doesn't account for all the facts."

"Such as?"

"Such as his telling other people he'd found a poaching center, asking Garret not to tell Robert, confronting you over lunch at Shabaan's."

"You've got it ass backwards. Garret told me what was going on, and I asked Emmet out to lunch. To tell him to lay off Garret. Phantom Ranch wasn't even mentioned."

"Really? Then why did Emmet pump Garret for everything he knew about Robert's setup at the ranch, especially where the money came from for all those buildings and trucks and fences?"

"You can't rely on Garret's word. Of course, Garret would try to deflect suspicion away from himself."

Kim was a skillful liar. I needed to stop her from monopolizing the conversation, blocking me from Robert. "If you pursue this line, you're making things worse for Robert, not better. The signs of poaching at Phantom Ranch are incontrovertible; so are Emmet's suspicions." I looked into Robert's face. "Kim warned you about Emmet, didn't she?"

"I knew nothing about Emmet's . . ." The first words of Robert's sentence came out fine, but then his voice got hoarser and hoarser. He cleared his throat and took a sip of tea. "Kim told me nothing . . ." Again the words grew hoarse, like a violent case of laryngitis. A look of surprise came over Robert's face. He couldn't complete the sentence. Robert let out a noisy exhalation of breath, a sound of amazement and disbelief.

Kim stared at him with a funny expression on her face, as if she didn't know whether to be angry or scared. "Is your throat okay?"

Robert massaged his larynx. "It feels fine." His full, rich voice came out true and clear. "It sounds fine now, doesn't it?" He gave a half smile. "It was like something caught the words in my throat. I just couldn't finish that sentence: Emmet did not suspect . . ." For the third time, his voice grew hoarse and faded out. "Emmet did suspect . . ." The words came out with no problem.

The magic worked.

Robert's expression was a strange combination of fear and satisfaction. "I am a certified son of the soil! You see—I cannot tell a lie. This is amazing. You may trust anything I say—until the magic wears off."

Just as I'd feared with Old Thiaka, I was caught in my own web. Robert could be faking laryngitis, to trick me into thinking he spoke only the truth. But that look of surprise on his face when his voice faded out looked genuine. I still had to rely on my own judgment and wits.

"Did Emmet confront you with what he found?" I asked Robert for the second time.

"Yes."

The confession hung in the dim room between us.

"Yes," he went on. "It was the day of the funeral. He set off in his plane, then returned a few hours later, almost sundown. He told me he'd gone up to the donga in the northeast quadrant, where the elephant migration route crosses the property, and found signs of a permanent poaching camp. I was unhappy to hear this, of course. As I told you, as part of my integrated scheme, we plan a scientific research center at Phantom Ranch, probably focusing on elephants. I have already talked with your friends the Darrows about this—in fact, as soon as the funding comes through, I plan to make it a top priority. I told this to Emmet, of course. He could tell I was deeply shocked and dismayed by his discovery. I'm sure he believed me. Our conversation was amicable."

"The ranch is huge. Isn't it possible that someone is running a poaching ring under your nose and you don't know about it?"

"Emmet suggested that also." Robert shook his head emphatically. "It is impossible. My nose is not long, but I manage to stick it in everywhere. There is not one facet of the project that I do not personally supervise."

"Emmet said he found bits of elephant skin in your trucks."

"He never told me that." Robert finished his tea in two big gulps. "I heard it later from Kim. I don't know, perhaps he didn't trust me enough to tell me all the evidence."

"Or maybe he made a second, secret visit to the ranch to search the dam site," Kim said. "From the way he talked, I got the impression he'd gone back to get more evidence."

Robert shrugged. "In any case, Kim told me what Emmet said about the trucks, and I checked them all very carefully myself, including the dam site. It wasted a whole day. I did not see these gouges he spoke of in the floor of the truck, which he presumed were from tusks, nor did I see bloodstains. All of my foremen arc handpicked, from Enderit. I have known them all my life." He gestured outward from the mud hut where we sat. "Do you see any signs of conspicuous consumption in this village? Any Mercedes parked in front of a hut? If any of these men had newfound wealth, everyone here would know about it, I assure you." He pointed to his throat. "You can tell by my long speeches, I am speaking the truth. Besides, if I had wealth from an ivory business, you would have seen my Mercedes parked down below next to your Rover. I would not have taken a bush taxi and walked the last ten miles to Enderit on foot."

There was nothing wrong with Robert's voice now.

"Where did you get the money for all you've done at the ranch?"

"From grants, international donors, foundations, even some from philanthropic individuals, like Garret's partner, Mr. Hanyo, who's interested in a future co-leasing arrangement with us."

"I'd hardly call Mr. Hanyo philanthropic. He wants to make ivory legal again and ranch elephants for their tusks."

"Well, we also have other donors, such as scientists interested in the elephants for research purposes. Like your friends the Darrows, for example."

"Would you be willing to give me a list of these sources?"

"Sure. They are all legal and aboveboard." His voice was steady and even.

His story was plausible. On the other hand, what if a dedicated person like Robert was faced with a desperate shortage of funds that threatened to destroy everything he had so carefully built? Wouldn't he be tempted to kill elephants as a short-term holdover? Wouldn't it make sense for him to bring in an outside poaching team, maybe from Somalia, that he could get rid of once his financial crisis was over? And once he'd ventured that far into criminal waters, wouldn't he be able to rationalize killing Emmet to protect a greater good?

"Going back to your employees, for a second. What about Husseini, the foreman of the dam site? He's not from Enderit, is he?"

"If you've met him, you know Husseini is a Somali. I hired him for that one specific project, but the work crew is local; they go home each night."

"Where does Husseini sleep?"

"He has a tent at the campsite."

"All alone?"

"He has a cousin who is staying with him, also."

There was a persistent rustling above Kim's head; there was something moving in the thatching, trying to get in or out. Rats, bats, a snake? For once I hoped we wouldn't get a wildlife viewing opportunity. Kim completely ignored the sound. Either she had nerves of steel or she didn't know enough to be worried.

"Emmet visited the dam site two weeks ago, and then you searched there, when?"

Robert thought a moment. "Last Monday."

"Last Monday, the day after Kim had lunch with Emmet." Kim nodded in confirmation. "Which means Husseini knew he was being scrutinized, maybe thought Emmet was closing in on him. If he was managing a poaching business on the side, he could have tipped off his boss."

"Husseini could have tipped off anyone," Kim said. "That widens the field beyond Robert, Garret, or me."

"Maybe, but the field isn't all that wide. The killer has to be someone who had access to Emmet's study, knew his habits, and could drop by his camp and be invited to breakfast. I can't rule you or anyone out until we've found more hard evidence. The sooner we can prove who's guilty, the safer you two will be."

"If you want to question Husseini, you'll have to go soon. His contract is up Friday and he's returning to Somalia."

"How convenient."

Robert showed his empty palms. "The dam will be finished midweek. The timing has nothing to do with Emmet's death."

Magic or no, I couldn't take Robert's word that all his trucks were clean, that there was no evidence anywhere of a poaching business. I needed to return to Phantom Ranch and check it out myself. This time, I'd go in alone and unseen.

28

I NEEDED DARKNESS in order to explore the dam site in secret, so it was a full twenty-four hours before I could put my plan into effect. An hour before dusk I backed the Rover in among some thorn bushes from where I could watch the workmen leaving. I'd passed through a big burned-out area on the way up, but the brush fires hadn't reached this far and there was still plenty of cover. An eagle owl lamented *hu-hu-hu-hu* from the riverbank as the sun did its vanishing act. Behind me some large animal bounded off noisily. I kept my eyes on the dirt road, as if I could miss a big truck going by if I so much as glanced away.

What I so grandly called a plan really consisted of nothing more than the idea of waiting after the local workmen left, until Husseini and his cousin were solidly asleep in their tents, sneaking into the worksite and checking out their one closed truck. Given the security that distance and isolation breeds, I was sure there'd be no guards, and because of wild animals, people tend not to take midnight strolls. After a strenuous day of construction work, the Somalis should sleep heavily, and their tents were far from where the vehicles were parked. If I was quiet and alert, the chances of getting caught were nil. Or so I reassured myself.

As if on cue, as the sun dropped below the horizon an open-bed truck carrying workers left, heading south toward the ranch headquarters and the main exit from the ranch. A

205

misshapen gibbous moon poked above the horizon, its bright silver light dimming the stars in the western sky. I ate the sandwiches I'd brought, followed by a cup of steaming coffee from a thermos. It was going to be a good few hours before I could count on the Somalis going to sleep. I didn't really mind waiting. I rolled down my window so I could smell the cool night air, with its hint of smoke from the brushfires mixing with the herbal smells of the grasses and shrubs around me, and I listened to the night noises of Africa.

A fatal hitch occurred an hour later. I stared in dismay as the closed truck I planned on searching came driving down the road from the dam site, preceded by a beat-up Suzuki. Instead of turning toward the heart of the ranch, the two vehicles lumbered off the road and headed north. Husseini was up to something. Dropping a couple of men off at a village in that direction? No, because in that case there'd be a proper car track showing signs of regular use, and besides, they wouldn't need a closed truck. They were driving cross-country, toward where we'd seen the elephants. I had to decide quickly whether to follow the truck or wait for its return. Waiting was safer, but if I followed, I might catch Husseini passing along a last shipment of ivory. Next week he'd be gone. This could be the one chance to find the next link in the chain. I slipped into first gear.

Without turning on my lights, I followed them, far enough behind so that they wouldn't hear my engine noise. The African night is not exactly still, between the loud trilling of tree frogs and the screeches of the tree hyrax sounding like escaped lunatics, but I kept a discreet distance anyway.

They used the same route Mikki, Henry, and I took two days before. To our right the donga was barely visible as a thicker darkness against the sky. Their lights suddenly spotlighted the trees as they turned right, then disappeared entirely into the brush. The area where we'd watched the elephants dig for water was only a few hundred feet ahead. I didn't want to drive in after them, figuring they'd have to turn around and head back this way, since the dry riverbanks were too high to negotiate. I left my car in the deep shadows and followed on foot. Maybe they were heading for that abandoned camp we'd found nearby. Did they have a cache of tusks near there, which I and the Darrows hadn't found?

The track under my feet was full of cement-hard ruts and animal footprints dating from the last rainy period, broken branches, and animal turds, all booby traps for the unwary. I allowed myself to switch on a pencil flashlight every now and then. They weren't likely to be looking back, and besides, the trail wound around so much, the light wouldn't show very far. The worst part was the darkness itself, pushing against my face like a thick spiderweb.

Walking at night along a game trail is one of the stupidest things you can do, but if I didn't use the trail, I'd be lost in minutes. Telling myself that the men ahead of me would have flushed out any waiting lions, I crept toward the donga's edge, listening intently for human sounds and angling to one side so I wouldn't come out on top of them. I heard nothing but the eagle owl's lament.

Then I heard the low rumble of an elephant's stomach. I dropped to my belly and edged out until I could see. The sandy riverbed was luminous in the moonlight. It was pocked with elephant tracks that made moon-shadow craters in the sand. The elephants slept on their sides like scattered glacial erratics, although of course the glaciers never reached this far. A giant snore buzzed peacefully in the night.

A pair of spotted genet, a nocturnal animal I'd never seen but recognized from field guides, crossed the moonlit sand looking like elongated cats with striped tails and spotted body. I was too hyped up and focused on Husseini and his men to care. I thought I heard some whispering, but it might have been the wind. There was an ominous metallic sound that my mind refused to decipher. Then all hell broke loose.

They had several assault rifles firing at once. The gunfire deafened and pummeled me, filling my whole body, the whole world, with noise; noise like knives stabbing into my flesh, into my heart. One or two of the elephants managed to scramble to their feet before being riddled with bullets and collapsing. One ran a few steps toward the gunfire, as if to protect her sisters, before she was mowed down. Most were killed as they lay.

"No!" I screamed. "Bastards!" Luckily my voice was lost in the maelstrom.

It only lasted a few moments. An elephant groaned, a startling sound in the sudden return of silence. Two baby elephants were left alive, and they ran here and there in a panic, touching their dead sisters and aunts with their miniature trunks, ears flapping, whimpering with distress. The larger shapes didn't move, would never move again. I could feel the babies' terror. Their whole family had been wiped out in less than a minute. They'd even killed teenagers with only the smallest stub of ivory showing. I fought for control to stop myself from breaking down noisily and completely; I didn't want to become one more addition to the carnage.

One of the larger elephants, the one who had groaned, lifted her head, collapsed back onto the sand, lifted her head again. She levered herself up to her feet, groaning deep in her chest. She managed to stand, but only for an instant before she swayed and tottered. The babies ran to her side and reached out to touch her face with their trunks. Her knees started to buckle, and the tiny elephants leaned against her, maybe trying to shore her up, but they were too little.

A staccato burst of gunfire smashed into the group. The larger elephant crumpled to the ground, a great dark stain of blood gushed from her mouth, and with a shuddering groan she died. One of the babies had been hit also, and was screaming in agony. The gunmen let it scream. I heard a guttural order, and men started to scramble down the steep wall of the dry riverbed. The last surviving baby whirled around and fled upstream. Without its protecting family, it wouldn't last the night.

I recognized the thin silhouette of Rashid Husseini. He climbed on top of an elephant's face and laughed.

If I'd had a gun, I'd have shot him dead. Rage coursed through me, hot and urgent, almost hallucinatory. My heart thudding and my fists clenched like stones, I watched three men hack off the elephants' trunks so they could get at the

208

tusks more easily. They gouged the tusks out of the elephants' faces, shouting to each other in the guttural sounds of Arabic as they worked.

I tried to fight through my anger and focus on why I was there. I had a job to do; I had to keep thinking. If they were speaking Arabic, that confirmed they were Somali, which supported Robert Thiaka's statement. The question was an important one, because if the Kenyan work crew was involved, chances were that Robert Thiaka had a hand in running the whole operation. If there were no Kenyans involved, Husseini could be running a poaching gang without Robert's knowledge. It was easy enough to import some unemployed Somali guerrillas, already prepared with their AK-47s, to come down as a temporary work crew and wipe out more elephants. I wished I'd asked Robert how he had found Husseini, if anyone had recommended him. I needed to find out who Husseini reported to, who he might have warned that Emmet was on to them.

I couldn't watch anymore. I knew I should wait and follow them, see where they cached the ivory, or where they delivered it, but I was too scared. Poking around an empty worksite or ranch buildings was one thing. Following armed killers was another. I headed back to my car. I could still hear the screams of the wounded baby elephant, growing fainter as its life ebbed away. If I didn't at least see where they hid the ivory, it would be hard to pin anything on Husseini, to keep him from leaving the country or repeating this night's work elsewhere. Without the tusks, there'd be no proof. I stopped in my tracks, started again. How could I live with myself if I just ran away now? I had to follow them. I made a deal with myself: I'd see where they dropped off the ivory, but that was it, then I'd cut out and head home.

I got to my car and smelled trouble before I saw it. The wind had risen strongly, coming from the west, and it carried the acrid smell of smoke. I climbed onto the roof of the car and could see a line of flames advancing toward me. It was hard to judge the distance with no landmarks to measure the rolling plain. Was it a half mile? A quarter mile? Was that close or far? I didn't know how fast fire could travel. The wind whipped dark smoke across the moon, which seemed to jeer through a tattered veil and then was eclipsed.

Damn, damn it all. Now I could hardly see my hand in front of my face, and my throat was beginning to sting from the smoke. Still afraid to put on my headlights, I slowly shifted into first gear and drove into the grass. I missed the tire tracks I'd followed before, but that was probably just as well, since the poachers might be returning the same way. The grass reared blackly above the radiator, a sea of swishing sound. Unseen branches of a fallen tree screeched against the side of my car as it pushed slowly but steadily forward. The smell of fire grew harsher in my nostrils, and I imagined I could hear the crackle of flames, but surely it was too far for that? Had I gotten turned around in the dark and started heading west, into the fire, instead of south? I climbed on the roof once more.

The dark mass of trees along the donga was to my left, so I was pointing toward the road and the way out of there, but the flames were now ahead of me, an encircling tentacle reaching for the riverbed. Flames hit a thornbush and burst a dozen feet into the air. This was getting scarier by the minute. Now I could hear the grass sizzle and snap. A herd of gazelle came rocketing out of the smoke and into the trees. Were they telling me something? They could head for the donga more safely than I. If I tried to drive in, I'd land right on top of the poachers—and I certainly wasn't about to leave my car to the fire and try to run to the donga on foot.

Once more I bulled my way forward. The fire hadn't reached the trees yet. I might be able to cut through the edge of the woods and circle around. The moon reemerged as the wind gusted from the south. Thankful for the light, I wound through the tangled shadows of thornbush and reached the sanctuary of the trees. There was a screeching and thrashing of foliage as a troop of monkeys, disturbed from their treetop sleep, moved overhead.

I took a deep breath, feeling a bit safer. Then everything around me suddenly speeded up and raced out of control. A hurricane-force wind threw itself against the woods, making

210

trees groan and snap. Flames leaped from nowhere into the crown of a fever tree right in front of me. The gust died for a moment, only to be followed by a wall of wind that swept through the trees with a roar, carrying fire with it.

I had to get out of here. Smoke scorched my throat, mixing with the taste of fear. I bent all my attention on driving forward, as if motion alone could save me. A burning branch was ripped from its place and smashed into my windscreen. Shards of glass exploded over me, and I felt a warm gush of blood on my face. Blood was in my eyes, I couldn't see where I was going. I lost control of the car, which careened into a wall of branches and stopped.

I pulled off my shirt, managed to wipe the blood off my face. The cut on my forehead was not deep, but it was bleeding freely, and there was no time to search for a Band-Aid. I twisted the shirt into a bandanna and tied it around my head to keep the blood out of my eyes.

The fire had blown into several trees now, illuminating the fallen tree I'd smashed up against. When I threw the car into reverse, the engine roared but nothing happened. I'd reached the end of my road. I leaped out.

Fire snaked through the woods in a demented fashion. I could feel the heat on my bare skin. Soon the flames would lap around my feet. Coughing, I ran for the donga, dodging the darker shadows, ignoring the branches whipping against my chest.

And then the riverbed lay below, a haven, a collage of sand and rock and shadow. I dangled from the crumbling edge, arms stretched to breaking point, searching for ground with no success. The bank gave way and I tumbled onto a bed of loose rocks. Above me, the Rover's gas tank exploded with a whoosh.

29

ON FOOT, AT night, you remember you're a primate, with six senses and an innate fear of the dark. I tried to look on the bright side: at least the fire provided some illumination. I started walking. It was slow going over the boulder-strewn surface. I fell once with shocking suddenness and banged my shin. After that I went even more slowly.

At this rate it would take me three days to reach safety. Where was safety anyway? Could I go to the ranch house? I had no proof Thiaka wasn't involved. Did I have to walk all the way to the next town? The scratch on my forehead was throbbing. I had no food, no water.

I didn't see a way out, but giving up was not an option, so I kept walking. I hadn't gotten very far when there was a rush of movement in the patterned shadows ahead. The dull beat of hooves on sand, a cry cut off abruptly. The hairs on the back of my neck stood up. There were streaks of movement from all sides. It was lions converging on a kill.

I hunkered down and froze, afraid to even breathe. I doubted they could smell me through the smoke. Lions don't have great night vision—they like to hunt after dark because they're sprinters and night gives them an advantage in surprising their prey up close. I had a chance of escaping notice as long as a lion didn't stumble right over me. They were quite busy.

Two males with imposing manes trotted hungrily toward

the snarling mass of sister lionesses. Their roar scared even their consorts, who backed away from the kill. One lioness snatched a bloody haunch and tried to carry it off. The lions charged her without hesitation. The female dropped her meal and fled. She joined the impatient circle of her sisters, growling and changing places.

I could smell the blood. I wondered if this was going to be the last wildlife viewing I'd ever do. Save the best for last.

As the males gorged themselves they slowed down, and one of the females edged forward and tentatively licked at the carcass. She was tolerated, and settled in to feed. The males retired. Soon there was a writhing mass of lionesses hiding the kill from view. A jackal showed up and darted in right under the lion's jaws. Cubs, too, tried to grab what they could. Lions are a spartan society: cubs compete with adults for food, and when it's scarce, they're left to starve.

As the carcass dwindled to bones and the lionesses lost interest one by one and disappeared into the night, I began to wonder about my future. I was in a worse spot than ever. The donga was full of lions. I had no way to defend myself if attacked. Night was my only protection, and for some reason it didn't feel that safe.

I kept still long after the last lion had disappeared, and then began walking, every sense alert for danger. I heard the bass rumble of the truck long before Husseini and his sidekicks came into view. What the hell? They must have found a way down the riverbanks and they were using the dry riverbed as an escape route from the fire.

Once again I dropped down and froze into the shadows, one more round boulder, slightly larger than the rest. My heart pounded loudly in my ears. This was giving me a greater respect for prey animals. It takes courage to hide in plain sight, to not lose your nerve and bolt. If I moved, they'd see me for sure. I could outrun the men, perhaps, but not their bullets.

The Suzuki passed me, its engine grinding as it pulled itself over the rough surface. The truck pulled even. I could see the glow of the driver's cigarette. It was past. They hadn't seen me.

A rock jumped up and hit their crankcase with an ominous clang, and the driver slowed to a crawl. I noticed a rectangular outline flat against the back of the truck. It was a ladder to the roof, which, like many African trucks, had a frame on top for strapping on extra loads. That's when I got my brainstorm.

I ran recklessly over the rough ground and jumped onto the rear fender. It was only a moment's work to scramble up and fall to my belly on the heaving roof. I grasped onto the baggage frame so conveniently provided. I was set. No more lions, no more three days' hike without food or water. I'd have a bird's-eye view of where they stashed the ivory, while I was perfectly invisible up on my high perch. The only challenge would be to pick a safe time to slide off undetected, but that seemed by far the best of all my alternatives.

The truck ground on through the night, humping its way over boulders and bulling through sand traps. By the time we left the flames behind and climbed out of the donga, I felt bruised and battered all over. At least the cut on my head had stopped bleeding, and I carefully unwound my shirt and got back into it. I could hardly imagine how awful I must look—bloodstained, filthy, and slightly crazed—but I wasn't planning on being seen for a while yet.

The dirt track across the grasslands felt as smooth as a superhighway in comparison to the riverbed. We headed straight for the ranch house. So Thiaka was in this, I thought, but then we detoured a half mile or so before we reached the ranch buildings. Did that mean Thiaka wasn't involved, or just that he was careful to keep the poaching business out of sight of his legitimate workers? Goddamn, this case was like a maze, twisting and turning back on itself, getting nowhere.

Hold on a second, I told myself, even if I got off the truck now, this night's work had confirmed which trail led out of the maze. Emmet had indeed discovered a poaching center, and Husseini knew that Emmet had discovered incriminating evidence. Husseini quickly tipped off an accomplice who knew Emmet's habits and had access to his house, and either singly or together they had planned and carried out Emmet's murder. The clues to the accomplice's identity still pointed in every direction, but Husseini was definitely the link. If I could just hang in there and see where this truck was going, the night's horror would be worth it.

The hours stretched out in a never-ending, bone-jarring monotony of truck smell, truck noise, and truck movement. And still, all I saw around me was the dark, whispering grasses. Every now and then the headlights caught the eyes of wild animals, reflecting a spectral red. After a while the moon set and all was darkness except for the cone of the headlights.

We reached a true road and picked up speed. We passed through a few sleeping hamlets too fast for me to bail out even if I'd changed my mind. I hadn't lost my nerve yet. I wanted to see where this ivory was headed. If I could stay awake that long. Despite the discomfort, my eyelids felt weighted with exhaustion and kept falling shut. It was way past my usual bedtime, and my body was playing its usual sleeping sickness act. Several times I awoke with a jerk of alarm, wondering how long I'd slept.

The last time, the sky was lightening, and on each side of the road rows of coconut palms flashed by like a strobo-scope. A coconut plantation? We'd covered a lot of ground while I slept. The only plantations I knew were near the coast.

That didn't surprise me. Much of Kenya's ivory ended up in the picturesque dhows that plied the coast along centuries-old trade routes once used for both ivory and slaves headed for Arabia and the Persian Gulf. The British blockaded the coast for twenty years before they were able to stop the sultan's traffic in human beings. Slavery persisted in the Arab island city of Lamu until 1907. The traffic in dead elephants' tusks continued, of course, and if we took twenty more years to stop it, there'd be no elephants left.

It was only a couple of years ago that a conservation team managed to find and secretly film the main ivory processing plant, run by three notorious brothers from Hong Kong out of Jebel Ali in the United Arab Emirates. You'd think the sheikh had enough money from oil without a side business in elephant extinction, but apparently he didn't think so. The ivory plant was shut down after the scandal broke on British TV, or rather, it was moved to an unknown location.

If this ivory trail from Phantom Ranch could lead us to the new processing center, it would be a tremendous coup, might even be the clinching argument for a permanent worldwide ban on ivory. Was that why they'd killed Emmet? Now that dawn was near, how long did I dare stay on the truck? Safety said get off at the first village we come to; but if I did that, we'd never know what cove, what island, was the transfer point. Still, with daylight came a saner sense of caution. I decided to climb down at the first chance I had. Better to live and tell what I knew so far.

A red sun pushed its way through the sea's flat horizon. The air was humid and heavy, and even the breakers on the white sand beach off to our right seemed listless. The beach was utterly deserted. This was an area of few villages and less traffic.

We turned inland and passed through a belt of monotonous forest that stretched for miles. Some baboons scattered off the road, and once or twice a bush buck stared from the forest's edge. The woods gave way to a grassland with scattered palms, when I first heard the sound of a vehicle behind us. I didn't realize it was the sound of disaster. It was one of those fateful moments that you're destined to replay over and over: what if? What if I hadn't craned my head to see?

But I did. And I found myself staring right in the face of a surprised driver. He pulled out to pass, and as he did so, he called out to the truck driver, "Hey, man, you have a white hitchhiker on top."

30

I WAS HEARING my death sentence. Before he'd finished, I was halfway down the ladder. The truck slammed on its brakes, almost wrenching my arm out of its socket and saving me the trouble of climbing to the ground. I landed hard, but I instinctively curled my shoulder and rolled with the fall. I heard the truck doors open and the shouts of the men as I scrambled up and started to run. I headed into the grass. It wasn't tall enough to provide cover, but plenty tall to slow me down. I listened for the shot.

None came. The passing car had sped on, but not so fast he wouldn't have heard gunfire. Instead of shooting, a big fellow with longer legs than mine ran me down. I could hear him gaining on me, and I had the horrible nightmare sensation of running in slow motion. My fastest sprint simply wasn't fast enough. He threw out his leg and sent me sprawling. Then he pulled me up and without pause gave me a tremendous whack across the face that knocked me to the ground. It opened up the cut on my forehead. Blood oozed into my eyebrow and down my cheek.

"No funny business," he growled. He was a barrel-chested black man, not Somali, with a triangular nose that covered half his face, and a massive jaw. It was a hard face overlaid by the soft baggy eyes and jowly cheeks of a drinker. A man who might be given to sentimentality, but not to empathy for a fellow human being. Under the right circumstances, I could imagine him being bluff and jovial,

217

in a playacting sort of way. I could tell that wasn't today's script. He shoved me around to face the road and said, "Go." He gave me another shove. I started walking. I could taste my own blood.

Husseini was standing there waiting, along with a third fellow with an AK-47 over his shoulder. I could see the faces of the two men clearly in the morning light. Husseini's aquiline face looked ferocious. No pity there.

I turned to study the man with the gun, but I felt so frightened I had to look away. My heart started to pound. He was a small-boned man, like most Somalis, but it wasn't his muscles that frightened me. It was his eyes. They had the flat, soulless ferocity of a crocodile. I'd only seen eyes like that in photos of serial murderers or military dictators. It was the face of a professional killer.

"Not very clever, Jazz Jasper," Husseini said.

"I had the feeling we'd meet again," I answered.

"Put her in the back," he ordered the big man.

I'd have preferred to talk, to cut some kind of deal, but I couldn't figure out anything I had to bargain with, so I kept my mouth shut. Muscles opened the back of the truck and shoved me inside. About a hundred flies took the opportunity of the open door to join me. There was still flesh from the elephants' faces attached to the tusks, and the smell was nauseating.

It was obvious they would kill me when we reached a more secluded spot. What wasn't so obvious was what I was going to do to get out alive. He clanged the door shut and I was in the pitch-dark.

We drove for what seemed like ages, but was probably only another hour. By that point death seemed an attractive alternative to the dark, the fetid heat, the flies, and the bloody tusks. When Muscles opened the door, I stumbled to the ground, blinking in the harsh sunlight. We were in a narrow cove. A dhow with dark red sails, the color of dried blood, was pulled up on the sand.

"Put her in the hold. Ahmed will shoot her once you're well away from the coast," directed Husseini. He spoke in English, no doubt out of consideration of me. What a thoughtful guy.

"Get some big rocks you can weigh her down with, and stow them below."

"Wait a second," I said, and Husseini smacked me across the mouth.

"Keep it shut," he told me. "Your only choice is whether to die fast or slow. Don't make me angry."

I turned away, only to meet Ahmed's flat crocodile eyes and notice the knife at his belt. I shut up.

"Go." Muscles took my arm and whirled me around to face the boat. The Indian Ocean glinted in the morning sun. They meant it to be my grave. The sail luffed in the breeze. An Arab in a long caftan and turban was curled up by the rudder; he looked the other way as Muscles roughly pushed me toward the hold.

I didn't stop to weigh alternatives. I leaped toward the hold, feinted left, then dashed right and jumped overboard. I sucked in a lung-bursting breath of air and dove. I kicked with all my might, driving myself forward and down. I stayed under as long as my lungs would let me, then let out my breath in an explosion of bubbles and surfaced. There was the flash of something large and dark hurtling at me. Before I could react, I was gripped around the neck by a steel-hard arm and frog-kicked over to the side of the boat. So much for the grand escape.

Husseini peered over the edge at me. He had a pistol in his hand. With his other hand he flung a rope ladder over the side. "Get in. No more tricks, if you please."

My options seemed limited, so I climbed up as invited. Ahmed pushed me with the butt of his gun, hard enough to make me lose my balance and fall hard onto the deck. It was a piece of petty sadism. I sat up, rubbing my neck and gasping air in big lungfuls. Water ran down my clothes in salty rivulets and formed a puddle on the deck.

I pushed myself slowly to my feet and stood there swaying. I was weak and dizzy from the letdown of adrenaline, the exertion of the swim, and not having eaten much of anything since one small sandwich in what seemed like another lifetime. My vision went dark for a moment and I staggered.

"That wasn't very smart, Miss Jasper, was it?" said

219

Husseini. He gave me a rude raking look from head to toe, focusing on my breasts, which were visible through my wet blouse. I did my best to stare back with disdain—and almost managed it.

"Who are you working for?" I asked.

Unfortunately I had swallowed water when Muscles grabbed me, and it chose this moment to come back up. I retched painfully. A wave of blackness came over me and once more I fought it back.

The man with dead eyes approached me with the length of rope.

"Put your ankles together and your hands behind your back," Husseini said.

I didn't move. "The police are on your trail. You don't want a murder sentence added to poaching, do you? Why not just leave me on shore while you make your getaway?"

Ahmed's answer was to knock my feet out from under me so that I fell heavily to the deck a second time. I swore and began to push myself upright, when he put a knee in my back, seized my wrists, pulled a slipknot over them, and tightened it until I cried out from the pain. Then he looped the other end around one ankle, grabbed my flailing free leg, and bound my feet together. There was still a length of the rope left over. He pulled it up and tied it around my neck. If I struggled against the bonds, I'd strangle myself.

I was terrified and furious. If they were going to kill me, at least I wanted to die with dignity. The cut on my head was throbbing, and I could feel blood coursing warmly over my cheek. "Why are you hobbling me up like a camel?" I demanded, craning my neck around. The rope dug into my skin. "Take this rope off my neck."

Husseini barked an order. Muscles reached down with one hand, grabbed my two bound wrists and without strain lifted me straight off the deck. The pain in my shoulders was intense. I swung back and forth at the end of his arm, watching blood fall from my head onto the deck in dark red drops.

I don't mind blood, but swings make me nauseous. This time the blackness came over me in a deep, whirling vortex. I fell through space.

* * *

I don't think I was out for long. When I came to, I was lying in several inches of stinking water in the hold, next to a pile of elephant tusks. Through the hatch I could see Ahmed's baggy Muslim knickers and his slim hand fingering the rhino horn handle of his knife. I'd always wondered what those Somali knives looked like. Rhinos were being hunted to extinction so Ahmed and his buddies could each have one. Now I was seeing one, and unless I did something, I'd soon be personally extinct.

Muscles came to the hatch and dropped an armload of bloody tusks that clattered down next to me. Fetid bilge water splashed onto my face. The two other men were out of sight, but I could hear them talking. I guess Husseini and the gunman were white collar types, above physical labor. That was better for me. The longer it took to load the boat, the longer I'd remain alive.

I didn't waste any more time thinking about not escaping. I was too busy figuring out my next move. Actually, that wasn't too hard. The first thing I had to do was get out of the way of the hatch, so I wouldn't be conked on the head by a falling tusk. I was able to roll myself farther back into the hold without too much difficulty. Good, step one completed.

The next priority was harder: I had to get out of these ropes. Harder, but not impossible. Ahmed had trussed me with a series of slipknots. All I had to do was cut the rope in one place, and the whole thing would come apart easily. I couldn't bend my head to see the rope without choking, but I'd noticed before it was made of hemp, neither thick nor new. If I could find a sharp edge, I thought I could cut through it—if I had enough time.

I eyed the tusks. One of them had a jagged end, but of course it was in the middle of the pile, with the sharp end poking up, out of my reach. This was like playing tiddly-winks with no hands and a death sentence for losing the game. Once more I rolled through the bilge water till I was next to the pile of tusks. Maneuvering awkwardly, I managed to hook one of the bottom tusks with my ankles and shift it. Nothing happened. I heaved with my whole body

221

and pulled the tusk out of the pile. For a moment nothing happened, then slowly the whole pile started to shift. There was a loud clatter that I prayed wouldn't be noticed on deck. I was hit on the shoulder with a bruising impact, and another tusk landed on my leg. I lay still for a moment, listening for footfalls above me. There were none. Why should they care if an avalanche of ivory fell on me?

I twisted my head, looking for the tusk with the sharp-looking broken end. At first I couldn't see it, and my heart sank. I rolled and heaved my trussed-up body as best I could, checking every direction. Had it fallen underwater? I maneuvered myself around the periphery of the pile, which took an incredible exertion of energy. The water wasn't that deep, but the tusk wasn't that wide, either, and the water was opaque with filth. Halfway around I found the broken tusk by rolling onto it and feeling the jagged end stick into my belly.

I turned onto my back and, by rolling side to side, drew the rope that linked my ankles and neck back and forth over the tusk's end. Back and forth, back and forth. Every now and then I'd tug my ankles down to see if the rope was giving. All that happened is that the loop around my neck tightened. Didn't Ahmed know any knot other than a slipknot? I felt a new sympathy for camels, hobbled like this night after night. I rocked myself and pushed the rope against the tusk, straining to sense if it was being cut. It seemed to catch and then slip over and over, accomplishing nothing. I kept it up for quite a while before admitting defeat.

Another load of ivory came clattering down into the hold. We might take sail at any minute. I'd wasted a lot of time. I desperately searched the walls of the hold for something sharp, a handy nail or bit of metal, anything I could use. All I saw were patches of tar near the bilge line in various stages of disintegration, signs of ancient efforts to stop leaks. One of them was leaking a small but steady rivulet of seawater. Great—I could drown right here inside the boat. No need to throw me overboard.

There was nothing I could use to cut the rope. My teeth? I pictured myself curling like a pretzel and biting the rope around my ankles. And then I realized I wouldn't have to bite it. The ropes grew tighter the more I struggled against them. But if I didn't struggle, if I curled up instead, they would loosen. Ahmed was clearly not a sailor. They should have had the old man at the rudder tie me up.

I brought my knees up to my chest, trying to get my ankles within grasping distance of my hands so I could pull open the slipknots. I couldn't do it. My legs were simply not flexible enough, I couldn't arch my back enough, my arms weren't long enough. I strained with every muscle in my body, but the closest I could get left a foot-wide gap between my hands and feet. This is why I never took ballet.

If I couldn't reach my ankles with my hands behind my back, what if I moved my hands to the front? Lying on my side, I folded at the waist like an accordion and stretched down with my arms. The rope slackened and I managed to slip my arms under my butt, all the way to the back of my knees. Then I rolled onto my back, and it was child's play to pull my feet through the circle of my arms, and presto, my bound arms were now in front of me.

I'd done it! I curled up in a fetal position and loosened the loops around my ankles, then off my wrists, and finally, from around my neck. I was free. A free captive.

Now I had to figure how to get out of this boat alive. Two of the men, presumably Husseini and Muscles, were driving the two vehicles and weren't coming with us. That fit in with Husseini giving Ahmed instructions on when to shoot me and weigh my corpse down with rocks. So if I waited until we were well away from shore, I'd only have two men to contend with instead of four. Although I wasn't a fast swimmer, I was slow and steady, and the water was warm. On the other hand, in the clear, calm water, Ahmed would be able to shoot me easy as a fish in a barrel. If only I could create a diversion to grab their attention while I slipped overboard.

I wondered if the Somalis knew how to swim. As desert dwellers, probably not. If Ahmed was in the water himself, swimmer or not, he could hardly fire off a round from his semiautomatic. But how to get him in the water? I couldn't very well seize control of the rudder and capsize the boat,

223

with him patrolling up there. Should I try to use a tusk as a battering ram and smash a hole in the side of the hull? I doubted I had the strength, and it would be too noisy.

I went over to inspect the patch that was leaking. That jagged tusk might come in handy, after all. I was going to do the reverse of the little Dutch boy's finger in the dike. Using the tusk, I gouged off the tar patch. It didn't take long. Under it was a bit of wet canvas stuffed into a gap in the boards. With a crash of sound, Muscles dumped another load of ivory into the hold. I levered out the canvas plug. The trickle of water turned into a gushing stream. The wood looked a bit punky around the hole, and I enlarged it with the tusk. The die was cast. It would soon be sink or swim for all of us.

The hold was a big space, and it would take a while to fill with enough water, but that was all right. It would be worse for me if they discovered the flood before we set sail. There was nothing for me to do now but wait. I felt a sudden and crushing desire for a cigarette.

Muscles dumped in a last load of ivory. I heard a creaking of·ropes, shouts, the sound of the sail luffing in the wind. The boat floated free. I was heading out to sea in a sinking ship, with one old sailor and the man with crocodile eyes.

31

For a long time nothing seemed to happen. The water was getting imperceptibly higher, the boat was holding a steady course. When the water was halfway up my calves, it seemed to me that our progress slowed. The boat felt logy and less stable, but it might have been my imagination. I waited till the water was knee high, then I stripped off my clothes and shoes. My captors would be at a disadvantage swimming in their baggy Muslim knickers.

The weight of water was definitely having an effect. A bulkhead in the stern kept the water in the forward part of the hold, and the weight was tipping the dhow forward. We wallowed from side to side in a sickening way, and the swells made a slurping sound against the hull as if trying to swallow us whole.

There was a sharply worded exchange above me between the boatman and Ahmed. Footsteps tramped up to the open hatch and then withdrew. Ahmed shouted in an angry voice. The boatman's turbaned head appeared. He took in the seawater sloshing against the pile of tusks and gave a cry of fear. Ahmed pulled him back and began smacking him. Both men were shouting.

By now the water was up to my thighs. I scrambled onto the pile of ivory and looked through the open hatch. Ahmed had flung the boatman to the deck and was unslinging the AK-47 from his shoulder. A wave of fear washed over me, as physical as the seawater around my legs. I'd miscalculated. It was in Ahmed's nature to shoot me and the boatman first and then try to save himself.

Ahmed crooked his arm and held the semiautomatic in two fists, ready to shoot. His eyes locked on mine. Crocodile eyes filled with fear and murderous rage. The boatman at his feet, thinking he was Ahmed's target, kicked upward with all his strength. His naked foot caught Ahmed in the balls like a hammer pounding into a nail.

Ahmed clutched his groin with a cry and doubled over in a spasm of pain. His gun clattered to the deck. This was it. I didn't hesitate. I hoisted myself over the edge of the hatch, grabbed the AK-47, and flew across the deck and onto the rail in one continuous rush. The two men's shouts mixed with the thudding of my heart and of my feet on the deck.

Ahmed flung himself at me and grabbed my ankle. He

225

yanked me back onto the boat. I fell on him, knocking him down. His head hit the boards with a loud crack and his grip slackened. I kicked free and scrambled to my feet. He pushed himself into a crouch and rushed me. I swung the AK-47 like a bat, aiming low and putting my whole body into it. He put his right arm up and the gun butt connected with a bone-breaking jar. He cursed and tried to grab me with his left, but I leaped to the rail and jumped overboard.

A cool avalanche of water closed over my head. I did the frog kick, driving myself deeper as I let go of the semiautomatic. The long black shape turned wavery and dim as it disappeared into the depths below me.

When my lungs felt like they would burst, I kicked up to the surface. The dhow was listing badly, and the whole stern was raised out of the water. The dark red sail was a bloody splash of color. Ahmed stood at the stern. He saw me and yelled, shaking his fist. No matter. Without a gun or a lifeboat, there was nothing he could do to me now.

The sun was halfway up the eastern sky, and I headed away from it, setting myself a slow crawl that I knew I could keep up for as long as necessary. A line of long-tailed cormorants swept by inches off the water, also heading for shore. They were out of sight in minutes. I plowed on, conserving my strength.

The worst part was thirst. I was already thirsty when I started out, then I swallowed saltwater more than once, and my tongue felt swollen and burned. Could thirst swell your tongue until you couldn't breathe? I kept my mind off it by trying not to think about the saltwater stinging in my head wound. Or about blood in the water and sharks. The turquoise waves bobbed gently in the sunlight, with not a ripple or a fin to disturb the mercurial surface, but it was no use telling that to my imagination.

All was quiet, except for the occasional cry of a seabird. Every now and then I'd look behind me, but there was no sign of Ahmed and the boatman. My arms started to tire, so I switched to the backstroke. After a while I got bored with imagining sharks, and instead began to think about the human variety.

Who had set Husseini up in business at Phantom Ranch?

Whoever it was had killed Emmet, or ordered him killed, and would come after me the moment I reappeared in Kenya.

I closed my eyes, blotting out the empty sky above me. Kick, glide, kick, glide. I felt like a water bug on the surface of the bottomless deep. Thoughts swam up in my consciousness, turned and disappeared like a school of fish, only to reappear from a different angle. Emmet, Mikki, Henry, Joseph, Omondi, Robert Thiaka and Old Thiaka, Kim, Garret, Alicia, her boyfriend Greg, Striker, the waiter at Shabaan's, even the old cabbie who hadn't wanted to disappoint me. The disordered jumble of faces and conversations slowly took on a coherent shape.

I already knew all I needed to trace Emmet's path to death. It started when he'd gone to his old manager's funeral at Phantom Ranch, poked around, and saw signs of poaching. He confronted Thiaka with the poaching camp at the dam, but Thiaka claimed ignorance. On his return home, Emmet looked through Garret's things, discovered the carved tusks, and jumped to the false conclusion that his only son was running an ivory business under his very nose. He returned to Phantom Ranch a second time, discovered the truck Husseini used to transport ivory, then flew to Lamu to check out Umar Island as a possible smuggling base. As it turned out, Umar Island wasn't part of the smuggling scheme, but to the poachers it must have looked like Emmet knew even more than he did.

Garret told his sister Kim that Emmet was threatening to turn him in as a poacher. Kim feared that Thiaka might be the guilty party. She invited Emmet to meet her for lunch at Shabaan's. She tried to deflect him, but they quarreled, as usual.

Meanwhile, Alicia got confirmation she was pregnant and approached Emmet for a divorce. Emmet turned around and asked Mikki to marry him, but she stalled, asking for time. He and Alicia fought about how much of a settlement she should get, and she followed him down to his camp to argue about it some more. The next day someone that Emmet knew and trusted flew a small plane to Emmet's camp, and while Emmet was frying eggs, pulled out a gun and forced Emmet down to the water hole and shot him.

Who? The killer struck because he feared being caught for poaching. That meant he knew what Emmet was up to. When Emmet flew to Lamu right after searching the dam site, the killer must have feared that Emmet had discovered not just the trucks, but the whole smuggling network, and moved to silence him.

The killer was part of Emmet's intimate circle: knew about his camp, knew he'd be down there, had access to Emmet's study, and knew enough to remove Emmet's ivory files—also knew where Striker lived and that he might have records of Emmet's discoveries. And the killer obviously knew about Phantom Ranch, maybe through Garret, maybe through Robert Thiaka. With all those philanthropic donors, the ranch could have served as a convenient cover to launder the ivory money.

Who? My legs were starting to feel like water-logged posts. I was moving slower and slower, and still no land in sight. Who? There was no evidence that Alicia was involved in ivory poaching; all her actions could be explained by the conflict over her divorce settlement. Garret's suspect ivory came from his Japanese investor, who had also pledged a hefty sum for Umar Island before the killing, removing a patricidal motive. Besides, if Garret had been the poacher, he'd have had huge ivory profits to invest in Umar Island long ago. Thiaka, too, had no personal wealth. He was planning to set up an elephant research center at Phantom Ranch with Mikki—something he wouldn't do if he was also exterminating every elephant in sight.

Mikki was the one person to benefit directly from Emmet's death. She now had sole control of his fortune. Although it was all earmarked for Save the Elephants, it gave her unlimited research funds, a scientist's dream. She knew more of Emmet's moves and plans than anyone. But it was ridiculous to think either that Mikki was running an elephant slaughter business or that she'd kill the man she loved, or rather, one of the men she loved. Ridiculous. I thought of her irrational insistence that Alicia was the killer, how she tried repeatedly to deflect me from the ivory track.

But that was jealousy. Surely that was jealousy? Jealousy could lead people to do the most irrational things.

The faces and conversations swirled behind my eyelids. I opened my eyes. Suddenly it was clear as the cruel sun-drenched sky above me who the killer was. I could fight the waves, my fatigue, my thirst, the sun, but I couldn't fight the truth. I tried not to think of Mikki, but bits of memories kept surfacing: her bitten-down nails, her auburn hair bending over her clipboard as she recorded the elephants' behavior, her little girl laugh when she was happy.

The rest of the swim felt very, very long.

32

WHEN I HEARD the loud nasal *kuark* of a heron and felt its great shadow pass over me, I knew land was near. I forced my wooden legs to bend and kick. A quarter of a mile more and I could hear the surf lapping against sand. I did the breaststroke the last lap, soaking in the sight of palm trees and beach figs. Then there was water-ribbed sand below me, with sun ripples washing over it in a golden web. I put my foot down and touched bottom. I'd made it! I was alive. I stumbled onto land, half crawled to a patch of shade under the broad-leafed fig, and collapsed.

I lay panting there for a long time. It was a larger cove than the one where we'd set off, with not a single human footprint in sight. I was almost too tired to move, but my thirst drove me on. My face felt broiled and I hoped my tan had protected me from sun poisoning. If I didn't find something to drink soon, I wouldn't have to worry about the killer or anything else. I hiked out to the road.

The sight of a sand-covered, stark-naked white hitchhiker should have been a car stopper, but it was over an hour before the first car came down that little-used stretch of coast in order to stop. I was lucky. It was the Fanta delivery truck, bringing a load of soft drinks to Lamu. He gave me a drink, a second one, a third, his shirt, a towel to tie around my middle, and a ride to the Lamu landing strip. There I talked a pilot into lending me a pair of pants and flying me back to Nairobi on credit. He charged double for the privilege, but I was in no mood to quibble.

My last act before getting on the plane was to call Mikki at her office at the university. I'd thought of calling Omondi first, to tell him what I knew, but I have an overdeveloped sense of loyalty to friends. I thought I owed it to Mikki to tell her myself. Now that I knew, for some strange—okay, stupid—reason, I was no longer scared. You don't play around with murder, but that's what I did.

The phone rang on and on, and finally the department secretary picked it up.

"Professor Darrow? She's gone down to the Laird camp to pick up her things. I think she was trying to reach you earlier, to see if you could go down with her. . . . No, she was going to go home directly afterward. . . . Well, I'm sure you could catch her there. She'll be glad to see you."

"Thanks. May I leave a message?"

The secretary didn't answer immediately, and I thought I could hear Mikki's voice in the background. What was going on?

"Wait." It was the secretary's voice, "Wait a minute, here she is. She must have forgotten something and came back. I'll buzz you through to her office."

Mikki picked up the phone on the first ring. "Jazz. How are you? Any news?"

"Lots. We need to talk. May I come by your office?" I looked at my watch, but its salt-crusted face told me the hour I was swimming to shore. "Say in a couple of hours?"

Mikki hesitated. "Listen, I was literally halfway out the door. I have to go down to Emmet's camp to pick up my

230

stuff. How about I pick you up and we drive down together? I'd appreciate your company."

"What if I meet you there? I'm not at home, and I've rented a plane—I'll explain all that later, in person."

Next, I called Omondi and told him about my last twenty-four hours. To his credit, Omondi believed me and didn't waste time on useless questions. He was impressed with my conclusions also.

"Finding the corroborating evidence should not be too hard, now that we know where to look. It sounds like you should go see a doctor first, get that head wound cleaned up. Come into the office afterward, and I'll take down your testimony. We'll pick up Husseini on kidnapping charges."

"I'm still on the coast. Is it okay if I come in tomorrow? I think I may want to just collapse tonight."

"Yes, of course. You must rest and recover from what you have been through. But Jazz, let me ask you . . . ?" His tone softened.

"What?"

"May I come over to see you tonight, as a friend? I will make you a hot meal and bring you tea in bed." He laughed. "Or anywhere else. I was very worried, very personally worried, about you, and I just want to see you are all right."

I felt half pleased and half pressured by the attention. I liked being able to come and go, with no one to know or care—or did I? "Why were you so worried? I was only gone for twenty-four hours."

"Ibrahima called me after he couldn't reach you last night—we'd both left messages on your machine to call immediately, and then when you never called, we asked around a bit. No one had a clue as to where you'd gone. You'd better let Ibrahima know you're okay. He was very worried also."

"Thanks for the offer to come by." I planned to say don't bother, I'll be fine; but instead I heard myself saying, "It would be nice to have someone fuss over me a bit."

"Someone?"

"You. Yes, you. That would be very nice."

Anyway, after all that, I didn't want to be pressured not

231

to see Mikki on my way home, so I didn't tell Omondi I was meeting her at Emmet's camp. I hung up and stared at the heavy black pay phone. Should I call Striker? I decided it could wait. I didn't feel like talking to him right after that conversation with Omondi. I walked to the two-seater plane without remembering to be scared and I strapped myself in next to the pilot. Lamu grew small. We banked and turned, and the coast disappeared behind us. At least now I could tell Mikki that Omondi knew everything, and that gave me an extra illusion of safety.

Emmet's camp looked utterly deserted as we circled before landing. Mikki's plane was there, but she didn't come out to wave. Our landing was no bumpier than most, and after all I'd been through, I had no adrenaline left anyway. Maybe at last I was over my fear of small planes. I'd arranged with the pilot to wait, and he settled down for a cigarette in the plane's patch of shade, while I trudged up the hill to the camp.

When I got to the top, Mikki still hadn't appeared. Odd. There were no elephants down at the water hole, either, although I heard some crashing in the woods that straggled along the hill's crest. It was obvious the elephants had started coming into camp. The kitchen lean-to now leaned at a raffish forty-five-degree angle. The refrigerator was in the middle of camp, half crushed. The straw enclosure for the camp shower was flattened, and the latrine enclosure was now thirty feet away. A large mound of still redolent elephant shit was in front of the dining tent, and the acacia was missing half its branches. The camp would soon revert back to the wild.

I was surveying the damage, wondering where in hell Mikki had gone, when I heard a footstep behind me. I whirled around.

Henry stood there with a rifle cradled in his arm. Its muzzle pointed in my general direction.

I froze. The adrenaline, far from used up, surged through my body like a tidal wave. My heart was beating so hard I could hear it.

Henry pointed the gun more emphatically in my direction and laughed his big yellow-toothed mirthless laugh.

"You were expecting Mikki, so you could tell her about me?"

"Quick work, Henry. She phoned you after talking to me?"

"As luck would have it, I was standing right next to her. It's the first time in years I've visited her at work. My luck—not yours, of course."

"As soon as you heard I was alive, you realized something must have gone wrong."

"Yes, Husseini telephoned me a couple of hours ago and explained how your next stop was going to be the bottom of the sea."

"What about Mikki? What have you done to her?" I asked.

"Don't worry about her. You're the one who's going to die."

I clenched my teeth. The game's not up yet, you bastard, I thought. "Where is she?"

Henry nodded downhill toward the two planes, looking like models against the vast African plain. "She's sleeping off a sedative that got into her canteen by mistake. Ha! Ha!" Again his braying laugh. "By the time she awakes, we'll be in the United Arab Emirates. Women there can't get an exit visa without their husband's written permission. No elephants in the Arabian desert, but the expatriate's life can be very comfortable in Moslem countries."

"Henry, you're raving. You can't get away with this. I've reported everything to the police."

"By the time they issue an arrest warrant, I'll have a new identity. My contacts in the UAR are very high, in the emir's intimate circle. I have quite a nice nest egg there, too. The ivory business has been good to me."

I wanted to smash his ugly face.

He laughed again. "I'm having the time of my life. You look so angry!"

"Very funny. You're crazy to think you can get away with this." I was playing for time, not that time could do much to help me. But if these were my last moments on earth, quality time or no, I wanted to draw them out as long as possible. "There's a plane waiting for me down there, Omondi knows where I am."

Henry hefted the rifle, its beady black holes aimed once more at my chest. "This can take care of the pilot also. Or else I'll pay him off and say you'll be returning with me. It doesn't really matter, does it? I'll be long gone by the time the police find you, or what remains of you."

"I have one question, Henry. Why did you do it?"

"Kill Emmet, you mean, or start my ivory business?"

"Both."

"I killed Emmet because I thought he'd discovered my whole setup, from Phantom Ranch to the coast. Then he tells me he'd missed it all! Isn't that ironic?"

"Missed it?"

"Well, most of it. He had a lead on Husseini, but if that was all, I could have simply whisked Husseini out of the country. The only network Emmet discovered was a fantasy he built out of a tusk in Garret's room. He jumped to the conclusion Garret was running a poaching business and using Umar Island as a staging area. Utter nonsense. That little spit of land is too close to Lamu to be used for smuggling. Anyway, by the time he told me all this, I had my gun on him and there was no elegant way to bow out. I had to kill him. Now it's my turn to ask a question. How did you figure it was me?"

"Thiaka told me he had plans for an elephant research center at Phantom Ranch, but I didn't link it with the project you told Omondi about that time in his office, until today. Thiaka kept saying the Darrows whenever he mentioned his plans, probably because I was with both you and Mikki that day. For a moment I thought it was Mikki who wanted tons of money to start a new research center, but then I thought, why would she kill Emmet for that money when he was willing to fund whatever research she wanted? I realized the bill fit you even better. You couldn't get funded, could you? So you decided on some self-financing through the ivory trade, and then the research center would have laundered the dirty money for you, and also be a poke in Emmet's eye. Did you think you could get Mikki back if you had the primo elephant center in Kenya?"

"Clever girl. You figured this all out yourself?"

"The clincher was your nasty sense of humor. Who else close enough to Emmet to track his actions and kill him would have chosen to set up the poaching center on his son's ranch and use his daughter as the conduit for funds? You didn't do it just for the money, did you, Henry? It was your own little way to get revenge."

"Ha! Ha! I did try to set up a legitimate research center to study elephant aggression, but as you know, it's impossible to get funding these days. When I was looking for suitable locations, I remembered Phantom Ranch—I'd been a guest there when Garret's mother was still alive—and thought it would be a delicious location to set up my rival research station. Rub Emmet's nose in it a little. I explained to Thiaka that I didn't want the embarrassment of anyone knowing my plans until the project was fully funded. He was very sweet. He didn't mention it to a soul." He cocked the rifle. "Get going."

"Don't you want to hear how I escaped, and what happened to your ivory cargo?"

"You can tell me as you start walking downhill. I'm going to do it better this time, and make sure the vultures and jackals are finished before I let the elephants back."

I didn't move.

"I said get going. You have two choices. Stay up here and I'll shoot you in the stomach. You'll have a nice long, slow death. I saw some hyenas at the water hole a few minutes ago. No doubt they'd enjoy a snack. You know they don't kill their victim, they tear them apart alive."

He raised the rifle and shot into the air. I flinched at the loud report. "Ha! Ha! That was just to keep the elephants away. Did it hurt your ittle widdle ears?" He sneered at me. "The next time you hear the nasty loud sound will be your last. Now move."

There was the sound of breaking branches behind Henry, where the woods along the crest came up to the edge of camp. The sounds grew rapidly closer. Breaking branches, thunderous footsteps, a whoosh of air—and Broken Tusk

235

charged into the clearing. The gunshot must have frightened her. Her huge ears were out to the side, her trunk was raised and writhing around as she emitted a blast of fury. I could see the ugly scar on her shoulder where she'd once been shot, many years before.

Henry swirled around and raised his rifle. I dove for his legs and knocked him flat. Henry turned and brought the rifle butt against my head. I was momentarily stunned. He scrambled to his feet. I reached out to grab his legs, but he was out of my reach. Broken Tusk was almost on top of us. I could see the pink inside of her mouth, the course hairs on her trunk. Henry took aim. Then he lost his nerve. He started to run.

Broken Tusk kept right on coming. She broke her stride for a moment as she stepped over me with delicate precision. A great wrinkled stomach blotted out the sky for a second. She reached Henry and swiped him with her trunk. He landed amidst the broken bits of the kitchen. Still trumpeting shrilly, the elephant ran after him and thrust at him with her broken tusk. His scream didn't last long. He was briefly impaled. Then she shook him off her tusk like an annoying gnat. With one long glance at me, she turned and headed back into the woods.

33

IT WAS ODD to walk down the hill and find the pilot calmly drinking an orange Fanta in one two-seater plane and Mikki, slumped over, unconscious, in the other. Her burnished hair was gleaming in the sun, and her hands, with their bitten nails, lay limply in her lap. I yanked open the door and was relieved to hear her breathing gently and evenly.

The bad part would be when she woke up. I briefly tried on the idea of lying to her about Henry, but put it aside. She was an adult, had the right to know the truth about her own life. Mikki was a strong person, in her way. At least Henry's death spared her an agonizing murder trial. I imagined he'd be easier to forgive dead than alive, and Mikki would bury herself in work. She might even use Emmet's money to set up the elephant research at Phantom Ranch. Perhaps that might soften the senseless waste of two lives. Meanwhile, I wanted to get her to a hospital where they could make sure she woke up.

"Your friend is one big sleeper." The pilot had come up behind me. "She didn't even move when that rifle went off."

I looked quickly at his face. It matched his voice: bored and patient.

"There's been a serious accident," I told him. "There's a man up on top of the hill." He nodded. "His name is Henry Darrow. He was just gored by an elephant he tried to shoot. He's dead. Can your plane handle his weight? We'll have to put his body in the luggage space behind the seats."

He blinked unhappily, and one hand moved up to touch a small black goat's horn he wore on a thong around his neck. "You want me to carry a dead man back to Nairobi?"

"The dead can't hurt you."

"And what about you?" He looked at me with concern. "Did you shoot the elephant?"

"Don't worry about me. I'll wait here." I gave him instructions, jotting down the phone numbers he'd need. "This lady is Mrs. Darrow. She has taken some sleeping pills by mistake. Please radio from the plane that the police must come to the airport to pick up Mr. Darrow's body and take Mrs. Darrow to the hospital. You've got that?"

He looked dubious. "I agreed to fly you here and back, not carrying bodies and calling police. They will think I'm up to no good. Besides, it is dangerous for you to be here all alone. It is better for you to come with me and leave the dead body here. The needs of the living come before the dead."

"We can't leave him here. The animals will get him."

"And what if I leave you and the animals get you?"

"I have a rifle. I'll be okay." The pilot finally nodded his assent. "When you radio the landing tower to get the police, ask for Inspector Omondi, and tell him my name. Tell him you must turn around immediately to come and pick me up. The police will not bother you, I promise." I *hope*, I repeated to myself. If Omondi wasn't there, it could be a god-awful mess and confusion.

The two of us trudged up the hill, wrapped Henry's body in a couple of blankets from Emmet's cot, and lugged his corpse down to the plane. Mikki felt light as a doll in comparison. We sat her in the passenger seat and strapped her in. She stirred but didn't wake.

The pilot leaned out his window to shake hands goodbye, when I thought of one last instruction. I didn't want Mikki waking up in the hospital with only a policeman by her bedside. I asked the pilot to call one more person, Louise Carruthers, a Save the Elephants stalwart and old friend of Mikki's, to tell her that Mikki was in the hospital, was all alone, and didn't yet know that Henry had been killed in an accident. He repeated Louise's name and gave me a firm handshake. I stepped back and waved the plane off.

Now I was in for a long wait. I returned to camp, built a fire to let the animals know a human was in residence, found the water barrel still intact, and heated a kettle on the blazing fire. Emmet's sleeping tent was untouched, so I scooped up clean towels, soap, shampoo, and a set of Mikki's clean clothes. It was wonderful to wash the salt off me, wash away the horrors of the last night and morning. My watch was full of seawater and I threw it away. I towel dried my hair, looking down on the water hole. A young male elephant was standing up to his knees, sucking up the muddy water in his trunk and spraying it over his back. He was enjoying himself so much, he had a partial erection some three feet long. I knew how he felt. It was good to be alive.

I pulled a straw mat outside and lay in the dappled shade

of the acacia tree. The golden grasses of the plains whispered and stirred in the hot afternoon breeze, extending to the distant horizon. I rolled over on my back and looked up at the sky through the feathery canopy. My own future was completely murky. Emmet's murder and this investigation left me in a different place than where I'd started off. It was time to face some unpleasant truths.

First of all, I had to stop kidding myself about running my own safari company. Jazz Jasper Safaris wasn't making it. With the economic slump and all the revelations about poaching driving away tourists, I simply didn't have the capital to ride out this slow period. I hated the thought of giving up my independence. I sighed. Would I rather leave Kenya than be a tour guide for some commercial outfit that did eight parks in seven days, turning what should be a magical experience into a predigested blur?

A Bataleur eagle sailed low over the tree, coming in for a landing at the water hole. I wasn't ready to give up on Kenya, not yet. I wondered if private sleuthing could earn me enough to hang on to Jazz Jasper Safaris a bit longer. It was worth a try. If the international commission lifted the ban on ivory, everything would go down the tubes. If the ban held, maybe both the elephants and I could survive here.

A distant buzz in the sky grew louder, and I started down the hill. I can hardly tell one small plane from another, but even to my eye this was a larger beast than the one I'd rented. It taxied to a halt, and before the propeller had stopped whirring, out jumped Omondi. He bounded up the slope toward me, face lit with a smile.

"My dear Jazz! I am so glad to find you in one piece!" He grabbed me by both elbows, twirled me partway around and finished with a little shake. "The pilot you hired told me a rogue elephant had killed Henry Darrow, that he had an ambulance coming for Mikki, and that he'd left you behind—as too much ballast." His laughter was filled with relief. "I really should scold you. Did you arrange to meet Henry down here, knowing he was the killer?"

"Believe me, if I'd thought there was any chance that Henry would show up—but I wanted—"

". . . to tell Mikki yourself. Yes, I know you by now. Well, let me quickly examine where Henry was killed, and then we can go."

We reached the crest of the hill and Omondi surveyed the damage with a look of dismay. "What in the world went on here? You lived through an explosion!"

"The elephants trashed the camp before we got here. The only thing I saw damaged was Henry." I described Henry's attempt to kill me and flee with Mikki to the United Arab Emirates, his fatal mistake in firing into the air, and how Broken Tusk had delicately avoided stepping on me as she rushed Henry and saved my life. "I wouldn't call her a rogue elephant. She acted very specifically, one could say in self-defense."

Omondi frowned. "I must report that Henry was gored. The wildlife people will be told to shoot her. You can't let a man-killing animal run around loose."

I sank down on the picnic bench where Emmet used to eat his meals. "I can give the wildlife department a detailed description. It was a bull elephant I've never seen before. I'd estimate twelve feet at the shoulder, in his prime, maybe twelve thousand pounds, two long perfect tusks, and a very noticeable notch at the top of his left ear." There wasn't an elephant like that left in all of Kenya.

"I thought you called it *she* and her name was Broken Tusk."

"Did I say that? It must have been a slip of the tongue."

Omondi nodded imperceptibly and dropped the subject. He walked over to the crushed refrigerator lying on its side and nudged it with his toe. "It's as if they knew Emmet wouldn't be coming back."

"It's best it ended this way, don't you think?"

Omondi shook his head emphatically. "No, not in the slightest. It would have been better if you'd stayed out of it and let the police do their work."

"If I hadn't called Mikki when I did, she'd be in the United Arab Emirates by now."

"Only because Henry knew you were breathing down his neck."

240

I arched an eyebrow. "Tell me, Omondi: would you have discovered it was Henry? Were you even close?"

"Ow, you are hurting my pride." Omondi put a hand to his chest as if struck. "I admit Henry had hidden his trail pretty well. We knew about the existence of Phantom Ranch and the poaching evidence Emmet had discovered there, from the files you so kindly helped me find. We were following up Emmet's own suspicions of his son, Garret."

"In other words, you were on the wrong track."

"Well, it is over now." Omondi sat down next to me and took my hand. "I want to talk to you about something else. In finding Emmet's killer, you have been as fierce and focused as a lioness stalking an antelope in the long grass. But when it comes to love, I sense you are floundering. In this past week you have drawn me close and pushed me away, more than once."

"God, Omondi, I'm sorry. I guess I have been jerking you around. My business is a mess, me and Striker are a mess—I didn't mean to drag you into it."

"I wasn't completely neutral, either. I think I walked forward quite happily, and with my eyes open."

"I really value your friendship."

Omondi brushed the back of my hand softly with his fingertips. "There is more between us than friendship."

I looked into his dark eyes. "It would be great fun. I really like you—you're warm and wise and funny—*and* sexy. But when I think of us starting a love affair, I can see the ending as clearly as the beginning."

"Once the wonderfulness of getting to know each other is past, you think we would be done." Omondi's hand was warm on mine.

I said sadly, "Don't you?"

"I can't live in your world of constant safaris." He looked out over the distant plains. "You wouldn't be happy in my world of city life and extended family. If we stayed together, one of us would have to leave our world for the other."

"I had love affairs like that in my early twenties, before getting married. They were great—then. They helped me to find out who I am. But now I know who I am. I don't want

241

a six-month amorous adventure exploring another person's reality. I want to build something with someone."

"With Striker."

"I don't know. I'm having doubts about that, too. Striker seems to want everything on his terms."

"You only do things a hundred percent, don't you?"

"I tried a hundred percent—when I was married. Striker and I are trying for fifty-fifty and we can't even manage that."

I sighed and watched the animals below. A giraffe trailing three six-foot giraffe babies—babysitting for the mothers who were off feeding—was ambling toward the water hole with her funny loose-jointed gait. I wanted to reach out and rub my fingers over their smooth, beautifully marked coats. I remembered feeding a giraffe at the zoo, feeling the insistence of its rubbery lips on my palm. Giraffes are solitary or gather in loose and shifting groups. They don't try for one-on-one relationships.

"I've been mad at Striker since the day I found Emmet dead, when he wouldn't come stay with me in Nairobi." I explained to Omondi why he'd found me crying in the car that evening, after I'd called Striker.

"You are writing him off as one more selfish man."

"Striker wants me to mold myself to his world and cut off the pieces that don't fit." I pulled my hand out of Omondi's. Mikki solved the same problem by having two men to fit the different parts of herself. That was a terrible solution, but jumping from one man to another seemed only slightly better.

Omondi spoke softly. "What would have happened that night if instead of saying 'Fine, don't come,' you'd said, 'Striker, it's important to me. I want to be in my own bed and have you here.' What if you'd said, 'I need you'?"

"Those last words stick in my throat." To say *I need you* stripped me bare. I couldn't even blame it on my divorce. I'd never been very good at that kind of stuff with Adam, either. Maybe it was time for me to start learning.

"I think your hand with Striker is not played out yet," Omondi said. "You may know who you are, but you are not yet all you will be."

"You sound like Robert Thiaka's uncle, the soothsayer."

Omondi smiled. "I told you my grandfather was a famous sorcerer, specializing in love potions."

I smiled back. "And his own best customer."

Omondi leaned over and gave me a small, goodbye sort of kiss. "I am still going to hold you to your offer of taking me to see the mountain parks."

I stood up. "It's a deal."

When I got to my apartment door, I could hear Willie Dixon, my favorite musician, singing "I Am the Blues." It was Striker's favorite album, too. I turned the key in the lock, and the door was pulled open before I could turn the handle.

Striker pulled me in and crushed me to his chest. Then he was kissing me—urgently, passionately, harsh and soaring as a hawk.

Finally I pulled back for breath. "Striker! What is it?" I looked into his hazel eyes, flecked with gold and green. "What are you doing here?"

"I'm cooking dinner."

I followed Striker into the kitchen, amazed to smell a stew simmering on the stove. Cooking was never one of Striker's favored activities, and when we were together he usually played helper to my chef. "You're cooking? Something must be up."

Striker sprinkled in some thyme and gave the stew a stir. He was wearing an old pair of jeans and a faded flannel shirt. He never looked better. "Louise Carruthers called me from the hospital," he explained. "Told me Henry was dead and the police were picking you up from Emmet's camp."

"And Mikki?"

"Still unconscious, but she'll be fine. She just has to sleep it off. What happened down there?" He put the lid on the pot.

"Henry killed Emmet." I waved my hand. "It's a long story. I'll tell you later. He was about to shoot me, too, when Broken Tusk charged out of the woods and skewered him."

"Henry killed Emmet." Striker paused a moment to let

that sink in. "And Broken Tusk killed him." He gave me another kiss. "Darling, I'm proud of you for solving the murder. Thank God you're all right."

"Thank Broken Tusk."

"I'll drink to that." He picked up a bottle of red wine, already open and breathing. "Want some?"

"Please."

Striker poured two glasses.

"I'm a little the worse for wear." I laughed. "I must look like a wreck."

"You look wonderful. To our love," Striker toasted. We both drank.

"I still can't get over you being here. I'd practically forgotten I gave you a key to this place."

"After Louise called, I couldn't stand waiting at home to hear from you. I wanted to be with you tonight. I gambled you'd feel the same."

"Did you have any trouble remembering where I live?" Striker looked rueful. "I deserve that one."

He put his glass down on the counter, then did the same with mine. He encircled me with his arms and gave me a slow, appreciative kiss. His mouth tasted sweet as wine. Willie Dixon was singing "I don't trust nobody."

Our bellies pressed warmly together. I leaned back so I could see his face. "You really hurt me, not coming down the night we discovered Emmet was killed." I took a deep breath. It was do or die. "I needed you that night."

Striker pressed his cheek against my hair. "I know, baby. I don't know how I could have been such a jerk." He fell silent for so long, I wondered if that was all he had to say, but then he began to talk softly, into my hair. "I had a lot of time to think about us when I was out at Lake Baringo this week. The last time we were together—I could feel you slipping away from me, giving up on me in disgust."

"But I came back."

"Jazz, don't give up on me. I really do love you, even if I'm not very good at it sometimes. It's up to you also. Don't tell me it's okay when I'm fucking up. Fight it out with me."

I nodded. "You're right. It's both of us."

"Well, a lot of it is me, I can admit that, but I need you to hang in there and demand I act right by you. You know what I mean?"

"Darling, I love you."

"I love you, too. Anyway, this is all a roundabout way of saying I came here because I thought you could use some taking care of after all you've been through."

I gave him a wicked smile. "What kind of taking care of did you have in mind?"

"The stew needs a couple of hours to cook."

"That's what I figured." I took his hand and led him out of the kitchen.

*Coming to bookstores everywhere
in August 1994 . . .*

THE CHEETAH CHASE
by Karin McQuillan

Published in hardcover by Ballantine Books.

*Read on
for the exciting opening pages of*
THE CHEETAH CHASE . . .

1

I WAS IN the cheetah barn grooming Gin, lulling myself into a state of silken reverie, when she perked her ears toward the house, grew taut in every sinew, and took off. I ran after her in time to see her black-tipped tail disappear behind the house. I rounded the corner, and for a moment I thought Nick Hunter was on his back, roughhousing with the cheetah, a favorite game. Then I noticed that Gin was still, and only Nick was moving. He was thrashing about as if in intense pain. Gin chirped in distress. Her brother, Tonic, came racing around the corner of the house.

"Wynn!" I bellowed. "Quick!"

I could hear running footsteps in the kitchen, and thanked God that Wynn was a former nurse, confident as a child that she would make everything better. I dropped to the ground, cradled Nick's dark, elegant head on my thighs, and felt his brow. It was frighteningly cold, yet slick with sweat. His long, tan hands clutched at the dust. Gin sniffed Nick's face and chirped, the birdlike cheetah distress call. Nick's eyes were open, but he didn't look at us. A froth of saliva gathered at the corner of his mouth as he labored for breath. Tonic sniffed Nick's face and backed off, chirping. My own breath seemed stopped in my chest.

Wynn burst through the door and crouched beside me, her face set and intense. She touched his cheek, picked up his right hand and examined it closely. It was bluish, swollen to the size of a grapefruit.

Nick's sister Viv and her husband Roger Porter were right behind Wynn, both dressed for their country weekend as if they'd stepped from a whiskey ad in *Vanity Fair*.

"What is it?" Viv's eyes were two big O's of fear. "A snake?"

A chill ran through me. A snake. I'd been running safaris in Kenya almost three years now and had never had to deal with snakebite. Viv and Nick were born here, grew up on a big farm west of Mount Kenya. I seemed to remember a story of both brother and sister stumbling upon a viper as children, Nick saving his older sister and being bitten.

"I don't see a double puncture," Wynn said. Nick had a bit of gauze taped to one finger, protecting a cut. His other fingers were unmarked.

Gin pushed her tawny head closer to see what Wynn was doing, and wriggled in protest when I pulled her away. I knelt down and hugged her long, thin torso. I could feel the cheetah's heart beating rapidly against my chest. Tonic was nowhere to be seen. He must have run off in fright.

"Nick! What bit you?" Viv shouted, her voice panicky. He didn't answer, didn't even turn toward her.

Wynn raced back to the kitchen to pull the antivenin kit from the fridge. I followed her and went for the shortwave radio.

"What are you doing?" she asked.

"Calling the flying doctors."

"Right."

She ran outside. I explained the situation tersely to the dispatcher, and followed. Roger had found a big stick and was circling the outhouse, poking at the foundation, eyes raking the ground.

Wynn knelt in the dust and kissed Nick's brow. "Nicky, I'm here. We have antivenin. You'll be okay." With the rapid, experienced movements of a nurse—her job before coming to Kenya—she filled the hypodermic.

Viv caught her wrist. "Wynn, don't."

Wynn paused, hypodermic pointing at the sky.

"He's allergic to antivenin. He never told you? He was bitten when we were kids. He . . ." Viv's voice trailed off at the sight of Wynn's face.

250

At that moment I realized that Nick was going to die. The nearest clinic was Isiolo, the nearest hospital Nairobi. The flying doctors couldn't get here in time, and we had no way to get anywhere.

Isiolo, several hours' drive from here, was the only thing passing for a town in this vast region north of Mount Kenya. Beyond Nick and Wynn's house, scrub desert stretched out in a rolling wilderness that kept on until it hit the Sahara. The Hunters had chosen this land as a refuge of solitude and peace, with only cheetah and oryx, lion and kudu, as neighbors. Their plane was their link to civilization, and right now the plane was out of commission, being overhauled down at Wilson Airport in Nairobi.

Nick's breathing grew more labored and his legs and arms began to twitch and jump. The full horror of our situation pressed in on me. We had no way to get Nick out in time. Roger and Viv had come up on a commercial flight as far as Isiolo, and my boyfriend, Striker, had flown the Hunters and me up in his four-seater, spent the night and flown back to Mount Kenya after breakfast.

We didn't even have a car at the moment. Kaji, the Hunters' assistant, had taken it for a desert drive; there was a lone female cheetah she'd been watching closely, as part of a research project. We didn't expect her back until after lunch. Every way I looked, we were hours from help. Nick's life was ebbing away in minutes, not hours.

Wynn took Nick's pulse. Her usually laughing face was grim, deep lines of pain etched from brow to chin. "No pulse. He has no pulse. We have to counteract this venom," Wynn said, her eyes fixed on Viv's. "Do you remember what happened to him as a kid?"

"I'm not sure. He was seven and I was eleven. I remember Mother saying the cure was worse than the bite. They almost thought they'd lost him." Viv's eyes filled with tears.

"If only we knew what bit him," I said, "we could weigh the risks."

"I don't see a snake track anywhere." Roger's voice came out rough and jerky. "And I can practically tell where an ant walked, in this dust." He circled the wooden loo, poking with his stick at the foundation stones.

"Look inside," Viv said. "That loo always made me nervous."

Roger opened the door gingerly with the stick, staying out of a direct line of fire in case a spitting cobra was inside. They can spit nine feet with deadly accuracy; their saliva blinds you. Roger looked in from the side and scrabbled at something on the floor with his stick. "There's a dead scorpion in here. A big one."

I went over to look. A black lobster-shaped insect as long as a man's thumb lay in the doorway. A few legs were broken off and the abdomen was crushed, but its deadly curled tail was intact. "Nick must have stomped on it after it bit him."

Roger gingerly picked up the black horror by a front pincer. One of the segmented legs dropped off. It was a nightmare out of the mists of time, born when all the continents were one big happy island called Pangaea. I hated the creature, wanted to pulverize it, make it disappear as if it had never existed. Roger must have been feeling something similar, for with a curse he hurled it into the desert. It caught on a bush and hung there like a deadly fruit.

Nick's breathing grew more labored. Before our eyes, his face, chest, both his hands, every patch of skin we could see, turned the blue of veins. The hackles rose on Gin's back, and I shivered as goose flesh stood up along my arms.

"His blood isn't carrying oxygen anymore," Wynn said. "We've got to try this." She inserted the needle. Nick's whole arm jerked, but she had a solid grip on his biceps and was able to push in the plunger.

She wiped his wet brow. I inwardly prayed, Don't let him die, don't let him die. The twitches in his legs ceased. I felt a moment of hope. Nick couldn't die. Then his body stiffened, his skin turning purple-black. His heels drummed on the ground in a rapid senseless rhythm. It was a sound of doom. Green spittle frothed at his mouth. Viv began to sob. I gripped Wynn's shoulder. It was hard as a rock.

"Nick," Wynn called. That's all she said. Just that one

word, but it carried all the pain in the world. Nick, I love you. Nick, you're dying. Nick, don't go. Nick, I can't live without you. Nick. Please. Don't go. Nick, I love you. Nick: goodbye. It was the sound of someone's heart being torn open.

Nick Hunter self-destructed before our eyes. It was agonizing to watch. Gin whimpered and crawled forward. I had to turn my head away. Then the frantic sound of Nick's breathing stopped, bam, like a light switched off forever. Viv's sobs couldn't hide that silence.

Roger and I looked at each other in shock. Is this the way it happens? One minute you're alive, and the next you're dead? The whole thing didn't take ten minutes. I realized my mouth was hanging open, and closed it. I opened it again to speak, but found nothing to say. Gin whimpered and inched forward on her belly until her nose touched Nick's arm. Wynn tried and tried to revive him mouth-to-mouth, until we had to pull her off. Gin slunk away. By the time we heard the approaching whine of the flying doctors' plane, there was only a corpse for them to carry back to Nairobi.

2

I FELT LIKE rubble left behind after an explosion.

Wynn returned to Nairobi with the flying doctors and Nick's body; Striker was going to pick up the Porters and me around four. After Wynn left, I fell apart. I cried nonstop for an hour, cried for Nick, for Wynn, for myself. It felt so wrong. How could he be snatched away without a moment's warning? Crying that hard left me sick and dazed. I went to the kitchen and stuck my head under the pump. I could hear Viv sobbing in her room. From the sound of a bottle clinking against the slate-topped bar, Roger was still in the living room, drinking steadily. I didn't want to talk to him, so I slipped out of the house. I thought I'd finish grooming Gin: it might soothe her, and it would certainly soothe me.

As soon as I stepped out on the porch, I sensed something was wrong. There was Tonic, lying in the shade all by himself. The two cubs usually stayed within a few feet of each other, and if they were lying down, liked to be in body contact.

Feeling uneasy, I walked to the cheetah barn, calling, "Gin." No sign of her. Tonic followed me, giving his high-pitched distress chirp. I fought down my rising alarm. I went into the barn's shadowy interior. "G-in!" Nothing. Around the barn and the house. Had she snuck inside the house? I went back in.

Roger was on the couch, finishing off his whiskey and

soda. Ever the gentleman, he got up when I entered. "Hullo, Jazz. Been outside?"

Roger Porter was a big man, with a hefty bone structure and a middle-age paunch. He was looking uncharacteristically wilted at the moment, with a decidedly reddish hue to his tan face, but that might have been from the heat. Living in mile-high Nairobi, he wasn't used to the desert in August. He didn't show any outward signs of being the least drunk.

"I can't find Gin," I told him.

"She's not in here," he replied. "What can I offer you?"

"Nothing, thanks."

He went to the bar and added two fingers of whiskey to his glass, a short spray of soda, and an ice cube from a bowl. "No ice bucket, I'm afraid."

"You seem to be managing."

"I have the misfortune of having been born with a hollow leg," he said. "I've been trying to drink myself into oblivion, but it's not working." He whooshed the ice around and raised his glass. "Cheers." He took a big drink. "I say, may I ask you a favor? It would be very kind of you to look in on Viv."

"Sure." I listened: she seemed to have stopped crying. I went down the hallway and quietly knocked at her door.

"Yes. Come in," said a weak voice.

The blinds were drawn, but the afternoon sun had found a chink, and dust motes swam in a beam of sun that cut through the dim room. Viv was lying on her back, staring up at the ceiling.

"Roger?" Viv's voice quavered.

I quickly glanced around the room. No cheetah. "It's me, Jazz. Sorry to barge in. Can I get you anything?"

"Thank you. That's kind of you, but I don't think so. I'm all right." Her voice was weak, as if her throat hurt from crying, and she looked terrible. Her eyes were almost swollen shut and mascara was smeared under them in a racoon's mask.

"A cold drink? Or a compress for your eyes?" I offered.

"A compress? That would be lovely, if you could manage it."

255

I got her set, and continued my search of the house. It didn't take long. I hated to bother Kaji, but I was worried about the missing cub. Kaji had returned from the bush shortly after Wynn left with Nick's body, and I'd had to break the news to her. She'd reacted with disbelief and then cries of protest and grief. We'd talked only a few minutes—what was there to say?—and then each of us had crawled into our rooms like wounded animals.

I knocked on her door. "Kaji?"

She opened it immediately, took one look at my face and asked, "What's happened?"

She was in her usual outfit: khaki chinos and a slouchy olive sweater, despite the eighty-five-degree heat. Kaji's skin was smooth medium-chestnut. Her face was bony enough to be interesting, framed by the neat dome of her hair. Right now she looked drawn, years older than her age of twenty-five.

"I can't find Gin. Tonic is lying alone on the porch."

Kaji didn't waste time asking me if I'd checked here or there. "I didn't see her when I got back." She headed for the front door and I followed. "I should have realized something was wrong."

Nick had been the cub's favorite person. When he was home, she liked to follow him around. She and her brother were orphans. Nick and Wynn had found them chirping next to the skinned carcass of their mother when they were only bits of spotted gray fluff, one month old. Somehow they'd managed to keep them alive. Now Gin and Tonic were sleek youngsters, almost a year old, at the age when their mother would be teaching them how to hunt. They wouldn't be mature enough to survive on their own for another six months at least.

"She was the first one to get to Nick. Tonic took one sniff of Nick and ran, but Gin stuck with him the whole time."

Kaji clicked her tongue with annoyance. "I should have looked for her."

"Let's hope she's hiding somewhere close by."

We checked out the cheetah barn again, even looking

into open boxes in the storeroom. Tonic trailed us, chirping anxiously. He poked his head into the boxes, too.

"Where's your sister?" I asked him. "How come you let her run off alone?"

He looked at me with his clear amber eyes and chirped.

Kaji held her hands together as if in prayer and pressed them against her lips, thinking. "There's that big silver thorn near the airstrip where they like to lie sometimes."

The acacias and thorn trees in the nearby scrub were all leafless at this time of year, and shade was scarce. We hopped in Kaji's Land Cruiser and drove the short way to what we called the airstrip: a flat runway where the brush had been cleared and a wind sock erected. There was no sign of the cheetah.

"This is bad," I said, thinking of the inexperienced cub all by herself for the first time. Thinking of lions.

A pride of lions had moved into the area last month, drawn by the abundance of game around a marsh on the Hunters' property. For some reason, lions treat cheetah like an implacable foe, systematically searching for cheetah cubs and killing them with a single bite to the throat. It doesn't make sense: cheetahs pose no competition for lions—in fact, the lazy king of beasts steals the cheetah's kills, forcing the lighter cat to expend twice as much energy for a bite of food. The problem was frightening, because the game parks were full of lions, and cheetahs were losing ninety percent of their cubs. That's why private reserves like the Hunters' were crucial to cheetah survival. There weren't many of them.

Kaji and the Hunters had been carrying on a lively debate over what to do about the pride. Nick argued that they shouldn't interfere with the natural order on their land. Kaji countered that cheetahs are close to extinction and lions are not. Now it would be up to Wynn to decide.

"Gin can run faster than a lion, can't she?" I asked Kaji.

"Only if she sees it first."

Lions are short sprinters. They rely on stealth to creep up on a victim undetected. Would Gin know enough to avoid thick scrub, where a lion could surprise her? Or would she head for the shade, right into danger?

257

"If a lion gets her . . ." Kaji didn't finish the sentence.

"We'd better find her first. Do you think you can track her?" I asked Kaji.

She lifted her chin. "I'll have to."

We got back in the car. This time I took the wheel, so Kaji could stick her head out the window and study the ground. I ever so slowly circled the house and barn. It hadn't rained since the spring, and the ground was covered with a fine dust that took prints well. Too well.

There wasn't six inches of ground that wasn't covered by tracks, one on top of another: the deep furrows of zebras in single file, the sharp points of the impala's delicate hoof, the dinner plate tracks of elephant. It took a sharp eye to pick out the cub's prints on top of the confused pattern, and I had to keep to a crawl. Fifteen minutes passed. And another fifteen. Sweat started to trickle down my back.

Would Kaji be able to do this? She knew a lot about the bush, but most of it she'd picked up the last few years. Her tracking skills were nothing compared to the local Samburu people, herders in this semi-desert, who grew up observing the wild animals and their signs all around them. Kaji grew up as a city girl in Nairobi.

Most kids in Nairobi never venture farther than the city zoo, where the favorite attraction is a chimpanzee that smokes cigarettes. They know nothing about the wilds, and could care less. Kaji was unique, especially for a woman. Her parents' house was only a short walk from Nairobi National Park, and she and her brother had spent all their free time there, illegally sneaking in on foot. Her father had encouraged it, thinking that animals were safer company than the street kids and loafers. I wonder if he regretted that decision now, when college-educated Kaji had thrown over a white-collar career to be the foster mom to two cheetah cubs.

The Hunters hired her so that instead of being house pets, the cubs could spend most of their waking hours in the bush. The challenge was to teach them the lessons they'd naturally learn from following their mother, so they'd be able to return to the wild when they were old

258

enough. Meanwhile, Kaji and the car were always there as a refuge if a lion or hyena got too close.

"I got it! It's Gin's print. Very recent." Kaji's voice rose in triumph.

I hopped out of the car and walked around to study the track. Cheetah have the round four-toed pad of a cat, but their claws don't retract, so the track has a doglike look. "Great. Now, we've got to stay with it."

The next two hours were long, hot, and frustrating. We lost the track twice on rocky ground and it took ages to find it again. We drove and called, and Tonic trotted alongside, adding his chirp to our cries. Gin had followed an erratic course, winding among the scrub, now trotting, now making a short burst of speed after a bird or a lizard, now slowing to a walk. What worried us were the numerous pug marks of lions, including ones ominously recent.

To add to our misery, Kaji had half a dead impala in the back of the car that attracted a horde of flies. She'd stolen it from a hyena on her morning drive, to use in a hunting lesson for the cubs. Blood-gorged flies bumped and buzzed against my sweaty arms and face until I wanted to scream. "These flies are driving me crazy," I said. "Should we take a break, and give the impala to Tonic?"

"I hate to waste it. I was going to tie it on the car and race down the airstrip, give them the experience of running after their supper."

"So let's do it for Tonic now. It won't take long. I just won't be able to go as fast on this rough ground."

"Okay. Let me tie it on and get in back. Wait until we get to a long flat bit, where you can pick up some speed," Kaji directed me. "Start slow and easy. When Tonic starts to chase it, I'll yell. You hit the accelerator and go as fast as you feel safe. I want him to realize he has to run full out if he wants to eat."

Cheetahs do not instinctively know how to catch antelope. It's not easy, not even for the fastest animal in the world. Playing tag with your sister is different from catching a gazelle at sixty miles per hour, or picking out a vulnerable wildebeest calf from a stampeding herd and bringing it down. In the wild the cubs would observe their mother and practice on small wounded game she'd get for them. With all that, hunting is still so difficult, they often go hungry after Mom kicks them out to raise a new litter. Hunger is the final teacher.

Kaji tied a rope to the back of the Cruiser and to the leg of the carcass. Tonic approached the impala and swatted it with his foot. Kaji got in the back, waited for him to give it a tentative lick, then signaled for me to start up. I slowly accelerated, circled around a rocky spine, and came to a fairly clear and level area.

"Is he following?" I glanced in the rearview mirror, and could see for myself Tonic's sweet round face jogging up and down on those long elegant legs, with his black-tipped tail floating behind.

"Yeah, he's definitely interested. Get into third if you can."

I reached a bone-jarring forty miles an hour, the steering wheel vibrating like crazy under my hands, and Kaji threw out the meat.

"This is great! He's really moving," she yelled. "He's closing the gap!"

"Hooray!" I felt a surge of adrenaline. A patch of dense bushes with tiny hard-looking leaves was coming up on the right. I readied myself for Kaji's shout to stop.

"There's a lion!" Kaji yelled.

"Oh, shit!" As we whizzed past I quickly looked right and glimpsed two lionesses rousing themselves from their midday snooze among the bushes. One of them had her nose raised in a sniff, and the other was on her feet and bounding toward Tonic with a low growl. *"No!"* I yelled.

Tonic spurted into top gear, flying at sixty mph past my windshield. He crossed his legs under him, then stretched full out, covering fifteen feet with each leap. It was so beautiful it took my breath away. Those lionesses would never catch him.

Kaji peered out the back hatch. I could hear a lion growling. "Stop, stop," Kaji yelled. "She's being dragged."

I stopped the car and put my head through the roofhatch to watch. The first lioness had jumped on the impala's back and gripped its neck in her powerful jaws. The second lioness was only seconds behind. She reached the carcass in a muscular sprint, seized it by the throat and held on, growling at her sister. They were nose to nose, their jaws only inches apart, muscular tails lashing the air. The first one laid back her ears and snarled. Blood matted her chin. She had an impressive set of teeth, but so did the second lioness.

"Look at those thin bellies. They must be hungry." Kaji couldn't help sounding interested. She was fascinated by every scrap of animal behavior.

One lioness growled deep in her throat. The sound raised the hairs on my neck. The other one didn't budge, except for the flick of one ear, bothered by flies. They were matching their wills. Neither one could eat, but neither wanted to be the first to let go. This was going to take longer than a few minutes.

I looked at my watch. "Now we have two cubs to find."

"This is bad. I'm also worried about my adult female: today I saw her nipples are swelling, so she's pregnant. It's the newborn cubs the lions really go after."

"She's pregnant already? Too bad." Kaji must have been disappointed.

In addition to working with Gin and Tonic, Kaji had a personal goal of gathering data on cheetah reproduction; that's why she'd been following this lone female so assiduously. A female without cubs was either newly pregnant or soon would be. Kaji had hoped to be there if and when males came courting. Very little was known about male-female interaction. No one had ever seen cheetahs mate. That information was vital to save cheetahs from the big E: extinction.

With parks providing no safety to them, thanks to the lions, and the intense population pressure, many people were expecting cheetahs to soon be wiped out, or close to it, in Kenya. That's one reason Nick and Wynn and Kaji were making such efforts to return the cubs to the wild. Every cheetah was precious. There were only ten thousand left in the world, less than the number of people living in a big Nairobi housing development.

For other endangered animals, zoos could function as a

last refuge. Not for cheetahs. With rare exceptions, they wouldn't breed in captivity.

The problem, scientists discovered, was that cheetahs suffered a devastating calamity ten thousand years ago. Every cheetah on earth was killed, except for a single, pregnant female. We don't know how it happened, or how she survived, but the proof is there: all cheetahs are as closely related as Siamese twins—hardly any genetic variety. As a result, their sperm count is so low, it's a wonder they can reproduce at all. Many matings are unproductive. But zoos can't even get their cheetahs to try, and that's where Kaji got her idea for her research.

We needed desperately to learn the social interactions that triggered mating, so that zookeepers could reproduce the proper conditions. Do males need to fight for the female? Should the two sexes be kept apart? Or do males need to have a territory that the female moves into and out of at will? Until we learned the answers, zoos would be helpless to stave off full extinction.

Kaji was hoping that once she got some interesting data on her own, she'd be able to win funding for a long-term project, get together a staff, go out there and spend the time necessary to find the answers. Wynn and Nick believed in Kaji's research, and were proud to support it. For all three of them, saving the cheetah had become a mission.

One of the lionesses tried to pull the impala out of her sister's grip. Her sleek muscles bunched powerfully under her tawny hide, but the sister growled and held on. Two pairs of yellow eyes glowed balefully at each other.

Meanwhile, Gin and Tonic were alone among the rest of the pride. I looked at my watch again. Chances were, the rest of the lion pride was scattered around in small groups in this corner of their territory. What would happen if Gin or Tonic ran into another lioness waking up from her nap feeling grouchy? Kaji and I were not doing a good job of being Mother.

"I've got to break this up," I said. "Let me try moving forward a few feet."

I eased forward. Neither one let go, but the sleeker lioness shifted her grip to a haunch, and no longer nose to nose,

262

they tore hunks off the carcass with gusto. In a few minutes the impala was gone.

I drove slowly, while Kaji and I hung out the windows, looking for the cheetahs' tracks.

"I've got one on this side," Kaji said. She pointed. "To the left of this black thorn. It's Tonic."

"You can tell by his print?" I was impressed.

"It's a bit wider than Gin's, and he has longer claws. I'll show you when we get back."

We drove on, passing a family herd of Grevy's zebra and a few scattered giraffe.

Kaji straightened and rubbed her neck. "Listen. There's a car ahead."

"Got it."

"Let's see who it is."

I headed toward the noise of an idling motor, feeling nervous about bandits but embarrassed to show it. Nick and Wynn's place was miles from the main road, far enough north of the Samburu Game Reserve to be out of the radius of even the most enthusiastic tourist. You could drive around on their land for weeks and never see anyone but the occasional Samburu kid herding goats or cattle. Somali bandits, the *shifta*, had raided nearby tribes for centuries—but since clan warfare erupted a few years ago, they were crossing Kenya's northeast border in greater and greater numbers, armed with automatic weapons and a savage readiness to kill animal or human, whatever was unlucky enough to cross their path.

So I was initially relieved when we rounded a dense clump of white thorns and there was another normal Land Cruiser, no bandits, with Tonic on the roof. He was nose down and haunches up, peering into the open hatch.

"There he is!" Kaji shouted.

"Is he terrorizing people?" But even as the words left my mouth, I noticed the upstretched hand with a sandwich luring him into the car. Tonic delicately took it, swallowed it whole, and jumped into the Cruiser, looking for more.